Innamorata

(in love)

CONTESSA

PAGE PUBLISHING, INC.
New York, NY

First originally published by Page Publishing, Inc. 2019

ISBN 978-1-64350-917-4 (Paperback)
ISBN 978-1-64544-094-9 (Hardcover)
ISBN 978-1-64350-918-1 (Digital)

Copyright Registration # TXu 2-095-833
Effective 4/16/2018

Printed in the United States of America

Per mio padre, mia faglia e mio nipote

Introduction

From the time we're young children, we hear stories of fairy tales, of knights in shining armor who save the princess then walk down a path of happily ever after into the sunshine. That may be the start of being in love, but it's unlikely things remain in fantasy mode for the duration of the relationship. I am a romantic. I believe love to be the most incredible emotion of all, but it has many dimensions. Love can surely be described as blissful, uplifting, peaceful, rewarding, the ultimate happiness, and a host of other adjectives. I've found love to be all those and more, but for me love has mostly been a teacher, a classroom, a life shaper, and an ever evolving growth experience. I've had the most amazing and fortunate experiences while being in love, some great, some not so great. But most of all, the loves of my life have taught me more about myself, about my life and how to live it, than any academic environment ever could have. Wouldn't it be fabulous if an actual Love 101 course were available and we could get all the rules and playbook we need to be successful in the love department? Unfortunately, no such thing exists. The only way to learn about being in love is to experience being in love. Hopefully, whether it works out or not, the journey will always be worthwhile. I know it was for me.

Husband #1

The first cut is the deepest.

The thought of entering high school was thrilling to me and I couldn't wait to get there. Always anxious for the next step in life, I thought of it as my passage to independence, a chance to explore who I was, establish myself, and quite frankly, just breathe in a way I hadn't been able to yet. I didn't get much insight about the high school experience from my older brother, mainly because he was a brainiac who attended a school that was geared toward the academically gifted, an arena I had no place in. Don't get me wrong; I was a very good student and high grades came naturally to me, but I was nowhere near my big brother's league. My older sister, on the other hand, attended a public high school about four blocks away from our slightly under-middle-class little home. Many of her neighborhood girlfriends went there as well, and I reveled in overhearing her telephone chatter about who did this, that, and whatever else. I couldn't wait for my glamorous sister and her "chic" girlfriends to congregate in the bedroom we shared (it was an equitable fifty-fifty arrangement; she messed it, I cleaned it) so I could study what they wore, how their hair was fixed, how their makeup was applied, all while listening to them jabber on and on about the day's events at school, nothing of which had anything to do with academics. Their banter was an essential part of the high school curriculum I needed that I wouldn't have access to anywhere else but in our bedroom—so long as I stayed out of sight, but just within earshot. From some of the stories I heard, *Animal House* could have been filmed at this school without a script. Listening to them told me that high school

9

was a blast, and it was mainly due to hearing their antics that helped me prepare for it.

For as long as I could remember, I heard a voice inside me, constantly telling me to get prepared to go beyond the mental and cultural barriers that existed in my strict, conventional blue-collar Italian environment. I yearned to blast past the cookie cutter role that was cast for girls growing up here, which equated to high school, marriage, and family. I dared to dream that I could explore and even succeed in areas far beyond the realm of our existence, things that others would find ridiculously unattainable. I had no idea how, but I was determined to carve a path in life that would allow me to experience a broader sphere of the world than what currently existed.

That said, I decided to attend St. Columbus High School, an all girls, three year business Catholic high school that offered only major business and marketing classes, no secondary or minor subjects. A few of my friends decided to go there as well, but only because it was a three year school. While my agenda was focused on obtaining business acumen, all they cared about was getting out of high school one year earlier than the rest of our friends. It was relatively inexpensive compared to other Catholic schools, but I still felt guilty about my parents having to dish out the money for tuition, plus the cost of books, uniform, lunch, and bus expenses. Money was always tight in our house, and any additional expense required a sacrifice in another area. We wore the traditional Catholic school pleated skirts, wool blazer, and white Peter Pan collar blouse. My father agreed to pay, although he informed me that I would have to work and contribute to my school expenses. This was not a shock to me, and I expected to do exactly as my father instructed; that was typical of the way we were raised. In an attempt to save money, I only bought two blouses and alternated them every other day. Wear one every day, wash one every night. I lied about my age and got a part-time job as a cashier at the drug store on the corner of our house, so I was able to pay for my own lunch and bus fare.

I settled in quite nicely at my new school and quickly realized St. Columbus was not your typical Catholic school. My classmates were "neighborhood girls," which meant that they were from various areas, each defined by the boys of that neighborhood, gangs who named themselves. If you said you were from the Jokers, C-Notes, Gaylords, Latin Kings, etc., one would immediately know where you lived. Streetwise, very savvy and tough! I got along well with most everyone and soon made lots of new friends. I was elected freshman class vice president, which was somewhat of a status symbol, but the real badge of honor came after I got into a fight. An actual fistfight.

There was an obnoxious little bitch named Connie from the Gaylords. Connie fancied herself as quite the tough cookie, always throwing her weight around and bullying anyone smaller than she was to do whatever she wanted. Connie was constantly making trouble, especially in the lunchroom. Long story short, Connie didn't like me for two reasons: First of all, she also ran for vice president and lost to me, hardly getting any votes. Second, she knew I was not intimidated by her at all, which drove her crazy. Connie kept getting on my ass about one thing or another, but my quick wit and penchant for sarcasm usually caused her to back down and retreat. Eventually, though, her relentless taunting became more than just annoying, and I warned her once to stop, warned her a second time that she was walking on thin ice, emphasizing that there wouldn't be a third warning.

One day, in the lunchroom, she started up again, and without a minute's notice, I slammed my fist right between her eyes, sending her flying across the table. The friends I had from childhood were familiar with my temper; they were well aware that I could be pushed only so far, and when you provoked me enough and crossed my line, you had better run. It was a side of me that I didn't like to show, but undeniably there when I needed it. Connie got the message this time, along with everyone else. Connie's older sister, a senior, came running to her defense. There were a few other seniors there who were friends of my older sister; they saw what went down, and they quickly rallied around me, just to let Connie's sister know that I wasn't alone. It was a gesture that required no words. It was a neighborhood thing. The sister backed off.

"You did your neighborhood proud, Contessa," the seniors assured me as we watched Connie and her sister retreat with their tail between their legs, back to their own group. I knew I'd get detention for this, but hey, the added acclaim to my already great status was worth it. In addition to the glowing reputation I already achieved through student government and general personal interaction, now everyone knew not to mess with me or any of those I was close to. My dad always told us, if we ever came home crying that someone beat us up, he would kick our ass again!

"I'm not raising any sissies!" he would say. "Strike first, strike quick, and strike hard."

Words to live by.

I was in a very good place and loving high school. I was well liked and respected, I had my own identity, and for once, I was nobody's "little sister." I was just me, and for the first time, that was good enough. I was truly happy. The ax fell, though, just as we were about to leave for Christmas break. Our principle announced that due to financial severities, St. Columbus would be closing at the end of this school year. *Ugh!* I was crushed. I discussed this with my parents over the break, and we decided it would be best for me to transfer right away, so I would then only be down one full credit instead of two if I stayed there for the remainder of the school year. That made sense, so I agreed to transfer to Thorr High School, where my sister and cousin attended, which scared me to death. This was Chicago during a period where guys still had short hair and girls dressed in a feminine manner, with hair and makeup done to perfection, every day! The hippie movement, which would eventually give way to relaxed, more casual dress, hadn't hit just yet. How could I go to a much larger public school, having to wear street clothes I didn't have, with no sense of even how to dress in the first place, not to mention fix my wild hair, apply makeup every day? Not to be melodramatic, but I'd always been a realistic person, identifying my strengths and weaknesses. A raving beauty I was not. The only thing I had going for me was big boobs, which I didn't even consider an advantage, as they just didn't go with my skinny frame, wild hair, and overall look. Suddenly, the confidence and stature I had achieved and became so comfortable with at St. Columbus just evaporated. At an all girls school, these things didn't matter, but in a public school, they were everything! Ugh, the anxiety!

The decision and all necessary paperwork had been completed, and I was soon scheduled to start at Thorr High. The entire weekend before, I frantically scrambled through my closet, trying to put at least two weeks of outfits together. I thought that would give me enough time to whip up a few new things on the sewing machine. My mother had taught me to sew at a very young age, and I was getting to be pretty good, even creating my own patterns. Never were those skills more warranted than right now. My sister spread the word that I was coming to Thorr soon. As I settled into my new environment and class schedule, I met several of them. I was pretty surprised at how many people recognized me, noting the resemblance between my sister and me, something she had always balked at. Several girls and guys nicely approached me and introduced themselves, welcoming me to Thorr High. I was a bit shy, though, constantly reminded that my sister was gorgeous, was chic, and had it all together, as did her friends. They were the "it crowd," and it was pretty overwhelming for me. I knew I didn't belong there. Not that anyone made me feel unwelcome; I just felt so inadequate around them. We had a beautiful, perky, and sassy cousin named Jen, who also attended Thorr, in the same grade as my sister, and they both hung out with the same crowd. There were also a few of my grammar school friends there, so between those I knew from grade school and those I came to know from both my sister and cousin Jen, I soon acquired a nice circle of friends. The angst that I had at the first thought of transferring to this school soon diminished, and I realized I wouldn't die of shame as I originally thought I would.

Across the street from Thorr High was a little diner named Alice's Café. This charming little sandwich shop catered to the high school kids, much like Al's in *Happy Days*. Alice's was the focal point and hangout for the cool kids, as well as many others from various neighborhoods, some even older and had been out of school for years. Alice's was where the action was, and you went there more to hang out rather than have lunch, as the cuisine was not fine dining. A few older guys from the area who were in rock bands also hung out there. I was aware of Alice's and its allure from the start, but I didn't make it over there for some time. I had two study periods, one of which was spent working in the school office. I did clerical work for the school counselors. I used the other study period to actually complete my homework. I hated bringing books home. I became pretty comfortable with my schedule, and I soon felt more at ease at my new high school. I met and made plenty of new friends; however, there was one name that kept popping up, which really piqued my interest. He was called either Mousie or just plain Mouse by everyone. His real name was Michael, but many who knew him never knew it. He was simply Mousie, and up to this point in my life, I had never known anyone with such a significant reputation. The stories I heard about this guy were hilarious, unbelievable, and some so ridiculous it would have been impossible to make up. There are some names we all know that need no description as to their character; you just say the name and, boom, that's it. Dean Martin, John Wayne, Gregory Peck, Mel Brooks, Jonathan Winters, Robin Williams. If you compared someone to any one of them, enough said. That was Mousie. Say his name and you immediately knew what you were getting. Every group has their type A personality; one alpha dog, one person that commands the crowd, one person who everyone wants to be, or at least be around. Mousie was that guy. He was a legend at our school. The best dressed, the best card player, the best bowler, the best prankster, the best gambler, and by far, the best bullshitter, even conniving with his teachers to sign him out of class so he could go to the racetrack—and make bets for them! He was what *swagger* is. Mouse was the funniest, the sweetest, and the naughtiest.

After months of being on the scene, I still had not had the pleasure of meeting this Nicky Arnstein of Thorr High and wondered when or if I ever would. Honestly, though, I didn't think I'd have the confidence to speak to him if I did meet him, as his reputation made him larger than life and I was not prepared to encounter that quite yet.

One gorgeous spring day, Jen came down to the office to ask me if I could swipe an "Excuse from Class" note pass, which all the counselors had. I was pretty close to Jen, thought of her as my other big sister, and she always took a loving interest in me. Jen was one of the few people who actually knew I worked in the office and what I did there. Leave it to Jen to figure out any angle to get out of a class. She knew I had access to those passes, as well as the name stamps for each of the counselors. Of course, I would do anything for Jen and assured her I'd have it at the end of this period. Jen suggested that while I was at it, why not take one for me as well and the two of us would go hang out at Alice's? Sure, why not? I thought. I was secretly dying to go there and would be much less timid being there with Jen, so what the hell! I got both of our passes, and Jen was waiting for me outside the office after the next bell rang. Off to Alice's we went. It was the first really nice spring day so far this year, which was most likely the reason there was a full house at Alice's. It seemed like everyone who was anyone was there.

Just off to the side of Alice's front door, we noticed a large group of guys laughing, some even bent over in stitches, really cracking up. The jester in the middle of it all was a tall and slender, medium built guy, definitely not muscle bound or athletic, but most assuredly a guy who had control of the crowd. He was impeccably dressed, had neatly styled straight sandy brown hair, with dark large round eyes that glistened with mischief, set quite close together. He was not a head turner, just what you'd call a cutie, but a sharp dressed cutie at that! And just as ZZ Top said, "Everybody's crazy 'bout a sharp dressed man!"

I knew immediately this guy was the notorious Mousie, the pied piper I'd heard so much about. In a neighborhood full of people with nicknames, it was easy to see how and why he got his. He looked like a mouse, plain and simple. Mousie was cute, cuddly, and comical looking, like a cartoon mouse. He had such a suave manner, very polished, which was sort of unusual for the guys we grew up with, and his style really distinguished him from the rest. But more than his sophisticated clothes, trademark enormous diamond pinky ring, and playful banter, what you immediately noticed was his personality. His magnetism. He made sure he was noticed, drawing your full attention and focus to his antics. Part of Mousie's allure was his class and unparalleled ability to make you laugh your ass off instantly.

Didn't matter what the subject was—to be with him or around him was to laugh. He was a little rascal, a little boy who knowingly did the wrong thing and was spared punishment due to his charm and comedic prowess. A blind person could easily see the spell he put everyone under. The consummate prankster whom you never got mad at, for even if you were the butt of his jokes, you wouldn't mind but rather be happy to be associated with his high jinks.

Jen noticed me gazing Mousie's way and asked if I had met him yet. "No, but I've certainly heard plenty about him," I replied. "He's one of a kind, that's for sure." Jen laughed. Mousie, my sister, and cousin Jen were all very close friends. Mousie cut many of his classes, and Jen did quite a lot of his homework. Mousie often cut school to go to the racetrack. He frequently got some of the teachers to go along with him as well, offering to wine and dine them, pay for everything once they got there. Nice, huh? If any of the teachers couldn't go along, Mousie would offer to take bets for them; sometimes he gave them "winnings" they really didn't win, just to keep them under his spell.

The owner of Alice's, Miss Alice, as she was known, was a short and fat crusty old gal who fed the kids as if they were all her own. Alice was quick to reprimand anyone who got out of line. She didn't take any shit from anyone and wasn't above chasing you with her broom if you were disrespectful or got out of line. Although Alice was always yelling at her patrons, she really loved them all, especially Mousie. He had a knack of aggravating her and cracking her up at the same time. Jen and I were sitting adjacent to the front door, talking, when Mousie walked in and announced "Alice, I'm parched. I need some water. Not too much ice, I don't want to irritate my throat." As Alice handed him a tall plastic glass, he grimaced. "Not the plastic glass. Where's my glass glass?" he said as he put a ten dollar bill in Alice's tip box. Although rolling her eyes at Mousie's request, she apologized and got him a fresh glass of water, with just a few ice cubes, in a "real" glass. Before his signature move of raising his pinkie (which displayed his famed enormous diamond ring—who the hell has a diamond ring that big in high school?), Mousie was sure not to let Alice see him wipe the rim of the glass off before drinking it.

Had she ever noticed him do that, Mousie would have surely been on the receiving end of her broom. Indeed, he was quite discreet. As he drained his glass, carefully wiped his mouth with several napkins, he nestled up to Jen, staring me up and down.

"Hey, Jenny," he asked, "who, may I ask, is this young flower?"

"This is Jan's sister, Contessa," Jen said, making our introduction.

"Oh, yeah, I heard you were new here," Mousie said, as his eyes seemed to penetrate right through me. "How come I haven't seen you here before? Don't tell me you eat lunch in the cafeteria!" He laughed.

"No, I work in the office for lunch," I shyly replied.

"*What?* You work in the office?" he screamed. Jen explained what I did, that I had access to the counselor passes and stamps, which was how we were both sitting there at that moment.

"*Really?*" Mousie said, partly a question and partly a confirmation as he put his arm around me with the sweetest yet devilish smile on his entertaining face. "Well, hello, there. My name is Mouse, and you, my sweet pet, are my new best friend." All I could do was burst out in laughter. Mousie wasted no time in asking me to stamp a bunch of excuse slips without dating them. I hesitated, but he canoodled and countered every point of apprehension I demonstrated. Yep, easy to see why he was always the center of attention.

"Okay, okay, I'll get them for you," I surrendered, "but please don't tell anyone else, all right?" I was practically pleading.

"Oh, don't you worry, my pet, this will be our little secret, and you'll do it for me and only me!" Mousie declared.

Hence, my heart was captured for the very first time, as well as what I eventually came to realize was my attraction to the showman, the alpha dog, the one with the style and the flair, the one who commanded the room. Perhaps my eventual burning desire to be with this type of guy came from my own insecurities, my always feeling like the underdog, the ugly duckling, the never-good-enough; therefore, if I was with this person, I'd get the security and recognition I craved, as well as the guy too. Win-win, right?

Mousie and I became close, and before I knew it, I was doing most of his homework. How the hell that happened is beyond me, but chalk it up to his unparalleled powers of persuasion. I don't know if it was my passion to please him or desire to be needed that resulted in my dedication to his homework, but suffice it to say that if neither took place, he never would have graduated. Academics came natural to me, and I breezed by, always a straight A student, so doing Mousie's homework didn't place a hardship on me. More to the point, I actually felt important and needed, that I actually had purpose. I was completely fascinated by him and his lifestyle.

While only a junior in high school, he played cards all weekend, went to the racetrack almost every day, and most of his nights were spent at the bowling alley, either bowling or shooting pool for money. He was a superstar. Guys were eager to play him, knowing they would never beat him, but the experience and the show he put on for you while he was beating the pants (and paycheck) off you erased any care you would've had that he did. Going to the racetrack with Mousie was an even better experience and considered a privilege. The entourage that usually accompanied him always came back with big smiles and even bigger stories, of his expertise, if nothing else. Mousie handed out fifty dollar bills for this one to go get him a racing form, that one to get him a soda, more to anyone who would stand in line to get him something to eat. He often joked that if he could pay someone to take a piss for him, he would have, so long as he wasn't disturbed or didn't have to do anything to break his concentration while at the racetrack. The only thing he did himself was place his bets, after significant mental deliberation. Whether he won or lost, his game face, mood, and impish manner were set, solid and constant. Mousie was a walking party, and everyone was invited. Blackjack and Casino were his card games of choice, and that was where he really shined. No matter how many hours ticked away on the clock, he was unreadable and unwavering. Crazy as it might have been, I later heard guys admit that it was almost a pleasure to lose to him, just to say you played him.

It was hard enough for me to imagine anybody throwing money around the way Mousie did, but the fact that he was still in high school made it even more difficult to wrap my head around. However, the more I came to know him, the more comprehensive and accepting of his lifestyle I became. For his "hard work and efforts," Mousie rewarded himself with the finest and most fashionable attire money could buy. He was rarely seen wearing the same thing twice, except for that distinctive pinkie ring of his. More than anything else, though, it was his biting sharp wit, his quick, relentless humor, and his little boy charm that could turn any dastardly deed to his favor, which together heightened his appeal. I was taught to watch and learn, to be aware and observant before making an assessment or move. After a while, I realized that, although Mousie had more friends than you could count, many females included, he never showed evidence of a steady girlfriend. Once I overheard him say that he didn't have one special girl because he hadn't yet met one that could thrill him more than ponies or cards. Hmmmm, interesting.

By this time, I was a regular at Alice's. Mouse and I established a schedule there where I would get his homework assignments, deliver those I had finished, and he would have Alice prepare a special lunch for us. I got over my feelings of inadequacy around the Alice's crowd, largely due to Mousie and all the attention he bestowed upon me. His notice consequently bolstered my confidence, gave me a little more status of my own, and thus gave way for a bit more of my own personality to blossom. He treated me with respect not only for my academic abilities (hey, he was a junior, I was a freshman doing all his homework, and he was getting A's!) but as a lady as well. Mouse was always courteous and well mannered, but whenever girls were present, he also made sure that all the other guys were as well, even reminding them to watch their language whenever ladies were within earshot. Our regular, special lunch did not go unnoticed by others, but I dismissed it by saying that we were merely just good friends and I helped him with his homework, so he was paying me back. I wanted to believe it was more than that but was afraid to, just in case it turned out not to be true. Until one day.

Our special lunch at Alice's was every Monday. I was always anxious to hear the stories of what gambling scenario dictated his weekend. I would sit there mesmerized as he rattled off his latest tale, how he out strategized, outfoxed, and outplayed his opponents. He would go on and on about this card game, that bowling match, that pool game, etc. But this Monday, he told me that his usual Saturday night card game didn't go very well.

"Oh, I'm sorry," I whispered softly.

"Well, you should be," he snapped back. "After all, it's your fault!"

"*What?*" I shockingly replied.

"Come with me, my little chinchilla, we're going for a walk," Mouse ordered. Don't ya just love when a guy gets his feathers ruffled and he starts demanding? No argument from me—no, sir. As we walked, he explained.

"I'm the most focused card player you'll ever know."

Right, like I know a whole bunch, I thought.

"Last Saturday night," he continued, "I just couldn't get you out of my head and I had no concentration. All I could think about was you and what you might be doing."

I couldn't help but inject a little of my growing and nicely developing sass. "I was doing your homework. What else would I be doing on a Saturday night?" I exclaimed.

He laughed out loud over that. Without a second's notice, he had me in his arms and kissed the shit out of me. Your first kiss usually tells you if this will go anywhere. At that moment, I would have gone to Siberia with him.

He broke away and declared, "Next Saturday night, you'll be going out with me."

All I could do was bob my head up and down. Well, all righty, then. *I guess I have my very first real date next Saturday night with one of our neighborhood's most popular guys.* He walked, and I floated back to Alice's, barely able to speak or get my wits about me. As soon as we got there, I had to run to the ladies' room to check the stupid grin I was certain was all over my face. *Oh my god! I have a date with Mousie!* I couldn't believe it. However, just as my feet were hitting the floor, I began to sink below it. Reality hit. I had literally nothing to wear, nor did I have a clue as to how to fix myself up for a date! *Ugh!* Talk about mixed emotions. Now what?

The rest of the week, I couldn't get home fast enough to study my closet, trying to put some kind of outfit together that looked worthy of being out with Mousie. When I wasn't agonizing over the clothes part, I was practicing hair and makeup in the bathroom. *Ugh,* I was totally void of primping skills.

Quickly Saturday morning came, and while I was ecstatic over having a date tonight with the man of my dreams, I found myself sitting on the floor of my bedroom, fighting the tears. I was no closer to a solution as to what I would wear or what to do with the wild, frizzy mane I was staring at, compliments of our Midwest humidity. The doorbell rang, and being home alone, I ran downstairs to answer it. I opened the door to find my sister's best friend, Alexis, standing there like an absolute angel. Alexis sat atop the "it" list. She had everything, plus. A tall, slender, platinum blonde, stunning beauty with a fantastic figure, blue eyes, and the longest lashes, which she knew exactly when, where, and how to flutter effectively. Alexis was our neighborhood femme fatale, oozing of style, poise, and elegance. She immediately noticed something was upsetting me, and I quickly poured out the whole story. Did I mention she was an angel? Angels perform miracles, and Alexis did just that.

"Come with me," Alexis ordered as she took me by the hand and pulled me to her house across the street. Talk about an ambush makeover! Before I could blink, she began a step-by-step process that took over five hours. Alexis knew exactly what to do, and her expertise showed. Hair and makeup were done to perfection; she put me into one of her own pants outfits that was a little too big and a little too long, but we made it work. When she finally let me look into the mirror, I honestly didn't know whose reflection that was staring back at me. Now, I was really excited. Now I was ready for my date with Mousie.

Upon arriving at my house to pick me up, Mousie immediately commented on how gorgeous I looked. A first for me. I squirmed while he met my parents and chatted with them a bit, schmoozing with both of them as only he could. He turned the charm on big time, and while my mom was a shoe in, my dad was a tough nut to crack, and Mousie knew it. Mousie was quite aware of the protocol and offered that he was taking me to a known, prestigious Italian restaurant for dinner, which, of course, would please my dad. Mousie also made it a point to reference his uncle who was also very "known" and quite high profile in a way that some people only think of as characters in a movie. Because my dad was the neighborhood bookie and knew many of "those guys," his realizing who Mousie's uncle was allowed him to breathe a little easier and give us his blessing to date. As we were leaving, my father couldn't resist giving Mousie one more stern reminder as to what my curfew was and that he better make sure I was home on time. Mousie respectfully assured my dad he would and that his daughter was in good hands.

That night, I was Cinderella, unable to recognize my own reflection, dressed in someone else's clothes. I didn't need a carriage to transport me as I was floating on air. I wondered if I would lose one of Alexis's shoes! Would her clothes suddenly turn to rags at midnight, or rather my curfew of eleven o'clock? As we dined in grand Italian style, I barely remember eating, but I certainly remember Mousie being flawless at the dinner table and seemingly aware of my intrigue for his every move. He ordered for us both and ate with such impeccable finesse, never failing to raise that diamond pinkie ring at the appropriate time. I became more relaxed by mentally repeating to myself, *We're just at Alice's, we're just at Alice's*, over and over, which seemed to do the trick. This was not only my first real date but also the first time Mousie and I were actually together anyplace other than Alice's, having a real conversation, which turned out to be a very good ping-pong game. I listened so intently as he narrated many enthralling accounts of his strategic ability to win everything he put his gambling mind to. It was a perfect balance between talking and listening, something I wasn't used to. In my home environment, we weren't allowed to be very verbal, or too inquisitive. Unfortunately for my parents, I happened to be both, and I usually got punished for it. I felt that the only place my thoughts and feelings were welcome, recognized, and appreciated was in the classroom, which probably accounted for why I thrived at school. Mousie seemed to enjoy my inquisitive nature, easily and naturally responding to my barrage of questions regarding his thoughts, his life, his aspirations. While he wasn't shy about telling me everything, he was also just as interested in my thoughts, my aspirations as well. He listened as well as he spoke, which always remained key criteria for anyone I would become involved with.

While mindful of time, Mousie informed me that we wouldn't be having dessert because we had to take a ride. He said he wanted to take me someplace to show me off. Okay, I'd never been "shown off," so I guess this was my night of firsts. I was pretty surprised to pull up in front of the local bowling alley.

"*What* are we doing here?" I asked.

The voice and face that responded to me was of a more serious nature. "This is where I spend most of my Saturday nights. This is my life and livelihood. If you want to know me, you have to realize how I spend my time and be comfortable with it and in it." He put it right out there, honest and forthright, which I respected and, to this day, maintain as part of my own character. I don't blow smoke up anyone's ass; I tell it like it is. And if you aren't happy about it, oh, well, at least I'm honest and you can just move along. It was a "this is who I am, take it or leave it" moment, plus he wanted to flaunt me in front of it. *Bonus!*

Mousie entering the bowling alley was like the Red Sea parting. People practically saluted him while moving out of the way for us to walk by. He introduced me to everyone as his girl, and each encounter chipped away at the inhibitions I walked out the door with that night. The entire evening, his actions showed me it was not about him at all; this night was about me as he paraded me around, explaining that I was the reason he wasn't there for the usual Saturday night of gambling. Instead of music playing in the background, there were bowling pins clanking about, but in my head, I was still Cinderella this night, dancing with her prince as we waltzed out the door and into the coach waiting to take us home.

As we were parked in front of my house, I thanked Mousie for a fabulous time and joked about how I'd have to work all through the next day to get his homework done for Monday. I thought it best to keep talking so he wouldn't hear the loud pounding of my heart. Instead of laughing with me, he reached over and kissed me ever so tenderly. Although it was just that one kiss, it went on forever, and I can still feel it to this very day. That first date kiss was truly a first

I would never forget, and as a first date kiss should be, it was perfect! While stroking my cheek, he let me know there would be more evenings like this, as we'd be spending much more time together. On this night of firsts, Mousie also made it clear that I was his girl, his *first* girl. At that time in my life, I couldn't even have dreamed of what the perfect night, perfect date, would be. But I did now. He showed me. I was truly in love, and there would be more "firsts" to follow, each with their own magic and all in due time.

News certainly does travel fast. By Monday, everyone at Alice's knew Mousie and I were now an official couple. There were lots of "Congratulations!" to me, but I wondered if anyone was congratulating him. There were also plenty of jokes to Mouse relating to me being his girl as insurance to get his homework done in order to graduate. It was all in good fun, and it didn't bother me. For the first time in my life, I was proud. I felt significant, and I was deliriously happy.

Italian men are a funny breed. They set the stage, court you, wine you, dine you, and just when you fall head over heels, they become cavemen who forget the prize they've been playing for. I respected the fact that Mousie put his lifestyle right out there in front of me, expressing that this was his life, take it or leave it. I accepted it and didn't mind not going out with him every single weekend. After all, we saw each other every day at school. Fine, go ahead and play cards, win your bowling and pool tournaments, go to the racetrack. I had no problem with any of it. However, while on those weekends when he did his thing, I surely wanted to do mine. I was fourteen years old, for Christ's sake. I wanted to do the things that normal teenagers do with their girlfriends, and I had several pockets of girlfriends from various neighborhoods—my two different high schools and friends of my cousins in other areas. We'd go to a dance now and then, have a pajama party once in a while. Suddenly, that became a big problem with Mousie. He felt that his girl should not be going to dances in other neighborhoods, especially followed by a pajama party. Nope, not acceptable to him. He expressed that I should stay home so he knew exactly where I was, that worrying about where I was, whom I was with, and who might be trying to hit on me broke his concentration. *Oh, I'm sorry, master, but how many fathers do I have?* Bad enough I had to wrestle with my dad about going out where, with whom, a million details, strict curfews, etc. Okay, a pain in the ass, but after all, he was my dad and had the right to being strict with me. But I certainly was not going to allow anyone to lock me up in a closet while they were out doing what they wanted. No way!

As much as I knew I was in love with Mousie and wanted to be with him, there was no way I was going to take orders from him on this subject. I felt I was being pretty diplomatic, allowing him free rein to do whatever he wanted without bitching or ever saying a word about it. I didn't complain about one thing he did or how much time it took away from us being together, and my constant response was "Do what you need to do, but do *not* expect me to be locked up in the house, waiting for you to let me out." This was our one bone of contention, the only thing we argued about. He vehemently disagreed with my feelings, as did all my friends, who felt I should do what Mousie expected; after all, he was my boyfriend! I guess this was my first sense of being inherently different in nature from others I grew up with. I could never be bossed around by a man! I would not budge and continued to hang out with my girlfriends on the weekends Mouse and I were not together, which resulted in us arguing all through the following week. He couldn't—or wouldn't—see that I was true to him, understood his lifestyle, and had no other intention but just to have some fun with my friends, as he did himself. Jeez, I was just getting a taste of my teenage years, and damned if I would let someone else take them away from me! No fucking way! After a while, I had enough of it and broke up with him.

Our breakup became even more appealing to the Alice's crowd than that of our playfulness and joking while we were dating. The show between Mousie and me became a battle of wits, sarcasm, sharp tongues, and a contest to determine who could be sassier. I think I won that round (ha, ha, ha!). If I am to give Mousie credit for everything he did for me, I'll admit that I owe being crowned the queen of sarcasm in later years mainly to him. Our banter and teasing exchange amused the Alice's gang, which was not only enjoyable to me but really also opened the door to my confidence. Looking back, I think our daily display made our feelings for each other evident to everyone, but the two of us, or at least neither of us, would give in and admit it. I really didn't want to be without him, but I refused to allow him (or any man, ever) to order me to sit in the house and not enjoy my life while he was out enjoying his. I sensed he still had feelings for me but was just as stubborn as I was. And so we stayed connected in this way until school got out for the summer that year.

I embraced the coming summer with a newfound assertiveness and was determined to have an unprecedented season in the sun. While I missed Mousie terribly, I shook the sentimental feelings off by reminding myself of his Neanderthal attitude. If he wanted me, he could come and get me, but it would have to be on my terms. That self declaration made me feel a sense of maturity and empowerment, a confidence I had never yet experienced. I sometimes couldn't believe that I broke up with the guy whom everyone wanted to be with and I knew I was in love with. It wasn't a sense of vanity, but principle, that I broke up with him, and that was what gave me the attitude and edge I felt this summer. I was going to have a blast.

I was hanging out with the Reve Park girls, whom I met through one of my cousins. They were a little more upscale than I was, but my newly found *aplomb* leveled the playing field for me and we all got along great. Summer dances were everywhere in their neighborhood, and I was at every one of them, being sassy, dancing up a storm, meeting boys and making new friends, also enjoying a change of pace and scenery.

Just as this sizzling summer began and I was in the midst of dancing many a night away, I met a guy named Mark through the new group I was hanging out with. Although Mousie held an indelible place in my heart and my head, Mark was the kind of jaw-dropping, stop-dead-in-your-tracks, fucking gorgeous hunk that would erase any thought in your head, except how mesmerizing it was to gaze upon him. My epic summer came and went with Mark being a large part of it. So large, in fact, that he gets his own chapter later on in this book—be patient! I found that nothing mends a broken heart like a new heartthrob! But as it all came to an end, I realized it was merely a Band-Aid that temporarily allowed me to put my feelings for Mousie aside. I missed him desperately and was certain he had forgotten all about me over the summer.

Although I returned to school a sophomore, I felt more like the senior Mousie was, being promoted a few years for excellence in personal growth. I was both excited and nervous to head back to school, thrilled to see Mouse again, but a bit tense as to how it could or would turn out. Did he miss me? Did he still love me? Would he want me back, but without the attitude? I believed that our first encounter would tell me. Mousie excelled at strategy in game play-ing, although mainly when those games involved money. However, he applied the same strategies to the way he conducted his life. One very important characteristic trait that was effectively demonstrated by both Mousie and my father was simply to say what you mean and mean what you say. No games or guesswork, no drama, no bullshit. Lay it out there and deal with it; you'll be respected for that approach in the end.

As I walked to Alice's this first day back, I knew I'd find the answers I sought. *Okay, deep breaths and stay cool.*

Most of our friends were already at Alice's, and the chatter of everyone's summer fun filled the place. I sat in the middle of several girlfriends, joining in the conversation. Mousie wasn't there, yet. I hoped that if he did show up, it would be while I was engaged in the midst of all this laughter with the girls, so as not to seem as if I were looking and waiting for him. All of a sudden, one of my girlfriends nudged me. "Contessa, don't turn around, but Mouse is outside, staring a hole right through the window at you." I gave her a casual "who cares" look and kept right on talking, although my heart began beating so loud I thought the girls might hear it.

Keep breathing, I told myself and continued chatting with the girls. It was time for me to put on the game face and attitude that Mr. Mouse himself taught me to maintain when feeling cornered. Suddenly, without even turning around, I knew he was standing right behind me. I could literally feel him there.

"Excuse me, ladies," Mouse said to the girls in his oh-so-very-polite voice. The girls scattered. I swiveled around on the barstool and found serious Mouse greeting me, no joking, no banter. I had never seen his eyes so dark and deep. He wasn't smiling either, which I wasn't used to. Kind of scary and exhilarating at the same time. His voice lacked its usual lighthearted tone. Not cold, but not warm either. Kind of monotone, which for him was so unusual. Quiet, but stern, and serious in a way I had not ever seen or heard him before. Another little tip I learned from him was, when you're unsure of what your next move is, don't do anything until you are. Just keep still and let the action around you happen; your move will come as the action unfolds. That said, I sat there silently and was prepared to just listen.

Without a hello or any other pleasantries, he got right into it. "Did you have a good summer?" his monotone voice spilled out. I was actually sort of scared to speak, so I just nodded. "Well, I didn't," he declared, "and I'll tell you why. Contessa, I love you. You're my girl, and you're a part of me. You always will be. I want to be with you and only you from now on. I mean forever. Okay, I get it, I under-stand what your issue was. It's not fair or realistic for me to expect you to sit home when I'm out doing my business. Fine. But I learned my lesson, and I realize what a prick I was being. So we're back together now, and we're going to stay together, *forever*, you understand that? I'm gonna talk to your father and let him know that as soon as you graduate, we're getting married. We're gonna have kids and I'll give you everything you've ever dreamed of, I promise. It's you and me from now on. Got it?"

I had always said before then that you gotta love an action man, but *wow*! This was Rhett and Scarlett on the bridge in the middle of the Confederate war, as he left her to join the soldiers. Totally blew me away, leaving me speechless. Never in a million years did I expect this. Shakespeare himself couldn't have written a better solil-oquy, and who was I to argue with Shakespeare? Once again, all I could do was bob my head like an idiot, indicating "yes" I got it. I was unable to speak. My bobblehead nod seemed to have lifted the veil of seriousness that Mouse was wearing, and in an instant, he was back to his regular self, offering to buy everyone in the place lunch as a welcome-back-to-school treat. Talk about going from zero to sixty in five seconds—the place was jumping again.

He never mentioned any of this again, and I soon did see the evidence that he really did learn a lesson. He went about his usual business, as did I, doing the normal things high school girls do on the weekends: dances and pajama parties. Only now, Mousie made it a point to drive me to my friends' houses, come in, meet the parents, charm the shit out of them, and give them all a few laughs before taking off to conduct his own affairs. We were completely compatible in every way and developed a perfect balance between each other's individual activities and those we created together. We talked of our future constantly. He gave me every reason to believe that all the things we planned would materialize. Life was so good.

Mousie did speak to my father about getting married just as soon as I graduated. My dad was a little surprised yet realized Mousie was serious. Dad just listened and said nothing, which was his signature style. Never let anyone know what you're really thinking, Dad taught us, and when you aren't sure what to do or say, do nothing, say nothing. Wait it out, think it through, and don't act until you are absolutely certain you're making the right move. So Dad said nothing. Mousie just blew that off, but I knew better. I knew Dad was "thinking," which made me a little nervous.

It was as if we were engaged the whole time and were planning out our wedding. Open discussion of our future together was so natural and frequent it was no surprise to either of us when, in the spring of my senior year, just one month before graduation, at seventeen years old, I became pregnant. We received the news with great joy, as if we'd already been married and trying for years. No shock at all, as we worked pretty hard at achieving this goal. It was what we both desperately wanted. The only hard part now was breaking the news to our parents, particularly mine. Mousie was petrified. My dad was the one and only person, or thing, that he feared, and with good reason too. My dad was a very scary man. He was not necessarily a large man, but my dad's small athletic frame was rock solid muscle, completely chiseled from his perfectly placed cheekbones right down to his toes. His overwhelmingly handsome face had such definition, especially his piercing gray-green eyes, which could freeze you with one glare. The man had a very distinctive presence and was held in high regard. Although he was small in physique, Dad's nickname was Big Lou, big as in strength and discipline, which was what he stood for. All the guys in the neighborhood had a great deal of love and respect for him but were also scared to death of him.

Someone once told my dad that one of the neighborhood guys said something derogatory about my cousin Jen. My dad searched the neighborhood for this guy and found him in the middle of the pack, hanging out on a street corner as the guys normally did. My dad got out of the car, broke through the crowd, and literally picked up this guy by his throat with one hand until his feet literally dangled, telling this kid that if he ever said anything bad or disrespectful to any of the young girls in our neighborhood again, he would come find him again, only next time there would be no warnings, no words, just action.

"Okay, Big Lou, whatever you say, Big Lou. I'm so sorry, honest, Big Lou," the kid stuttered as he dangled there, shaking. "I'll apologize to Jen, honest, Big Lou," he added as all the other guys cracked up. With that, Dad put him down and left. The kid kissed my cousin Jen's ass for years.

I wanted to get "the talk" over with as quickly as possible. I took my mother aside one Saturday afternoon and broke the news. She did freak out a little, but it had more to do with what my father's reaction would be. While she did smile at the thought of becoming a grandmother, she couldn't help but show how scared she was about my dad finding out. He was going to explode! I told her that Mousie was coming over in a while to talk to Dad and suggested that she go visit one of my aunts while "the talk" was taking place. She agreed and couldn't get out of the house fast enough.

My dad had two jobs. By day he was a very skilled, innovative carpenter and had done remodeling work for everyone we knew. When nighttime came, he was the neighborhood bookie, which meant he took racetrack bets over the phone and collected money for...um, "businessmen" in the neighborhood. After dinner, he had about two hours before the phone started ringing with people wanting to place bets. This little break was his nap time. I think it was a good thing that Dad was still in nap mode on the living room sofa when Mousie arrived. Without ever even rehearsing what we would say, we woke him up and asked to talk with him. While still in a bit of a stupor, Mousie took the lead and broke the news that I was pregnant and that we wanted to get married right after graduation (which was in two weeks) but, of course, wanted his blessing. *Whew!*

There, it was out.

In one split second, my mind flooded with years of my dad's own voice. I heard his many lectures over the years about believing in yourself, never letting fear prevent you from doing what you feel you need to do, to be a leader, be confident, and all the stuff that boils down to being strong enough to take your own steps knowing you may fall but that you'll be able to pick yourself up and move on.

Dad sat there silently for what seemed like forever. He reached over to his pack of cigarettes and lit one up. Those piercing gray eyes of his were burning a hole right through Mousie, who, I knew, was shitting in his pants. It seemed like Dad took an hour to light his cigarette. I was really nervous too, because I knew Dad was pondering his move. Mousie took the bold step of reminding Dad that he had already declared his love for me and our plans to marry, having asked Dad's permission some time ago. While Dad took a drag from his cigarette that took forever, Mousie continued to plead our case, and we later joked that the real pleading was for his life. Of all the times I might have been proud of my husband-to-be, this was his finest moment. I knew how scared he was to face Big Lou with this news, yet he spoke calmly, distinctly, and with heart. I never really knew what surprised my dad more, the news itself or the manner in which Mousie delivered it. I think Mousie's approach might have disarmed my dad a bit, but then Dad always said that he admired people who just put their cards on the table. Dad admired courage. And so after Mousie's brave monologue, Dad lit up another cigarette, only this time even slower than the first one. On purpose, I think, so as to make us both sweat a little. Now it was Dad's turn to speak, and we were squirming.

Dad aimed his piercing eyes directly to Mousie and began. "You've come to me several times telling me how much you love my daughter and you want to marry her. I respect you for that and what all you've said here tonight. But you need to know I don't like you and you are not the choice I would make to marry my daughter. I know what you do for a living. I've been around gamblers all my life and I know that in the end you never win. It's no kind of life for a family, but you're too young and arrogant to know that. You'll find out one day, though, and it better not be at my daughter's expense. Now you're going to have a baby. If I didn't know how headstrong my daughter is, I'd have my hands around your throat right now. But I know she would never let anyone talk her into something she didn't want to do, so I know she must have wanted this, and you can bet that's what's saving your life at this moment. So you want my permission to marry her. Okay, you got it, *but*"—and this was a huge *but*, as he leaned in closely to Mousie—"if you *ever* hurt my daughter in any way, I will find you and I will put my hands around your throat and I will squeeze and squeeze until my fingers meet in the middle. I won't stop squeezing until your eyeballs pop right out of your head. Do you understand me?"

Mousie bobbed his head, managing an "Of course, Big Lou, I understand."

Dad continued, "And be thankful that I know your uncle. I know you come from a good family, so that's in your favor. But don't you ever forget what I told you here today, capisce?"

Another bobblehead nod from Mousie.

And with that, Dad extended his hand for a handshake, the symbol of a closed deal. As they shook hands, Dad lightened it up a bit by telling Mousie, "I have to admit, though, it took guts coming to me like you did. I admire your courage, kid, but don't let it go to your head, you hear me?"

"Sure, Big Lou. You'll never be sorry either," Mouse told my father, with all sincerity.

Dad's retort to that was, "You're the only one who has to worry about being sorry. So don't be."

Case closed.

We were officially getting married, and the news spread like wildfire. To learn that most any other "just turned seventeen" girl was getting married and expecting a baby might have been quite the shocker, but not in this case. Everyone who knew me well knew that being a wife and mother was my calling, my dream, and all I ever really wanted since falling under Mousie's spell. Not the path for most girls of this age, but certainly a fit for me. And so we planned a small, simple wedding which Mousie paid for entirely. I designed and made my wedding dress, a simple, fitted white dress with yellow embroidery on the bottom, with a matching headpiece. It was very appropriate for both the times and our reception, which followed our short and sweet church ceremony. As no wedding would be complete without a little drama, ours was due to the ceremony being delayed almost two hours because the priest we chose to marry us was late due to being at the racetrack with some of the neighborhood guys! While I was freaking out, Mousie later dismissed it as no big deal; after all, you don't walk away from a winning streak! Our wedding was not the grandiose affair that Italians are known for. We had what was called a peanut wedding, held in a local VFW hall. Simple in decorum and at the cost of less than $1,000, Mousie saw to all the details. We had a neighborhood band and a mouthwatering Italian feast as supplied by a few of Mousie's gambling buddies who owned an Italian restaurant and owed him money. The drinks flowed all night, and a room filled to overcapacity of wonderful family and friends enjoyed what was to be remembered as one of the most fun weddings ever by everyone who attended. It was all magical, all right. The only thing that could enhance this moment would be the arrival of our baby, which we were both so anxious for.

Our next step was to set up house and prepare for our big "next step," our little one. We took the apartment above Mousie's parents' home, which worked out great, as it was only four blocks away from where my parents lived. I was immediately grateful to have had a typical Sicilian upbringing, happily gravitating to the role of wife and homemaker with natural ease. This might have been a difficult transition for most girls my age, but since I was always a very domesticated girl, it fit like a glove for me.

We were the only married couple among our friends, and our little apartment was constantly filled with them. As I listened to the antics and partying stories of our friends, I realized more and more that I was exactly where I wanted to be. It was the early seventies, the days of sex, drugs, and rock 'n' roll. It never was my bag, so there was not a moment of regret on my part for the path I chose. The only real problem I had was the horrific morning sickness that seemed to consume me all day long. I had always been a healthy eater, yet everything made me sick to my stomach. Other than that, life was perfect.

Mousie had a regular routine down that I actually came to think of as his "work schedule." Call it youth or just plain naïveté, but I honestly didn't mind his lifestyle choices and accepted them. All the things we planned, everything he promised me, were materializing, and we were so happy, so why wouldn't I?

Each night was dedicated to one aspect of his many gambling skills, and he went off to do his thing while I made and maintained our home. Sometimes he didn't come home until the next morning. The Friday night card games often lasted through Sunday afternoon, but that was okay with me too. I accepted all this, as he promised it wouldn't always be this way, that things would change later on. I believed him. The time we spent together, though, was time well spent. Mousie talked and taught me strategy, and I listened intently as he gave me blow-by-blow accounts of everything he did, and it was actually interesting and very entertaining. We laughed so much, talked a lot, and most importantly, the conversation was always a two way street, an exchange between us, never one-sided. Mousie always wanted to know what I was experiencing as an expectant mother, how I was feeling, what my thoughts were about the baby coming. Crazy as it sounds, I settled into my new lifestyle quite nicely. I wanted for nothing and had money for whatever I wanted or needed. The only disappointment I experienced, which was pretty minor, was the response I received when I expressed my desire to go to community college after the baby. Although Mousie understood my thirst for learning, he merely replied, "Don't worry, baby, I'll teach you everything you'll ever need to know," which was not said in a cocky manner, but in one of his many hilarious, put-on voices, Mousie's own brand of seduction that always worked like a charm. We were so very happy.

There is no way to fully prepare for the birth of your first child. You can ask all the questions and get all the right answers, but nothing prepares you for the actual birth. It's probably a good thing too, because labor is something that you're better off not knowing about beforehand! It really is true, though, that you forget all about the pain once you hold that precious angel in your arms. We didn't have that pleasure for a while, though, because our Little Contessa decided to present herself two months early. She was a beautiful little preemie, weighing in at a mere three and a half pounds. We had to leave her at the hospital, in the high-risk nursery, for just over two weeks, as she needed to be kept in an incubator to support breathing and digestion. As that was accomplished, we finally got the go-ahead to bring our angel home.

My father insisted on being the one to pick up his granddaughter. He didn't even want Mousie to come; when I got word from the doctor, my father gave that paralyzing gaze to Mousie and announced to both of us that he would be the one to take me to the hospital to bring his granddaughter home. It wasn't my dad's way to show emotion, but his announcement told us how proud and excited he really was to be a grandfather. My dad wasn't around much when we were kids, and I could instantly tell that he planned on being a hands-on grandfather. He gave me parenting tips all the way home. Funny thing, this car ride was the longest and most detailed conversation we ever had, and it was wonderful. I suddenly saw my father in a light I never had seen him in before. It was amazing. Here I was, a mother, for just a minute, and all of a sudden, as if a veil was lifted from me, I could see the how and why of so many things he had done and said over the years in the name of being a good parent. How lucky I would come to realize I was to have had this one day, this one car ride with my father.

We drove straight to my parents' house, where the whole family waited to see the gorgeous but oh-so-very-tiny Little Contessa. She weighed just under five pounds. She wore Cabbage Patch doll diapers. I didn't blame Mousie for being scared to hold her—we all were—but that subsided quickly once we got our Little Contessa home and began caring for her. Soon we both became proficient in handling our little premature bundle of joy. Little Contessa was the best baby; she slept in long increments, allowing me to get back on my feet quickly. She was bright, happy, alert, and it was noted by everyone that she was the spitting image of her daddy. Mousie also resumed his regular schedule, which I had absolutely no problem with, as it allowed me to hone my mothering skills and create an action plan of my own. Thankfully, I had two grandmothers at my fingertips to help out when I needed to do grocery shopping and errands. I was also new to driving, so I really only went out when I had to, as I was still a little shaky, particularly with the baby in the car. I actually never even took a test; Mousie taught me to drive while we were still dating, and after we were married, he had a friend who worked at the DMV fix my license. For a mere one hundred dollars, all I had to do was show up with my identification, stand in the right line, and poof, there was my driver's license.

Mousie chose his words carefully. He said that once I got my license, he'd have me driving a new car in no time. Well, one would think he meant he would actually buy me a car. Not the case. One day, Mousie's good friend and gambling partner, Nick, came over to show us his brand new car, a gorgeous light blue Pontiac Catalina. It was slick and had all the latest features. We wished Nick all the best of luck with his gorgeous new wheels. Just a few days later, Mousie came home after a night of playing cards and plopped a set of keys on the table. With that undeniable impish grin of his, he announced, "Your new car is waiting for you outside."

I ran to the window. "Is Nick with you? The only car I see out here is Nick's new Catalina."

"Well, it's yours now," Mousie said, laughing.

"*What?* I'm confused. What's going on?" I asked.

"I told you I'd get you a new car, and I did. It's yours," he quite proudly declared.

"Mouse, I could never take your friend's car. It's brand new, he was so excited about it."

"You can and you will. Nick gambled and lost. I won. The car is yours. Period. That's the way it goes. There's no hard feelings either.

He knows the rules. It's an awesome car, too, you're gonna love it. Now go make me some breakfast, I'm starving!"

And just like that, I had my new car.

Five weeks after bringing Little Contessa home flew by quickly and very merrily. The major changes that took place in my life in this past year were positively significant and seemed natural and effortless to me. I was confident that nothing, absolutely nothing, could rock the bliss I found myself in the midst of.

It was just before eight o'clock on a Sunday morning when the phone rang.

Oh, shit, I thought, *who's calling so early?* Still in somewhat a stupor from a long middle-of-the-night feeding with the baby, I jumped out of bed and ran to the phone. My brother was on the other end, barely coherent, telling me that our father had a massive heart attack and died instantly. Big Lou was dead. I was hysterical, and there are still no words that adequately describe my feelings at that moment. *Shock, devastation, disbelief, numbness* perhaps. I was just now starting to bond with my dad for the first time. I was just beginning to see the wisdom of his words and his ways. I screamed for this to be a dream, but it wasn't. My father was gone, and I immediately realized that I would live the rest of my life never telling my father how much I loved him, needed him, and admired him for his courage and the relentless lessons in life he gave to all of us. There would never be anyone in my life who would have such a powerful impact, and I would live the rest of my days never letting him know that.

We quickly went to my parents' house. As I sat there in a fog, listening to the details of my dad's final evening and moments, I tried to take it all in, but I couldn't. Other family members and friends began to arrive as we all attempted to console one another. My poor mother, still young, vivacious, and gorgeous, was in a catatonic state. The house was soon filled. At one point, Mousie whispered to me, asking if he could turn on the TV to watch the game. Completely befuddled, I asked what the hell he was talking about. As if I weren't pretty close to the cliff at that moment, his response put me right over the edge.

"The Super Bowl, it's starting pretty soon," he said way too nonchalantly.

I pushed him into the bathroom, as that was the only space nobody else was around. "Are you fucking kidding me? You want to watch a fucking football game now?" I was half whispering, half screaming. And the look on my face should have told him of the seriousness of his misstep.

"Hey, I got five grand on this game! I have to watch it," he very coolly replied.

A chill ran up my spine, and I felt ice daggers spew from my eyes.

"What, what's that look for?" he so stupidly asked.

"You know what? Why don't you just go home and watch the game. Go ahead, go. The baby and I will stay here so you can concentrate on your business." I walked out of the bathroom, and he sneaked out of the house completely undetected. Talk about a life changing moment. In that one instant, I realized why my father was so opposed to Mousie and his gambling ways. Nothing will take precedence over a gambler's bets; everything else is secondary, my dad would say. I thought I was so smart. I thought I knew so much. I didn't know shit. My father lived the gambling life; he knew it well and had enough experience to know that in the end, as he so knowingly put it, a gambler never wins. How could I be so stupid to not realize my father was giving me the wisdom of his own mistakes? It all became clear to me this day; today was my real graduation day, for I lost the one most integral figure in my life. Suddenly I realized how hard it is to be a parent. All the things he tried to teach us instantly registered. His strict and unwavering nature was his way of showing us strength and courage, for he risked his own children not "liking" him in his relentless attempt to ensure his kids had the fortitude to go out into our tough world and make it. "I'm the only one who has to give a shit about the way you turn out," he would always say. A little quote I often used on my own daughter whenever I needed to lay down some rules. It took this one singular conversation with my husband to shove this reality into my face.

Mousie attributed my quietness over the next few months to dealing with my father's death, but he went about his normal affairs. Of course, I was still recovering from the reality that my dad was gone, but I was also in deep thought over that disgusting display of selfishness Mousie demonstrated. And by the way, he won the Super Bowl, and although he won a ton of money, it really pissed me off that he did. I started looking at him a little differently, noticing a little more of a cocky attitude and swagger. My father was the only person who could keep Mousie in check, the only thing that kept a boundary on him. I was starting to fear what would happen now that Dad was gone. He had nothing to fear now, nobody to rein him in. If I thought I was all grown up and independent before, it was only now that I realized I crossed the threshold into adulthood with only the memory of my father's words to guide me when I needed direction. My father taught me to look at more than what was in front of your face, to look beyond the surface. I never knew how important that was until now. Now I knew that life changes in an instant and you have to be able to quickly adapt to the curveballs life throws at you. Secure your own place in life and never depend on anyone else to make your life for you; you have to do that yourself. Also, never take anything or anyone for granted. Always let those you love know it, not just by your words, but, more importantly, by your actions. I promised my father that I would be sure to teach his granddaughter all the same things.

I became less accepting of Mousie's lifestyle and before long, sat him down for a serious discussion, telling him it was time to make some changes. I told him I wanted more stability now that we were a family and insisted that he get a normal job, something we could count on. Mousie assured me that he was working on something big, a new business venture that would change our lives, and that he was was waiting to get a few details ironed out before telling me more. Within another week or two, he finally disclosed those details. Here's the short version.

As each decade brings about a new recreational drug, something new was about to explode onto the scene. Quaaludes, or "ludes," as they became known, were a central nervous system depressant that promoted a very relaxed, euphoric feeling when ingested. With great pride, my entrepreneurial husband joyously announced he became partners with a supplier of this new wonder drug. Mousie met a man who was part of the national distribution arena for the drug while playing in a weekend card game. I never knew many details, nor did I even want to, but apparently, the two put their heads together, forming this new partnership. The man was responsible for the Midwest distribution. Mousie's fame for making shrewd deals did not fail him, and he negotiated a deal with this guy for unprecedented profit margins. He bought ridiculously low and sold sky high. He would store them in a warehouse and hire several "salesmen" with actual territories. Lord knows he had many disciples who would do anything for him. So you're sitting around, chatting with your married girlfriends, swapping husband stories, and someone says, "My husband came home and I asked how his day was. 'Fantastic, honey. I just closed a deal that's gonna make me the top illegal drug dealer for a new controlled substance that will inevitably become the most-lusted-after street drug of the decade!'" Can you imagine that?

"ARE YOU OUT OF YOUR FUCKING MIND?" was my response. There are no words to describe my rage. Okay, gambling is one thing, but drugs are certainly a whole other level. *No way!* I didn't even drink. I never smoked pot. I had a child to raise. "Absolutely not!" I protested.

"Aww, there's nothing to worry about," he assured me. "I got it all worked out, you'll see." He was determined to go forward with this partnership, and there was no stopping him. I was a wreck. Nobody needed to tell me this was the beginning of the end. I knew it.

Talk about a tidal wave. Ludes hit the streets and took off like a flash fire. This was the height of hard rock bands, and everyone was getting high. Seemed like everyone was living according to Ziggy Stardust, Led Zeppelin, The Who, and the Rolling Stones. Pot was merely an appetizer. Quaaludes were now the main course. Profits were colossal. In no time at all, the demand far outweighed the supply, and prices went higher and higher, profits got bigger and bigger. I saw, I watched, and I panicked. There was more money rolling in than anyone could ever imagine, and Mousie was spending just as fast. Money was stashed everywhere in the house—in the freezer, in suit jacket linings, under the carpet, I mean everywhere—and I was a nervous wreck over it. What if one of these wacko customers decided to rob us, knowing he wasn't home all that much? After all, Mousie was known as an easygoing guy, certainly not anyone you would be afraid of.

I soon saw the end of one chapter and beginning of a darker one almost overnight. Yes, there was tons of money rolling in, and with it rolled plenty of extravagances that I enjoyed as well. But I honestly felt so guilty, even dirty, using that money to sustain our home life. But what else could I do? I was actually disgusted by it. The friends who used to stop over and hang out at our house were now showing up totally wasted or desperate to get that way, looking for ludes. I don't know if I felt more rage, repugnance, or both over the thought that these people would actually show up at my door looking for drugs, thinking they were kept in our house and I would dispense them at a simple request. That, along with having all this money hidden everywhere, wondering if anyone else knew about it or thought about it, haunted me. If people out there thought we kept anything in our house, what would stop the freaks who got high on ludes from plotting and planning to break in, rob us, hurt us, or whatever else?

I was going out of my mind. I had enough, and I sat Mousie down and told him I was leaving. I couldn't stay there trying to raise a child with all this going on right in my face. He begged me not to go and assured me that he would take care of everything, that he would ensure nobody ever came to the house anymore, just please give him another chance to fix things.

"Fix things? How about getting out of this business?" I pleaded. "That's all the fixing we need."

But he assured me everything would be all right if I just gave it a little more time; after all, didn't he keep every other promise he ever made me?

If you sell candy, you better not like sugar. If you are a baker, you better not like pastries. We all have a weak spot; we all have an Achilles' heel. Know yours and keep it in check. If you have a business, no matter what that business is, you better keep your focus, or soon you'll be out of business. It was only a matter of time before Mousie started dipping into his own cookie jar. The later known phrase "Don't get high on your own supply" hadn't yet been coined. I pretty much overlooked it at first; after all, he didn't even drink alcohol, and I thought it was just an occasional thing. But I soon noticed that he, along with so many others, was eating these things like candy. With my father gone, Mousie had nothing to fear anymore, and I was getting frantic. I saw friends I'd known for years constantly high and incoherent, deteriorating over these little white pills. One of our friends was in so many car accidents due to becoming hooked on ludes they nicknamed him Crash. Funny, huh? I saw women I knew were on public aid sign over their monthly welfare checks and/or food stamps in exchange for ludes. Sex for Quaaludes? You bet! Did people try to warm up to me merely hoping to score free ludes? Absolutely. Almost overnight, our environment and most of the people in it changed, and not for the better. Unfortunately, even Mousie, the one who I thought was so in control, so together, succumbed. And so began his downward spiral.

My husband had it all. At this point, he had even more than even he ever imagined. His mannerisms, taste and style, humor and reputation for throwing money around were all part of the image he loved and thrived on. It was only now that I began to realize just how important that image was to him. This latest venture of his added yet another element to his overall persona. He was crowned the Quaalude king and wore that crown as if it were a 20-carat diamond ring. If what had transpired already didn't disgust me enough, watching Mousie get higher and higher made me want to vomit at the sight of him. I knew him better than he knew himself and knew he didn't know what a boundary was. Nothing was ever enough for him. And these days, I was hearing my father's voice more clearly now, remembering him telling me to look beyond what's in front of you, to see the big picture. Although Mousie denied popping Quaaludes as often as he did, only a complete idiot couldn't see it. The slurred speech, eyes at half-mast, nodding out, dropping lit cigarettes on the furniture. Then there was my personal hair-raising favorite of hearing his crackly Quaalude voice, which sent shivers down my spine. He shouldn't even have needed the Quaaludes. The high he got from knowing he was idolized by everyone should have, weirdly, been enough.

But I was learning about addiction and its insatiable appetite. There's never enough of whatever it is that's got its grip on you. Was it arrogance, addiction, or both that fed his addiction? And if all this weren't enough, he had even begun to hit me. If anything was so totally against his character, it was physical violence toward me. Mousie was a lover, not a fighter by nature, but these days, any little thing would cause him to slap me, kick me, or even punch me. Thankfully, my little girl was still a baby and didn't see any of this; however, it was a little trickier to hide the occasional bruises and marks from friends who would stop by. I frequently had to discourage company, as I didn't want anyone to know what was happening.

I knew it was the effect of the Quaaludes. I hated the Quaalude king. I hated him so much that one night, while the king was bobbing his head and drooling all over himself, he ordered me to make him an ice cream cone. *Yes, Your Highness, I'll make you an ice cream cone you'll never forget,* I said to myself. I went to his secret stash and grabbed a handful of Quaaludes, mashed them up with a rolling pin, mixed them up into the ice cream, and stuffed it all into a cone. *Fuck it,* I thought, *he wants to get high, I'll get him high!*

As he licked away, he slurred, "Hey, this ice cream tastes funny, it's a little bitter."

"It's got pecans in it, that's probably what you taste." I laughed.

He ate the whole ice cream cone and passed out shortly after. He slept for three days, stumbling out of bed once in a while to pee. Ahhhhh, three days of peace and quiet for me and my baby girl. At one point, he got up to go to the bathroom but, in his hazy condition, wandered into his closet. He was still so fucked up I'm sure he wasn't even conscious. With his eyes half open—he was still swaying back and forth—I watched him piss all over his very expensive, meticulously placed shoe collection, and roared with laughter. I really needed a laugh, and this was it. I washed up the piss from the floor but left his shoes all wet and "pissy." They eventually dried up, and I cracked up every time I saw him put on a pair. I know, what a bitch, right?

We were on a sinking ship, and I was desperate to find the life jackets. It was all so sickening to me. How quickly life changes. This was what my father was trying to prepare me for. Here I was, still trying to find my way as a new mother, having just lost my dad, the only income I had was illegal. My young, single friends, who were all getting high as well, thought being married to the Quaalude king was the most awesome thing in the world. The man I was so in love with was deteriorating before my eyes. I felt there was nobody I could talk to about the nightmare that my life had become. However, in my dreams I could call out to my father for help, and I did very often during this time.

"Daddy, Daddy, help me, please tell me what to do and show me the way," I would pray to him as I lay awake at night. And he came to me each time. Just as clear as I saw my surroundings, I saw my father sitting at the foot of my bed, calmly reminding me of my strong will, that I never showed fear, not even to him. He reiterated the oration I heard many times as a young teenager, reminding me to be a leader, never a follower, to never ever let anyone lead me down a path that was not my choosing. These "conversations" with my father are among my most cherished memories of him, for they actually did tell me what I knew I had to do and fortified me with the strength to do it.

I saw less and less of Mousie, and more and more of the Quaalude king. Our dream was over. Yes, life changes, and you better be able to change with it—sink or swim, period. Thankfully, my beautiful, delightful baby girl filled my days with immeasurable joy. She was my whole focus, and planning a future for us became my priority. As I put her to bed each night, I sat beside her crib, watching her sleep. I softly whispered to my Little Contessa, "I promise I will not let you grow up around this craziness. I swear I will take you away from here and we will live a normal life, one that you will be proud of. I don't know how yet, but I promise you, my sweetheart, I will never let you down."

I began to siphon money from Mousie whenever possible. Normally, he was sharp as a tack and extremely focused when it came to his money, but he got pretty sloppy these days and was usually so fucked up he never even realized anything was missing. My many yet feeble attempts at trying to convince him to redirect himself ended up in arguments and eventually led to physical abuse. I had no interest, time, or patience in trying to be a rehab counselor. My sole focus was to get the hell out of there and build a life for me and my daughter. I learned firsthand that if you use, you lose, and Mousie was using not only his own product but had also graduated to other, more sophisticated drugs as well. His "salesmen" had gotten just as sloppy, also from using, and just as the Quaalude king soared to a meteoric rise, the kingdom began to crumble. *Go ahead and trash your life,* I thought, *but I'll be dammed if I let you take me down with you.*

My mother was still in a state of shock and recovering from the sudden death of my father, who left nothing behind but a pile of bills. My brother and sister both still lived at home with Mom. My siblings and I were all contributing to maintaining my mother's household as well as caring for her personally. Going back home to live with Mom was not an option. Besides that, I felt a strange sense of independence consume me, and I was determined to forge ahead completely on my own. I felt my father's blood, a huge force of nature pulsing through my veins, telling me this was the way to go. In an attempt to show me that things would change, we moved to a new apartment almost a year ago. Mousie really thought I bought that bullshit, but in reality, I knew he moved us just so his parents wouldn't see the constant stream of people related to his business coming and going. Our new place was relatively inexpensive, spacious, and beautifully furnished. Little Contessa and I were quite comfortable here, and at a year and a half old, she was aware this was her home. I didn't want to disrupt anything for her.

One day I thought, *Hey, why should I be worried about finding a place for Little Contessa and me? Mousie's the problem, so he should be the one to leave.* After thinking about it long and hard, I thought that demanding he leave the house would be the wake-up call he needed. Not so.

I finagled enough money to pay the next few months' rent and the household bills. By this time, Mousie was so frequently fucked up he wasn't even aware of any such thing as bills or even groceries. He was frequently gone for days at a time, and as I continued to plot and plan my future, I was constantly on edge. Our landlords were a young Italian couple who heard more than their share of our arguments and were witness to the physical results of those arguments on my face and body. I approached them for help, indicating that I wanted to throw him out but needed their help to do so. I offered to pay to have the locks changed so he no longer had access to our apartment. They immediately agreed. They had two small children of their own and didn't like the constant noise and disruption that Mousie brought into our building, so they had no problem with helping me execute my plan.

Throwing my husband out was the first step. But what then? How would I support us? Even though I had stashed away a little money, it would only last for so long. Then it came to me one day. I was the quintessential neat freak, always cleaning, with everything having to be in just the right place. Why not put that to work for me and clean houses for others? By talking to my landlady and a few neighbors, I was able to line up a few cleaning jobs. The landlady watched Little Contessa for me while I worked, and I reciprocated for her when she needed to run errands. My plans were falling into place. Mousie had no idea what was going on, as he left one day and hadn't been back since the locks were changed. But then he reappeared. He was pretty wasted and couldn't figure out why his key didn't work. I allowed him in just to talk, firmly informing him the landlord was aware of everything and if he heard the slightest bit of arguing, he would immediately call the police. I told Mousie that I just couldn't go on this way, and while it was my wish to have him clean himself up and rejoin us, hopefully getting our lives back on track, I would not allow his lifestyle or behavior in the home I was raising my daughter in any longer. I wanted him out of the house. All that had already transpired kept me in a constant state of shock, but his response was the lightning bolt that snapped me right out of it and laid the groundwork for the tenacity and intensity I am known for to this day.

"What? Who the fuck do you think you are telling me to leave? You'll do what I say when I say it! You'll take whatever I dish out and like it, you hear me? You were nothing when I met you, and you'll never be anything without me! What the fuck can you do on your own? *Nothing!* You owe everything you have to me, and you can just kiss my ass and be grateful I don't throw your ass outta here now! You think you can tell me to get out? What the fuck would you do without me? What the fuck can you do? You're worthless! You need me! How the fuck do you think you can get along without me, you stupid bitch? Now shut the fuck up and make me something to eat!"

With that delusional rant, I realized the man I fell in love with, the man I married, was completely gone. *Dead!* That was it. I was done. I offered to let him take whatever he wanted right then and there and demanded he leave immediately. I also told him that as long as I had even the slightest suspicion that he was using drugs, he would never be allowed to see Little Contessa. If everything else weren't enough to convince me I was on the right track, this second declaration of his surely was.

"There's not a fucking thing here I want, so yeah, I'll leave. And don't even kid yourself to think you can get money from me, 'cuz I promise you, I'll never give you a fucking dime, not for anything. I'll make sure you come crawling back to me, and when you do, maybe after you suck my dick for a while, I'll let you kiss my ass before I throw you a little fucking bone. Yeah, then you'll see how stupid you really are, telling me to leave, you fucking cunt! And I'll see my daughter whenever I want without any shit from you!"

I felt the force of my fictional guardian angel give me the strength and conviction to adequately convey my feelings to this monster, with the intensity in which I felt them. This was my defining moment, my Scarlett O'Hara scene, and I played it with all the fire she was known for; fist clenched and raised high in the air, I vehemently proclaimed that it would be over my dead body he would see Little Contessa, that while there was a breath of life left in me, he would never have the opportunity to expose her to his world and all his vices. I begged him to hold his breath waiting for me to ask him for anything, because he'd surely die while waiting for that to happen. "So get the fuck out and don't let the door hit you in the ass!" And after he did, in true Scarlett fashion, I took the same vow she did: "I'll do whatever I have to for our survival. I will answer to nobody, and I will never depend on anyone for anything, ever! And I *will* succeed!"

Thankfully, Little Contessa was napping during this exchange.

Mousie did leave, and hearing the door close made me feel like a building was lifted off me. I sat there in what I felt was the most peace I had felt in quite a while. I was calm as I clearly saw a vision, an epiphany. *I will do whatever it takes to succeed. I will learn, I will grow, and I will keep moving forward. Nothing will stop me from creating a positive, productive, and privileged life for my daughter, one that is void of all this bullshit and drama. God help the person who gets in my way! My Little Contessa will have a life that doesn't include drugs, gambling, and the rest of the street vices that destroy lives. A life that will allow her to pursue her own dreams, chart her own course. Yes, whatever it takes, with no regrets, and anyone who doesn't like it or understand can fuck off! I will be my own person and never ever depend on anyone for anything, ever!*

The years passed with each of us staying true to the last words we exchanged.

Although I tripped and fell many times, I always managed to pick myself up and remain independent, while Mousie contributed nothing either financially or emotionally to raising our daughter. In my plight to raise a confident and strong child, I learned to let go of any anger I harbored against Mousie; instead, I chose to provide Little Contessa with countless stories of how and why her father and I fell in love, our fun times and escapades, and the positive elements of our short life together. I wanted her to know and understand that while her father was not in her life, he did love her, that God makes all kinds of people, short, tall, fat, thin, weak, and strong. Her father, unfortunately, was one of the weak people who couldn't even care for himself, let alone take care of someone else. I wanted her to know that she was wanted and loved by us both, and as she grew older, I was able to provide more details as to what all transpired. In time, when I was sure she was old enough, mature enough, and mentally equipped to handle the story, I would tell her everything and prayed she would agree that the life he chose was not conducive to what would be the best world to raise a child in. I desperately wanted her to understand that while I loved the man I married, that man fell to addiction and got lost in the shuffle, and if I wanted a better life for her, I had no choice but to leave him and all the bullshit he brought into our lives. I believed then, and still do, that children are a product of their environment. I did not want my daughter to see her mother succumb but to stand strong and independent and have that example to live by. To this day, I pray I achieved my goal.

Time passed, and through mutual friends, we would hear tidbits about Mousie and his ongoing shenanigans. We came to learn the he eventually fulfilled his lifelong dream of living what he called the high life in Las Vegas. Still a gambler, still dabbling in drugs, but still fun to be around, or so we heard. I had long since shed any ill feelings toward Mouse; I worked hard and was fortunate to realize much success in a career anyone would be proud of. I came to learn that the best revenge truly is your own success and there is no place for anger or acrimony in achieving that goal. Bad karma. I sometimes proposed to my daughter that if she should ever want to seek her father out, I would surely help her. I would welcome the opportunity for her to get to know him on her own, thus enabling her to form her own opinions.

Now grown, Little Contessa and I were vacationing in Las Vegas, and I spontaneously sought him out, wondering if I would find the Quaalude king or the real Mousie. A chat on the phone revealed no sign of the Quaalude king, only the good old Mouse, so I managed to arrange a meeting between him and his beautiful, intelligent young adult daughter, who had already embarked on a successful career path herself. She was still the spitting image of her father and was receptive to meeting him. We met in the lounge of our hotel, and I immediately knew that it was Mousie we were meeting; the Quaalude king was gone, hopefully forever. Without having seen him in so many years, I was happily surprised to see how good

Mousie looked, that he had aged quite well. Even better, he had his best accessory with him—his undeniable humor, wit, and charm. Our encounter began with Mousie immediately and, seemingly, genuinely apologizing for not being much of a father, for the way he treated me, as well as for neglecting her and admitting that losing us was the worst mistake of his life, confessing he had nobody to blame but himself. I had never seen him so humble, and I have to admit, it was particularly endearing. It actually turned out to be a fun and somewhat magical night, which left me hoping that perhaps, maybe, after all these years, we could actually be a family again. Call me crazy, but for one brief moment, I truly believed, and hoped, it could be. They exchanged contact information, and the ball to keep in touch was now in his court.

However, that ball was unfortunately dropped in a relatively short period. The one wonderful thing that did transpire, though, was that during the course of their short lived reacquaintance, Little Contessa was able to realize most of, if not all, the things I tried to convey to her over the years and thus seemed to have fully understood what I did and why.

And then one day, years later, I received a call that Mousie died from a drug overdose. I was numb for some time, replaying our entire relationship over and over in my head. Nobody would have believed how deeply I was affected, saddened, of course, that he was dead and because it was an addiction he was never strong enough to shake that took him. I grieved the very first love of my life, who had such an impact on me. I was also furious. Angry at the waste of what could have been an incredible life. Mad that another chance for us to be a family again, a chance for my daughter to have both parents in her life, my precious grandson to have a grandfather as well, was gone forever. While most women wouldn't have even cared—and honestly, many friends and relatives expressed shock at why I did—I felt a very strong sense for what I needed to do. I decided that I would bring him back home to Chicago for a proper memorial service and burial. As a parent, I've always tried to show my daughter the right path, and I believe that responsibility continues as a parent no matter how old our children are. In addition, my Italian upbringing taught me that in death, you put your own feelings aside and do what's respectful and proper to honor the deceased. Was Mousie a shitty husband? *Yes!* Was he a negligent father? *For sure!* Did he make my life miserable and cause me a great deal of pain, both physically and mentally? *Absolutely!* However, wasn't he the one who gave me the confidence I lacked to become my own person all those years ago? Wasn't he my very first and most important love? This might be a twisted sort of logic, but after we split, wasn't it his horrid treatment of me that evoked and ignited the fire and drive in me to forge ahead independently? And more than anything else, more than all the material things he either gave and/or took away, or that I acquired since, it was Mousie who gave me the most wonderful and cherished gift of my entire life, my Little Contessa, for which I would always and forever love him and remember him for what I knew was his core, rather than who he eventually became.

And so the chapter finally closed with saying goodbye to this man who was once a superstar, who was loved and highly regarded by everyone who knew him, but not without a little comedy or drama, depending on how you viewed it. Little Contessa, who was by now a married woman, mother, and cancer survivor, was still undergoing chemotherapy treatments. We had only a short window of opportunity to have the funeral services. At this time, Little Contessa was in the middle of significant medical treatment. Recovering from breast cancer, she was on a strict chemotherapy schedule that could not be deviated from. While difficult, we figured out a way to proceed with services and maintain her medical treatment plan. We had everything set, including his obituary notice in the newspapers, with all the details. Mousie had to be embalmed in Las Vegas then flown to Chicago. His body was somehow misplaced. I called every mortuary in Las Vegas to find him, and after one whole day of frantic phone calls, I finally did. I was able to get him on the last flight available that night, and thus enabling the services to go on as planned and also allow Little Contessa to get to her chemo appointment as scheduled. The services were a mixture of joy in seeing old friends and sorrow of losing one. While I played the role of the hostess at the services, it was an effort for me to keep a straight face. Nobody would have believed it, but I was fighting back tears all day, hurting that Mousie was gone, as well as being mad at him for letting the happiness of what could have been a real family slip away. He had such potential as an individual; we had such potential for family life, particularly now that we were all grown up, not to mention a beautiful grandson to share. Mouse gave me the spunk to dare to dream and realize a life of my own. He could have made his life so worthwhile, as well as ours together. But it was not to be.

The night before his funeral, I wrote him a long letter, pouring out all my feelings, telling him that I would bury my disgust along with him if he did one last thing. I begged him to keep a watchful eye over our daughter, keeping her healthy, happy, and safe in a way that only he now could. I placed the letter in his coffin before it was closed.

Little Contessa's health continued to improve, and while she had fought this dreaded battle courageously and magnificently, I can't help feeling that her dad is lending a hand with her ongoing good health. Although there were some who felt Mousie did not deserve the memorial services, I never regretted providing them. Looking back on this relationship, I smile and recount the blessings from its experience. Most notably, my daughter, but I also believe that it served as the stage for me to learn, grow, develop, and express who I was. When we enter into a relationship, we are naturally optimistic for its evolution, and we all have to be the willow once in a while in order for that to happen. If we at least try, we'll find we won't break! I learned never to allow yourself to be completely dependent on anyone. Every aspect of any relationship should be give and take. It's up to us to equip ourselves with survival tools and our own responsibility to be prepared and know when to use them, as well as have a plan B. Let go of anger. It won't get you anyplace. Put your energy into moving forward, keep your focus and leave the drama behind. That will help you know how and when to forgive. And most of all, find the lessons, the humor, and the honor in all your relationships, and you will no doubt allow people to see the same in you.

The first cut really is the deepest, or at least it was for me. While I moved on positively, I can still feel the hole it left in my heart. The lessons I learned from this entire episode provide a Band-Aid for the hole; maybe that's a good thing in order for their reminder to remain. But should I ever say "I love you" again, it will be just like the song: I would give you my whole heart, but there's a piece of it forever gone to someone else.

The Lawyer

Know where you're going and what you
need to know in order to get there.

As I sat in a church pew, attending the most elaborate funeral services ever, all I could do was pray as I reflected. A friend of mine, a lovely lady, had just passed away after many years of being plagued by illness. I was very sad that she had passed, but glad that her suffering was over, for she had been sick for a very, very long time. I was praying as sincerely and profoundly as I knew how. I was praying—no, actually begging—for forgiveness from my dearly departed friend. I mentally begged for absolution from this lady, and, of course, from God, for something I did a very long time ago. Something that would have prevented us from ever being friends in the first place had she known about, and something I prayed she would never find out when we ultimately did. But now she was with God and knew everything. I was truly and genuinely sorry for what happened so many years ago, and I realized now I could no longer hide behind youth and ignorance.

It seemed like an eternity ago when I made that silent pledge to do anything I had to in order to succeed and make a better life for myself and my daughter. Decades had passed when I took on the persona of my fictional champion, Scarlett O'Hara, and vowed that if I had "to lie, cheat, steal, or kill," I will pursue my ambitions without conscience and answer to nobody in order to provide a fuller, richer, and more successful life for us. A mirror of divine intervention was now being shoved in my face. I didn't like it at all, but I knew I deserved it. All I could do now was mentally beg, pray, and remember so that I would never repeat this mistake.

Rewind to the end of my first marriage. The mouse was out of the house for about a year, and my main focus was earning a living for us. I started cleaning houses; I brought Little Contessa along with some toys, and she played nicely while I cleaned with the speed of sound and utmost precision. I sometimes had up to four houses a day, but that still wasn't enough. I was barely scraping by. These were the leanest times of my life, but I look back on them with both gratitude and laughter. I am grateful for this period, as being so poor allowed me to sharpen my wits, think outside the box, and become evermore willful in achieving my long-term goals. I hate to admit to some of the things I did during this period, but these were desperate times and consequently called for desperate measures. With money extremely scarce, on several occasions, I took Little Contessa to the grocery store, perched her in the child seat of the cart, and walked the aisles, allowing her to pick out whatever she wanted to eat. I opened her selections and let her munch away. I didn't even consider that I'd get in trouble for doing that. My thought was, if anyone said anything, I could just fall back on "Don't worry, I'm going to pay for it." That was my version of taking my daughter out for lunch. I also stole food. I don't mean a jar of peanut butter here and there. I mean I managed to snag whole beef roasts from our local grocery store. I was friendly with a butcher just a few blocks away who knew I was going through a rough time. I would bring him the stolen roast and he would divide it up into ground beef and other cuts, which allowed me to make a few heartier dinners. During this time, Little Contessa and I ate a whole lot of scrambled eggs; therefore, having meat for dinner was like having a holiday meal. This was also a time when I had to decide between toilet paper and Kleenex; we couldn't have both. I usually just went for the toilet paper because it was more versatile. You could blow your nose with it and even fold it into napkins. Forget about paper towels, which were way too extravagant at that time. Only the absolute necessities were purchased. To this day, I am a freak about stocking an abundance of toilet paper, napkins, Kleenex, and paper towels. I can never have enough! I've always been grateful that my daughter was too young to know about any of this. I did my best to keep her happy and entertained.

Yes, this was the most impoverished time of my life, and yet I remember more laughter than pain. I look back and think of the games I made up to play with my little girl, and nothing could ever replace those cherished moments. She took my worries away and put a smile on my face. Little Contessa gave me the will to go on and the strength to do whatever I needed to. I read a lot during this period and came across a quote that I remind myself of to this day: "That which does not kill us, makes us stronger." So true. I never would have known the power of this statement if this period in my life had not occurred. I survived it all, and the experiences certainly did make me stronger. More so than even I realized I could be. I am not proud of some of my actions and have remorse about the unethical things I did back then. Consequently, I've tried to make up for those things. Through the years, I have donated much of my time doing volunteer work, as well as considerable sums of money, to charitable organizations in an attempt to pay back the necessities I took when I had no money to pay for them. I hope I am forgiven.

News that the neighborhood men's club burned down streamed through our area. A light bulb went off in my head. I had an idea. Every neighborhood had a men's club, where the guys would go to play cards, play pool, chitchat, have a drink, and hang out. An early version of today's "man cave." A men's club usually had food catered when marathon card games were underway, which was pretty much every weekend. I knew several of the guys who frequented this club; friends of Mousie, my brother, and even some older friends of my dad. I approached a few of those I knew with my proposition. I offered them the use of my dining room to hold their weekend card games, and I would provide ongoing food for them while they played. In exchange, they would pay me one dollar per hand for the duration of their card game. Crazy, you say? Card games usually started on a Friday night and lasted through Sunday afternoon. I had a large dining room, with furniture able to seat eight comfortably, which was about the right seating they usually required for a good game. At one dollar per hand, the house usually cleared several hundred dollars from one weekend game. All I had to do was keep the food coming. I was known for my cooking, mainly Italian dishes and particularly my spaghetti sauce ("gravy") and meatballs. I started out small, as I had little working capital for the first game. I simply made a big pot of gravy with meatballs, sausage, and all the fixings that went with it. It wasn't hard to keep the pasta boiling, serve it up, and take the plate away when required. Before long, I was making a decent amount of money from the games and the meals got more and more elaborate and delicious. It was a win-win for both the house and the players.

Understand that I knew these people who camped out at my house all weekend. There was no fear of anything bad happening. Some even knew what a hard time I had with Mousie, and they admired how I stood up for myself as well as my independent nature. They were even a little protective of both my daughter and me. This was not a little card game with a few buddies getting together to blow fifty dollars. You've never seen serious men until you've seen them gamble for serious money. They were friends, and they were quiet and respectful, aware that Little Contessa was present, usually playing with me in her room or in the living room or even sleeping. All they wanted to do was play cards and eat when they were hungry. To amuse Little Contessa and somewhat explain to her what was going on, I taught her simple card games like Go Fish, as well as made up a matching game, to help her identify and add up numbers, which she really enjoyed. The players knew that Mousie was an absentee father and was not contributing financially. Usually, the big winner would throw in a little bonus for me, particularly as the meals got better. So for just a few days a week, all I had to do was cook, which I loved doing anyway, serve, and clean up while I played with Little Contessa in between. Not only did this allow me to ease up on cleaning houses, but it also enabled me to start taking a few night classes. I realize some people would frown upon a situation like this, but for those of us who grew up in our environment, it was no big deal. I was surviving.

I knew the card games wouldn't last, and I socked away as much money as I could before they ended, which was a few months later. Since I became comfortable with serving, I thought I'd try out for a waitress job. How hard could that be? I thought. I heard about a new nightclub that was about to open. This new club was not too far from my apartment, and rumor spread that it was to be quite posh and the new "it" place. The owner was a friend of my father's, and several of my friends suggested that I speak to him about a job as a cocktail waitress. Never really much of a drinker, I knew nothing about alcohol or mixed drinks. But the more I thought about it, the more I was convinced, saying, "What the hell, I'll give it a shot!" I went in to speak to the boss. I have to admit feeling a little guilty, lying to the boss about having cocktail experience, but then I really don't think he even heard me, as he was mainly focused on my boobs while showing me what a sexy uniform I would be wearing, telling me how hot I would look and what draw that would be for his patrons. I think that was more his focus than my experience, and therefore, I can't say I lost sleep over my little lie. I was to start that next weekend. I didn't have to be at work until eight o'clock, which was great. That start time allowed me to play with my daughter all day, feed her, and have her bathed and in her jammies before my cousin, the babysitter, arrived.

Call it naïveté, desperation, or just plain old balls, but I really didn't think twice about how I would perform on my new job until I actually got dressed to go to work. Yep, this sure was a hot, sexy uniform. Skintight and slinky, with a slit up to my waist, complemented by black tights and the highest heels I'd ever worn. Honestly, my biggest concern was walking around in those heels! It actually never occurred to me that perhaps I should have studied up a bit on mixed drinks and their ingredients. Oh, well, into the lion's den I went, and I nervously awaited my first customers. I had no idea that there's a systematic way to write a group drink order on your pad that would tell the bartender how to place the drinks on your tray, allowing you to serve the right drink to the right person. The way I learned that was by taking my very first drink order from a group of six, two ladies and four gentlemen. They were seated by our hostess, and I approached them with great enthusiasm. They were a very classy looking group; however, one of the men instantly showed he lacked any class at all by declaring he could stay there and drink all night, as long as it was me serving him, while caressing my leg up to the slit of my uniform as he spoke. I was cool about it, though; just goes to show you that you can buy expensive clothes but that doesn't buy you class. Oh, well, welcome to the nightlife!

I gave their drink order to the bartender, who was pretty frustrated because I didn't have it written in any special order. I didn't understand why. I collected their drinks and brought them to the table, placing one drink in front of each guest. The asshole with the wandering hands sipped his drink and made a funny face. He told me there must be a mistake, that this wasn't his drink. Flustered and completely unaware how to handle this situation, I relied on my quick wit.

"Are you sure? Can you taste it again?" I seductively asked.

He sipped the drink again.

"Do you like it?" I asked as I bent over and leaned into him.

"Yeah, sure, but…," he started.

"No buts," I interrupted. "You tasted it, you liked it, so shut the fuck up and just drink it!" I finished.

With that ballsy show, the group roared with laughter, and one other man added, "Honey, you're the only one who's ever been able to shut this guy up!"

The asshole stood up and grabbed my arm. "Feisty little girl, aren't you? I love it. Gimme your phone number, honey. I gotta see more of you."

I gave him a long, hard glare and responded "Beat it, shorty, I'm working" while I shrugged my arm back and walked away as the rest of the group howled with more laughter. They finished that round of drinks, left me a fifty dollar tip before leaving. *Piece of cake,* I thought to myself. *I can do this.* However, many of my other patrons didn't see the humor in my mistakes, and I was fired within two weeks.

I quickly got another waitress job at a well known and popular pancake house called Teddy Bear's not too far from my house. I was certainly more suited to serving breakfast and lunch as opposed to late nights and the alcohol crowd. I learned fast, made several friends, and more importantly, made lots of money, and since Teddy Bear's was a corporation, I also got medical and dental insurance for Little

Contessa and myself. I was able to maintain a regular daytime sched-ule and soon was even able to send Little Contessa to a very nice day care, where she could play with other children all day. We had a nice routine going, and soon a waitress friend of mine got me a job as a fill in girl at the Italian dining room where she worked. I managed to get a few night shifts in that restaurant several times a month. The owner saw how hard I worked and liked me, and soon he offered me a regular part-time schedule. I worked Teddy Bear's five days a week, then two nights at the Italian dining room, plus alternating Saturday and Sunday evenings. Those two days a week I worked both were pretty funny. I would fly out of Teddy Bear's, rush to pick up Little Contessa, then pick up my cousin the babysitter, and bring them both home. I made sure there was dinner already cooked and in the fridge for them the night before so all my cousin had to do was warm it up. I would drop them off, rush to the Italian dining room, and make a mad dash to their ladies' room to switch uniforms and get on the floor. It was all a whirlwind and hard work. I was always tired, but the money was good, and we were starting to live a real life, so it was all worth it. I was able to get an extra day off here and there, which I devoted to Little Contessa, and I always tried to treat her to something special on that day. She was the happiest little girl you ever saw. While she napped and slept in the evenings, I sewed for people, gaining a little extra money as well. I also still cleaned a house here and there, but that really faded out, as my two waitress jobs proved to be more profitable. Things had really shaped up nicely. Having my household finances finally under control allowed me to start planning one important thing I had on the back burner for far too long: a divorce!

I've never denied my OCD tendencies in all areas of my life, personally, professionally, and mentally. I live by an eternal checklist. A messy mind is a messy life. I do my best to keep my life clean, neat, and uncomplicated. It had been almost two years now since Mousie and I split up. Although I knew our marriage was irrevocably over and he had been completely out of our lives, it nagged at me that things were just left hanging. I had lots to figure out and get into place, and I had to be patient, but patience has never been a virtue of mine. A divorce cost money, and I didn't have any excess. Jeez, I'd been choosing between toilet paper and Kleenex for some time and I had finally grew my finances to allow for both, but paper towels were still out of the question. And so was paying for a divorce. Until now.

My family had friends with a relation who was a divorce attorney. They knew my situation, and after a few inquiries were made, the family friend agreed to take my case without charging me a left lung. After all, this would be a noncontentious divorce—no assets or property division at all, so pretty cut-and-dried. I made an appointment to see this attorney, without a thought except that I just took one more step to get my life on the right track. As I dressed for the appointment that morning, it dawned on me that I hadn't been downtown in such a long time. It also occurred to me that I had never been to an office before, not anybody's office of any kind. *Hmmm, this will be interesting.* I proceeded to dress in attire that was currently fashionable: Nik Nik blouse, French-cut jeans, and how-did-I-ever-walk-in-those platform shoes. This was the seventies, and I was styling!

I arrived at the lawyer's building with just enough time to locate his office and present myself. Such a fancy building! Marble, gold, and crystal everywhere. It was astonishing to me that people actually worked in such a lavish environment. As I entered the office, a very sophisticated receptionist greeted me, showed me to a seat, and offered me a wide variety of refreshments, which I declined. I was instantly fixed on the receptionist—not only her physical appearance, but also her poise, her manner of speech. She was so naturally elegant. I listened as she called into the lawyer's office to let him know I had arrived. She came over to me and advised me the lawyer was on another call and would receive me as soon as he was finished. I thanked her and sat there frozen, afraid to move while sitting on the most sumptuous sofa my ass had ever been on, trying to take in these surroundings. Marble walls, Italian leather furniture, silky area carpets, crystal lighting everywhere. I noticed reading material on the burl wood coffee table that was so above me I wouldn't dare even pick any of it up. While I sat there, I watched the receptionist do her job, answering phone calls, interacting with coworkers. She was so polished in both her appearance and manner. Her tone, her delivery, and her dress were all so impeccable. I thought I looked pretty good when I left the house, but being here right now, watching her, I felt like Julia Roberts walking down Rodeo Drive before she had her makeover. I was certainly not dressed for this atmosphere, and what really made me want to hide under the sofa was knowing my wardrobe at home was void of anything like I saw here today. The only time I had seen such posh surroundings was in the movies. Although so overwhelming to me, I was making mental notes.

Finally, I heard her phone buzz, and she said, "Okay, I'll show her right in." She asked me to please follow her. As we made our way through the thick frosted glass doors into the array of cubicles, I walked in wonderment through the aisles of knowledge and intelligence that permeated the air. This was my epiphany! Knowledge is power, Dad used to say. Like a bright light going off in my head, I instantly knew I needed to be in a place such as this. I immediately realized I needed to learn more in order to do more, be more, have more! Yes, the only way to grow and develop is through education. A million thoughts flooded my head, but I tried to shelf them, so as to concentrate on the conversation with the lawyer that was seconds away. Finally, we reached his office and the receptionist showed me in and made the introduction.

The lawyer was not a very large man. He was not particularly handsome either. He did, however, have an immediate and overpowering presence. Not too tall and a little stocky, the lawyer had very pronounced stereotypical Italian features. His thin, dark hair was styled in a "swirl" in an attempt to hide it's thinning. He had a very thick, Godfather-like mustache, which he caressed throughout our conversation. Although framed in dark glasses, his deep raven eyes pierced right through me, as if to intimidate me. Was that real, or was I just feeling insecure? I called upon my fictional champion, Scarlett O'Hara, for instantaneous help, and her swift response became a stare back of my own that let Mr. Lawyer know I was not intimidated and, although in unfamiliar territory, I would hold my own here. I came to learn, though, that his penetrating glare was a tactic of his specifically intended to weaken whomever was sitting on the opposite side of his desk. I gave as good as I got, and it seemed to make a difference. In time, he learned that maneuver didn't work on me. Style, taste, and savoir faire exuded from every inch of him, starting with his tailor-made silk suit to his soft Italian leather shoes, to the diamonds and gold glimmering from his pinkie ring and watch. The tone of his voice was soft and quietly strong, with deliberate words eloquently rolling off his tongue. Yet even with delicacy, he commanded attention. I had never heard such diction and enunciation, and their mesmerizing combination left an indelible mark on me. There was an aura about him that was electrifying. I was almost more focused on him than the reason I was there, but I was determined to get through this meeting leaving just as much a favorable impression on him as he had on me.

We reviewed the specifics of my divorce case, the lawyer asking many questions and taking notes. It was mainly just the basic facts of our marriage as well as the demise of it. I didn't have the yellow legal pad that the lawyer did, but I was taking notes of my own. Mental notes of his demeanor, but also of several words he used that I didn't quite understand. I was pretty good at improvising and got through the conversation, but just barely. When I got home later on, I did cerebral replay of our conversation, recalling and writing down each word I didn't understand. I pulled out my favorite book, good old *Webster's Dictionary*, looked each word up, then recalled the conversation in order to get the correct context per our discussion. In doing so, I experienced the same epiphany I had earlier while in the lawyer's office, only now it was even clearer, more distinctive. I imagined myself working in the same type of setting as I experienced today. This experience was such an awakening. Not only did I realize an ambition but also the road that would lead me to achieving it. I would work toward someday being employable in such an arena and having all the required skills to be successful in it, including being aptly conversant among my peers in such a way that I could speak and carry myself with the purpose, clarity, and distinction I was part of this memorable day.

I didn't know much about the law or its process, but I did know that my divorce was an easy case, no assets or distributions, no contest, no real issues. That said, I became curious with the frequency of Mr. Lawyer's calls. More particularly that their content became completely unrelated to the divorce. When I questioned him, the lawyer simply said he found me quite intriguing, and he was trying to get to know me better. Hmmm, I wasn't exactly sure what he meant by that or how I should take the comment, but I thought I should just go with it in order to find out. Besides, I was becoming more curious about him as well. For me, his allure was the apparent vast knowledge he possessed. His demonstrated panache didn't hurt either. I learned something from each conversation with him and even began writing down things that he said to look certain words up later. Finally, one day he asked me to meet him for lunch, indicating that we needed to review our case before we went to court. I agreed.

Now that I had a taste of what was not appropriate attire to be in the lawyer's company, I chose what I would wear more carefully. Not that there was anything really wrong with the clothes I met him in; I knew now they were atypical for him and for anywhere he planned on taking me to lunch. I was certain of that, and my instincts later proved correct. I had a very plain, simple, yet formfitting navy blue dress I reserved for wakes and funerals that I thought would be perfect. I arrived at his office right on time, and once again, the lovely receptionist greeted me. I was so much more confident this time, having a sense of what I was walking into. I even engaged in conversation with her and made her laugh. The lawyer suddenly appeared in the lobby, letting his receptionist know he was leaving for lunch and would be back in about two hours. He addressed me with a warm embrace, holding my hand in his while explaining it was such a beautiful day he wanted to enjoy the fresh air, suggesting we walk over to a nearby favorite Italian restaurant of his. We left his office, and fluent conversation followed along as we walked. Yes, it really was a gorgeous day! The lawyer complimented me on my appearance and also told me how much he enjoyed our telephone conversations. He added that he was quite intrigued by me. I had to ask him why.

"I have to know what it is about me that intrigues you," I asked, partially from innocence and partially from my curiosity to learn more about what makes this man tick. "I mean, our lives are worlds apart, and right now I'm at such a crossroad. What could possibly interest you about me?" I innocently asked.

"You're unlike anyone I've ever met," he quickly replied, "and I mean that as a compliment. I don't know much about you, but between the background my family gave me plus what I've learned through our phone chats, I sense a very strong will and determination, which is rare to find in women. Especially young women of your background. I want to know more." He had finished as we entered the restaurant. I didn't know how to react to that, so I just remained calm and figured I'd let the information keep flowing, remembering Big Lou's words: "When in doubt, keep still."

The restaurant was fabulous, very downtown chic, and we were immediately seated at a table waiting just for him. I watched his every move intently, copying most of his actions, interactions with the waitstaff as well as his table manners. I think I pulled it off well. He ordered one lunch for both of us, indicating we would share it. I thought that quite odd. Maybe I wasn't as polished as he was, and the only person I'd ever been out with at this point was Mousie. Ordering one meal to split was not something Mousie would ever do. More to the point, he would have ordered the entire menu, if for no other reason than just to impress me. He didn't even ask me if I even liked what he ordered; he just did it. Hmmm, curious. The conversation continued with the lawyer asking me some very personal questions about my background, work, and future plans. Now, I realized I'd been out of the loop for a while, but my instincts told me he was genuinely interested in me personally, aside from any divorce info. Not necessarily by what he was asking, but his tone and how he was asking. This was definitely date talk! *What's his game?* I wondered. To know me at all is to know I wear it all on my sleeve—no mincing words, just a put-your-cards-on-the-table type of person. Now I was intrigued, and I needed to know what he had on his mind.

"Do we have a court date yet?" I politely yet firmly asked.

Looking a bit surprised, he calmly responded, "No, not yet."

"Why not? I mean, it's been some time now, and you said yourself this should be a pretty open-and-shut case."

"These things take time, Contessa. I am a man who takes his time planning my strategy. I'm enjoying getting to know you, and the better I know you, the more efficient I can be at pleading your case. Strategy is everything in life if you want to be successful in whatever your endeavors may be, and I never lose. Ever. So be patient, we'll get there." He finished in a very knowing tone.

Gee, I guess strategy really is important in life. I heard that from my father, then Mousie, now the lawyer. *Okay, that info is now filed.*

"I didn't mean to be rude, but it's so important for me to get this over with. I just want to put it all behind me and move forward. I'm kind of a checklist person, and this is at the top of my list. Part of my strategy, you might say," I said, apologizing.

"You're a girl with a plan, all right, I can tell. You're also very brave, and I admire that," he responded as he reached over for my hand. "I've never known anyone like you, and I'm enjoying getting to know you better."

His silky soft hands are holding mine, and he is caressing my arm. What the fuck do I do about this? Be cool, Contessa!

"Brave? What do you mean?" I coyly asked.

"Isn't it obvious? Such a young girl like you having to deal with everything you've had thrown at you? Plus losing your father and not having anyone to take care of you and your child. That is quite admirable, and I see such determination in you. I really applaud and respect you for that," he explained.

"Thank you, but to be clear, most of what has happened in my life so far was because of deliberate choices that I made. I chose to have a baby. I chose to get married. The only thing I didn't choose was to have my marriage end this way, but when my husband became the Quaalude king, I chose to leave him. I refused to have my daughter be brought up in the environment her father created. I learned a lot through all this, but mostly that you can't ever depend on anyone else but yourself to make your life what you want it to be, and I won't ever do that again. I would say I'm more determined than brave— what's the word? *Tenacious?* I'm only doing what I need to in order to make a good life for us. The kind of life I always dreamt about, for both me and my daughter. I don't quite have everything figured out yet, I'm still working out the details, but I'll get there, just watch and see," I confidently explained back.

"I'm certain you will! So what is your plan?" he asked.

Instantly a wave of Scarlett rushed through me, and I heard myself say, "It's coming along as we speak, so just sit back and enjoy the show. But don't worry, I'll make it." I was assertive in my response.

The lawyer smiled, stroked my hand, and said, "I believe you will, and trust me, I will be watching. You're quite a girl." By then he watched our server approached us with our meal.

"Ah, wonderful. You're going to love this." He grinned.

With a sarcastic smile right back at him, I responded, "I'm sure I will."

Lunch was just as delicious as the banter that accompanied it. I could never explain it, but the lawyer always brought out the sassy, sarcastic side of me. Maybe due to us both being Scorpios, maybe it was my competitive nature to challenge his bravado, but at any rate, it was pretty entertaining. As we left and walked back to his office, I was not entirely surprised when the lawyer told me I must meet him again, and soon. Emphasis on *told me*, not *asked me*! Without hesitation, I reminded him that I worked breakfast and lunch shifts, so taking day off as I did today meant losing a day's pay.

"Okay, forget lunch," he said as he put his hand around my waist and pulled me to him. "I'll take you to dinner next week." His arm around my waist tightened.

Dinner? What was this about? Don't get me wrong—I liked him. Maybe even more than just like, but not in a romantic way. I was so impressed by him I was in awe of him to the point that I studied his every word and move, learning so much in the process. But I was not looking for romance here. My goal was to get divorced and that was it. The educational element that I encountered in the process was pure bonus, and that only added to my game plan for enhancing my life. Although I had very little experience, it was nice to know my instincts were sharp and working properly. My interest in the lawyer was more to study him rather than date him. *Scarlett, help me out here!*

"I'm not sure if that was an invitation or a command, but either way, I'm afraid next week is impossible. My work schedule is pretty full. I work every day, I'm on the night schedule in the dining room three nights, and I'm on call Sunday. Plus, I have a ton of studying and a paper due. That doesn't leave me much time to be with my little girl. I have two babysitters that I rotate, so I have them on a pretty tight schedule as well," I coolly explained.

"I'm impressed, my lovely. I'll call you and we'll talk."

As he pulled me extremely close, all I had to do was put my lips into position and he would have pounced on them. But I defiantly didn't. Instead, I merely whispered, "Call me with a court date," as I gave him a peck on the cheek. "Thank you for lunch," I added as I disengaged from his tight grasp and walked away.

I had always been a list maker, writing down my thoughts on whatever decisions I had to make. To me, the simple logic of creating a list of what needed to be done each day helped create and maintain a forward moving path, plus writing down positive and negative elements of a situation side by side in order to visualize an outcome was the only way I knew to keep order in my life. I replayed this afternoon in my mind over and over, trying to sort it all out just to make sure I was thinking straight. Yes, he really was interested in me. I was sure of that. I revisited my list of objectives for the future, and as you can guess, at the very top was "finalize divorce." Beyond that were various educational goals, to complete certain classes that I felt necessary to enable me to try for other jobs. I vowed my food service days were limited—not to demean the food service industry, as it is hard and a respected work, but I yearned and aspired for much more. The lawyer didn't strike me as someone who gave up easily. No, he definitely gave me the impression that he got whatever he went after, and I think my reluctance to fall into his arms made him all the more determined. More to that point, I think he thought I was some stupid little girl so impressed by him he could do whatever he wanted. True, I was impressed by him, but realistic enough to know that he would never fit into my world, and while I was enticed by all the elements of his scene, I merely wanted to grasp it, master it for my own self. He was Professor Higgins to my Eliza Doolittle, period! So that pointed directly to the "educational" portion on my life goal list. *Okay, I can run with this. Let's see what his next move is.*

Regular conversations ensued, and before long, we got to know each other well. Very well. Not only was I no longer intimidated in any way by him, but more to the point, I also became a very quick study and learned many things from him. For instance, a person's exterior is in no way a mirror into their heart, soul, or mind. Also, never to be threatened, frightened, or even fooled by that exterior. Stay true to yourself and keep confident. Believe in yourself, learn the vernacular and ways of the playground, and you'll be fine. I came to realize that underneath all that polish and pizzazz was just a man, and an insecure man at that. He had money, and he had power. Our conversations revealed to me that he used both to control people. Reflecting upon many conversations with him left my naive little head thinking, if you had to use money or influence to manipulate people to do things for you, then those people didn't really respect you. If they did, you wouldn't have to use any kind of leverage in order to get whatever it was you wanted. It appeared to me that the lawyer was a major control freak, and my unsophisticated mind told me that when one feels the need to control everyone around them, they are not confident enough in themselves to manage things without using an iron fist or bribery as a tactic. But I was not wise to the ways of the world and just shrugged it off to something I simply didn't understand. I found the lawyer to be needy. I felt that the budding relationship with me somewhat empowered him. To him, I was an uneducated, uncultured little girl who looked at him as a god on a pedestal. I assumed he thought I was still in complete awe of him. Not the case. Not anymore. Although we were very different and worlds apart in many ways, our connection lay in our similar Italian background and heritage, where there were many similarities that we took pleasure in sharing. It was actually surprising to me that I even had these thoughts, that I even realized all this. I didn't think I was that smart, but I did realize I was experiencing new things, new surroundings, and new people; all of which were feeding my insatiable appetite to learn. But I knew I was right about all of it and decided to just go with it and see where the road took me.

The lawyer asked me out constantly, but I rejected his offers, always pointing to my hectic work schedule and studies, which wasn't a lie. I was keeping my focus, but truth be told, I realized that he couldn't stand not getting what he wanted. I was also enjoying being the one who was not giving in to him. I realized that was a power I had, and I liked using it. So the phone calls continued with playful and some deep chatter, sugared with a little divorce talk here and there, just enough for him to have something to hide behind. Now that I'd come to know the lawyer better, I laughed at how intimidated I was by him when we first met. Isn't it funny? He came into my life as such a force of nature, one that I was so instantly taken with, wanting to emulate his mannerisms, knowing I could learn so much from him. Yes, he was a force, all right, but as I got to know him better, I learned that he was a force I could certainly handle and deal with. I found that fact humorous indeed. I was learning and growing as a person too.

Finally, we had a court date to finalize my divorce. It was next month. I was so relieved to hear that. The biggest objective on my list was about to get crossed off.

I hadn't seen or heard from Mousie in a very long time. He was keeping his word on not giving me a dime, and I didn't care one bit. I wasn't even mad that he made no attempt to see his daughter either. Of course, it would have been nice for her to have a dad, but this dad had no clue as to how to be one, so I felt in my bones it was all for the best. Through mutual friends, I kept tabs on his shenanigans and knew he was still up to no good, and I wouldn't have my little girl around that shit anyway.

I met the lawyer at the courthouse, and we went into a room to review the procedure. This was my first time ever in a courthouse, and instead of being nervous, I was excited. So glad to be getting this over with. We sat in a small room, waiting to be called. After what seemed like an eternity, a lady entered our room and told the lawyer the judge needed to see him in chambers. After being gone for some time, the lawyer returned with a smug look on his face, his chest puffed way out, a bunch of papers in hand.

"All you have to do is sign these papers and you are a divorced lady. I'll let you thank me later," he said.

"What do you mean? What happened?" I innocently asked.

"Apparently, your husband informed his attorney he is leaving the state, has no intention of contesting the divorce, and also has no intention of paying child support, but we'll go after that later. First things first, just sign these papers and you are a single woman. Let's get this part completed, then we'll investigate where he's gone to and go after him for support," the lawyer triumphantly declared.

He still didn't realize the nature of this situation, and I didn't want to bother explaining it all again. I was just glad that my divorce was granted, that I didn't have to confront Mousie and there was no drama to it, so I immediately began signing away. The papers were then stamped and filed. Done. We were free to go. That was all it took to end what was supposed to be my fairy tale life with my first love. Oh, well, no time to dwell on it. Just move on.

As I got to know him during our many long chats, I became aware that the lawyer was a man of certain stature in his field and highly respected by his peers. However, as we left the courthouse that day, I experienced something notable about attorneys in general that both captivated me and repulsed me at the same time. The twist, the spin they put on a situation to make it their own. I could see how convincing they could be, too. We walked along arm in arm as I listened to him praise himself and his expertise in getting this case won so easily.

What the fuck are you bragging about, asshole? I thought. *We had an uncontested victory because Mousie didn't show up! I'm gonna check your pants for a wet spot, 'cuz I'm convinced you're giving yourself an orgasm getting off on your own words!*

But I let him go on, now insisting we must have a celebratory dinner that night. That was not necessary, but I thanked him nonetheless. He stopped, pulled me very close to him, and held me tight.

"Yes, it is necessary," he commanded as he pulled me hard and closer to him. "You're in my life now, and we're going to be spending more time together, alone. Do you hear me? I want to be with you, I have plans for us." He leaned in to kiss me. His black-as-coal eyes pierced right through me, certain I would succumb to whatever his wishes were, but I held him off. Like my guardian Scarlett, never was I better than when I was cornered, and never would I be told what, where, and with whom I would spend my time.

I stubbornly reminded him that I was a mother first and foremost and, in addition to a child, was juggling two jobs and night school, which didn't leave much time for evenings out. And besides all that, he wasn't even offering me anything but telling me what he wanted. Oh, yeah, I got the whole picture and ended it with citing the time, noting I had to get back home, as my sitter had to leave soon. Reluctant to let me go, the lawyer pulled me tighter and even closer. Only this time, without even a nanosecond to think about it, I leaned into him and kissed him hard, long, and with a fiery passion he would never forget. Make note, I kissed him, not me succumbing to his kiss. There's a definite difference. It was my choice. And it was I who pulled away when I wanted to. He might have had plans for me and I let him know what he could have, but only if I allowed it.

I thought long and hard about the situation and decided that yes, I did the right thing. First of all, I threw him off guard, and I liked that. I enjoyed knowing that a guy would never know what to expect from me. Second, not that I knew exactly what he had up his sleeve, but at least he now knew I wasn't afraid of him, I was certainly not a puppet, and most of all, I could handle myself. What the hell did he mean by "you're in my life now," anyway? Realizing you can catch more flies with honey than vinegar, I took his constant evening calls with an obnoxiously sugared demeanor, in an attempt to have him spill a little more of the guts he thought he had out to me. Deceitful? Perhaps, but I was using a tactic I actually learned from him. In his constant soliloquies noting his legal triumphs, the lawyer shared many of his strategies with me. Most notably, if you take the proper steps to ensure the enemy's comfort and confidence, you will be able to obtain the information you need from them. I'm not saying the lawyer was my enemy, but he was certainly someone I wanted information from, and so I made sure he was extremely comfortable and confident in my "mutual" feelings for him. My own twist on this was that egotistical men have a major weakness: their ego. They will fall for just about anything if you stroke their ego well enough. Basically, they let their guard down around ass-kissers. This theory of mine was tested, tried, and true by virtue of me using it over and over. And so I'd prefer to think of it as applying the lessons I'd learned while doing my homework.

Our many long conversations did reveal that the deep feelings he confessed for me were genuine, that he longed for a relationship with someone of his own culture and background. It could have been music to any girl's ears, if it weren't for one minor detail: he had a wife! I never mentioned it, always giving him the opportunity for some sort of explanation. They didn't get along, they were separated, they had this or that irreconcilable issue, or perhaps even "I'm going to divorce her because I am in love with you." Something crazy like that! But no explanation of any sort accompanied all his declared feelings for me and the life we were going to build together.

Finally, I decided that I would meet him for dinner. Mainly because I was completely befuddled by what I was hearing as opposed to what I knew to be fact. My instincts told me there was something worth pursuing here, and I wanted to find out what. I even entertained the idea that maybe, just maybe, if he explained what his intentions were about his wife, I could possibly see him differently. How would I feel about him if he were free? I began to daydream about what it would be like to have an actual relationship with him.

He was certainly a man of substance, in several ways. Once I got past the initial intimidation and my own insecurities toward him, I realized he was a person with a significant education in areas far beyond me but whom I could learn quite a lot from. I was no longer timid around him, now more confident in myself to be around him, certain I could be at ease in his world. At the same time, my hunger for the knowledge he had in all areas obviously attracted him. In addition, my sassy attitude and refusal to be one more of the many who idolized him became a challenge for him, which I believe he really enjoyed, particularly as it was coming from someone clearly not his intellectual equal. I also think that grounded him a bit, which he secretly didn't mind. Yes, I'd meet him for dinner, if for no other reason than to find out what he had in mind for "our future together." I certainly had nothing to lose. So in my attempt to prepare myself for what might be forthcoming, the question was, could I see myself in a relationship with him? Not sure, but I would be willing to try. Again, I was now more confident of myself in his arena, but skeptical of him in mine. I just couldn't see him sitting on the floor, playing with my daughter. But at this point, all I had to do was sit back and enjoy the show he was about to put on. I gave it a lot of thought but could come to no conclusion, as the fate of the situation rested with him.

Date night, I made sure I would look absolutely irresistible, perfection from head to toe. Not to brag, but come on, ladies, we know when we put it all together properly and we know for sure when we're outfitted to get the job done. Sassy but a classy, clingy summer knit dress with just enough reveal to guarantee the allure I sought to get the information I wanted in order finish this one way or another. I met the lawyer in the restaurant of his choice, another place where he had his own table and was known by all the staff. He ordered champagne and appetizers. He never asked me what I wanted; he always just ordered for both of us. Another thing I noticed and didn't like, he only ordered one entrée, indicating to the server that we would split it. Hmmm, for someone who was always trying to impress, I thought that was a little on the cheap side, and I remembered what Dad always said about not trusting cheap people! We toasted to me being a newly single woman, thanks to, as he put it, his "inimitable legal expertise," hearing about which made me struggle not to crack up. I stopped myself from giving into laughter by initiating a more serious conversation.

"This is a lovely restaurant, but I am most impressed by my host," I began. Nothing puffed up the lawyer's chest like someone letting him know that he took your breath away.

"I knew you'd like it," he responded, "and we'll be coming back here often, you'll see. From now on, we're going to be spending a lot more time together."

"Now that's something we need to talk about. I'd like for you to explain what you mean by that," I informed him, purposely sounding naive.

"What don't you understand? Like I said, you're in my life now, and we'll be going out much more frequently and seeing each other more intimately. I have plans for us, plans that I'm very excited about," he arrogantly responded.

"You are, huh? Well, don't you think it would be utterly fabulous to share those plans with me? I mean, in all the time we spend on the phone, you mention things about our future together, which makes me wonder what exactly you're thinking about. So put it out there now, what specifically are your plans for us? I would really like to know," I half-asked, half-stipulated.

We were seated in back of the restaurant in an elegant corner booth. The lights were dimmed and soft music pervaded, a setting fit for a marriage proposal. As he poured more champagne for each of us, the lawyer unveiled his plan for our future, which he so proudly concocted.

"How could I know what fate had in mind for me when I agreed to act as counsel for your divorce?" he began. "Never in my wildest dreams did I think I would meet the future mother of my child."

"WHAT?" I screamed so loud that several patrons looked over at us. *Oh my god, did he just say "future mother of my child"? What the fuck is this about? Is he fucking crazy? Someone, please help me pick my mouth off the floor!*

"What the hell do you mean?" I demanded.

"Shhh, quiet down. Everyone knows me here," he whispered.

"Rewind, counselor. From the beginning. What the hell are you talking about?" I repeated.

He poured more champagne for each of us, clutched my hands, and began, "When I agreed to represent you in your divorce, I had no idea of how I would be affected by you or what an impact you would have on me. I met a young girl whom I thought was limited and in need of help. Once I had the opportunity to get to know you better, I realized you were not just a girl but a young woman with a passion and hunger for life I've never known. You are amazingly determined, wise beyond your years, and I believe nothing will stop you from achieving your goals and dreams."

"I really appreciate your words, but…," I interrupted, still waiting for him to mention his wife and his marriage.

"Let me finish. I admire you for your determination in overcoming the many obstacles you have been dealt, and the fact that you attack and overcome them one by one is really something I feel privileged to watch. You are blessed with fortitude. You will go far, I just know it," he continued.

I interrupted again, "Thanks, but I still don't—"

"Shhh. I have much in my life. Many material things that I admit give me pleasure. However, there is one simple joy that has eluded me, something that all my success and wealth cannot buy me. Something I desire more than all the things I have amassed put together, which I'm afraid I am helpless in obtaining on my own. That's where you come in," he said, seemingly about to cry.

I was starting to get the feeling this was not going to end well, but I let the lawyer go on. Only now I grabbed the champagne bottle and helped myself while he continued this crazy ass story.

"I want a child more than I can tell you, but up till now, that has not been possible. My wife has not been fortunate enough to carry a child full term. She has been pregnant several times and has miscarried each pregnancy. She's never made it past the fourth month. We know the problem is with my wife. After all, I was able to get her pregnant several times, so we know for sure I'm all right, that the issue is not with me. After many tests, the doctors still cannot pinpoint a reason that she's not able to see a pregnancy through. Plus, the older she gets, the more the chances of her doing so decrease," he finished.

"I'm so sorry, but honestly, I can't see what this has to do with me. This is the first time you've ever even mentioned your wife at all," I responded.

"I know. Probably because I am completely captivated by you whenever we meet, whenever we speak. It's been a joy for me to listen to your thoughts, your aspirations, and your plans for not only your future but your daughter's as well. You are an amazing mother in spite of the many difficulties you've already experienced in your young life," he continued.

"Wrap it up, counselor. Where are you going with all this?" I impatiently asked.

"I want to be with you. I want to make love to you. I want you to have my child," he confessed.

If ever my mouth literally and realistically fell to the floor, it was at this very moment. I could not speak. But I did manage to down another full glass of champagne and sat silent for what seemed like forever.

Finally, I came back to reality and said, "Would you mind pinching me? Because I think I am in a dream and you just told me you wanted me to have your baby."

The lawyer smiled, put his hand on mine, and confidently, proudly declared to me, "You are not dreaming, although I could make this situation surpass your wildest dreams."

Wow! He was actually serious. This was insane, but crazy as it was, I just had to hear the whole plot. "Okay, so tell me, counselor, how do you think this would work? I mean, do I just pop out a child and hand it over to you or what?" I sarcastically asked.

"Of course not. I'm a married man! I couldn't let my wife ever find out I have a child by someone else! Not only would that devastate her, but she could also ruin me financially for it. No, she could never find out, nor anyone else, for that matter. It would have to be our little secret. Just between you and me," he finished.

I wasn't this stunned when I realized I needed to get rid of my husband! Nothing in the world could have prepared me for this. This well educated, renowned attorney whose intelligence I did admire was out of his fucking mind!

"I'm dying to hear the rest of your plan. Please continue, counselor."

"Don't be so flip about this. I've thought this through very carefully, and I know this is the answer for both of us. I've told you how I feel about you, but I left out that I also find you extremely attractive. Perhaps the other qualities you possess make you even more attractive. Being intimate with you with the objective to conceive a child would truly be a labor of love for me, and I know I can make it pleasurable for you as well. I realize you are struggling now. I'll see to it that you are financially secure. Your life can be so much easier if you would just do this one little thing for me. I'm telling you, you would want for nothing, and consequently, neither would your daughter. And if we have a son, there will be extra perks, you'll see. As I said, I've thought this through very carefully and its a fantastic deal for you, and a win-win for both of us. Of course, the only stipulation is that I cannot allow you to engage in other relationships. I just couldn't allow my child to be exposed to another man in the house," he finished.

"I can't believe what I'm hearing. I am struggling for words." was all I could say upon hearing this absurd proposal.

"There's only one word you need to say. Just say yes, and we can leave here and get right to it. I'm a fabulous lover, you can bet on it. I know how to please a woman. Your kiss told me just how passionate and responsive a lover you are, and I know you'll be satisfied. And once you become pregnant, I will make a significant deposit to your checking account, with monthly deposits to follow," he went on. As I sat there in complete disbelief of what I was hearing, the lawyer continued, "I can see how surprised you are at what I am proposing to you. I can't imagine you've ever had such a promising offer, or ever will, for that matter."

I picked up my purse and slid out of our booth, announcing I needed to go to the ladies' room. I couldn't walk away fast enough. Once there, I did a quick replay of the lawyer's entire monologue just to make sure I heard it all correctly. Yep, I sure did. Who the fuck did this arrogant asshole think he was? More to the point, what kind of an asshole did he think I was? I had to think fast in order to put an adequate comeback together, one that was fitting enough to put him in his place and let him know exactly what I thought of his benevolent offer as well as exactly what I thought of him for making it. I took a few minutes as well as a few deep breaths. My first instinct was to just leave, but then I thought no, he needed to hear face-to-face what an asshole he was. One more long deep breath, and I was ready to come out swinging. I approached the booth he called his own, but instead of nestling back into it with the lawyer, I stood there on the side next to him and explained I wouldn't be staying for the main course, that the appetizer he served me was quite enough for me.

"I know your brand of sarcasm, Contessa, and this is not the time or the place for it. Just sit back down, and let's continue our discussion," he whispered.

"I don't know how long it took you to hatch your ridiculous plan, but you didn't even have to finish in order for me to realize how insane you are for allowing it to roll off your tongue! I don't know who you think you're dealing with, but trust me, counselor, I'm not someone who would be thrilled to take whatever tiny scraps you might throw at me. And my big reward to let you fuck me? Go fuck yourself, counselor, because you'll never have the pleasure of screwing me! Take your fantastic deal and shove it up your ass. I'm outta here!" I strongly whispered right back.

He grabbed my arm. "Wait, sit down, let's talk this out over dinner. You're making the mistake of a lifetime," he pleaded.

I broke free of the grip he had on my arm. "You wanted a celebration? Eat the entire entrée yourself, you cheap bastard!" I left.

As I stood outside, waiting for the valet to bring my car around, the lawyer approached me and began pleading with me to come back inside. I was furious that he even came out after me, and shrugged him aside.

"Newsflash, counselor, I don't pick up crumbs, and I don't take bullshit like your fabulous offer! I know you're used to everyone kissing your ass and doing whatever it is you want, and I hope you don't fall off that pedestal you obviously put yourself on when you hear this, but you don't have one fucking thing that's appealing to me, especially your dick or anything I might get for playing with it. So fuck off, leave me alone, and don't you ever dare call me again. Capisce?" Just then, my car was pulled up. I threw the ticket at the lawyer and told the valet, "He's paying for it," as I got in and pulled out of there as fast as I could. To say I was angry would have been a severe understatement. I don't know what I was, if only just glad to be out of there and out of the lawyer's presence.

I hardly slept that night, replaying that whole scene over and over in my mind. I was glad I didn't just leave, glad I told him off.

I doubt that had ever happened to him before, especially in public where he was "known." Major asshole! The lawyer was not a stupid man, not by any stretch of the imagination, so what was that story all about? Could it really be true? He certainly wasn't dumb, but could his overinflated ego have taken over his brain? Or as in many cases, was he just being a guy and thinking with the wrong head? Even if he just concocted some stupid plot to try to get me into bed, thinking he could bribe me with being his kept woman, did he actually believe it would work? Do women actually fall for that bullshit? Yikes, maybe some women actually do, but not this woman—that's for sure!

Although I got very little sleep, I woke up that morning feeling like a lion ready to take on the world. As I made breakfast for me and Little Contessa, watching the sweetness of her morning shenanigans and listening to her angelic but squeaky little voice as she fluttered about, playing in our apartment, I mentally recited my vow never to allow anyone or anything to prevent me from achieving my goals, or interfering with the plans I had for us. I knew the lawyer wouldn't take no for an answer or, at the very least, try to rationalize his stupidity with me in some way. I was certain he would definitely be in touch with me again.

I was right. It only took a week, but he called me one evening, just after I put Little Contessa to bed. I immediately let him know I didn't have anything to say to him, nor did I want to hear anything from him.

"Please, just listen to me," he begged. "You didn't even give me a chance to tell you everything. You just left in such a huff."

"I heard all I needed to. How do you expect someone to respond to the offensive suggestion you gave me? Have a baby for you and keep it a secret? Are you kidding me? A win-win? You're out of your fucking mind!" I snapped.

"Calm down and let me finish," he pleaded.

I have to admit, while there was absolutely no chance of my going along with this outrageous idea of his, I was curious to see how far he would take it, so I let him continue.

"We can each give each other something we both want. I can make sure you are financially secure if you would just have my child.

I'm completely enchanted by you, and I know you must have feelings for me. I know you're struggling financially, and I'll see to it that you never have to worry about money again once the baby is born. I told you, if we have a boy, I will give you a bonus. When you become pregnant, I will make the first deposit to your account, and trust me, it will be significant. Monthly deposits will follow after that. The only stipulations are that you can never disclose the fact that I am the father and you must agree never to become involved with another man. That just wouldn't be right," he finished.

None of this is right, you dick! I thought. But for just one fleeting moment, I expected him to burst out in laughter, saying something like, "Ha, ha, ha…gotcha! This is a joke, of course." But no, the lawyer was dead serious about this entire situation. He needed to see once and for all that I could never be bought or bribed to succumb to his wishes, like the many others in his life who were willing and able to go along with his whims. Nope, not me.

"Are you finished?" I asked. "Or is there anything else you'd like to add?"

"That's the whole story. That's my offer to you," he said so dryly.

"Okay, now it's my turn," I responded. "First of all, I have to tell you, I really thought you were joking at first. But then I realized you weren't, and I think I'm still in shock over this whole thing. You want a baby conceived from a business transaction? You're crazy! I have one child that I worked long and hard in order to conceive. She was wanted desperately by both her parents, who were madly in love. And now I'm a single mother, and yes, a struggling one at that, but I'm struggling with dignity and I love every minute of it because every single day I come a little closer to where I want to be. I answer to nobody, and I never will. Counselor, there is no carrot large enough for you to dangle in front of me that would ever allow me to even consider such a ridiculous proposition. Not for ten times the money you have, not for anything. I just divorced someone I found to be dangerous in several ways, but at least his negative ways were out in the open. But you, you are much worse because you hide your flaws behind expensive suits, your position, and your money. You say you love your wife, but you are willing to lie to her and cheat on her in the hopes of conceiving a child to hide from the world just to satisfy your own greedy ego. I will confess, though, I actually gave thought to having a relationship with you. I really thought that was where you were going with your invitation to dinner. And my big reward would be being your kept woman, another person for you to control! No, thank you! I'm going to hang up now, and I really don't want to hear from you ever again. I mean it, don't waste your time by calling me. Should I ever answer the phone and hear your voice on the other end, I will just hang up. Goodbye, counselor!" I slammed the phone down.

It took me a long time to shake off the anger I felt toward him. Imagine actually thinking you can buy someone's life like that. *Ugh!* In the end, though, I began to realize it was that anger that pushed me to another level. I studied harder, I took on another shift, and I saw once again how mistreatment from another man fueled me into action and made me even more determined. I thought about it now and again, and the one thing I learned was that men may feel it's okay to suggest things like that because there are women who will allow them to, I suppose. Oh, well, that may be appealing to some, but I will never allow myself to be under the thumb of anyone, ever, especially a man. If my experience with Mousie didn't teach me enough about independence, this certainly did. *Bye-bye, Counselor. We are done.*

Years passed with several chance meetings between the lawyer and me. Certain family events brought us together over the years, but I made a conscious effort to avoid him. I never noticed him with his wife. The family said she was away on business most of the time. Through some conversations I came to learn that she was a senior manager for a very prominent cosmetics company, which required her to travel much of her time. I became very close to a niece of the lawyer. Her name was Cassie, and after Cassie's husband passed away, my aunt and I would often go to Cassie's house to visit. It's what Italians do after a death, just to keep the family close and support the survivor. At Cassie's house, I finally met the lawyer's wife, Sallyanne, whom I found to be absolutely darling. A tiny, petite little blonde that oozed of style, sophistication, and personality. Although she was always drenched in designer labels and made up to the nines, she was very down-to-earth, very personable, and tons of fun to be around. She was impeccable, sheer class from head to toe, but she was also very embracing. I started to see Sallyanne at Cassie's house regularly, and we became fast friends. I learned that Sallyanne was sick frequently. She had a number of health issues and had been riddled with various female problems over the years. She also talked about her difficulties sustaining a pregnancy. At one point, Sallyanne confided to me that she was aware of her husband's cheating ways throughout their marriage but found it easier to turn her head away from it, rather than confront it. Her rationale being that in the end she was completely confident he would always be there for her. Sallyanne also revealed that she was very insecure about herself, that nobody else would want her because she was not able to bear children. My heart broke for her. I felt so bad for her in several ways. I was sorry for this beautiful, intelligent, kind woman, who was a bright light and breath of fresh air, that she was so doubtful of herself and what all she had to offer, that she would settle to stay with an unfaithful man because she lacked confidence in herself. Very sad. I also felt very guilty for already having known of her husband's philandering ways, but I certainly would never divulge what I knew.

One day I was visiting Cassie and the lawyer was there alone, as Sallyanne was out of town. While helping clean up after dinner, the lawyer got my attention, pulling me over into a room that was empty. He wanted to talk to me privately and asked for my phone number. By this time, years had passed and I had long since let go of my angry feelings toward him. Harboring anger never gets you anywhere; it's never a positive thing. My life had been on a very progressive track, and I had nothing to be mad at really. Truth be told, knowing what an asshole he was, I actually felt a little sorry for him. I had long since moved on to prosperity, and on my own terms. I was in a great place in my life. He, however, seemed to be stuck in a huge rut and extremely unhappy. So what would he want to talk to me about privately? Surely not to ask me to have a baby again! So when he asked me for my phone number, I vehemently refused.

"There's no conversation we need to have that everyone else, including my dear friend Sallyanne, shouldn't be able to hear!" I told him. I left the room, as I didn't want anyone to take notice that we were in a room alone together.

I finished helping to clean up and began to gather my things, preparing to leave. I cooked dinner for the group that day, and consequently, I had several bags of platters, containers, etc. to bring home. The lawyer announced he would help me out to my car with them. I had no choice but to let him, as I didn't want to cause a scene in front of everyone. Once outside, the lawyer confessed that he never stopped thinking of me, that seeing me now and again over these years made him realize what a fool he was, that he should have pursued me in a different way, asking if I would please, please give him another chance and meet him for a drink one night soon. Boy, some people never learn, do they?

He leaned in to kiss me, and without a thought, I kissed him right back. I'd been told I was one hell of a kisser, and I gave it all I had, long and hard. I knew that was wrong, but I did it anyway. Mainly just to bust his balls. I know, I know, I just couldn't resist. He deserved it. He was responsive to my kiss, as though he felt confident that he got to me. Finally, I broke away.

"You surprise me by your kiss, Contessa, but it's power didn't," he said softly. "I knew you'd come around someday."

"I just wanted to give you a taste of what you'll never have, counselor! That's all of me you'll ever get! You're still the asshole you always were!" I snapped.

"I don't understand. What's the problem, anyway? We have such history together. I know we could make a go of it if you would just give us a chance," he muttered.

"You delusional fuck! You didn't deserve me all those years ago, and you certainly don't deserve me now. I'll never have all the material things you do, and I don't care. What I have, all your money could never buy—it's called integrity, which is something that surely won't be engraved on your tombstone. I feel so sorry for Sallyanne being stuck with you. She really deserves so much more!" I snapped back.

"Yeah, I noticed how chummy you've become with her. What's up with that?" he demanded.

"I like her so much more than you! You don't even realize that it's you who married up! Now get out of my way, I have to go." I pushed my way past him, and I left.

Not too much longer after that encounter, I was devastated to learn that Sallyanne had passed away. I sat in the church pew along with so many others who truly loved her to say goodbye. As I stated earlier, it was definitely the most elaborate funeral I had ever attended; however, I knew it was true to the lawyer's nature. Spare no expense and put on a big show. I'm certain he believed that if he threw a big enough funeral, perhaps he would be forgiven for being such a shithead to his wife while she walked the earth. The lawyer demonstrated some disgusting behavior through the years, but this last incident sank him to an all time low. While I addressed him at Sallyanne's funeral services, I embraced him appropriately and conveyed my condolences. Mainly for show to the others I was with. While expressing my sympathy, he actually whispered into my ear, "Now I'm free, it's our time," to which I whispered back in his ear, "You'll never have what it takes to have me. Stay the fuck away from me, you piece of shit, before I rip those little balls and tiny little prick right off you!" And I smiled as I walked away.

As I ponder this longtime association, several thoughts come to mind. There are people in this world who truly believe they can buy everything, including other people. Stay true to who you are and never succumb to a bribe, no matter how tantalizing it may be. Never lower your standards merely for material gain. Although a very attractive carrot may be dangling in front of you, never take the bait and compromise who you are or what you believe in for it. Never envy anyone for what they have or a lifestyle that differs from your own. Not everything is as it appears, and nobody's life is perfect. We all have issues and problems. Know where you're going, what you want, as well as what assets you'll need in order to get there. And probably, most important of all, never let material things or wealth of others encourage you to do things you normally wouldn't. Stay your course, maintain focus, work hard, and have enough confidence in yourself to know you'll achieve your goals. That will allow you to look yourself in the mirror every day and smile, knowing you've stayed true to your principles and you're moving forward on your own terms.

I look back at this episode with mixed emotions. Sadness, of course, that in the end a lovely lady passed away far too young. But in addition, I can't believe that I was once in such awe of a man who was merely an arrogant asshole. But then, I remember that I actually did learn quite a lot from him and he opened my eyes to position and a place in life that set me on a new course. Through the lawyer, I became aware of the corporate world and immediately knew that was where I wanted to be. In addition, I learned the necessary personal skills as well as academic requirements I would need to equip myself with in order to climb the ladder in this arena. Education, manner, style, speech, tact, diplomacy, and of course, an ever sharp instinct will always serve you well in the industry of your choice. Those are the basic fundamentals of any business environment, but you'd be surprised how many do not realize the need to master those skills in addition to the knowledge needed in the specific field. Through the lawyer, I learned the direction I wanted to go in, plus the tools I needed to travel with. For that I will always be thankful to him. In addition, he pissed me off enough to further ignite the flame for learning and life that was already burning inside me. So in a strange way, I am grateful for this episode, as I learned a great deal from it.

Through the years, I had had no choice but to interact with the lawyer, at various family functions. He never stopped chasing me, and I'd taken great pride in sharpening my wit and sarcasm, aiming and firing directly at him, hitting him smack between the eyes every chance I got. Mean, bitchy, you say? Hell no! He deserved that and more; it was the only way to deal with people like him. He never lost his arrogant, condescending nature, the "I'm so much better than you" attitude, and I cut him at the knees with sheer delight. After all these years, he finally realized he was no match for the verbal prowess I had developed, admitted it, and retreated from battle. I'm not being vain or conceited in saying that he chased me all these years. I know better. I'm positive it had more to do with the fact that he knew

I wasn't one of his worshippers who believed he walked on water, and I'm certain all he ever really wanted was the thrill of the chase and a conquest. However, the lawyer eventually got himself an intro-verted little girlfriend, a definite "yes" girl. Someone who seemed very subservient and apparently didn't mind eating half a meal when she dined out with that cheap bastard. But some things never change. Even though he had his girlfriend, a new worshipper, he still tried to worm his way into my life whenever he could, although to no avail. Once a liar and a cheat, always a liar and a cheat, I suppose. At least I successfully continued to channel my life toward happier, more pos-itive, and more productive endeavors. I'm sorry for him that I can't say the same. And at the end of the day, after all is said and done, I will still credit my experience with the lawyer for providing me with course and direction, as well as how I would get where I wanted to be, which I ultimately and proudly did.

Husband #2

Signs!

I once saw a plaque in a home decor shop that said, "God drops pebbles on your head before He drops the brick." As I reflect on this relationship, I could have used the brick first, as the many, many pebbles the good Lord dropped on my thick head didn't even make a dent! I was blinded by emotion and desire instead of clear vision and good old common sense. I could not, or maybe just would not, see what was clearly in plain view, right in front of my face.

Things were going well for me. I had a good routine in place, working two waitress jobs, making decent money, with good healthcare benefits. Little Contessa was happily situated in day care, and I had several babysitters that I rotated to cover my night shifts. I didn't mind my hectic schedule, so long as I managed enough time to play with my little girl, keeping her happy in whatever way possible. I was even able to get studying done and continued with my educational pursuit as well. My social life consisted of coworker chat, and that was fine with me. High school girlfriends kept in touch and got me up-to-date with what all was going on with them. I was way too busy to be lonely or bored. I was also too busy to have thoughts about dating, a boyfriend, or anything even closely resembling a relationship, not until that fateful night at my cousin Jen's party, which changed everything.

I had known husband #2, Will, mainly through his neighborhood reputation—handsome, fun, and the life of the party. As a teenager, he and his family lived down the street from mine. Will was a friend of my older brother, who eventually married a good friend

88

of my older sister. We did like to "keep things in the neighborhood," and that was not a joke. They were young, she became pregnant, and they had a very quick wedding (not judging, just saying).

The relationship with Will was a situation that took great pain, both physical and emotional, to run its course. While this guy lacked all of Mousie's savoir faire, humor, and heart, Will was strikingly, even devilishly, handsome, magnetic, and well built, with quite a beguiling way of talking to a lady. Although married just a few years prior, Will was now separated from his wife. Knowing his ex just a bit as my older sister's girlfriend, I found her to be an arrogant bitch, based on the after school girls' gathering in the bedroom I shared with my sister. The ex-wife placed herself high above the other girls, not shy at all about announcing her finer style and manner of dress, that she was so much prettier and sophisticated than the others, and of course, how every guy in the neighborhood lusted after her. For someone who considered themselves so superior, her reputation these days was pretty inferior. Rumors spread she was an easy lay, as discussed in detail, from experience, with quite a few of the neighborhood guys (PS: yes, guys do talk). I had heard such awful things about her that I naturally assumed the reason for their split was based on her own activities. The neighborhood chatter was that she screwed a few of Will's friends. One of her most notorious liaisons was with a very close friend of his right in their own home—actually, in their own bed! The couple threw a party, everyone got high—hey, it was the seventies!—she chose the most handsome guy in the neighborhood, who had just broken up with his childhood sweetheart, and the ex took the soiree upstairs to her empty bedroom, while hubby, Will, was passed out downstairs. That was the big gossip for some time and proof that their split was due to her promiscuous shenanigans. So of course, it never occurred to me that I was wearing rose colored glasses when we first gazed into each other's eyes. I even felt sorry for him, that he was betrayed so badly by both his wife and one of his longtime best friends.

My cousin Jen threw a party, and the whole gang would be there. I hadn't been out in such a long time, and Jen insisted I get a babysitter to join her party and the fun. It was indeed a good time, and I really enjoyed being out among my friends. With an evening of nothing but laughter and good times, it was late and the party was winding down. I was helping my cousin clean up when Will asked me for a glass. He was drunk and wobbling, but holding his own. We sat, talked, and I don't recall what worked faster, my fluttering eyelashes or his undeniable magical charm. Maybe one fueled the other, because before I could blink, we were an item. I was from an environment that advocated being a couple. A woman's place was with a man. It wasn't the norm for a young woman to be on her own. You were more popular if you were partnered with someone. I was working so hard, and while I didn't complain about anything, being included in this group of friends made me realize I was lonely. This encounter with Will made me aware of just how lonely I actually was. Being with him would be, could be so easy. Both from the same neighborhood, knew all the same people, were so familiar with the Italian ways and our culture. What more did I need to know? Having a daughter of his own, he was very good to Little Contessa and also understood my priorities—mother first, work second, playtime dead last. That was no problem for Will, and he constantly praised me for my ethic, citing how his ex-wife put her own social life first, leaving their daughter mostly to the grandparents to care for, something Will said ate away at him.

However, there were many signs glaring in front of me, but I guess I was blinded by his light or just didn't want to see them because I wanted him so bad. First of all, at the time we got together, he didn't have a job. Will was an insurance salesman with a very reputable firm for several years, before and during his marriage. Will was not shy about telling people he earned a very good living but had just left his company as he just got tired of the insurance business. His divorce was about to go through, which caused him to sell his house. Will said he was weighing his options before making his next move. The stars in my eyes were more evident than the smell of his bullshit, I guess, and before long, he was all moved in with me. I actually don't even remember us having the conversation about doing so; it just seemed to have happened. Looking back, that was surely another sign that I'm very embarrassed to admit I failed to see.

Second, Will was an all-too-easy drunk, void of conscience regarding any ramifications of his intoxicated state, but again I stupidly didn't realize the full extent of this vice of his until much later. I don't know if he just couldn't handle whatever he was drinking or just plain drank too much. Whichever, he was quick to get very loud, boisterous, and just plain obnoxious. I heard about his drunken antics more than I experienced them, as he was out way more without me than with me, as I was either working or caring for my daughter. We were able to have a date night once a month, maybe twice if I could get a sitter. That left him much more time to be out with the guys, playing sports, watching sports, talking sports, or just "hanging." In time, I would discover how much he loved betting on sports, which made me cringe. But more on that later. So I really didn't see much wrong with him hanging out with his buddies since my priorities didn't include going out much.

Will made it very easy for me to fall madly in love with him. When we were together, he was fun, attentive, and loving to Little Contessa. We shared many interests, particularly music, and sometimes we just listened to music very low, so as not to wake Little Contessa, while lying in each other's arms, talking. Now that was pretty amazing! We were an electrifyingly passionate couple; our love life was explosive and continual. Will taught me, and I was a very willing pupil. I was so enamored with him I failed to look down the road and see where he was going. He was not putting much effort into finding a job and was able to cover his bases on that by handing me money every week to go toward "our" household. I stupidly didn't question where that money came from but just assumed it was from his "savings." Double bonus for me, I thought—I had a fabulous guy who was helping to support me and Little Contessa. Ugh, what a dumb ass I was!

Golfers allow themselves a mulligan now and again, and eventually becoming a golfer allowed me to immediately think of Will whenever I heard the term. He was surely my mulligan, my extra shot after a poor stroke that would not be counted on the scorecard. A fitting explanation of this relationship. While I never considered myself the smartest person in the world, I certainly wouldn't say I was the dumbest either, particularly after what I had just been through with my first husband. I thought I learned a thing or two. Apparently not. If I did, I never would have fallen for my mulligan in the first place, who was merely a similar version of my first husband—just as charismatic, only much more handsome. Another neighborhood guy who, I must clarify, shared certain traits all the neighborhood guys had but lacked the sweetness and class that Mousie was so known for. Why couldn't I see that right from the start? I guess I was swept away and held by the spell this Svengali placed me under. Where is a psychic when you need one? A good medium could have told me Will was the devil incarnate, completely void of any conscience. I believe if you looked up the word *sociopath*, you would find Will's picture there. Yes, a fortune teller would have been a definite benefit, but then I wouldn't have learned what all I did in the process.

Aside from his drop-dead-gorgeous looks, sex appeal, and personal charm, Will had something else, something that was critical and spoke to the very core of me. He was a father himself and had a heart for children, which was numero uno on my "must" list. A vitally important second for me was family. My love of family and the growth of one was something immensely dear to my heart. Family was what we were all about. The traditional Sunday dinners we grew up on, big, loud family holidays together, and all sorts of family gatherings year round were just as much a part of me as my two feet were. Friends and neighbors dropping in and out, sharing a meal or coffee and treats, were how we lived our whole lives. I hoped that my next relationship would include a family, one that my little girl and I could easily transition into and become a real part of. Not only was the family element very present with Will, but his family also welcomed the thought of a grounded, family oriented Italian woman in his life, joining their family as well, something they did not have with his first wife. That said, the family component only added to the allure and my overwhelming attraction to him. Coming from a neighborhood where everyone knew one another well was a plus, as we shared the same background, same culture, same traditions. An easy situation to nestle into, I told myself. It would be so ideal. Another set of parents for me, grandparents for my little girl, and a sister-in-law who, being divorced with kids herself, related to me. In addition, Will's daughter could become a big sister for my Little Contessa to play with, and maybe, hopefully someday, dare I think it, we would add one more to our new family. I believed that Will was the be-all, end-all, absolutely perfect catch for me, and the new family dynamic clinched it.

Signs. We see them every day, but do we really pay attention to them? Think about it. You're driving along a familiar route, and you see a DETOUR sign. You ignore it and keep on going, as you've driven this route so very often. Suddenly you come to a dead end, a barricade, and another sign: ROAD CLOSED FOR CONSTRUCTION. You are pissed off, but then you remember, *Oh, yeah, that's what the detour sign was for!* Looking back, Will was one great big *detour* sign that was glaring right in front of my face, one I just didn't pay any attention to. Only long after this chapter of my life closed could I finally admit, to my discredit and embarrassment, that I created a scenario in my head and my heart and I wanted it so bad I told myself I could make it all happen.

When we first got together, I was working two waitress jobs and taking classes at night. Soon I was very fortunate in obtaining my first office position at a Holiday Inn in a Chicago suburb. I was completely absorbed in my work and my new work environment. This was what I was preparing myself for, training for, and I soaked up anything and everything I could that might help me move on and up to the next rung on the ladder. It soon paid off. We were now living together in an apartment building belonging to my very dear aunt and uncle, second parents to Little Contessa and me. That next step and ascent into the corporate world followed about one year later. I miraculously secured a position with Four Seasons Hotels, downtown Chicago. More on that later. This forward-thinking company offered a wide variety of paid management courses, and I took advantage of all that I could, which meant more night class time. Little Contessa was attending a very nice Catholic school near our house, and my relatives often helped me out watching her while I attended evening classes a few nights a week. I made sure, though, that I was always home on time to put Little Contessa to bed. That was one thing I was certain not to miss. Mine was an aggressive schedule, but the more reward I received from this hard work, the more invigorated and, yes, more assertive I became.

By now you should be wondering what Will was doing while I continued my professional journey. Simple. He was enjoying himself! At the time our relationship began, he was just about done with his marriage, and divorce followed soon afterward. Will said he had to sell his home and split the proceeds with his former wife. He went on to tell me that he was tired of the insurance business and was "thinking" about what he wanted to do next. The thought that perhaps Will did not leave his firm voluntarily entered my mind, but I didn't dwell on it. Hindsight being I didn't want to allow negative thoughts about him to linger. While Will was "thinking," I was working my ass off, educating myself and making a home for the three of us. And in my bliss, it didn't immediately dawn on me to ask myself what Will's contribution to the party was. I was so in love with his good looks and charm, in love with the idea of our little family as well as his. However, I always did have a breaking point, and eventually a sarcastic word or two began to roll off my tongue about his not finding permanent work, his partying, and that his financial contribution to the household needed to be increased and more regular. Will's answer to my sarcastic comments was answered by more charm, more seduction, and more sweet talk. The humiliation I now feel for being so blind and falling for it all is immeasurable and something I shall never live down. Shame on me!

Throughout my twenties, I was plagued with ongoing female medical issues—cysts, tumors, and other related problems that caused my periods to become a bit erratic. After not feeling very well for some time, I found out, much to my shock and horror, that I was pregnant. Devastated, I left the doctor's office in a fuzzy state, went home, and said nothing. After putting my Little Contessa to bed, I sat alone, thinking back to when I discovered she was on the way. Mousie and I were jubilant and filled with excitement about the new life as parents we would embark on. Little Contessa was brought into the world with great anticipation, jubilation, and more love than any child could possibly have. Even though the marriage went south, our start was wholeheartedly embracing her coming into and enriching our lives. Such was not the case with news of this pregnancy.

The brick I needed to wake me up just landed on my head, and I instantly saw things in a way I hadn't previously. I pulled myself up from nothing after my divorce. I had been working round the clock at building our home life, increasing my ability for career opportunities, and all the while, trying to be the best possible mother I could be. I was fortunate enough to have overcome every single obstacle that presented itself to me, only fueling the fire in me to do more. And now this news. I thought long and hard, and I realized that as much as I wanted more children, especially with Will, this was not the time, completely out of the question right now and not subject to negotiation. But I kept thinking. Suddenly and for the first time, I took a good, hard look at the facts. Was Will good to my daughter? Yes, but I began to believe it was a convenient opportunity for him. Little Contessa was right in front of his face, there to play with when he was around. While we did do things as a family, he didn't have any real parental responsibility for her, and that was by my design, but he always showed great affection for her. Thoughts that Will was substituting a relationship with Little Contessa for his own daughter—whom he did not go out of his way for, did everything he could to avoid paying child support for, and certainly was no role model for—became more apparent. He demonstrated that he did not have the conviction, dedication, or strength to be a real dad to his own child, as it was a harder situation. Thinking through this scenario caused me to realize that Will was only capable of handling simple, easy circumstances. All that said, I knew sharing the news of my pregnancy would not be met with the same excitement as when Little Contessa was on the way. I felt strongly then, and do still to this day, that my first obligation was to the child I already had. I wanted to give her the world. The very core of my ambition and work ethic was targeted at my Little Contessa, so she could have choices I didn't, that she would not have to struggle as I did, that her life would go far beyond mine ever could. Having a child now would only have all the progress I'd made this far instantly disintegrate.

These thoughts led me to the only conclusion I felt would remedy the situation. My first priority and solid commitment was to the child I already had. I would have an abortion. I felt that I should tell Will, but in my heart I already knew his reaction would be similar to mine, and I was correct. He was not happy at all and was quite relieved when I told him of my decision. That was that, decision made and mutually agreed upon. I went through with my plans and felt nothing but relief when it was over. It was behind me. Without getting political, I would just like to say that I was quite relieved and appreciative to have had a choice and be able to exercise it, making this decision as it related to me, my body, my life, and my future. I'm also very grateful I had been fortunate enough to have the procedure done properly and safely. I asked God to forgive me, and through the many blessings He has bestowed upon me since, I feel that forgiveness was given. When I'm ultimately at the pearly gates, begging forgiveness for all my sins, I'll know for sure.

This episode was clearly a wake-up call for me, truly one I was in desperate need of. It made me see that our relationship was a one-way street and changes had to occur immediately in order for it to continue. I developed a mental Q&A, a sort of a checklist for me to decide next steps. This process is one that I follow to this day whenever I am confronted with a dilemma, asking myself questions pertaining to the problem.

> Q: In a perfect world, what's my ultimate goal?
> A: Tweak, fine-tune, and straighten out my relationship with Will and eventually get married.
> Q: What's preventing that right now?
> A: Will needs to get his life in order, become more responsible.
> Q: What can I do to steer the situation to the direction I want it to go?
> A: Sit him down and lay the law down. It's shit-or-get-off-the-pot time.

I realized having a confrontation such as this might (gulp!) drive him away, but I heard my father's voice in my head: "You may not like the truth, but the truth will always put you on the right path." I realized I needed to put my big girl panties on and confront the situation, come what may. If he didn't like my ultimatum, he would leave, and I guess after a good cry and a period of sadness, I'd be no worse for the wear as my life was in order, and very good order at that. If he did heed my warning, great! We would then be on our way to the next phase of our relationship.

With pride, determination, and a feeling of empowerment, I sat down and delivered an ultimatum sermon to him in a tone Will had never heard from me before. While Will was engrossed in a football game, I turned the TV sound off and began.

"We need to talk," I said quite soberly.

"Well, go ahead and talk, but turn the sound back on, will ya?" he answered.

That made me so mad I turned the TV all the way off.

"What the fuck—"

"What the fuck, is that I need your full attention! Listen up, because I'm only gonna say this once!" I snapped.

He sat up straighter, looking a bit more serious upon hearing my tone.

"I can't believe I'm saying this, but after really thinking it over, I'm actually glad this pregnancy occurred. It caused me to think—I mean *really* think—about our relationship, our situation, and where we're going," I began.

"What do you mean 'where we're going'?" he snapped.

I didn't like that smart-ass interjection before I even got through my introduction. I felt my sassy pants knot up a little. "You need to check your tone, honey, because this conversation is going to decide our future, and if we even have one," I threw back.

"Well, what do you mean 'where we're going'? Where are we going? I don't get it," Will asked.

"I know you don't, and that's the problem. I know where I'm going, that's for sure. I'm going forward. I'm going up! I'm working my ass of to make something out of my life, something that I can be proud of. Something that will result in a better life for all of us."

"I know, sweetie, and I'm so proud of you," he said in a much softer tone.

"Will, we've been living together for some time now. I love you and want to, hope to, be with you for a long time."

"I love you too, Contessa, so what's the problem?" he interrupted.

"You're the problem, Will. You need to get your shit together, get a job, and start taking more responsibility for this relationship if you want it to continue. You need to get a steady job, one with a future. You need to beef up your contribution to our household, both financially and personally! The late nights, the drinking, the gambling, all of it has got to stop. And I mean immediately! Either you get real serious real fast, or we are done. I'll give you two months to get a job. And if you can't make that happen, you're out of here! I need commitment from you, Will. I'm not demanding marriage, but I am demanding that you start acting like you're committed to us creating a life, a good life for both of us and our children. If you can't do that, just say so and leave. If I find you aren't even trying, you will come home one day to find your things packed and out on the street. Trust me on this, Will. I've never been more serious," I concluded.

Will sat there shocked. "What's come over you? Where did this come from?" he asked.

In somewhat of a threatening tone, I finished "You think you know me so well, don't you? Will, you better start paying a little more attention, because obviously you didn't know that I can only be pushed so far before I push back! Did you forget that I got myself to this point from nothing? Did you forget what all I went through with Mousie? You're a fool if you think I'd ever allow anyone to drag me down. Not you, not now, not ever. So the ball's in your court, sweetheart. It's all up to you. And the clock starts ticking right now. We don't need to talk about it anymore, just know I'll be watching!" I went to bed and slept like a baby.

I was pretty frosty to him after that night, and soon he realized my demands were not to be taken lightly, not negotiable. Laying the law down as I did was at first difficult, but I immediately felt a weight lifted. I actually felt as though I grew an inch or two! Now I knew what being empowered meant, and I liked the feeling. Even though I was a bit nervous about what the outcome might be, I felt so much stronger having laid it all out as I did. The end results were quite positive, though, as Will immediately seemed to heed my warning. Not only did he turn on the charm big time, which I reveled in, but within that month, he secured a union job at one of the most popular Chicago newspapers. It was a labor job with different shifts, paid well, with great benefits. He would start in a few weeks. One small glitch, though: his ex-wife became aware of his new job and immediately filed a suit to have his wages garnished for back child support. He and his family were furious! I hated to admit it, but I certainly understood her actions. Even though she was a shitty mother, she was still entitled to child support. I was disgusted by Will's attitude to try to avoid paying, even hiring an attorney to try to get out of it or pay as little as possible. As usual, I couldn't hold my feelings in.

"That's your child! How can you be upset over contributing to her support? You should want to! You say you want a relationship with your daughter, but you don't want the responsibility that comes along with it. Your ex-wife has every right to expect that you pay your share of the costs relating to having a child, and I know that firsthand!"

This declaration did not lead to me being the most popular family relation, but I didn't care at all. I went about my busy days walking a little taller and reveling in this newfound feeling of authority. When things aren't going your way, it's up to you and you alone to initiate change and take the reins and actions that will get you where you want to be. Come what may, you will always feel stronger knowing you took the steps to do so.

It was during this period that our relationship really took off to the next level. As Will embraced his new job, I noticed a sense of pride come over him. He began to act more responsibly, toward us, our home life, and his daughter. While his financial contribution to the household wasn't all that significant, due to his wage garnishments, I respected it and let him know in several ways how much I appreciated his turnaround. By this time, I had moved up a bit within my company, having received two promotions. I was now earning a very good salary, doing work I enjoyed and was very proud of. Little Contessa continued to be her happy self, and all was well on the home front. Life was good, and we were in a wonderful place.

We were spending the weekend at the home of Will's parents, in a lovely western suburb of Chicago. We always had such good times there. Mother Betty was the typical Italian mother, living for her family, something always cooking, ready to sit you down to feed you. Father Tony was quite a handsome man, a retired truck driver. He was a street guy who made good after leaving the street life behind him and focusing more on his family life. He was kind, funny, and loved nothing more than being surrounded by his family. Sister Irene, a divorced mother of three great teenagers, also lived in the building. Irene and I immediately clicked, and her kids were absolute darlings. They lived in a gorgeous condo development with tons of room for children to be outside playing, enjoying the park, pool, and fresh air. The family welcomed Little Contessa and me with open arms. We all got along wonderfully; if I were fortunate enough to have "in-laws," they were what I wanted. Collectively, the family let me know how thrilled they were that Will was in a relationship with me. Other relatives told me that Tony and Betty bragged that their son was very fortunate to find a strong, independent Italian who had her priorities set, one who would make a great partner for him as well as a nurturing stepmother for Diana, Will's daughter. It was a dream for me, and I had every reason to believe it would continue to get even better.

And soon it did. The parents arranged to have Diana stay with them for this weekend, which was the reason for our visit. Little Contessa and Diana played nicely together. The girls were still getting to know each other as we were not able to see Diana very often. Diana was two years older than Little Contessa and seemed a bit shy around us at first. However, it was the comical and fun loving nature of my Little Contessa that won her over. Soon Diana's shyness diminished and the two girls got along wonderfully. With all the kids outside playing, the adults sat around talking. Betty, the condo building's Nosey Rosey, informed us that one of her neighbors was selling their condo; it was a second home for the owners to use when in town, visiting their grandchildren, and therefore was hardly ever lived in. Betty had a discussion with the owners and found they were selling it for a very low price. Ever the schemer, Betty told the owners to hold off on listing it, that her son would probably be interested. She also convinced the owners to drop their price a little more, as they would be saving the cost of a realtor fee. They agreed. Betty got the keys from the owners in order to show us. We all took a walk down the hall to see it.

The condo was awesome! Excellent condition, not a thing needed to be done. A new owner could move right in. I couldn't believe we were actually discussing buying it. We sat down and began crunching numbers. As my salary was the meatier of the two, I realized the heavier burden would be on me. I wasn't sure I could handle it. I was also quick to point out that we had no savings, nothing to use as a down payment. Tony and Betty took great delight in announcing they would be very happy to lend us the money for an adequate down payment and we could pay them back a little at a time. They added that it would be a wonderful opportunity for the family, that they would be so happy to assist in making it happen. It was a dream for me, but I had to think this over a bit. I thanked them and let them know I had to think it through a bit more. None of them, particularly Will, could understand why I was hesitant.

My head was spinning all the way home. Will was pretty psyched up about this opportunity; in his mind it was a go and had us already moved in. I conveyed that we needed to discuss it more, that I had to think it over. He didn't understand why I wouldn't jump at the prospect of owning our own home, especially in this beautiful development, surrounded by his family.

"You're like a kid in a candy shop," I told him.

"What's wrong with that?" he said back, laughing.

"How about paying for it, for one thing?" I sarcastically asked.

"What's the big deal? My parents said they would lend us the down payment, and you just got a big raise," he quickly responded in too cavalier a manner for me.

"The problem I'm having right now is that you aren't as good with budgeting as I am," I snapped back. "It's one thing to borrow the down payment, but you're forgetting *borrow* means it has to be paid back as well. You know I'm completely against borrowing money from anyone. I need to think this through, and I really don't want to talk about it until I have my thoughts together," I finished.

"Fine!" Will snarled. We finished the drive home in silence.

I spent the next several days eating lunch alone with my notebook and calculator so I could think in peace and play with numbers. There were other issues besides finances as well. Did I want this? Absolutely! Would it be a step toward my ultimate goals of making a better life for Little Contessa? No question. Better living conditions, better schools, tons of kids her age in the development. However exciting these benefits were, my main concern was that the bulk of financial burden would be on me. My recent promotions escalated my salary considerably. I had just started realizing the comfort of not just making ends meet but actually saving a little. Will's take home pay was not much at all, given the union dues and wage garnishments, making his household contribution minimal. I knew he wasn't considering payback to his parents. Will was a taker, and he rarely, if ever, paid back. I didn't want to be part of that. Not my style. I thought back to my vow of never getting into a dependent situation, and taking money from his parents would put me there. I was certain Will would neglect any payback obligation to them. I wouldn't do this unless I was confident I could handle it on my own. The financial portion was certainly a significant drawback. The second issue was, to me, just as significant. We were not married. Living together was one thing; if you broke up, one just packed their things and left. Buying property together without the benefit and commitment of marriage would create quite a different situation. While owning my own home was a dream of mine, marrying Will was too. My dilemma was how to present the marriage issue without seeming like it was an ultimatum. I would never, under any circumstances, try to force a guy to marry me—who would want a marriage that had to be forced? Surely not me. I thought long and hard about the situation. By the end of the week, I was ready to discuss it and sat Will down to roll out my plan.

"It's a big step, and I'm a little nervous, but I think financially we can swing it if we stay focused and committed. I have a two-part plan to show you."

"That's my girl, always thinking! Okay, lay it on me," Will asked.

I showed him the numbers I worked up on a notepad. "This includes all expenses related to owning the condo. I divided the total by two, so it's half for each of us. The commitment, Will, is for you to realize this can't happen without your full dedication to paying your share."

"What makes you think I wouldn't?" he interrupted.

"Ah, let's be realistic, Will. You know you have a tendency to get stuck at the bar and do a little gambling now and then. Those things cost us money that we won't be able to do without. Besides, with your new job you shouldn't be concerned about hanging at the bar or gambling anyway! If we buy this condo, there's not going to be a lot of extra money, so if you want a little extra cash, you're going to have to get some overtime in and earn it. Or maybe even a second job, like I've done. Your choice, Will. If you really want to do this, you need to convince me I don't have to worry about any of your old vices, that they are gone and I can depend on you for your full contribution," I explained.

"Of course, you can!" he said as he rolled his eyes. He sat there looking over my budget.

"What's this set of numbers here?" he asked.

"That's part 2 of my plan," I answered.

"Explain," he asked.

"This part is about the down payment and payback," I began.

"My parents already said they'd take care of it," he interrupted.

"You're using the wrong phrase, Will. They offered to loan us that money, not take care of it," I corrected.

"Yeah, so what's the difference?" he stupidly asked.

"The difference is that 'take care of it' implies a gift. *Loan* means borrow, and you have to pay that back. This section here outlines the extra deduction from your check that you'll pay your father back with," I explained.

"I already talked to my parents. Dad said he doesn't need it back right away. He said we can take as long as we need to. Mom said as long as we put the deed in their name, its not even an issue."

I actually threw up in my mouth a little when I heard that, but I had an inkling that was what the lady had in mind, based on some of the comments she had made while rolling her plan out. As I said, his mother was quite the schemer, and this one little revelation had me realize she was going to play me. She knew damn well that her son never paid anyone back for anything. She also knew that financially, I would be carrying the bulk of this deal. So why not—or so she thought—put the deed in their names, have me pay for it, and let them be secure in knowing they owned another property as well as security for their son? Nice new "in-laws," huh? Already using me for their own gain and son's benefit. No fucking way! Which was why I came up with a genius plan of my own. Take that, Nosey Rosey! *So it's gonna be like that, huh? Bring it, honey, I'm ready.*

"And what do you mean 'I pay my father back'?" he questioned.

"I have something a little different in mind, Will. We're going to split the down payment in half. You can certainly take your half from your parents if you want. I plan on using the loan program from my company. The payback is deducted right out of my check, and that calculation is factored in over here. See how I included everything into the budget? And the best part is"—I was quickly learning how and when best to put on a really good act, for my benefit—"the deed can be put in both our names so we don't have to burden your parents with that. We'll truly be homeowners, Will! Isn't that great?" I triumphantly finished.

"I can't believe you figured all this out on your own, Contessa. Jeez, I can see what you're learning in all those classes you take! I have to admit, I'm really impressed," Will lovingly said while embracing me.

"I'm learning how to plan for our future, honey. Now get over here and tell me if we have a deal." I pushed all the paperwork aside, and we made mad, passionate love on the living room coffee table. Done and done!

My plan was designed to keep us together, but financially separate, plus maintain my independence and percentage of ownership in this property, married or not. This way, I had no responsibility or obligation to his parents—that was completely up to him. What was I learning in my classes? Strategy, for one thing! Subsequent conversations with his parents on the subject didn't go quite as smoothly. Tony was very complimentary of me, letting me know how happy he was that his son was with such a levelheaded, smart business woman. Mother Betty, however, was pretty pissed off. It was as if she really wanted to hold that deed over our heads, or at least my head, to have something over on us or me alone. Oh, well, not an issue now as it was finally all a done deal and we prepared for the move.

It was a fast and furious pace, but we were able to make all the necessary preparations for our move. I was excited beyond words to have this opportunity; for so many reasons, however, moving away from my dear relatives did tug at my heart. They were wonderful people, like second parents to me and grandparents to Little Contessa. Knowing we would not see them as much made us sad, but they were very understanding and excited for us as well. Other than that, it was full steam ahead, and before we knew it, moving day arrived. Little Contessa was pretty excited as well, knowing she would have a much larger, nicer bedroom and a big beautiful park and swimming pool to play in, with friends throughout the development. She looked forward to starting a new school, making new friends she could have playtime with, even sleepovers now and again, which she was not able to do in our little city apartment. Living right next door to us was a divorced mom with a young girl the same age as Little Contessa. My daughter and I knocked on their door to introduce ourselves and were greeted by Liz and her daughter, Candy. We all became instant friends.

The move seemed to go pretty well. Getting settled wasn't so difficult either, as we really didn't have much furniture. That would come in time. Will had the shopping bug. He wanted to go out and charge up a storm, but I stuck to my guns—bare essentials only. We needed to get used to this new financial setup before we went nuts on furniture, I maintained. Everything seemed to be going smoothly, except for my commute to work every day. I didn't mind taking the train; I actually liked it as it gave me a chance to eat breakfast and even get caught up on work that I brought home. The big pain in the ass was having to take two busses after getting off the train. What's more, the return trip at night became increasingly difficult with ongoing city construction. As the snow began to fall, traffic to the train station got even worse, often causing me to miss my train, consequently making me late to pick up Little Contessa from the after school program. Thank God for my neighbor Liz, whom I was able to call for help, asking her to pick my daughter up when I knew I would be late. Little Contessa was welcome to stay at their place until I arrived home. I reciprocated by taking the girls out for ice cream, roller skating, and various other activities. It was great to have a neighbor whom I could relate to and depend on, and we did so with each other regularly.

The commute was getting progressively worse, and soon I realized I had no choice but to start looking for a new job in the suburbs. That was a tough one, as I currently held what I always called a dream job—great company, excellent benefits, wonderful training programs, with a clear path for growth and development. I began my job search, registering with several employment agencies. Each of the recruiters seemed to be impressed with my résumé and credentials, indicating I would be easy to place. I was going after a new rung on the corporate ladder and was very aggressive with my résumé and presentation, even stretching things a bit. Maybe a bit arrogant, you might say, but nonetheless a style I was developing. Even so, I was surprised at how quickly the responses came in for interviews.

Will, on the other hand, had no problem easing into our new situation. His job was going well; he didn't mind the long ride to and from the city. He demonstrated a noticeable sense of pride in contributing to our household finances, as well as making our new house a real home. Will helped paint, wall paper, and decorate. As finances allowed, we were able to buy furniture, piece at a time, and we had a lot of fun shopping for things. He seemed really happy and didn't appear to miss hanging out with the boys at the bar back in the city. He did find a new hangout at the restaurant where his sister

Irene worked, quickly making friends there with other regulars. He would go there on occasion to watch a sports game. I didn't mind, so long as he wasn't drinking and stayed on this positive path. Little Contessa was enjoying her new school and having girlfriends to play with within the building and around the development. She and I became very close to Irene's children, who were good kids and fun to be around. They were also helpful to me when I needed someone to watch Little Contessa and Diana. I began waitressing at the restaurant where Irene worked one night a week. It was a nice restaurant with fabulous Italian food. One night there earned me a good amount of extra cash, and I didn't mind the exercise. We were managing our new financial situation just fine. This was a very happy time for all of us.

Soon I secured a position with Citibank, as they were opening a Midwest regional office in a neighboring suburb. It was a fantastic position, offering spectacular benefits and a phenomenal internal growth path. The office was a short ride into work each day and thus allowed me to better manage after school care for Little Contessa, who, by now, was in middle school. My new position offered a wide array of paid management courses as well as mandatory enrollment in the American Institute of Banking, which meant more night classes. Somewhat rough on my schedule, but I was certain it would be worthwhile, as I quickly learned my new company opted to promote from within before looking outside. The mantra of this company was "swim with the sharks." The philosophy behind it was, sharks move forward, crabs move sideways—do you want to be a crab or a shark? It took me all but a nanosecond to declare my alignment to the sharks. The tone of the company was not to merely meet your goals but how far beyond them you can go. It couldn't have been a better fit for me, and I reveled in the opportunity I had just been given.

During this blissful period, Will and I became closer than ever, as well as he and Little Contessa. I encouraged and welcomed the opportunity to have his daughter, Diana, stay with us more often, and that was slowly beginning to happen. This was the last piece of our family puzzle, and I wanted her to truly feel part of it. I hoped that Diana and Little Contessa would become close and feel like real sisters. Just when I thought things couldn't get any better, Will gave me the surprise of a lifetime. The kids were asleep, and we were snuggled up on the sofa, watching a movie, a comedy, and we were laughing our asses off. At one point, we knocked heads as we were doubled over from this hilarious movie. As we both held our foreheads, Will took me in his arms.

"I am so in love with you, Contessa," he declared as he kissed me passionately. "Look at what you did for us."

Amazed, I responded, "What do you mean? What did I do?"

Will waved his arms all around the room. "You made this happen. You put it all together. You kicked me in my ass when I needed it most and made me see the things that were most important. For me and for all of us."

"And what's important to you, Will?" I coyly asked.

"We are. You and I, our kids, and our families. That's what I want, that's what I know we can have, all because of you. I love you, and I want you. I want you forever," Will gently told me.

"You have me, Will. Trust me, I'm not going anywhere, except for an occasional business trip here and there," I joked.

"Ha, ha. No, I mean I want us to be together, always. I think it's about time we get married."

It took a lot to make my jaw drop, but this did the trick. Was he really proposing to me? I couldn't speak. I began to cry.

"What's the matter? Don't you want to get married?" he asked while hugging me a little tighter.

I found my voice. "Oh my God, yes, of course, I do. I mean, I've thought about it, even dreamed about it. Things have been so good for us for quite some time now I didn't dare to want for anything more. I didn't think we needed to change anything. I guess I'm just a little surprised. Where did this come from? I had no idea you were even thinking about it," I sniffled out.

"Actually, I've been thinking about it a lot lately. I know you don't think I pay much attention to you or what all you do, but believe me, I'm very aware of everything you do for us, for me, for our kids. I see the work you put into our home, all the attention you give to our kids. I watch you work on stuff you bring home from the office, after the dishes are done, after the laundry is done, and after the kids are sleeping. I'm amazed at what I see you working on. You blow me away, Contessa. I don't know how you do it all, and you never complain. I couldn't ask for more in my partner, and I don't think things can get any better than this, except to know that we will be together forever. So what do you say? Let's get married," he finished.

At this moment, I had every reason in the world to believe my dream came true, that he meant every word of what he was saying. I trusted and believed that he truly and completely turned around and his vices were behind him.

And get married we did. We had a lovely celebration with both families and lots of friends present. Our daughters were flower girls, looking adorable in matching dresses. The food and drink flowed, the music played, and laughter, dance, and good spirits filled the room. It was quite a celebration. Until…

I was in the lobby of the party room, saying goodbye to a few guests. I noticed Will and a friend come out of the men's room and motioned for him to come over and say goodbye as well. As he got closer to us, I was mortified to spot white powder around his nostrils. Thankfully, the people we were saying goodbye to were elderly and probably couldn't see it, but my eyes were perfectly fine and I knew exactly what was going on! My brand new husband was snorting cocaine in the bathroom on our wedding day!

I didn't need the lightning bolt that pierced my heart at that moment, nor did I need a fortune teller to predict this future. The man who melted me from the start, the man I watched make a concentrated effort to be everything I said I wanted, the man I dreamed of marrying and just became my husband got his first taste of the newest vice of the eighties. Dear God, here we go again! Jumping to conclusions? Absolutely not! Been here before, and knowing the times, the players, and in particular, having full grasp of Will's lack of ability for control, I was confident his appetite for this new party favor would surge. *Dammit!* I didn't think anything would have to happen or change once we were married. We had been living together for some time, we were nicely settled into our new home, kids were comfortable with each other, and both of our jobs were going very well. I wouldn't even have considered that there would be anything else to get used to, or new to manage. Until this very second. Happy wedding day to me!

I decided not to say anything about the cocaine right away. I thought it best to wait and see how and when an encore performance would occur. In the meantime, I had a full plate with my new job, my evening classes, and our home. Little Contessa was growing, as were her homework needs, and I was determined to spend time immediately after dinner to work with her on assignments. She was a very good student and was well liked by classmates. Reports from school and her teachers were always glowing. Diana, on the other hand, was quite a handful. She was one of those kids who instinctively knew how to play people to get her way. She mastered the "poor me, my parents are divorced and my mother is never home, nobody loves me" game whenever things didn't go her way. Thankfully, she was only with us on weekends! She was quite challenging, and her demonstrative behavior soon began to create problems between Will and me. It was hard enough to be a parent, and a single parent at that, let alone be a good stepparent. I had no guidebook for reference on how to be a stepmother. However, I did know that what was good for one child was good for both kids, and there was only one set of rules in our house that was to be adhered to by both children. Although my daughter was a model child, I was a strict parent; my constant words to Little Contessa were "Nobody else has to care about how you turn out but me."

As Little Contessa grew into those dreaded early teen years, which came with hormones erupting and the typical girlish smart mouth—to which I immediately thrust some sort of lightweight punishment—she heard my mantra regularly and stomped off into her room upon hearing it. I pretty much laughed those times off, knowing they would pass. Diana, on the other hand, was not used to rules at all and threw constant tantrums whenever confronted with even the slightest form of authority. Both girls were required to set the table for dinner, help me clear things up afterward, and do dishes.

Cleaning up their bathroom after use, maintaining a neat bedroom, taking care of their clothes were my absolute must do's. Instead of embracing these fundamental chores, Diana not only rebelled but also threw tantrums over. I let her know if she kept it up, she would be sent home. Diana's response was to run down the hall to either her grandmother or aunt's house, spinning tales of how her wicked stepmother was abusing her. The in-laws expected me to give in to Diana, which I absolutely refused to do, causing many heated discussions between them and me.

Adding to this problem, Diana was to spend the next entire summer with us. Will's way of handling his unruly daughter was to have his shift changed to nights. He just didn't have what it took to handle the hard part of parenting. That was his gift to me. Will's new work schedule had him sleeping during the day, up and around later in the afternoon, with just a bit of time to play with the kids before he left for work at about five o'clock. I hired a sitter to watch the girls during the day as he slept. Surprisingly, the sitter reported that the girls got along well and there was never any problem between them. The dramatics began once I got home from work, when chores and rules were enforced. Go figure!

That summer was immensely taxing on me. My new job was extremely demanding, but I was managing it. While I was earning a salary I never would have imagined, I had to work ten times harder than my counterparts to keep up to speed with the knowledge they walked into their positions with. Having adopted the motto of the organization, I found it wasn't enough for me to be just as good as they were; I pushed myself to be better. I thrived on my studies at the Banking Institute as well as the fast paced corporate culture I now belonged to. Citicorp was a well developed, progressive environment that kept the door open for upward mobility to anybody who demonstrated they deserved it. I was determined to be worthy of everything this company had to offer. In one way, I was glad that Will was working nights, as I then had one less person to tend to. Sounds bitchy, I know, but my evenings were jam-packed. Prepare dinner, eat, and clean up. After that, I looked forward to entertaining the girls in some way, which could have been so much more enjoyable if it weren't for Diana's constant and chronic complaining and theatrical displays over every little thing. While the girls got ready for bed, I did some laundry, housework, and general cleaning up. When they went to bed, I addressed the work I usually came home with in order to stay one step ahead at the office. My engine was running a thousand miles per hour, and I pretty much lost track of any thoughts regarding Will getting into trouble or the whole cocaine thing.

With Will working nights, he normally returned home early in the morning, just as I was getting up for work. We sometimes even had time for a little morning intimacy, which brought me back to that good place between us. He would be fast asleep by the time the sitter arrived, as I left for my office. But as this summer progressed, Will began getting home later and later, explaining he was getting some overtime in. Wonderful, I thought. A little extra cash is always nice to save for extra things. However, this "additional" cash I expected to receive and put toward our household finances never seemed to surface. Even more frustrating was that his regular monetary contribution was beginning to decrease as well. I'd question Will about it, and he continually had some lame explanation. His car needed work done, his union dues increased, he gave his dad extra money toward the down payment payback. Bullshit! I knew he was up to no good, and decided I would confront him this weekend. Friday was payday, and I did the banking on Saturday. I planned on confronting him this Saturday morning, as I prepared my checks and bill payments.

Saturday morning, my temperature was rising with each hour that passed and Will still was not home. I fed the girls a great breakfast and sent them outside to play. I passed the time catching up on some work I needed to do in preparation for a major presentation at a very large bank holding company on the East Coast the following week. If this marketing proposal went well, I would attain a huge new client and could be in line for a fabulous promotion. Suddenly, the girls came in wanting lunch. Lunchtime already? And that bastard still wasn't home! *Just try to bullshit your way out of this one, Will!*

Lunch for the kids included the usual whining from Diana; she didn't like the sandwiches I prepared, she wanted soda (which I was against and never had in the house), and she put up a stink as to why

I wouldn't buy it for her. Little Contessa and I rolled our eyes at each other, thinking the same thought: *Here she goes again!*

"Diana, you're on my last nerve right now," I said as I used every ounce of self control I could muster.

"What does that mean?" she snipped.

"That means we better finish lunch and go back outside to the pool," Little Contessa offered.

With that, Diana just left the table.

Little Contessa finished her lunch. I hugged and kissed her and whispered how much I loved her. We had a little giggle over Diana. Thank God for Little Contessa, who lightened up many a tense moment between Diana and me. Off to the pool they went while I tensed up even more upon looking at the clock and Will still was not home. I fought to concentrate on my work. Hours passed with me entertaining the girls throughout the night. I thought dinner out at their favorite place followed by a movie would do the trick. That made them happy, and I could at least attempt to occupy my mind. At this point, I was beyond infuriated. I was actually kind of hoping that there was some sort of accident, which would be the only thing that would ease my level of rage. Add trying to mask my emotions in front of the kids. *Uggggh!* It wasn't too late after the movie, so I took them roller skating for an hour. I wanted them really exhausted in case Will stumbled home in the middle of the night. I managed to wear them out, all right, get them home, cleaned up, and into bed like nothing at all was wrong. I found peace in watching my daughter sleep, hoping I could right whatever was wrong for her sake.

Although my heart was racing the entire night, I dozed off for a while. I woke up to the sun shining and the birds chirping. Sunday morning, and Will still was not home, but it was a perfect summer day, too gorgeous to let anything spoil it. I decided to make the girls a big pancake breakfast, and so I began. As usual, Little Contessa was first to get up.

"Mmmm, I smelled the pancakes, Mom! Thanks! I'll set the table for you," she offered. As she began to set the table, I reached for her, hugging and kissing her all over.

"What's that for?" she laughingly asked.

"That's for being the best daughter in the world, my little lamb!" I said.

There are no words to explain to a child the joy they bring you, and when you're wrestling with something difficult, the mere presence of your baby comforts you. Children never understand that until they become parents themselves. My little girl always washed my tears, fears, and angst away. Today was no exception.

Diana stumbled in, demanding to know what kind of pancakes they were. Did I make bacon? Did I buy the syrup she liked? Where was her apple juice? Jeez, did this kid ever stop? We finished breakfast, and true to her nature, Little Contessa began to clean up. I was really nervous that Will would stroll in, and I didn't want the girls to be there when he did. I emphasized the beautiful day and that we shouldn't waste one minute of it. "So let's get out to the pool." I told them I had just an hour to hang out with them, as I had to get back to my presentation. I acted as coach to their diving board games and races. The sun was dusting my skin, and it seemed to take my mind off things. I did need to get back to work on my presentation, and by this time, Candy and some of the other development kids joined the pool activities so the girls wouldn't miss me at all.

I spread my work out on the dining room table and dived right in. I made good progress and, in fact, was almost done when I heard the key enter the lock on the front door. It was Will. As I looked up from the table, I was mortified to see my handsome husband looking like he had been on a week long drunken bender. The sight of him—bloodshot eyes, hair standing out on end, slurred speech, reeking of a bar, and not even able to stand up straight—both disgusted and infuriated me. I got right into it.

"What the fuck happened to you?" I demanded as Will tried to avoid me by going into the bedroom. Following him, I continued, "Where the hell have you been for the last two days?"

He turned around, and the demonic face I saw didn't belong to my husband. His physical features actually seemed to change as he turned to me, a bit still wobbly and slurring as he spoke.

"Who are you, the fucking police? I don't have to tell you shit!" he barked.

"I'm your wife, who has been here holding down the fort, working my ass off, while you're God knows where, doing God knows what! I told you before you left for work two days ago we had something important to talk about when you got home. Then you prance in here two days later like it's nothing?" I snapped back.

"I was out, that's where I was! O-U-T with my friends, having a little fun! That okay with you, bitch? 'Cuz you're no fun anymore! Miss Serious, you and your fucking job!" he slurred.

What was I hearing? Where was this coming from? Obviously, he was still high from whatever and in no condition to have a serious talk. At this point, I just thought it best to walk away, as he was in no condition to talk, and I didn't want to risk the girls walking in on this. I thought better to let him go to bed and sleep it off. We could start over again later.

"Fine, Will. I just need your paycheck, because I already wrote out this month's bills, and I need to deposit it first thing tomorrow morning," I demanded.

An eruption followed. "There ain't no check this week!" he lashed out.

"WHAT? What do you mean no check this week? You've been skimping on what you owe to the house more and more every week, with these bullshit excuses, which was what I wanted to talk to you about! So now what? Where's your check?" I demanded.

"Here's my fucking check, bitch!"

Pow! A hard punch directly to my face that knocked me out right onto the floor. The room was spinning, but I managed to pull myself up by grabbing hold of a chair. I fumbled my way into the hallway bathroom. There was a medicine chest in this room, the older kind, which was attached to and stuck out from the wall. It had mirrors that slid open on each side. I opened this chest to get an ice pack, and before I knew it, Will rushed behind me, punched me in back of my head, and shoved my face into the medicine chest. I heard the mirror crash and had to keep my eyes shut as it shattered onto my face.

I heard nothing but the pounding of my heart. I could not even feel myself breathe. It was like a dream where you see yourself running but don't feel your body taking the steps. I can't even say I remembered what Will did the seconds following these two annihilating blows. With my eyes tightly closed, I felt my way out of the house and down the hall, banging on Liz's door. Upon opening her door, I heard Liz scream at the sight of me. She immediately started brushing off the shards of glass that were on my face. I could not speak for some time. As Liz worked on my face, I heard her express what a bastard Will was, that everything would be okay, that she would get one of Irene's kids to watch the girls while she took me to the hospital. Working at lightning speed, Liz removed the glass from my face and handed me a towel to place on my eyes, warning me to keep my eyes shut until we got to the hospital. She called Irene's daughter Tina to come stay with all three girls. Thankfully, the girls were mindless of it all, enjoying a blissful summer day at the pool.

I didn't mind the mild concussion so much, or the slight cuts all around my face. I knew the swelling of my nose would eventually go down, that the black-and-blue around my eyes would get worse within the next day or so. So what. I could deal with that. What I did have a hard time with was how and why this happened. What switch got flipped that made Will turn into a monster who could do this to me? While it took a little time for my brain to even begin to "have thoughts," I was most grateful for the fact that none of the glass got into my eyes or mouth, as the hospital staff warned that could have caused significant damage. They gave me pain medication, which helped. Liz took me back to her place, and all I remember is falling to her sofa, drifting off to never-never land.

I woke up the next morning to the chatter of three young girls having breakfast in Liz's kitchen. Liz approached me and quietly whispered, "We had a sleepover here. I told them your medicine cabinet fell on your head. I haven't been in your house and have no idea where Will is. Just stay here and rest. I've got it under control."

"I owe you, girlfriend," I whispered back as tears gushed from my swollen, puffy black-and-blue face.

The girls bought the story Liz told them on how I got hurt, and as they ran in and out, I continued resting at Liz's house. By Sunday night, and still no word as to Will's whereabouts, I had to go home.

I nervously entered our condo and was delighted to find an empty house, with Will nowhere to be found. As I got the kids ready for bed, my loving Little Contessa gently kissed my cheek to console me. Her compassionate wishes for me to feel better gave me the lift I needed to take the next steps. With the kids in bed and their TV on, I announced, "Girls, I'm going down the hall to Gramma Betty's for a minute. I'll be right back."

"Okay, Mom," they said, giggling.

Betty's mouth dropped when she opened the door and saw my face. She didn't invite me in, but I walked past her anyway and began. "Liz told me she came here to tell you what your son did to me. And yet you haven't even had the decency to come see how I was doing or help care for your own granddaughter! Honestly, I don't even care, but you should know I filed a police report at the hospital. They took a statement from both Liz and me in addition to photos of me, so it's all on record."

The look on Betty's face told me she was more afraid of how I would retaliate against Will than be apologetic for what her son did to me. I smelled a rat and continued.

"I don't know where Will is, but I'm confident you do. I'm well aware of the lengths you've always gone to in order to cover up your son's bad behavior. So here's what we're gonna do. You're going to take that fucking little brat granddaughter of yours home immediately. I've had about all of her I can take. I have to go to the East Coast for a presentation, and my daughter will stay with Liz while I'm gone. You're going to make sure that your son stays far away from here, and don't even try to tell me you can't reach him. I put a restraining order on him, and you better let him know it. He's not allowed in or near our condo until I return from my trip. At that point, I'll have a police officer here while Will takes what he needs and gets out. Do I make myself clear?" I finished.

Betty didn't say a word, just continued her vicious glare at me. I left.

Tuesday morning, I was packed and ready for my presentation on the East Coast. I thanked Liz for caring for my daughter and said goodbye to Little Contessa, hugging her ever so tightly before I left. I had a pair of huge Jackie O sunglasses that hid almost all my bruises and black eyes. I really didn't care about my looks; I just didn't want to scare people on the plane. I actually thought of my bruises as kind of a badge of honor in a way; every day I looked at them gave me strength to proceed with what I knew I needed to do. My razor sharp focus was now centered at two targets. I would get this new client, confident it would send me to the next level of management. I would file for divorce and get far, far away from Will and his madness. With these two objectives consuming my thoughts, I met the clients and put on one hell of a presentation. My bruises were easily explained as a result of a car accident. Truth be told, they might have even helped me a bit as I wasn't ashamed to play the sympathy card to the clients.

"A terrible accident, but I was still able to get your presentation done in time, as I know how important this was to you." Hey, play the cards you're dealt, right?

My approach to them was, "Come rain or shine, my team and I would always be available for excellent customer service." It might have been enhanced by a little violin playing, but it worked, and I got the contract.

I called Liz to check on Little Contessa. She informed me that Little Contessa and Candy were at another friend's house, that they were being treated to dinner and a movie with the other friend and mother. I was able to catch an earlier flight, which would get me home in plenty of time to plop onto the sofa for just a little solitude and a chance to relax a bit. I got home, went to my mailbox, and found a huge pile of letters from our bank. *What the hell are these?* I thought, but I would open them later. As I got closer to my front door, I heard loud laughing and music coming from our unit. I stood in the hallway for a minute, listening. It reeked of cigarette smoke. I quietly and slowly entered. Horrified, I saw Will and an old neighborhood friend—Jimmy, notorious for using and dealing drugs of a variety of sorts—yakking it up and smoking cocaine. I stood there in shock, watching them laugh, light up their individual bongs (a new toy I'd never even seen before), inhaling and exhaling the disgusting shit. They didn't even notice me. My house was a mess. Liquor, pot, and a variety pills were all over the house. It smelled worse than a cheap bar. They looked like they hadn't slept in days, and immediately I knew they had quite a party here while I was gone. So much for laying down the law to Betty. So much for just a little bit of solitude! I went straight to the receiver and shut the music off.

"Well, look who's back! My big shot wife!" slurred Will.

"Hey, Contessa, long time no see!" Jimmy slurred right after Will.

"Party's over, boys. Get out, both of you!" I snapped.

With a wobbly walk, Will approached me. "The party ain't over till I say it's over. You got that, bitch?" he slurred.

"OUT, NOW!" I screamed.

Slap! Slap! I felt two harsh slaps to my face.

I screamed. Jimmy quickly ran out, telling Will he would wait in the parking lot, that Will better leave now as well. I quickly ran to my bedroom to grab my mighty *mattarello*, a long specially treated rolling pin Italians use to roll out pasta dough, which I kept under the bed. With all the force I could muster, I began to beat Will with it.

"You wanna hit me again, mother fucker? Now you better kill me, 'cuz I'm gonna kill you!" As I hit and hit and hit, he ran out of the house, down the hall, and I was right behind him, banging that rolling pin all over him as he screamed. Before I knew it, Liz came running out, grabbing me and my mattarello.

"Contessa, stop, stop! Think what you're doing! He's not worth it!" Liz cried. "I called the police, Will, they're on the way!" Liz yelled.

Liz held me, hugged me as I became hysterical. Will hobbled out of the building. It was a *Jerry Springer* episode if ever there was one. We walked back to my house, and the police arrived a few moments later. They took a statement from both Liz and me, making note of and photographing the drugs and paraphernalia that were strung throughout the house. I showed the officers my copy of the restraining order. I had to decide if I wanted Will picked up and jailed. "Absolutely!" I told them. I gave them a few tips on where I thought Will might be, and they left. Liz and I hurried to clean everything up before the kids came home. When they did, I couldn't hug my girl long enough or hard enough. I burst into tears.

"What's wrong, Mom?" Little Contessa so compassionately asked.

"I'm just so glad to be home with you, my lamb!" I cried.

Will was picked up and spent two nights in jail. The in-laws were furious with me, and I didn't give a shit. What followed in those two days was a series of discoveries, each one like another blow to my head, each one more wrenching. The pile of letters from the bank were NSF (Non Sufficient Funds) notices regarding recently deposited checks from my account. I found out Will was stealing blank checks from the new, unused checks that were still in boxes. He took the checks from the bottom, writing them out for hundreds of dollars each, payable to a friend who owned a bar and signed my name to them. The friend cashed them with full knowledge Will was forging my name to them. Will was actually fired from his job for poor performance, failure to pay his dues, and a host of other things. He started gambling again, owed money to everyone, and was robbing Peter to pay Paul. He was forging my name to these checks to give me cash for the household to cover for him losing his job. Did he actually believe I would never find all this out? What the fuck was wrong with him? In addition, he fell down the rabbit hole that was lined with cocaine. This was the mother lode and way more than I bargained for. I was carrying the financial burden of our household finances. I was caring for his fucking drama queen, spoiled rotten daughter, and this was my payback? *No way, it's over, I'm done!*

I used my presentation skills to put a beauty together for my case against Will. I combined the physical abuse pictures and paperwork, the police report and pictures of the drugs, statements from Liz, all the bank notifications, and related check forgery information together. The presentation was my action plan and bargaining chip for divorce that would take place immediately in the office of the attorney I just hired. The deal was simple. Will would have only one choice: either sign his half of the condo over to me or face charges on the several punishable endeavors he was was responsible for, which would most definitely land him in jail. What was more, his friend who cashed all those checks was also at risk for cashing checks he knew were forged. Cruel, greedy, unfair, you might say? I would respond *hell no*!

First of all, we had a deal whereby each of us was financially committing to half of all home related expenses. I found out Will made no attempt to pay back his parents for his half of the down payment. Payments from the loan I took from my work were deducted from my paychecks and documented. Will's financial contribution was considerably less than mine, as his salary was less. That would have been okay with me had he stayed on the straight and narrow. But when his antics started up again and his weekly contributions became less and less, offering bullshit, insulting excuses as to why, meant that I had to pick up his financial slack. I took on a second job in order to do so. Now add in the bulk of caring for his daughter becoming my full time responsibility, assuming paying for everything she wanted, increased payments to the sitter I hired, entertainment, etc. I wouldn't have minded that either, if Will had been more of a presence and took more responsibility with her. Putting up with her constant dramatic manipulations and exercises was exhausting, plus having to argue with his family over why I didn't just give in to the poor little brat wore me out. All this while I was coordinating everything in regard to the purchase of this condo, relocation, getting settled in, working, night classes, and ultimately, even having to find a new job, which I was successful in doing. And what was my payback for doing all the right things? Calculated lies, deception, and the added pleasure of being physically beaten to an almost unrecognizable state! Will's acceptance of this deal would certainly burden me with added financial obligation. Having to pick up all related costs meant I would have to work more at my waitress job to do so. But if it bought me freedom from this madness and independence, so what! Remember the story about the pebbles and the brick? Maybe I didn't feel all those pebbles, but I certainly didn't ignore this big, fat brick!

My attorney was impressed with all the organized information I brought to him. Will arrived with his own attorney as well as a cocky chip on his shoulder, ready for a fight. When confronted with everything, Will's attorney was notably disgusted, and it was clear Will hadn't disclosed any of his wrong doings. His attorney asked for a time out, dragged Will out to the hall, and gave him a loud lecture heard by my attorney and me. We both got quite a chuckle from it. Once they were back in the office, Will's chip was gone, as was his bad attitude. He began to cry.

"Contessa, please, please don't do this. I'm begging you to give me another chance. Just one more chance, and I promise I'll make it all up to you, to us," he pleaded.

I'm sure the look on my face plus my icy tone could have frozen a snowball in hell as I replied, "Screw me once, shame on you. Screw me twice, shame on me! Cry me a river, sweetheart. No deal!"

Will cried harder, begged more, but my lawyer carried on with the mission, reiterating there was only one choice for Will to make without me pressing charges on all the other issues. Will signed off on my proposal. He and his attorney abruptly left. My attorney congratulated me again for the information I put together, but also for not caving in to Will. He cited that many other clients he had represented would have succumbed to the tears of their husband even after so much abuse. I completed all the paperwork I needed to sign off on with him. I had no choice but to ask my attorney if he would allow me to make payments to him for his services.

"This has been one hell of an ordeal for you, Contessa, and I applaud you for the way you've handled it all. I'll tell you what… How about if I take you to a lovely dinner in the Chicago dining selection of your choosing, and we can discuss my bill for services rendered?" was my attorney's response.

I immediately threw my head back and laughed louder and longer than I had in a long time. "Touché, counselor!" Eventually, we did have that lovely dinner, as well as several others following. But that's another story!

Many years passed without any communication from or with Will. No real reason for us to be in touch, as I had moved on. While I kept in touch with old friends, I made it a point never to place myself anywhere he might be. However, there was a party being planned with many of the old gang, a reunion of sorts, people from our old neighborhood. My brother asked if I would attend with him. *Sure, why not?* I thought. The anticipation of seeing old friends, even as far back as grade school, warmed my heart, and I looked forward to it with anticipation. Without the slightest thought of encountering Will at this event, before I knew it, I heard that loud, raspy, and unmistakable voice of his. I turned to the direction it was coming from, and there he was, laughing and yakking it up with some of the guys. Handsome as ever, he had aged quite well. Good looks were never his problem, so that didn't surprise me at all. Not one to wait for the ax to fall, I approached him from behind and pinched his ass. He turned around, flashing his perfect white teeth with a huge smile, and threw his arms around me.

"Hey, it's my favorite wife!" he yelled.

The sight of the two of us embracing shocked the shit out of our friends. Several approached me later on, sharing their thoughts, having been witness to this phenomenon.

"I thought someone slipped some LSD in my drink!" joked a girlfriend.

"Jeez, I know this is a reunion, but I never thought I'd see a reunion between the two of you!" added another, chuckling.

"For a minute, I thought we all died and went to heaven, but then Will was there, so I knew that couldn't be!" One of the guys laughed.

And my personal favorite, a mere "Have you lost your fucking mind?"

Will and I hugged and cheek kissed. He complimented me on how well I looked and even stroked my arm, which repulsed me, but I let it go by. We chatted to catch up with each other, but I was extremely guarded and limited in what information I gave him about myself. Yes, I let the bad feelings go and was friendly, but that didn't mean I was dumb enough to ever forget what a liar, cheat, and extremely unscrupulous man he was.

In the end, he hugged me again and, in what seemed to be a genuinely apologetic tone, said to me, "Contessa, you're the strongest woman I've ever known. I realize how horribly I treated, you and you were right to divorce me. I wouldn't even argue over you taking the house. You had every right to do it. I've heard you've been pretty successful, and nobody deserves it more than you. You're a good woman.

I'm really happy to see you happy. You deserve it. I wish you well forever."

At that moment, I said a silent prayer, thanking God for giving me the will to move forward, not to dwell on negativities of the past, or waste time and energy on hate or ill will. I've always said the best revenge is to move forward positively with your own life, achieve your own success, and let the negatives of your past go. Keep your sights set forward, not behind you. If this doesn't prove my thoughts true, I don't know what would. Not that I was ever trying to, but who says you can't get even with the devil? I think I just did!

The moral of this story is, pay attention to signs! They appear for a reason, for us to see them and recognize something isn't quite right. Signs try to tell us something. In relationships, particularly new ones, things may happen that don't sit right with you. You may be so enamored by this new partner you're likely to dismiss these signs, thinking they'll just go away. Don't sweep them under the carpet thinking you can change or even stop them. The changes you want to see from your partner should be initiated by the partner, not you. If what you see isn't what you want, if the relationship is more negative than positive, that means it's toxic. Don't kid yourself into thinking you can change the other person into what you want them to be just because you want them so bad. Closing your eyes and pretending issues aren't there will only prolong the inevitable. Lastly and most simply put, if it looks like shit, smells like shit, it is shit! Move on and save yourself lots of grief. The next relationship is right around the corner.

The CFO

The only thing you should fall in love with at work is your work!

My relationship with Will was in its infancy, as was the entry-level accounting position I held at a suburban Holiday Inn. With my having been a cleaning lady and waitress up until then, this was my first encounter with the corporate world, which instantly captivated me. I fell in love with both it and the hotel industry. Something new and different everyday. New faces, constant challenges with different groups holding functions, meetings, and parties. We were still living in the city at this time, and it was a long commute between home and work, with the drive time sometimes over an hour. I enrolled Little Contessa in a very reputable private school near my office, which helped in various ways. First off, it was a quality education and delightful school environment. Second, I wanted to be near her while she was in school. As kids might often have emergencies, knowing I was physically close to where she was all day set my mind at ease a bit. Lastly, a long commute didn't matter so much if my little girl was with me. The tuition was pretty steep, but I rationalized it by virtue of the reasons just stated. Where there's a will, there's a way, right?

We were attending a family function at a cousin's house one summer Sunday. In addition to lots of relatives, there were many friends of my cousin attending as well. I met a very friendly lady, and we instantly hit it off. Carol was quite sophisticated, very intelligent, yet extremely engaging and down-to-earth. Carol told me she worked for Four Seasons Hotels, and I informed her I worked for Holiday Inn. I knew to point out that the two hotels couldn't be compared in caliber, of course, but we began a fluent and easy conversation centered on our mutual compassion for the various components of the industry itself. Carol remarked that she thought it admirable for me to undertake such a long daily commute, and having my daughter enrolled in such a prestigious school to have her nearby was quite impressive. Carol asked if I was satisfied with the company, if there was opportunity for career growth, if I saw myself there long term. My response was that as my first real position in the corporate world, I had nothing to compare it to, but I was learning a lot, had good benefits, and at the moment, was happy. Having just completed my first year there, I had my sights set on advancement. Carol probed as to what my future desires were, if I wanted to remain in the hotel business or move on to something else.

"I just love this industry! You meet so many people from different places, various backgrounds, and businesses. It's like getting an education just by doing your own job. You learn so much from all the diverse people you meet and work with. I just love it! I definitely want to stay in the hotel industry, but I think some time soon, I may try spreading my wings a bit and looking into other hotel chains. This was a good starting place for me, but I want to work my way up a notch or two, especially after talking to you!" I explained.

Carol asked to exchange telephone numbers. About a week later, I was clearing up the dinner dishes when I received a call from her. I was surprised to hear from Carol, and even more amazed as she disclosed the reason for her call. She explained that there was a secretarial position open in the accounting department at the Four Seasons. She thought I was well suited for this position, based on our discussion at my cousin's party. Carol asked if I would be interested in applying for this position.

"Are you kidding me? Of course, I'm interested! I'm so grateful that you would even consider me for this opportunity!" I screamed.

"Well, I can set up the interview, but the rest is completely up to you. I can't guarantee anything else," Carol explained.

"You'll never be sorry you recommended me, Carol! I promise I'll make you proud," I assured her.

Carol provided me with all details of the interview—date, time, and with whom I would be meeting. My interview was set for three days later at 3:00 p.m. I would be meeting with the head of accounting, a very strict and meticulous man who ran a very tight ship. Carol continued explaining the way this department was structured as well as how she felt I would fit in. This heads-up information was extremely valuable, and I thanked Carol profusely for it. I planned on telling my manager I had a doctor's appointment as my excuse for having to leave work early on interview day. I would pick up Little Contessa early as well. I asked my aunt if she could watch my daughter, if I could drop her off and head on to the interview. I did some role play with myself, rehearsing my strengths, team spirit, welcoming of challenges, and goals. I chose the perfect interview suit. Everything was all set. Until…

About an hour before I planned on leaving work, my aunt called to tell me she had a family emergency that could not be helped and therefore would not be home to watch Little Contessa. Yikes! Now what was I going to do? There was no way in hell I would call and ask for my interview to be rescheduled because my sitter canceled on me. It was the mid 1970s. Women were rising in workplace management positions. However, one fact was made abundantly clear: a single mother automatically had a stigma attached to her. At this point in time, the thought in the corporate world was that the single mother came with baggage; the single mother wouldn't be reliable, would have constant issues, particularly in attendance, as their children would always present problems, not conducive to a vigorous work environment. I repeat, *no way* was I going to highlight this stigma before I was even being considered for the job. Therefore, there was only one thing for me to do. Inhale, take in a big deep breath, then exhale. Little Contessa would have to come along with me to the interview.

How do you describe the perfect child except to merely say she is? My Little Contessa was every mother's dream. Always happy and smiling, she inherited her father's incredible sense of humor. As a dead ringer for him, she captured an audience and held it with comedic mastery. Little Contessa was a preemie, born in my seventh month of pregnancy. Physically, she was an itty-bitty little thing, but from day one, her personality was huge. Her large, deep dark brown eyes were lined with the most luxurious long, thick lashes. One bat of those lashes could melt any iceberg. She had a mass of thick sandy brown hair that fell into perfect wavy curls. Her hair was so thick in ratio to her tiny little face it sometimes appeared as though she had a wig on. Little Contessa had a knack for making a game about anything and could hold court with anyone, displaying her improvisational skills. At any moment in time, no matter where we were, she might break out in song, dance, and soliloquy. My daughter possessed a phenomenal vocabulary well beyond her years, consisting of both appropriate and colorful language that rolled off her tongue with ease. She was always spontaneous, and I never knew what might pop out of her mouth at any given moment, regardless of where we were or with whom. Her delivery was a high pitched, squeaky little voice that sometimes left people within earshot with their mouths gaping open. From an age as early as three, Little Contessa loved thumbing through magazines and was obsessed with "name brands" of all sorts of products. Even this young, she would comment on your clothes, your hair, your furniture, and ask anyone what brand of face soap or body lotion they used. She was the quintessential comic that nobody could walk away from. She was (and remains) a blessing, my joy, and my whole heart.

I had no time to dwell on the decision I made to take Little Contessa along on the interview with me. I picked her up from school, and as soon as we got settled into the car and on the road, I began trying to explain where we were going and why. My daughter was not the type of child you could easily pacify with a simple explanation. Little Contessa wanted to know everything, and nothing short of the whole story would do. I reminded Little Contessa of when we first went to visit her school, to look around, to talk to the teachers and look over the grounds just to see if she would like going there everyday. That proved to be an analogy she understood.

"Mommy is going to talk to a nice man, just like we talked to your teacher. If he likes me, he will be my new boss, which is kind of like your teacher. But you must pretend it's quiet time, just like at school. I need you to be very quiet while we are talking. We'll bring your coloring book and crayons for you to draw with," I explained.

"What's the man's name, Mommy?" Little Contessa asked.

"His name is Anthony Dade," I told her.

"Will he like you if I color him a nice picture?" she asked.

"Oh, I'm sure Mr. Dade would love a picture from you! You can work on it while we're talking," I said, trying to convince myself more than her.

"Will he like my dress?" she asked in her own style.

"Oh, my sweetheart, I'm sure he will, but please, please remember that we can't ask him questions about your dress, because this is about work," I pleaded.

"Will he like my naturally curly hair?" she asked as she "poofed" up her curls with her hand.

"Yes, honey, I'm sure he will, but please remember this is like quiet time at school and you must not ask any questions. It's very, very important that Mr. Dade and I have grown-up talk while you color him a pretty picture," I pleaded.

"Okay, Mommy, let's sing Joe Cocker now." Little Contessa suggested as she began to sing "You are so beautiful to me…" as she went on with the melody. That was my amazing little girl.

It didn't even dawn on me to find a place to park before pulling up to the hotel. I had no choice but to let the valet take it, and I gulped at the thought of what it would cost me. My main concern was answering the ongoing questions Little Contessa asked and ensuring she understood that it was most important for her to remain quiet and concentrate on coloring the very best picture for Mr. Dade. The hotel lobby was more glamorous than anything I'd ever seen in person. Little Contessa, ever the lover of beautiful, sparkly things, was very taken with the grand furniture, the huge ornate crystal chandeliers, and all the elegant decorations. She desperately wanted to sit, look around, and gaze at it all, and I explained we could after my meeting with Mr. Dade. We made our way to the accounting office. I could see the surprise on the secretary's face when she saw Little Contessa with me. I just took a deep breath and ignored her bewildered stare. I defiantly felt the only one I owed an explanation to was Mr. Dade himself.

Within a minute of my being seated, Mr. Dade came out to greet me. He was a man with an aura, a kind of presence that made you want to sit up straighter, speak your best, and be on top of your game. An impeccably groomed, handsome, and refined Englishman, he was, I'd guess, around fifty years old. He donned a well tailored, crisp, and conservative three piece suit, complete with pocket watch in the vest pocket. His shoes were so shiny I could see my reflection in them. This was the very first time I heard that spellbinding English accent in person, and I must admit, it was both hard to follow and enchanting at the same time. Rather than give a curious look regarding the appearance of a little girl accompanying me, he graciously bent down and asked, "And who do we have here?"

Before I could speak, Little Contessa offered her hand out to him. "I'm Contessa, just like my mommy. I'm going to color you a picture while you have grown-up talk," she offered.

I internally breathed a huge sigh of relief as Mr. Dade escorted us to his office. I explained the babysitter snafu, which Mr. Dade didn't comment on. He was pretty poker faced.

I finished my introductory portion of the interview with "This interview is extremely important to me. It's a fantastic opportunity for me and, I believe, for you as well. I am extremely committed, reliable, and a person who can multitask and adapt to change immediately. I can promise you'll see immediate proof of that upon hiring me," I declared. I don't even know where those words came from; they just seemed to fall out of my mouth. All the way here, I was so focused on managing Little Contessa I hadn't had a second to think about what I would say.

"I'm impressed with your confidence, Contessa," Mr. Dade responded as he proceeded with the interview. He began with the normal questions regarding review of résumé, past experience, goals and aspirations, as well as why I felt I would be an asset to the company. While I was sweating bullets on the inside, the exterior persona that I presented was cool, collected, and confident. The questions then took a surprising turn. He asked about my family background, my current homelife, and the inevitable plan I had for child care. Although I was a bit taken aback, I continued in a fluent manner. I gave him the short version of my being raised by strict Italian blue-collar parents, followed by a brief statement of being married and divorced at a young age, and that I was now a single mother. I elaborated on a plan A, B, and C for child care. If Mr. Dade had any reservations at all about hiring me, I wanted to ensure that inadequate child care would not be one of them. I made sure he knew I had that base completely covered.

And then the unimaginable happened. Mr. Dade asked Little Contessa if she had finished his picture. With such a confident feeling that I conquered the interview, I suddenly sunk and crumbled inside from surprise at this question and fear of what my precocious little girl might say.

"Yes, I did, Mr. Dade. May I get off your lovely couch?" Little Contessa asked.

"Of course you may," he said, chuckling, probably just as surprised at her answer as I was of his question.

This little girl knew no fear. She was not intimidated in any way when in new surroundings or in the company of unfamiliar people. She sashayed over to Mr. Dade and proudly handed him the drawing she made for him, explaining every detail. I was amazed at the patient attention he gave Little Contessa, even engaging in more conversation with her. He ended their little chat by asking her if she had anything else to say to him. I was not surprised when Little Contessa said yes, she really liked his office, his furniture, and also that the curtains matched the sofa! Mr. Dade let out a hearty laugh and took a minute to, I suppose, gather his thoughts. His serious tone returned, as well as the business at hand.

"Contessa, I don't even have to think it over. I'm offering you the position as my secretary and assistant right now, if you want it," he declared.

Completely shocked, I seemed to screech, "Yes, of course, I do!"

"Before you jump at it, let me explain a few things. I'm quite direct, don't sugarcoat anything. Many people have a hard time with that, but it's my style and you either deal with it or you don't. I don't believe in wasting time beating around the bush. I tell you everything up front. When you have questions, ask. Never guess, assume, or act if you aren't exactly certain. I'm very fast paced, and I expect my team to keep up with me. I will not accept any excuse for work not done on time. I can promise that you'll work harder here than any other place you've been. You'll have the latitude to make certain decisions, and you'll need to be confident of your choices, with proper rationale for making them. There will be overtime, and when the end of the month falls on a weekend, we'll all be working. You will have access to confidential information, and disclosure to anyone will not be tolerated. This office is known for precision, and you will be held to that standard as well. Do you accept?" Mr. Dade declared, more than asked.

"Absolutely!" I triumphantly decided, immediately convinced being part of this tightly run ship would catapult me right into the atmosphere I dreamed of.

"Good. You'll receive an offer letter in the mail within the next week with all the details of the position. Salary, benefits, and programs offered by Four Seasons will all be outlined. I suggest you provide your employer with your resignation. I'll want you to start right away," he finished.

No worries, I couldn't wait to resign from Holiday Inn and begin my new journey with Four Seasons Hotel!

I received the employment package, complete with all the information on my new position. I was amazed at the training programs Four Seasons offered and immediately started planning what courses I would take. I looked forward to starting this new opportunity with great anticipation. I planned my outfits for the first two weeks. The increase in salary would allow me to buy a new suit once a month and still have enough to put toward the house budget. I often thought about the interview. It was apparent Mr. Dade was a man of decisive ability, but he initially gave me the impression more thought would factor into his hiring decision. Surely there were more applicants that I was confident were more qualified than I was. Oh, well, I wouldn't question whatever it was that prompted him to hire me; I would just remain grateful he did.

I made sure I arrived early on my first day. The office was still dark, except for one light appearing from Mr. Dade's office. My work space was just outside his office, and as I was getting settled in, Mr. Dade suddenly appeared. He had the rigid stiffness of a mannequin. Perfect grooming and posture. Salt-and-pepper hair neatly slicked back. Suit, vest, shirt, and tie so crisp I thought wrinkles would be afraid of him. He walked with a style all his own, not leisurely, just as his thoughts and conversation. Direct and to the point.

"I had a feeling you'd be here early. Good. I'll have a few words with you in my office," he commanded. The solemn tone I first met him with was once again present. I immediately knew it was his norm. In anticipation of a significant conversation, I grabbed a notepad and pen and followed him into his office. There would be no easing into this position. I would hit the ground running, and I'd better deliver. In rapid, monotone sentences, Mr. Dade began as I took notes.

"First of all, welcome to Four Seasons Hotels. You'll want to learn about the company, our history, our corporate culture, our locations. Feel free to use my library here to study everything you'll need to know. No more Mr. Dade, call me Anthony. I arrive most mornings at six and work twelve hour days. I don't expect you to, but I do expect all required work to be done in a timely manner, so you will need to ensure that happens regardless of how long you are here. You are replacing Sue, who was just given a promotion. Sue will be in shortly. She will be responsible for training you. Sue was an excellent assistant to me, which was why she was promoted. I mentioned that you will work harder here than anyplace else, but your efforts will be rewarded. This department performs with the razor-sharp precision that accounting should be known for, and that will apply to you as well. Nothing short of my expectations will be tolerated. Any questions so far?"

"No, sir," I responded as I continued writing. Trust me, nothing he said needed further clarification!

Anthony went on with details of his work ethic, his required methods for communication between us, his in box/out box techniques, and several other dos and don'ts that I needed to be aware of, including specific instructions as to monitor the way his desk was left to ensure housekeeping did not mess anything up when they came to clean in the middle of the night. *Whew!*

As I left Anthony's office, Sue arrived. A very cheerful young woman, Sue introduced me to the rest of the accounting team as they came in. Sue was a polished professional, yet very friendly and embracing. She emphasized Anthony's expectations and even demand of accuracy in all things, that mistakes or excuses were not tolerated. Sue also stressed Anthony's robot-like style. "He's like the Eveready battery—he just keeps going and going and going. Not only do you need to keep up with him, you'd also be wise to try to be one step ahead of him." She also told me how giving he was in recognition of hard work and accomplishments. Not the effort of but dedicated, precise, and proven results were what he focused on and rewarded, hence her recent promotion. She was to spend the first week training me in all aspects of my job, also explaining what her new position was within the department and how each of our jobs would interact.

To say this was all a whirlwind would be a gross understatement. I took books from Anthony's library home every night, studying the history of the company, learning its culture, locations, and principles at headquarters, with whom Anthony interacted regularly. I took notes all day long, reviewing them each night. My position required me to dive into the world of numbers, which didn't come naturally to me, but I was surprised at how I began to get along with them. My first priority was managing Anthony's schedule, consisting of both business and social engagements, sometimes having to shuffle people around, which was actually entertaining. I studied Anthony's habits and learned all the eccentricities that made him who he was. He had his morning coffee in one cup and afternoon tea in another. He required each to be placed in a specific spot on his desk. Never think of setting either down without a coaster! I hand washed each after use and replaced them in their designated area in his office. His office was to be meticulously maintained. I began leaving notes for housekeeping to make sure they didn't touch this or that, whatever he was working on that he might have left out on his coffee table, always in a specific order. He would know if anything was touched.

Anthony repeatedly said, "Success begins with organization, first in your own mind and person. If one is not meticulously organized in their thoughts and daily actions, one will struggle to find success." It made sense to me, and I must admit that I myself adopted this philosophy, amused at the realization that this was the start of my OCD tendencies. His correspondence was sometimes difficult to interpret; his British version of certain words was spelled differently than in the American dictionary. Also, whom the letter was addressed to made a difference as well. If it was to another Englishman, I would have to maintain that version of spelling. A bit confusing, but I eventually got the hang of it as well.

All deposits for banquet and meeting rooms came to me, as well as the final payments. I was to ensure all aspects were charged correctly and paid in full. I was responsible for the rental of glass showcases throughout the lobby and hallways that displayed products from various Michigan Avenue stores. I drew up and executed contracts for the various case sizes and managed their monthly rental payments. I received daily proceeds from the parking garage, gift shop, and spa. I was to log all cash and turn it in to the cashier, reconciling all receipts at month end on the general ledger balance sheet. I could certainly see why Anthony would accept nothing short of perfection. The solvency of the entire hotel relied upon the shoulders of this department. There was a vast amount to learn, and it was a grueling pace, but I reveled in every bit of it.

On the home front, things were okay. Little Contessa had adjusted well in her new school, a local Catholic school with a good reputation. Attending the same school were a few of our relatives and the daughter of an old friend of mine, whom Little Contessa got along with well. I asked my friend Rose if she could pick up my daughter along with her own and have Little Contessa stay at her house until I got home from work. She agreed to help me out, and in appreciation, I was always bringing the kids treats from the hotel, as well as entertaining them whenever I could. Will was still "finding himself" and was out quite a bit. Truth be told, I kind of didn't care, because after dinner, cleaning up, doing homework, and getting Little Contessa to bed, I was studying everything I could get my hands on to become more learned and competent in my position. In a way, you could say that I enabled him to be lazy, and I wouldn't argue the point. I was just so eager to master and juggle it all; I really relished in the nighttime quiet to do what I needed to. And it seemed to be working. I often doubted myself, having to make quick decisions while holding my breath and praying they were the right ones. But each week got a little easier. Each month demonstrated more confidence in my own efforts and abilities. Before long, it was time for my first performance review. Anthony scheduled lunch for the two of us in one of the hotel restaurants.

I was both excited and nervous. Excited as this would be the first time I experienced our hotel dining in one of the actual facilities. While I learned my way around, discovered what was where and who was who, I had not yet had the privilege of the high caliber dining service that our guests enjoyed. The hotel defined luxury, class, and elegance. Austrian crystal adorned and sparkled every ceiling and hallway wall. The only sound you heard in the lobby was that of the fountain, sprinkling drops of what I was certain to be champagne throughout the air! The hustle and bustle of people going to and from, conducting business of all sorts, people working and people playing, were muffled by carpeting so thick and plush that no sound upon this lush flooring could be heard. The grand ballroom boasted a million dollar ceiling covered by crystal spirals. A famous Italian painter was brought out of retirement to hand paint a beguiling mural throughout the lobby leading down through the halls, luring guests into the shops and restaurants. Employees were treated to the experiments and tastings of chefs in training from around the world, in addition to left over banquet cuisine of the highest quality. This was my workplace. I was surrounded by the epitome of luxury, wrapped in the finest things money could buy, things I never would have dreamed of even knowing about, let alone being encompassed by. This day I would find out if my performance was pleasing enough to my boss in order for me to stay put in this environment that immediately mesmerized me. Hence, I was also nervous.

Anthony was hard to read. He didn't say much except to give a directive or make a statement. Sue shed a little light on his personality and method, advising me that Anthony would not sing your praises but would surely let you know if you screwed up. Sue told me to think of his silent nature as "no news is good news" and not to take it personally. That was hard for me, as this position and everything that came with it often left me unsure of myself. I was desperate for Anthony's approval or acknowledgment that I was on the right track. So his suggestion to have my performance review at one of the finer dining facilities of the hotel rather than the normal review in his office made me even more nervous. Was he going to feed me an elegant lunch as my "last supper" before dropping the ax? Would Anthony allow me this one last treat to soften the blow before giving me the boot? Ugh, I was so anxious!

The morning seemed to be a hundred hours long. Finally, Anthony buzzed me through the intercom line to announce we would be leaving for lunch shortly. I quickly locked my desk up and prepared my telephone for the message center to take all calls. Just as I stood up, put my suit jacket on, and made sure I was picture-perfect, Anthony emerged from his office. In his very formal manner, he marched to the big glass doors that served as the gates to our accounting department, so gallantly holding them open for me to pass through. Anthony walked in a confident manner; his steps were very measured and deliberate. While he was not a very tall man, Anthony carried himself as if he were a skyscraper. His movements were somewhat regal, as if he were trained all his life to ensure every gesture, every motion, action, and or deed, was executed with precision. He both intimidated and fascinated me. He asked for a recap of the most current banquet deposits as we walked on. We were off to the dining room as I provided the information he sought.

The refinement and sophistication of The Dining Room were parallel to that of the entire hotel. The same sparkling Austrian crystal lined its ceiling, another exotic mural painted by the same Italian craftsman surrounded these walls, and the furnishings, china, and tabletop china were of superior quality. The maître d' greeted both Anthony and me by name, which took me by surprise. I came to learn that was one of the training elements of all dining staff: know the names of your guests and welcome them accordingly. Just as in the lobby, people seemed to glide along throughout this room without making a sound. Mere whispers of conversation were heard as we were escorted to our table. I tried very hard not to let on how overwhelmed I was. The worry over how Anthony would judge my performance, combined with the splendor of this room, had my heart rate at an all-time high.

"Normally, I would have ordered ahead of time so our lunch would be ready upon our arrival, but I'm not aware of your food preferences," Anthony announced. So typical. Order ahead, have food ready upon his arrival. Like I said, every move deliberate and calculated. Not a minute of the day to waste. I could not really see the menu all that well, as my nerves seemed to have taken over my vision. I ordered a bowl of soup, thinking it would be the simplest to get down while hearing my fate. Who could eat being so nervous?

"Contessa, I have extremely high expectations from all my staff the very instant I decide to hire them. If I weren't completely confident each would do the job I require, I would not have hired them in the first place. I've been disappointed here and there, but normally my instincts are spot-on," Anthony began in his refined, perfectly enunciated English accent. "I know a bit of your background, and now I'd like to give you insight into some of mine. This information is not for you to pass on to others, but relevant to our conversation here today," he continued.

"My family and I are from a very small depressed town in England. My father died way too young from a minor illness that would have been easily treated if only we had even a small extra sum for the simplest of doctors. After he passed, my mum took whatever work she could find to care for me and my siblings. She had no real skills but found work as a maid in a wealthier area. The people she worked for were quite hard on her, often keeping her quite late. She also took in laundry for others, hand washing the fineries of her employer. I saw her scrub and clean till her fingers bled. I once found her on the floor of our tiny cottage with the scrub brush still in her hand, having fallen asleep while scrubbing it late at night after working nonstop for over a week. I cared for my siblings while mum worked. As we grew, we found work doing odd jobs here and there.

My mother taught us the value and importance of education and made each of us promise to pursue higher academics no matter what. We learned from her that we could achieve anything if we developed and stuck to a plan, kept our focus, and worked hard toward our goals. Mum had a feeling she wouldn't live long and wanted to prepare us for a better life that she herself could not provide."

Divulging any personal information seemed extremely out of character for Anthony. He was all business all the time. Personal or lighthearted chatter seemed to never leave his lips. I wondered why he was telling me this.

He paused for a moment as our server meticulously placed rolls and starters on the table. They were aware of Anthony's preferences.

"And just as my mother predicted, she didn't last too much longer. She literally worked herself to death. She never complained and constantly reminded us not to either. Weak people whined, while people of strength made change, she would say. Mum instilled a serious work ethic particularly in me, as I would have sole responsibility for my younger siblings and pass the same onto them. She taught us that persistent ethics and dedication to them were critical keys to success, and I was to do anything in my power to ensure my siblings and I realized our ambitions. After Mum passed, her words were ever present in my head and all my deeds. I'll spare you the details of how we pulled through, but suffice it to say that what I encountered and endured for the sake of survival were things I would not wish on my worst enemy," he continued. "While my experiences were frightful, I came to look upon them as stimulus to keep going, to succeed. Each obstacle was difficult, but overcoming one after another was more incentive and fuel to take on the next challenge. I was hungry, both literally and figuratively."

I listened with the utmost attention. Anthony's facial expressions were different from what I had ever seen before. He seemed to have taken on an entirely different look and persona. I had not seen this softer, personal side of him, and something told me not too many other people had either. I found I was no longer nervous. The more Anthony spoke, the more relaxed I became.

"Consequently, I became the most driven man you'll ever know. I successfully raised my younger siblings, put them all through school, and saw each of them on their way to become positive, contributing adults," he went on.

I don't know what made me interrupt him, but I cut into his train of thought and interjected, "Anthony, I'm sorry you've had such a difficult childhood, and even more sorry about both your parents passing away so young. Trust me, I can relate to both hardship and losing a parent so young. But I must admit, I'm a bit confused as to why you're sharing this with me. I mean, I'm flattered that you are, but it seems out of character for you."

"Do you have any idea why I hired you?" Anthony asked.

"I have to admit, I did wonder. I mean, I'm certain you had more qualified choices," I confessed.

"On paper, yes, I certainly did," he quickly assured me. "But I saw something in you that none of the other candidates demonstrated even a glimpse of."

I'm sure I had a deer-in-the-headlights look on my face, as this revelation confused me more than ever. What in the world could he have seen in me that was more significant than all the other apparent skills of the other ladies vying for this coveted position?

"Anthony, what could that possibly be?" I asked.

He continued, "Your hunger. Your tenacity. Your strength. Contessa, I saw my mother in you. I saw the mama bear struggling to provide for her young. The mother who would stop at nothing for the sake of paving the way for her offspring to go farther, to have more, to secure a more fortunate life than she had. I sensed you had nothing to fall back on but your wit and gut instincts, and with that, I saw myself in you. Struggling, climbing, always reaching higher and higher, slaying each and every obstacle that had the nerve to present itself to you."

I felt a tear run down my cheek.

Anthony continued, "Don't be sad, Contessa. I mean to compliment you. I place a high value on academics and have great respect for education, but I know firsthand that life itself teaches more than any classroom to those who are smart and savvy enough to grasp the lessons. I can see you are. I get the feeling you've already fallen down many times, but you use whatever it was that tripped you up as a tool to rise above and start again."

I sat there mesmerized by Anthony's words, as if he were a fortune teller recounting my past and about to unveil my future. I was desperate to hear what would happen next.

"What else do you see?" I asked.

"I see a determined young woman with an insatiable appetite to learn. And I will feed that hunger. I will see to your continued education through our company training programs. I'll ensure you are prepared to take many steps forward, in a variety of directions. But, Contessa, let me also forewarn you. I will not go easy on you. More to the point, you'll feel more pressure than ever before. And I'll push you harder and longer than the rest of the staff, because of the promise I see in you. But in the end, you'll find confidence in your instincts, you'll make solid decisions and be certain of each and every step you take, and the pressure will be replaced with pride in your accomplishments." Anthony knowingly declared.

I couldn't tell if my mouth was hanging open or just watering with all Anthony just predicted. I was in awe of him.

"Anthony, this is a dream to me. I promise I will never, ever let you down. You'll see," I responded.

"I do not allow myself to be let down. I expect you will manage all responsibilities with precision, strategy, and always a smile. That's very important. Your salary will increase, and training will begin this month. There will be no need of another performance review. You will either meet my level of expectation or be let go. Period. Now, let's have some lunch, shall we?" Anthony finished.

I couldn't wait to get home to tell Little Contessa and Will the good news. Not only did I make it through the trial position for my job, but Anthony also mapped out a training program for me as well as the opportunity for additional management courses, both in-house and outside the company, which would prepare me for advancement within the organization. It was an aggressive platform, but I was chomping at the bit to get started. This was an opportunity of a lifetime, and I would make the most of it. In addition,

Anthony gave me a completely unexpected salary increase, which was the cherry on this dreamy cake. I did not lose sight of the pressure Anthony warned me about. I was certain he was going to crack a very hard whip, and I welcomed the opportunity to meet the standards Anthony would set forth.

I disclosed all aspects of my review with Anthony to my family, and they were very happy for me. Realizing I would have to attend night classes a few times a week, my aunt and uncle assured me they would help out with watching Little Contessa. They were my angels, always looking out for me and my daughter. I repeated the good news to Will, who expressed being happy for me but only focused on two words: *salary increase*. I explained that with the increase came additional responsibilities as well as night school and training courses. He didn't seem bothered by that at all, but looking back now, I believe he saw my night classes as opportunity for him to stay out without having to worry about explaining to me. Oh, well, I was too high on it all to see what his real reaction actually meant, or maybe I just didn't want to. I was on cloud nine.

As time flies when you're having fun, the next several months were first and foremost captivating and, yes, fun as well, because I so enjoyed acquiring more knowledge and skills. I was immediately immersed in learning and mastering more detailed elements of my position, our department, and our company. I embraced and agreed with Anthony's philosophy as to how all components work together and thus become a well oiled machine. I brought study material home every night, and after Little Contessa was nicely tucked away in bed, I dived into my homework. I made it a daily point to apply any newly retained application, and in a way Anthony would recognize. Although he never said a word, I remembered Sue advising me that "no news is good news." Anthony didn't hand out compliments but was certainly verbal if you fell short. I was soon enrolled in an accounting course and attended class twice a week. Anthony had just initiated a cross-training program within our department. It was a genius plan. We would each spend a month in one another's position, thus learning how one job affected and had an impact on the other. I had the "honor" of spending time in each member of our accounting team, as Anthony felt it necessary for me to have grasp of the entire cycle, even welcoming thoughts on improvements in any given area. During a discussion regarding the interaction between accounts payable and accounts receivable, I made a few suggestions to Anthony that would lessen duplication of efforts and thus streamline things a bit. I felt a tremendous sense of pride as I was leaving his office and noticed him smiling out of the corner of my eye. I knew I was on the right track! It was nothing short of a whirlwind, one that stayed close to my heart to this day.

All was smooth on the home front. My aunt watched Little Contessa on the nights I had class. My relatives were always glad to help me whenever they could, as they saw how hard I was working and were proud of me. Thank God for them! Upon leaving class on those two nights, I drove home like a lunatic to make sure I'd be home in time to put Little Contessa to bed. I cooked extra dinners, carefully packaging and labeling them whenever possible to allow for a little more playtime with my daughter on the nights I didn't have class. After bath and bedtime prayers with Little Contessa, I hit my books and studied the rest of the night. Will was out mostly every night, which didn't bother me a bit. I was consumed with my new job, new educational opportunities, and the management of it all to care. Besides, his not being in the house allowed me one less distraction.

One of my strong suits had always been to figure out a situation and work my way through it. Strategy was my gift, and I relied upon it to organize every minute of my time these days. I should have been exhausted, but I wasn't. I thrived on it. Yes, my days were quite long, but they were filled with substance and application. My workload and responsibilities, both existing and new, required precision if I were to make it all work. I ran a tight ship, everything by the clock and according to schedule. I had no choice. Little Contessa got right up out of bed when her alarm clock went off each morning. As she washed up, I prepared her breakfast. Upon finishing, she knew to put her Catholic school uniform on and gather her things for school. While she ate and dressed, I completed my own finishing touches then fixed Little Contessa's hair (there was always a certain style to it, with a bow, barrette, or something fancy to add!), and out the door we went. I dropped her off at school promptly and raced off to the office. Thankfully, her school had extended hours before and after school to accommodate working parents. Always anxious to get to work, I tried to get there as soon as possible. Now and then, I managed to get to the office before Anthony did, and while he never made mention of it, I swear I caught that approving smile of his.

While I was happily perched on the next rung of the ladder of success, Will was still "weighing his options." In other words, he was hanging out with the guys most every night, having a good time. Bowling league, golf league, and pool night occupied most of Will's weeknights. Will's interpretation of these activities was that they allowed him to mix, mingle (his specialty), and integrate with people in other fields so he could discuss potential career options and hopefully network himself into a new position. I don't know if he actually believed his own bullshit or if he was just bullshitting me, but regardless, I bought it hook, line, and sinker! In addition, Friday night was always considered "guys' night out," so add that in and Will's week was pretty much taken up. Because I was so busy with everything else, I never questioned him, his whereabouts, or what he might or might not have been doing. I just kept my mind and thoughts on the work I had to do. We did manage to have private time and loving moments where Will worked enough magic on me to remind me we were in a good place. A Saturday date night here and there, wee-hours-of-the-night intimacy, and an occasional family night at home did the trick for me.

One Saturday night, we were out with Mike and Gina, good friends of ours who were also from the neighborhood. They always wanted to see Little Contessa, who adored them as well and loved to put on some sort of show for them. After dinner, my aunt graciously offered to watch Little Contessa so we adults could go out for a bit. We went to the local Italian club, as many other friends of ours would be there. It had been some time since I'd been out to see anyone, and it was nice to finally have some adult time. The guys gravitated to one area, leaving the ladies in a cluster to catch up and have some girl chat.

"Contessa, I didn't want to interrupt Little Contessa's song-and-dance show during dinner"—laughter from all—"but I've been dying to hear about your new job. How's it going?" Gina asked.

Just then, Will approached our group to ask if any of us wanted a cocktail. He heard Gina's inquiry.

"My girl is movin' up! I'm so proud of her. She's working in the accounting office, taking classes, and kicking asses!" Will announced. "And if I know her, she'll be running that place someday, just watch," he continued.

He went on and on in that vein, boasting and bragging of me while I sat there with stars in my eyes, hearing him delight in my endeavors. I hadn't ever heard Will be so openly verbal with his feelings on my job and what all I was doing. This was Will's style. Be loud, be proud, and make sure everyone heard the things that should be said. It took me a very long time to realize that was a ploy of his, but in the meantime, I reveled in his remarks, particularly because none of the other gals had any such comparable accomplishments for their guys to brag about. To hear Will openly toot my horn was just about the best aphrodisiac in the world to keep me completely in love with him. This was just one of many other public demonstrations by Will that kept my rose colored glasses in place and me completely under his spell.

I continued to learn, grow, and thrive at work. A particular aspect of my job was to collect the rent payments on the vitrines (showcases) that lined our lobby. The payments were actually dropped off or mailed to the front office manager, as the point of contact for each company that leased our vitrines. The front office manager was often unavailable, tending to his duties, and his assistant was consequently running all over the hotel, doing God-knows-what, but one thing she wasn't doing was paying attention to her responsibilities. Tracking either one of the two down each month to get my hands on the actual checks was a nightmare. After experiencing this month after month, I approached Anthony one day and communicated my frustration. Before he had a chance to say anything at all, I quickly followed up my complaints (I remembered my dad's words: never complain unless you have a solution) with a well thought out strategy in solving the problem.

"Anthony, this may be way out of line for me to even suggest, but why don't we rewrite the policy for the vitrine tenants to submit their rent payments to us directly and cut out the front office confusion? All we need to do is write out detailed directions and communicate them internally. Then send written notice to each vitrine renter and include self-addressed return envelopes for them to mail their payments directly to us," I triumphantly offered.

Anthony sat there silently for a moment. "That's what I want to see from you, Contessa! Identify the problems and initiate a fix for them. Sometimes a fresh pair of eyes can paint a whole new and improved picture. I approve of your solution, and I'm giving you complete authority to design and implement new payment guidelines. Draft them up for my review, and once I sign off on your proposal, you can begin implementation, both in-house and to all tenants," he announced.

"Sure thing, Anthony. By the way, as long as we're talking about the front office, I have a few other suggestions that I think may help streamline some interaction with our credit department as well," I offered.

"You're on the ball, Contessa. Good work. Make notes of all your observations and include them in the draft of the new guidelines to me. I'll look everything over and respond accordingly," he directed.

I was floating. Not only did Anthony see merit to my vitrine payment suggestions, but he also welcomed hearing all the ideas I had in other areas as well. I put pride, time, and detailed thought into my notes on various timesaving and, what I anticipated to be, cost saving measures between our department and several others. As my first suggestive input on policy and improvement, my presentation had to be strategic and exact, showing positive results in the form of streamlining applications and procedures, which in turn would increase production and cut costs. I spent the next few nights working diligently on the notes. Finally, they were done to perfection—problems, detailed solutions, complete with estimated time and cost savings. I laid them on Anthony's desk early one morning, and within an hour after he arrived, he called me into his office.

"Contessa, I think you know I expected good things from you," Anthony began.

"Yes, I know that," I timidly answered. As I opened my mouth to begin an explanation, Anthony's words came out first.

"This proposal is not good—it's phenomenal! I certainly planned on seeing improvements from the cross-training program, but I didn't think anyone would take it as far as you did. Identifying overlaps, duplication of efforts between departments, streamlining procedures, cutting costs! The fact that you produced a well thought out solution to every issue you raised shows how seriously you took your interactive training. I'm impressed!" Anthony declared.

Wow! I suddenly remembered Sue's words: "Don't expect verbal praise, Anthony doesn't hand out compliments, no news is good news." I was blown away.

I fought hard to hold back my tears, of pride, joy, disbelief, whatever; they just welled up in my eyes. "I'm sorry, I'm just so excited. Anthony, I worked so hard on this. I saw things that I believed to be nonproductive, and at first, I questioned myself. But the more training I experienced, the clearer certain things became, and I really believed I was on the right track. I'm so happy you approve of my observations," I sniffled.

"Didn't I say you would learn to trust your own judgment? You picked up the ball and ran with it. Well done, Contessa! In fact, so well done that I'm giving you a raise, effective immediately," he said.

"Oh, thank you, Anthony, thank you so much!" I shrieked. "You'll never be sorry, honestly. I'll work so hard you won't regret it."

"You certainly will work hard! You may be sorry once you hear the conditions. Since you worked up such a phenomenal plan, I'm tasking you with its implementation. You'll start by writing procedure for each of the points in your presentation. You'll execute the departmental communications. Once all areas are aware of the changes in policy and protocol, you will personally be responsible to train all affected employees to implement each of the changes I'm approving. Any questions?" Anthony asked.

"When do I get started?" I wholeheartedly asked.

"That's my girl!" Anthony said with a laugh.

I immediately decided that I wouldn't tell Will about my raise. It was unexpected, and I thought this was an opportunity for me to do some saving. If he knew about it, he would find something to spend the extra money on. We were in an "okay" place with our household budget; we surely could have used more, but I felt strongly that should come from Will. He needed to get a steady job and increase his weekly contributions. Our company offered a direct deposit of payroll option as well as a Christmas Club whereby you could have deductions in the amount of your choosing to be withdrawn from your paycheck and automatically deposited into your designated account. My feeling was, if you have the deduction made before you receive your check, you'll never miss it. So I had my new raise split down the middle and designated half to go to a Christmas Club account, and the other half went into my 401(k). I felt quite proud of myself for doing that, and I was never sorry. Nothing like having a little extra cash tucked away that nobody else knew about to give a girl a sassy edge. It gave me such a sense of independence and, consequently, empowerment. For so long, I had scraped by. Never again. From this moment on, I'd always make sure that I maintained a little extra dough-re-mi for my own security.

I worked diligently on the cross-training program Anthony was allowing me to manage. From writing my own protocol, position interaction, and integration of responsibilities to communicating it all to the various departments, to the individual training in each position, it all came together beautifully. I was proud of myself, and even more importantly, I knew Anthony was proud of me as well. I heard him use me and my efforts as an example of "operational comprehension and innovation and putting your mind to work in a way that leads to creation." I sure did appreciate the raise, but Anthony's praise would have been enough for me. I was becoming a superstar at the office, becoming well known as Anthony's right hand. I reveled in it. I know this may read like an easy, seamless scenario, but believe that a piece of cake it was not. Although we worked in this fairy tale setting, we all worked our asses off. Upon leaving the office, I rushed to pick up Little Contessa, put dinner on the table, go over her homework, play with her, clean the house, do laundry, grocery shop, etc., followed by studying and work related material that accompanied me home most nights. Every minute was accounted for, planned right down the second. No time wasted on anything.

Once Anthony approved my implementation and training plans, I began to meet with the various department heads with whom procedural changes would be made in their respective areas. Even though this was my baby, my plan, I found myself in unfamiliar territory. At this point, I was only comfortable being in the background. I still wasn't at ease speaking directly to these managers. I was insecure around them, always afraid they would say things or use words I didn't understand. Which was why I added a "Speak for Success" and "Public Speaking" to my studies, which included increased vocabulary, diction, and enunciation. In addition to dropping my "street mouth," I learned a few basic principles that helped me immensely. First of all, breathe! We forget to do that when we are nervous, which can really screw up your thought process and timing. Next, make sure you always maintain direct eye contact with your audience. You don't have to use big, fancy words; just make sure your instructions are spoken slowly, clearly, and with distinction. That will hold your audience. With these lessons and much practice, I got my presentations down, and ultimately the perspiration rings under my arms got smaller and smaller with each completed training.

I was having lunch and studying in the employee cafeteria one day when suddenly I heard a cheery voice ask to join me. I looked up, and to my delight, it was Sue, whom I really liked but hardly ever had a chance to chat with.

"Sue, of course! Sit down, please. My God, it's been forever since we've had a chance to catch up." We laughed as we arranged the table for both our trays to fit on it.

"That's because you've been so busy being a rock star around here," Sue told me.

"Oh, stop!" I said shyly.

"Contessa, don't tell me you don't know the reputation you've made around here. The last management meeting Anthony held had particular focus on your cross-training program and everything you've done to put it all in place. Everyone was truly impressed," Sue told me.

"Sue, honestly, it was enough for me to have Anthony's blessing. I was a little hesitant to even present it to him at first, but I kept hearing his words on how he appreciates thinking outside the box, to not just do your job, but to always be mindful of how you can improve things," I confessed.

"Remember I told you that Anthony isn't one to hand out compliments? That no news is good news? Contessa, you need to know that Anthony has never been so verbally complimentary of anyone here as he has been of you. His praise is mainly reflected in our paycheck!" Sue laughed. "I understand why you would be hesitant. Anthony can be a pretty intimidating guy, and it took guts for you to approach him with a new concept. But now you get him, don't you?"

"Well, let's just say I'm getting there. At least he doesn't scare the shit out of me anymore!" I confessed as we both let out a huge laugh. "Anthony warned me—no, actually promised me—that I would never work harder in my life but also that I will realize great reward having done so. He was right on both counts. Sue, I actually cannot wait to get up in the morning and get to work! And the best part is that I can see the fruits of my labor. I can actually feel success. Crazy, isn't it? Anthony made this all possible for me, and I will never forget him for that."

Sue raised her glass of lemonade. "Let's drink to Anthony," she proposed. I joined her in raising my water glass up to hers. "Here's to the best boss we ever had." We clanked, we drank, and we laughed.

As time flies when you're having fun, the clock raced at the Four Seasons, and before I knew it, several years had passed. Anthony continued to crack a mean whip, and it always proved worthwhile. My responsibilities grew, as did my position, status, and paycheck. I was no longer referred to as Anthony's secretary, only his assistant. I still couldn't wait to get to work in the morning. I was completely and totally in love with my job. Who wouldn't be? Working in the lap of luxury, daily dining on gourmet cuisine, even meeting celebrities of a wide variety. Greeting, interacting, and servicing stars of film and television, politicians, prominent corporate leaders; notoriety of all sorts came to stay with us. My position allowed me to realize many things I never dreamed possible, including the normalizing of celebrity. We met with the rich, the famous, as well as the infamous. We were trained never to call attention to their fame or stature, that they were people just like everyone else, only their job or position put them in the public eye. We encountered them in their travels, and they relied on us to make their stay exemplary. Just as I learned to speak to and advise senior managers, I became aware that celebrities were nothing to become unnerved over. We saw their habits, good and bad; we recognized and dealt with their quirks, saw to their every want and need, even put up with much bad behavior. Like I said, we are all just people. It made for great conversation with my family and friends, but I could never imagine how this cavalier attitude toward "celebrity" would serve me well later in life. Wait for it.

Although I usually maintained one night class per week, my hectic pace relented somewhat as I became more knowledgeable, fluent, and confident in my role. Things at home were going well, just as finely tuned as my position at work. By this time, Will and I were married and had purchased our home in the suburbs. To say the commute between downtown and the suburbs was difficult would be an understatement. To begin with, I had to take two busses to the train station. Timing was everything, and while the busses were barely on any schedule at all, the trains departed on the dot. Racing against the downtown Chicago rush hour traffic was a nightmare on any given day, but Friday traffic was worst of all. Soon a major construction project began right in the midst the bus route to the train station, eating up more of my precious time to get to the station. On school nights, it was a million times worse. I tried to leave the office a bit earlier whenever possible but wasn't able to do so very often. These days, Anthony was traveling more than usual, and therefore I had some extra responsibilities to take care of in his absence. He was spending a great deal more time at headquarters in Toronto than his usual monthly summary meeting, but I was way too busy to contemplate as to why. It was all so confidential, and I had specific instructions from him as to how to handle any questions from any of the other managers. The additional duties I performed in his absence were distributing highly confidential budget information to each department head and to obtain their individual notes on forecasting for future budget alterations.

In the meantime, I hired a high school girl who lived in our building to stay with Little Contessa, who was now in middle school, until I got home. I was late more than on time, and the sitter became increasingly annoyed. As winter approached and the snow piled up, traffic got even worse, and consequently, I was getting home later than ever. The sitter ultimately quit, and I scrambled for alternate solutions, none of which worked out for very long, as I continued to be late. As much as I fought the realization, working downtown and living in the burbs was not working out at all. While each of the situations was ideal unto themselves, the two combined were not jiving. I agonized and struggled with the commute all winter, until I could no longer ignore the only remedy for this situation. The very thought of leaving Four Seasons was absolutely devastating to me, and finally I realized I had no choice but to leave my dream job and find employment in the suburbs. It was the only way for me to better accommodate my homelife and responsibilities there.

I thought it best to at least begin a job search before I even made mention of it to anyone, particularly Anthony. I contacted several recruitment companies to gain insight for what the job market was in my area that my skill set and experience would be compatible to. Each of the placement managers I contacted was very encouraging, indicating they had several great opportunities that would be a good fit with my qualifications and experience, particularly in relation to my current role at Four Seasons. They assured me significant interviews could be set up right away. Apparently, many companies were moving out of the downtown area to the suburbs for the same reason more people were. As most folks were getting more house for less money, businesses were getting more office space for far less than downtown real estate prices. In addition, traffic was more manageable, and as necessary for many business people, this also offered easier access to Chicago O'Hare Airport. After doing much research, I reluctantly agreed to sign on with one agency that appeared the most promising. I was pleasantly surprised to be sent on interviews right away, all to reputable, noteworthy companies with significant positions available. Leaving my office early was hard to manage, but I worked it out by coming in earlier and explaining a dentist or doctor appointment or school event. Anthony didn't seem to mind at all, as he was confident that my work was never neglected, every task completed to perfection.

Finally, I was offered a position within a Midwest regional sales office of Citibank, located about twenty minutes away from home. It was an excellent starting position with phenomenal benefits. The company offered an abundance of paid training and management courses, with an open path to advancement for anyone with the drive and ambition to go after it. While I was still heartbroken to have to leave Four Seasons, I couldn't have asked for more in a new position, and one with new promise. Or so I told myself. I accepted this wonderful new opportunity with mixed emotions of joy, excitement, and heartbreak. I didn't know how I would face Anthony or what words I would use to tell him I had to leave the most wonderful, inspiring, and encouraging opportunity anyone had ever given me. I agonized over it all weekend, rehearsing what I would say come Monday morning. It was more than letting go of a luxurious work environment; it was saying goodbye to a wonderful place and all the people in it who took me in, nurtured me, provided all the tools for me to develop and grow in ways I desired but never thought possible, and then welcomed me as part of their team. How fortunate and appreciative I was to have had this experience, one that allowed me to acquire and apply such a vast collection of knowledge for not only my own success but for that of our team, our company, as well. For the first time in my life, I felt that I actually belonged, that I was truly part of something significant. Yes, I was a lucky girl, all right. And now I had to put my big girl panties on and stop looking backward, because that was not the direction I wanted to travel in. I was moving forward, and I decided that was where I would focus, come what may.

Riding the train in this Monday morning, I was pretty nervous, reviewing my resignation speech to Anthony. I wanted to find just the right words that would adequately express how deeply I wrestled with this decision, why it was necessary, and most of all, how I appreciated what all he did for me. Articulating my appreciation for what all he taught me was vitally important to me. Anthony pushed me to learn, sharpen my intuition, and therefore, trust my own judgment, to think outside the box and not be afraid to suggest new concepts, so long as I had calculated their success. For the first time in my life, somebody looked inside me and saw what I felt—the desire, the drive, and the ambition to rise above everything and accomplish anything. He did that; he was successful, and consequently, so was I.

I saw the light on in Anthony's office when I arrived. I was getting settled in when suddenly I saw him appear before me.

"Contessa, please come into my office," he solemnly requested.

The serious look on his face and tone in his voice made me forget all about my speech. I immediately entered his office, finding him swaying from side to side in his big leather chair. I made myself comfortable in the chair on the other side of his desk, facing him.

Anthony began, "Have you wondered why I've been spending so much time at headquarters lately?" I was surprised that he opened a conversation with a question, particularly this one, but I didn't hesitate with an immediate answer.

"No, I haven't. I would never wonder about or question your schedule."

"I apologize for the extra burden of work I've placed upon you as a result of my frequent absences, and I need to compliment you on how efficiently and effectively you've addressed it. I've had very positive comments from several department managers as to how impressed they were with your communications and interactions concerning related budget issues," Anthony offered.

"There's no need to thank me, Anthony. I actually viewed doing all of it as an opportunity and a compliment. You never would have trusted me to do that if you didn't think I was capable, particularly with budget issues. So it is I who will thank you," I responded.

"Good answer on both counts, Contessa!" He paused and swiveled back and forth in his chair a minute. "I've made a decision. It was hard for several reasons, and it took much contemplation, but I made it and I'm settled with it." He stopped swiveling and seemed to be staring right into my heart. "Contessa, I've been asked to assume the role of Corporate Chief Financial Officer and will have to relocate to headquarters in Toronto permanently. The official announcement will be communicated by headquarters to the entire organization tomorrow, but I wanted you to hear it from me first. Senior management and I were also interviewing for my replacement, and we've made that decision as well. Larry Wotts, the Controller from our San Francisco property, accepted the position and will arrive here next week to start. I'll be leaving the following week," he finished.

My jaw literally dropped. My heart was racing, and I could barely breathe. I put my face into my hands and sobbed hysterically. Was it relief that Anthony was leaving as well as I was? Or disbelief over what a twist of fate this development was? Did his announcement soften the guilt I felt in leaving in the first place? I don't know, but all my emotions just exploded at once, and all I could do was cry. Anthony came out from his desk to embrace me and offered me a tissue.

"There, there now. I'm not worth all these tears. You'll get on fine with Larry, you'll see," he said as he compassionately dabbed my eyes with tissues. "Besides, you have a reputation to uphold. I bragged about your diligence and drive, told him he was getting the best assistant in the world!"

That led to another teary outburst from me.

"Anthony, I have something to tell you too," I said, sobbing. "I was going to tell you that the commute between home and work has caused significant problems at home for me and that after agonizing over it, I've had no choice but to leave Four Seasons and get a job in the suburbs, close to home. It was an extremely difficult decision for me to make. You know how I love it here—this is like home to me." My emotions were unstoppable. "Anthony, you've done more for me than anyone ever has. Nobody else has ever given me the confidence, the power to shoot for the stars, reach for and achieve my goals. You worked me, you trained me, and you gave me the ability to really believe in myself, that I could actually do whatever I set my mind to. And I love you for that. I will always, always have

155

a special place in my heart for you," I finished. There, I said it, and I was finally calming down. I took in a huge breath, let it out, and repeated, "Yes, Anthony, I love you and I will be forever grateful for everything you've done for me."

Anthony sat silently for a moment. "Well, it seems that our relationship turns out to be quite serendipitous, doesn't it?"

"Anthony, I'm not sure what that means," I confessed.

"That is an unplanned, unexpected encounter that results in a mutually lucky and fortuitous opportunity for both parties," Anthony explained.

"Well, now I'm really confused. I mean, I surely realize what all you've done for me, but if I get your meaning, I don't understand what the benefit was to you," I responded.

"You're my reciprocate," Anthony declared.

"You're going to have to elaborate on that one, Anthony. I'm completely lost," I confessed.

The hard core, all business facial expression and demeanor of Anthony Dade suddenly softened into a warm, compassionate, and dare I say it, a bit teary eyed, big old teddy bear. "Do you remember our lunch date for your first review?"

I certainly did, and this softer side of him immediately reminded me of that day. "Every word," I immediately replied.

"I gave you the short version of my early years and how they related to me hiring you in the first place. I want you to know that you have fulfilled every intuitive expectation I had of you and in some ways, exceeded them. I've never regretted my decision. But now I want to share another aspect of my life and how it relates to you. I spared you the anguish of my survival, but there's an element of it that you should know, as it's relevant," he said. "When I was at probably the lowest point of my young life, filled with despair, having to support my younger siblings with not much to go on, I met someone quite by accident who seemed to tap into what all I was going through and gave me significant assistance. I was working several jobs, constantly exhausted, and I think sometimes not even conscious. I was walking home on a long road one day when I noticed a lady about my mother's age up ahead of me, carrying groceries. All of a sudden, I saw her trip, fall, and her groceries spilled all over the road. I rushed to her and helped her up. She was okay, but quite shaken. I picked up her groceries and told her I'd walk her home. I carried her bags on one arm while she balanced herself by resting her weight on my other arm. As we walked, we talked and got to know each other a bit. I did tell her of some of my struggles. She was aware that I lived a distance from her in the much poorer section of the town. She was verbal in her appreciation of my helping her home. I spoke of my mum and how I would have wanted someone to help my mum if this happened to her. I saw her to her door, and she offered me some money in gratitude. I refused it, told her how I enjoyed our chat and company on my walk. She asked for my address so she could send me a proper thank you note. Sometime later, I received a letter in the mail from our town's most prestigious accounting firm. Apparently, her son Simon was the Chief Financial Officer of that firm, and his letter offered me an apprenticeship there. I was scared to death but took him up on his offer. He was an extremely harsh taskmaster, but I learned a great deal from him about business and life itself. He paid my expenses to college, and after graduation, I worked at his firm for many years. He also helped my siblings with obtaining employment in various areas. I stayed very close to both of them. When the opportunity to work for Four Seasons here in the States presented itself, I was hesitant to leave. Simon and his mum encouraged me to take it, that I must go in order to realize my fullest potential, that this new opportunity would allow me to better care for my family, even from a distance, plus pave the way for future career growth. Before I left, Simon told me a story with similar circumstances to mine and that my encounter with his mum was a gift, a way for him to pay the universe back for the kind and fortunate gesture he had received years prior. His benefactor had passed away, and he believed extending himself to me in the way he did would adequately show his gratitude. He called it the universe's reciprocal arrangement, to give back what good fortune you've received."

Anthony paused, and the anxiousness for me to hear more must have been apparent, as he took a few breaths and held up his hand as a give-me-a-minute gesture. He was a little choked up.

"And the instant I met you, sitting there with your darling little girl, frantically explaining why you had to bring her along, I knew you were my opportunity to pay back. That you were my reciprocate. The morale of this story, Contessa, is that you must always look for a reciprocate. You must actively seek out a way to pay back for a helping hand you've received somewhere along the road. You have to look for it and act, and in doing so, you'll realize it's giving back that is the true meaning, the key, and the joy of success. Of all the things you've learned here, I hope this lesson will be the most valuable. For you, my dear Contessa, will be successful, of that I am quite confident," he finished.

I didn't feel like crying anymore. I was unexplainably calm. "Anthony, as my time passed here, I frequently wondered how I could ever repay you for the many opportunities you've given me. Now I know. I fought having to leave because I absolutely love my job, I love this hotel, the people in it, and most of all, I love you. You've given me more than opportunity. You gave me focus, a direction, and a true sense of belonging to something. You encouraged me, something nobody ever did for me. So I will leave our little home here, and I'll take all the lessons you've taught me and carry them with me always. I will make you proud, I promise," I vowed.

I was no longer sad. We embraced and hugged a bit. "Okay, now go on and get to work. We've got things to accomplish before we make our exits," he said as he broke away. Typical Anthony!

Anthony always worked at lightning speed, but the next week he made his normal pace look like that of a snail. He wanted to wrap up several projects before he left. I was glad to be so extremely busy, as it made me forget that I myself was leaving, and I really didn't want to dwell on that. Anthony asked about my new position and was quite pleased that I accepted the job at Citibank, telling me he was proud that I would be entering the world of banking. He felt that changing industries was a bold choice many wouldn't opt for, but he would have expected nothing less from me. "Bravo!" as he put it. We had additional conversations about my new position, and he advised me on how I could apply training I received at Four Seasons to the new role I would soon undertake. In addition, that I should continue on with any of the paid courses my new company would provide. "Never feel as though you've had enough of the classroom," Anthony advised me.

News of his promotion and departure for head office spread quickly, and soon Anthony's farewell party was planned. The date for his party was coincidentally my last day at Four Seasons. Anthony's party would be a gala event in the Grand Ballroom. Dinner, entertainment, and even a comedic roast of Anthony by many senior management staff. Anthony insisted I sit at his table, which frowned upon by some but acknowledged by others as a compliment to me and the stature I achieved through him. In addition, Anthony expressed that it was fitting we spend our last hours together in celebration of a memorable career experience.

It was a magical night. The Grand Ballroom never looked more elegant. As I listened to the many speeches, my eyes wandered all around the ballroom. I wanted to take one last look at the grandeur of this room. The magnificent Austrian crystal chandelier that consumed the entire ceiling. I felt the hand painted Italian mural that circled the walls embrace me one more time. The finest china, the most impeccably trained staff, who introduced synchronized serving. These and so many more elements that captured the essence of this exceptional, opulent, and memorable environment. I took a mental snapshot of it all, and I'd keep it in my heart forever.

The evening was coming to an end, and I wanted to leave prior to its official conclusion. I said my goodbyes to many who wished me well and hoped we would keep in touch. I then tapped Anthony on the shoulder, and without words, he knew it was time to say goodbye. He gracefully put his arm out for me to take. We walked arm in arm toward the elevator. He stopped for a moment and gazed around at the luxurious lobby.

"It is majestic, isn't it? Never look back, Contessa. That's not the direction you'll ever be moving in. Keep the places, the moments, and the people in your heart, and they will always be with you. Now get out of here and go set the world on fire. I'll be watching for your flames." Anthony bestowed his last bit of advice to me. We hugged for a long time.

With my voice quivering and tears beginning to gush, I tried desperately to say a dignified and simple "Goodbye, Anthony!" I stepped into the elevator, and as the doors closed, he blew me a kiss and said, "And by the way, I love you too." The elevator doors closed. And I sobbed uncontrollably.

I carry all of Anthony's lessons with me to this day.

As my career progressed, I continually looked for a "reciprocate" of my own. I ultimately had the good fortune to extend that philosophy to not just one, but many, hiring several single mothers and putting them on an aggressive training path that ultimately led to their own growth and development. I think of Anthony often and still have a group photo of our original accounting department in my office, reminding me of that magical and enlightening experience. My time at Four Seasons remains among my most cherished memories.

In closing this chapter, dare to dream. Chart your course and go for it. Explore, embrace, and learn with an open mind. When a situation is not working for you, only you can make the changes necessary to turn things around, no matter how emotionally or physically difficult it may be. And while change and new challenges can certainly be daunting, never back down. The greater the challenge, the sweeter the victory overcoming it. Believe in yourself, and the magic will happen. To paraphrase Anthony's words, never look back; you've already been there. Keep your focus forward, for that's the only direction you surely want to be heading in. And most of all, always be on the lookout for your reciprocate and be ready to give back.

The Doctor

Bad Medicine

Having a handsome gynecologist is a crime against nature; having a drop-dead-gorgeous gynecologist is a crime against women! I mean, think of the things that take place in the OB/GYN office. The tissue paper gown, the stirrups, the instruments they poke you with. And if those aren't bad enough, how about the positions we need to get into in order to use them, add the fear of farting while they are poking and prodding you. *Ugh!* The cherry on that cake is having a gynecologist who is not only wickedly handsome but, in addition, also deliciously engaging, easygoing, funny, hypnotically charismatic, and compassionate to what women's issues are. Oh, and not to forget one who loves to listen to rock 'n roll while he's doing all the poking. Nope, just not fair.

The doctor was referred to me by my regular OB/GYN as a specialist who could help get to the bottom of years of my female problems. I had a history of cysts, tumors, and endometriosis, and this doctor was a specialist in all those departments and more. At that time, he was blazing a trail of innovation in female medicine. My files were sent to him, and the appointment this morning was for an ultrasound followed by a conference with him for his recommendation for treatment. I was fortunate to obtain a very early appointment and was grateful, as I had a pretty busy day at work, so being able to get in and out early was a blessing for me so I did not have to take a day off. It started out to be one of those rare mornings when everything fell perfectly into place. My long, thick, wavy auburn hair turned out like a shampoo commercial after this morning's shower.

As a manager in the banking industry, I wore suits that were simple, smart, and cut to emphasize a fit and trim figure without being too risqué for the conservative arena I worked in. Traffic was also on my side this day, and I arrived a little early.

The new patient paperwork had been filled out in advance, and I was greeted by a very personable receptionist, who explained that the doctor's assistant would be out momentarily to show me to the ultrasound room. Waiting for a new doctor to come in and introduce himself while you're lying there in the crinkly paper gown is a little nerve-racking. Especially when two seconds after you shake his hand, its up in your lady stuff. To my surprise, it was not the doctor who entered, but a female technician popped in, announcing that she would be performing the ultrasound. *Whew!* I instantly lay back and became so very relaxed I didn't even worry about farting air at her—but wait, would she tell the doctor if I did? Oh, well, she was pleasant and efficient while churning the dildo scope with the condom on it all around my insides. Watching the monitor, at least I saw a good show while I was relaxing. She was very explanatory throughout each phase of her probing. Actually, even though she was pointing out several things that weren't supposed to be there, I found it pretty interesting as well as entertaining. When finished, I dressed and she escorted me to the doctor's office, where he would meet me to discuss his findings and recommendations for treatment.

Now that the worst was over and I was sitting in a pretty plush office, waiting for the doctor to come in, I became even more relaxed. I sat there listening to the piped-in soft rock music. Unusual for a doctor's office, I thought, but being the rock 'n' roll girl that I was, I was diggin' it. Enter the doctor. I do believe the music changed— in my head, at least—to that worthy of the climax moment in an old romantic melodrama. This was the Jackie Collins novel, Lifetime TV Network, lightning bolt, when Rhett first saw Scarlett on the staircase moment. The very second he walked through the door, the doctor and I had a "D, all of the above" instant that seemed to last forever. I am not one who is rattled, shaken, or stirred easily, and I hate to admit that his entrance blew me away, but oy vey, talk about having an impact! This man had presence! He knew it, too, but not in an arrogant way. He was the naughty little boy who knows his charms allow him to get away with things. His smooth actions, his suave manner, never indicated he knew he was leaving you weak at the knees, but trust me, he knew.

With an unassuming yet penetrating approach, the doctor extended his hand to me and introduced himself. It was more than an introduction; it was an engagement whereby you instantly understood he was "not just a doctor." I say that not only in relation to me, but eventually, after our having such a close doctor-patient relationship for so long, I felt then and know now that each and every one of his patients felt the same while under his care. Yet something told me there was more to it with me; maybe it was all the violins and fireworks going off in my head! Although the doctor remained the consummate professional, the electricity was undeniably there.

You wouldn't immediately notice the doctor's relatively small physique, because his jaw-dropping good looks, charm, and magnetism seemed to have entered the room before he did. Impeccably dressed in the finest silk suit, the doctor had thick black hair with just the right amount of wave to it. His large, globular dark eyes were so commanding I couldn't look away if I wanted to. They were soft and gentle yet quite strong, very inviting and laced with perfect thick, sweeping lashes that could seal any deal under negotiation. Inimitable lips outlined his radiant smile, and together they screamed that the doctor was an out-of-this-world kisser. All this on a flawless face so perfect you'd think it was a handcrafted Ken doll. My God, I had never been so overwhelmed before. For a second I was feeling my clothes, because I was sure I was still at home in my bed and jammies; this was surely a dream, I thought. But no, I was awake and actually meeting a dream. It was a good thing I was sitting down, so he couldn't see my knees knocking together, and it was best that they already took my blood pressure, because right about then, my heart was pounding so loud I wondered if he could hear it. Jeez, it wasn't until he started asking me questions—and talk about a titillating voice!—about my health that I even remembered who I was. He took notes as I responded to his questions, while I eyeballed every molecule of him from head to toe along the way. My sizing up of him told me that while he was not physically a large man, he was huge in ability, reputation, as well as ego (hey, he was a gorgeous groundbreaker and knew it) and had mastered everything he pursued, regardless of what category his desires fell. He was confident and solid.

He extended his thoughts on treatment for me, and I had to give myself a mental pinch (*Snap out of it, girl*) in order to pay attention and ask a few important questions, while he graciously and fluently answered them all. My female related problems were not all that complicated, and certainly treatable by new techniques and procedures developed by him. He is taking me on as a patient. *Sweet!* It was easy to see how one could immediately think that because of his brilliant reputation and obvious sophistication, the doctor would be somewhat aloof and perhaps even cold. Ah, the price of brains and beauty! However, just the opposite was true; the doctor had a very relaxed and engaging manner about him that immediately put you at ease. And I was grateful, because this style of his completely disarmed me and enabled me to get through the rest of the consultation without seeming like a complete idiot who didn't even know her own name. After making arrangements for the next steps, I left his office completely comfortable, now being under his care.

After a period of tests and results, the doctor determined that I had a serious case of endometriosis as well as several cysts that needed to be removed. As long as I feel secure in the hands of a competent physician, knowing they've done all the necessary homework, I am fine with getting it over with as soon as possible. I'm not crazy about going under the knife, but because I've always been an active and fast paced person, I just can't stand not feeling one hundred percent. So be it. On with the surgery! As the doctor reviewed the procedure and arrangements to be made, he asked me what kind of music I liked. Surprised by his question, I laughed but quickly answered, "I'm a rock 'n' roll girl. Classic rock, to be exact."

"Really!" he exclaimed. "You know, I had a feeling you might be."

"Why is that?" I asked with a chuckle.

"I just had that feeling," he said. "You have a sort of edginess about you that seems to go with rock."

"Edgy? Wow, I've been called many things before, but never *edgy*. Is that a good thing?" I laughed.

"It's a very good thing, and I meant it as a compliment. I sensed it that first day I met you in my office," he said very confidently.

"I'm curious as to what would have given you that impression, especially when we first met, because truth be told, I was actually quite nervous," I confessed.

Those amazingly sexy, chocolate Kisses eyes of his speared right into me as he responded, "I knew it. I can always tell."

All righty, then.

He continued, "But I always ask my patients what kind of music they like so I can play it while I operate. I like to put my patients at ease as best I can. Music helps, particularly if it's what the patient likes. So who's your favorite group or groups?"

"Well, I don't know that I have an actual favorite, but I wouldn't be upset to know that Zeppelin, the Stones, The Who, or Beatles were with me during surgery," I declared.

"Yes, I knew it!" He jumped with excitement. "You just named all my favorites. I had a strong feeling we'd get along well! I have all of them, so we'll be there waiting for you, ready to roll."

"That's fine, Doc. Just don't let me find out you were playing air guitar while operating on me!" I finished, not even realizing how easy it was to have that crack roll out of my mouth.

That was the start of my nickname for him, which he never objected to. From this moment on, he would forever be *Doc* to me. He knew I was not being disrespectful, and that was the actual first sign that we were developing a friendship. Once he commented that normally he would have disapproved and never allowed being called that, but it seemed endearing coming from me. Doc said he admired how attentive I was to the information he provided (I actually took notes, which he laughed at), that it was refreshing to be treating someone who was really involved in their own treatment and actually paid attention.

"Well, wouldn't anyone be? It's my body, my health, and my future. Why wouldn't anyone pay attention?" I naively asked.

"You'd be surprised at how many people really don't get involved in their own health issues. They just accept the things they are told without questions, concern, and that's pretty boring for a doctor. I like my patients to be engaged. You are a refreshing change," he offered.

"Thanks, Doc. What else does my behavior tell you?" I asked.

"Well, based on how you've reacted to everything we've discussed, I feel you genuinely care about your own health and are paying close attention to your body. You ask many detailed questions, almost as if to challenge me, and I like that. It also tells me that you have high standards, and I admire that as well. I strive to have my patients feel comfortable in my care, and your attention tells me you really are. I appreciate that. I can't believe you even take notes! I have never had a patient take notes in all my years of practice. That's amazing!" He laughed.

"I have to. This is a lot of information, and I want to make sure I understand it all, so I read everything over when I go home, and as you are well aware, if I still don't understand, I will surely ask you again. Like I said, it's my body and my health, so I need to be certain of everything before you start removing things," I said with a bit of sarcasm.

Doc laughed. "I wish I had more patients like you. I can tell you're well versed and thorough, and I'm sure it applies to everything you do," he finished.

Did I see a little mischievous grin on his face while he said that? Yes, I do believe I did. So naturally I felt the need to respond in kind. "How insightful of you Doc. Like my daddy always said, if you can't be the best, don't bother."

Touché.

Doc laughed louder and harder at that one.

The first of what would be many, many surgeries the doctor performed on me was scheduled for later that month. Being a single mother, working several jobs simultaneously at that time, I was too busy and tired to give it a second thought. In my mind, I reviewed my notes, I thought it through, and it was now something on my calendar that had to be checked off, with every minute of my healing time scheduled for catching up with work related things to help make a smooth transition back. *Okay, let's get this show on the road.*

I am the Lucy Ricardo of *Murphy's Law*. If anything that can go wrong will, you can be sure that it will with me, but you will laugh your ass off when you hear the story. I'm one of those fortunate people who often experience mishaps, usually comical ones. This surgery fell right into that category. Surgery day arrived, and Little Contessa, who just got her driving permit, had to bring me to the hospital, as nobody else in my family was available. Driving rules say that one can drive on a learner's permit, so long as an adult driver with a valid license is in the car. Thankfully, I don't think the rules of the road indicate that the adult driver has to be conscious while in the car. Like I said, it was just my daughter and me, and we did what we had to do whenever we had to do it. The surgery was outpatient, so I was awake on the way in, but who knew what shape I'd be in on the return? Oh, well, we had no choice. That was the way we rolled.

The relatively quick outpatient procedure went according to plan. Everything that needed to be removed was, without incident. Doc came to the waiting room to deliver the good news to Little Contessa. Even my fifteen-year-old daughter was impressed with Doc's charming, charismatic, and engaging manner. Doc told his new fan that I would be in recovery for about two hours and ready to go home soon thereafter, although probably would still be be a little groggy. He asked if anyone else was with her to drive home. That was his introduction to how independent we were, and he told me later that he was deeply touched by this young, yet seemingly mature girl explain that there was nobody else, just "us two," proudly announcing that she just got her driving permit and could handle it. They chatted a while, and Doc conveyed he felt I was in good hands, that he must go as he had to leave town for a meeting in California. Little Contessa would reiterate their conversation and express to me how kind and personable he was. With the exchange between her and Doc over, my daughter returned to the book she brought along to read while she waited for me to wake up.

One hour passed. Two hours passed. Three hours passed. Finally, a nurse entered the waiting room and, with a very puzzled look, explained to my daughter that because I developed a high fever, they needed to admit me to the hospital. They were bewildered as to why this fever developed and needed to keep me there to find out what was going on. I felt awful when I eventually woke up in a hospital bed with several IVs going, realizing that my poor Little Contessa waited there all this time by herself and would have to go home alone. She called other relatives of ours, but they lived pretty far away and nobody could get there to go home with her. She assured me she would be fine. What could I do? I was burning with fever and in the hospital! True to her nature, she bravely and maturely handled it all like a champ! Indicative of any hospital stay, there was an ongoing parade of doctors, nurses, technicians, etc. pinching, poking while asking the same questions over and over and over and nobody seemed to be able to answer the only question I had: "What's wrong with me? I'm burning up! Where's my doctor? I want my doctor!" I was told he was not available as he had to leave town. Not known for being an accepting person, I insisted that my doctor be called and made aware of what was going on, for it was only his answers that would satisfy me.

"I want to talk to my doctor. He'll tell me what's wrong," I insisted to each and every staff member that entered my room. Although I was only semi-conscious, I remember not asking but demanding to speak to my doctor and nobody else. I thought that if nothing else, I would aggravate the shit out of them until they gave in and called Doc. I was relentless.

Suddenly, a nurse entered to peek in on me to determine if I was awake. When the nurse realized I was, she softly whispered she had a surprise for me, that she would be right back. In a few minutes, she returned, stood at the nightstand, and put her hand on the phone. It rang once, she answered and said "Just a minute," then she put the phone to my ear. It was Doc!

"The staff tells me you're being difficult," he said. "But I told them they must have my patients mixed up, because the beautiful young lady I just operated on is anything but difficult," he continued.

Oooooooh, great phone voice, Doc! I might have been semi-conscious, but I was alert enough to remember his velvety voice. "I'm not being difficult, I'm being specific. And I just want some answers, like you give me. It's your fault. You spoiled me. What's wrong with me? Why am I here?" I slurred.

"I'm so sorry, but you incurred a staph infection, blah, blah, blah," he said, explaining the nature and various causes of a staph infection. I heard his voice without the content and, at that instant, really didn't care. His voice to me was like an angel singing me a lullaby, and I just reveled in hearing it. I thought of everything under the sun to ask in order to keep him on the phone, but finally, he said he had to go. After all, he was the keynote speaker at a medical conference in San Francisco. Yet he took the time to call me! *Wow! Okay, nothing very serious, and I'll be released tomorrow, plus my follow-up appointment with him is all set. Great!*

Recovery was perfect, and the follow-up meeting was set, which resulted in Doc giving me a squeaky clean bill of health. We even had a few laughs over my demand to speak to him directly. He said he had never done that before, but then again, he'd never had a patient be so boldly demanding before. More laughs over it. Once he heard how adamant I was, he knew I would be unrelenting with the staff until he called me. "I think you're a pretty tenacious lady. I don't think anything deters you from getting what you want," he said to me with his big, dreamy, creamy dark brown eyes peering right into me.

"You'd be right to think that, Doc," I managed to reply.

"And that's why I think you're a very special lady," he spilled back, flashing those movie star pearly whites at me. I think I even saw one of them sparkle! *Ugh, be still, my heart!*

Following that episode, Doc became my primary physician. Over the next several years, I looked forward to each annual checkup as it always resulted in fun and whimsical banter between Doc and me, but unfortunately, or maybe not, he was always tasked with cutting out new cysts, tumors, whatever that had to be removed. All relatively quick, easy outpatient surgeries that should have been 1, 2,

3, done. However, Murphy's law kicked in with each one. To high-light a few…

Following the successful removal of some cysts, I simply never woke up from the anesthesia. As usual, Doc found my daughter in the waiting room alone, doing her homework. By this time, Little Contessa had her driver's license and was able to bring me to and from the hospital herself. Doc explained that I just had too much "twilight" and it would take a while to wear off. He thought it best that I remain in the hospital. It took two days for me to wake up. The staff, as well as my daughter, later told me Doc was extremely attentive, making personal stops in to my room, checking vitals and me personally.

Next year, next surgery, was the same "routine" thing. Only this time, everything seemed to go fine. I woke up and was released. *Whew!* My daughter was just as relieved as I was. However, my breath-ing became very labored, and by the time we got home, the situation worsened and my abdomen became quite distended. We called Doc's office and were instructed to get right back to the hospital imme-diately. It was discovered I had an ileus, which basically meant that due to having anesthesia, I woke up, but some of my organs (lungs) didn't! Once again, Doc had to leave town following my surgery, but called every day, speaking to me directly, assuring me that while not physically there, he had his eye on me.

Several years of the same followed. Always an unusual, unfore-seen circumstance, not related to the surgery itself but something that turned a "minor little surgery" into something larger that required Doc's further attention. Each experience resulted in additional checkups and office visits that became more and more fun, friendly, humorous, and bonding. Doc was married, with children, and just as he got to know my daughter in many waiting rooms, I got to know his family through much friendly, enjoyable conversation. The words didn't have to be spoken; we were now special friends with a mutual admiration and respect for each other. Also, we realized that we "got" each other in a way that was unique unto the two of us. I knew a lot of people who would think "Ewwww, that's so weird! Friends with your doctor?" But for us, it became a mutually cherished friendship.

Okay, I admit that I fantasized about him, but nothing was ever, ever acted upon, so big deal!

Finally, my medical issues subsided, and years passed. By this time, I was married to husband #3 (keep reading, that chapter is coming up) and lived in Michigan. Through his industry position and associations, #3 sat on several boards and charities, and consequently, we attended many black tie affairs. One December, I was particularly excited to be attending a charity event at the Four Seasons Hotel in Chicago, my hometown. By this time, I realized my marriage was lacking, had little in common with those we would encounter at this event, but anything that brought me back to my beloved city really perked me up. And if a stay at the Four Seasons wasn't the cherry on this cake, the fact that my daughter and her fiancé were able to come along with us surely was. It was Little Contessa's birthday weekend, so being together was an extra treat. I was a self proclaimed high maintenance lady, and nobody primps like I do. I was not going to let one single amenity the Four Seasons had to offer slip by me. Therefore, Saturday was spent in preparation for the evening function. A workout, massage, hair, nails, the works. I was the youngest wife of the group and was pretty much shunned by the old hags in it. Unlike them, I was not a country club wife. I actually worked for my living and was in the industry their husbands were in, therefore having more in common with the gentlemen, which really infuriated those snooty women. They were snobbish, tasteless, condescending crones. What pissed them off even more was that I didn't give a rat's ass about being accepted into their group, and they knew it. If that weren't enough to make daggers fly, seeing me at these events powdered, pressed, more youthfully chic, and tastefully to the nines while in the middle of their husbands' circle not only sent those daggers flying, but I think I also actually felt the sting in my back a time or two. Nothing I couldn't handle, though.

I returned to our room after my day at the spa to find it empty. Just as I wondered where #3 was, the phone rang. It was Little Contessa, very excited. "You'll never guess who I just saw!" she screamed. Being at the Four Seasons, I assumed it was a celebrity.

"Gee, I don't know, but it must be someone good," I answered.

"Doc!" she cried out. "We were siting in the lobby, people watching, and I saw him checking in. I ran up to him, and he was very happy to see me, making a joke that this was the first time he had ever seen me outside of a waiting room. He's here for a medical dinner. I told him you were here, and he wants you to call him as soon as you can," she finished, giving me Doc's room number. I missed my friend and the comfort he so naturally provided me, but I have to admit, my heart was pounding as I immediately dialed his room. I was too excited to even put on a reserved voice; I just screamed out, "What a coincidence, Doc!"

"How have you been? Where the hell have you been? You haven't been in to see me for so long. I've often wondered about you," he said in a longing tone.

"*Long* story, Doc. I'm married now, living in Michigan. I work with my husband, and we're in town for a business dinner here at the hotel tonight." *Oh, please let me see you, Doc,* I prayed. *Just a look would put a little spark back into my life.*

"I'm speaking at a medical dinner tonight. I'm here with my wife and would love to meet you and your husband. Can we meet in the lobby for a cocktail, say, around six?" he asked.

"Would I ever refuse you?" I quickly responded.

"You better not! Just tell me one thing: Are you still gorgeous?" he asked.

I almost couldn't believe my ears, but was even more shocked at my own response. "Far be it for me to make up a man's mind. Judge for yourself. I'll see you in the lobby at six." I just couldn't help myself.

Oh my God! How awesome is this! And I'm already dolled up, just need to slip into my gown. Uh-oh…now the hard part. I'd have to convince my husband to agree to this meeting, which was not going to be easy, although it would certainly be interesting. Oh, well, I always did love a challenge.

A pompous and controlling man, #3 tried to mask his domineering ways with good manners and a soft demeanor. He had his own unique style for getting his way, but by now I was wise to it. His ego told him that nobody was as successful as he was, and it was inconceivable to him that I could even know anyone remotely close to his professional stature. It was clear to #3 that I put my phenomenal doctor in Chicago on a pedestal, and consequently he made it equally clear that I was to be medically treated only by his family doctors. It was his insurance, so I couldn't ignore his ridiculous demands. I took extra care in applying my makeup. While I wondered where the hell #3 was, I planned out the conversation for when he finally arrived. What the hell, it was all a coincidence, and I just wanted to see an old friend. Most other people wouldn't have made a big deal out of it, but I was certain #3 would! He was averse to anything outside his circle or realm, and being the control freak that he was, he was used to managing every minute of our time. But I became well versed in his ways and had a trick or two up my sleeve to get around him. A man may think he's so smart by constantly tooting his own horn, boasting of how he rules his roost, but a smart woman will make note of his ways and silently learn how to turn that behavior around. Let the man think he's the big shot, so long as you know you're the one who whipped the game on him. Still, it would have to be some fancy footwork on my part to get #3 to meet Doc with me. I was confident that blowing a little smoke up his ass would do the trick. Make note: A man with a big ego is often easy to manipulate, because he is in constant need of feeding that ego. So go ahead and feed it, but be smart and keep it to yourself.

When #3 arrived, I told him the story, including meeting Doc and his wife for a drink at six tonight. "No way, we won't have time!" he immediately snapped. I could tell #3 was jealous; like most control freaks, he was insecure when out of his element, in unknown territory, so refusal to go there was his only option. I used reverse psychology. Feed his ego and pump him up, which would push him right out the door.

"Of course, we will. I'm ready now, and all you have to do is put your tux on. Don't you think I live for an opportunity to show my handsome"—*not!*—"husband off? Besides, you sit on a few medical boards, so here's a chance for you to strut your medical stuff off to someone who thinks he knows it all." Gag me!

Fancying himself as quite the medical expert, #3 responded perfectly, "Yeah, I guess I could stand the chance to show up one of those overpriced medics. Sure, why not?"

Whew! For many women, the bullshit about showing off your husband would have been true. In this particular situation for me, it was just the opposite. First of all, I really did want to see Doc. Second, I wanted to show him off to my husband—secretly, of course—who was under the impression that it was virtually impossible for me to know anybody of any substance on my own. My auburn hair was just touched up and finished off with a perfect shoulder length trim. Makeup…check, emphasizing my large, round dark eyes. The individual human hair lashes I just had applied really tricked the eyes out, giving me a sensual, alluring look with minimal effort. Kind of like putting the fur wrap over a sexy dress. Gown…perfect. A clingy, black panne velvet, backless knockout that accentuated a toned body in great shape. Only simple earrings and a sparkly bracelet to accessorize, and of course, a full length crystal fox coat over my arm. *Look out, Doc, here I come.* Floating down the elevator, I hadn't a clue what bullshit was spewing from #3's stupid mouth. What's the difference? He preferred me to just stand there and be arm candy anyway. Besides, my heart was pounding so loud I wouldn't have heard him if I were trying to listen.

Exiting the elevator exposed us to a sea of people floating throughout the lobby. And just like the Red Sea, they parted to reveal my Doc standing there with soft, searching eyes, looking for me.

"Doc!" I yelled out as he turned around.

Wait, was that Doc, or was it Rhett seeing Scarlett glide up the staircase? It surely was Doc, and while I knew I'd be excited, I had no idea what a thrill it would actually turn out to be. We had never seen each other outside his office or in the hospital, so this night was an extra special treat. Not that he needed any additives to be even more debonair, but in a tuxedo, pretty hard to walk away from. This was going to require award winning acting abilities. You've got to love a man in a tuxedo, and if dorky #3 could look even remotely decent in one, just imagine how good Doc Dashing looked, especially after my not seeing him for so long. For a split second, I forgot I was with

#3, and thinking that Mrs. Doc would be there, I stopped myself from running to him. Our embrace was so appropriate that not even #3 flinched. A handshake (secure, tight, and consciously held throughout the conversation), and an open, friendly hug, although his arm was tightly wrapped around my tiny waist, knowing my big fur coat would camouflage it. Shifty little devil that Doc, wasn't he? He caressed my toned back and squeezed me tightly. I quickly introduced #3 to Doc, and I could immediately see that #3 was intimidated by Doc's obvious good looks, polish, and panache. Whenever #3 felt compromised, his jaw twitched and his voice quivered. I was laughing my ass of in the inside, as I noticed both running rampant, and so to lighten it up and put #3 at ease, I quickly asked where Mrs. Doc was.

"Oh, she was running very late and apologizes. She really wanted to meet you," he responded as he extended his hand out to #3 and the whole introduction took place. Ever the gracious and perfect gentleman, Doc was flawless as he effortlessly conversed with #3, telling us both how good it was to see Little Contessa, meet her fiancé, that he appreciated Little Contessa bringing him up to date on both of us. Doc explained to #3 that he was originally from Iron Mountain so was very familiar with Michigan, which enabled a good bit of conversation between them. They talked about some of the scenic little boating towns in Northern Michigan. Doc also expressed how happy he was to know that I, one of his most favored patients, was married to a good Michigan man, that he got to know me and my daughter through the years and had a great deal of respect for us. I knew this really pissed #3 off, and to hear Doc say that he "admired" me was too much for #3 to bear. While #3 pretended to accept the comments graciously, I knew I'd pay a price for it later, but ask me if I cared. I was holding on to my Doc, and that was most important to me. As he always fixed what ailed me, I felt that just seeing Doc again was the medicine I needed at this particular point in my life, as it was not going well. But as Doc spoke, I fixated on his eyes; his normally strong, piercing chocolate Kisses were replaced by sad, longing, puppy dog eyes. Instead of penetrating, they were sorrowful and yearning. The more I stared into them, the more I knew I was right.

Doc was not happy. I would have given anything to tell #3 to just go, but sadly, I couldn't. Finally, after a forced (or perhaps, I should say, well performed) yet pleasant chat, we had to say our goodbyes. The men shook hands, and as I got another squeeze, I kept my eyes open, only to see his close tightly while he smiled. Goodbye, my dear friend! The ecstasy of our encounter enabled me to get through many anguishing events throughout the remainder of my marriage to #3. I played it over in my mind countless times and wondered what was really going on with Doc. He was definitely not in a happy place, and I knew seeing me lifted him up, just as seeing him surely did me. Oh, well, perhaps someday I would find out.

The next summer, #3 and I took a boating trip through Northern Michigan. Bad weather caused us to dock in a charming little town called Munising for several days. As I strolled about the town, looking at trinkets and treasures in various souvenir shops, I suddenly remembered that this was one of the towns Doc and #3 were talking about the night at the Four Seasons! I remembered Doc describing the waterways and coves he explored as a kid and how dear they were to him. While in one particular shop, I found a book of postcards that had pictures of all the areas Doc spoke of. I had to buy it. When #3 and I returned home, I thought of mailing the book to Doc's office, but something always stopped me. I put the book in my desk drawer and kept it there. In the meantime, marriage to #3 was quickly going downhill. Whenever I got depressed, I would take out that postcard book and gaze at all the pictures, which became very soothing to me. If I told anyone I did that, they might think it was because they reminded me of a beautiful trip with my husband. Not the case. They reminded me of Doc and comforted me. Very soon, my marriage was over, and it came about in a very abrupt and devastating way, but again (wait for it), that's another chapter.

While sitting at home one day, licking my wounds, I took out the postcard book and decided to mail it to Doc. I wrote a short note indicating I came across these pictures and thought he would like to have them. I also included my phone number. Within a few weeks, he called. He first explained that he was overjoyed to hear from me and also so appreciative to have those pictures. He went on and on about how they brought back such fond memories, asking where anyhow I got them and, most of all, thanking me for sending them. He then inquired about me, my husband, my daughter, and I gave him the short version on everything, closing with my official divorced status. He expressed his condolences, asked how I was doing, but without details, I just told him I was dealing with it all and I was fine.

"You're a tough girl, you can get through anything," he told me, but I was dying to hear more about him and remembered those big sad puppy eyes at our Four Seasons encounter. It was now his turn to bring me up to speed on his world.

"Well, I've been better, that's for sure," he began. "I'm actually separated from my wife."

Without even a split second to think about how this would sound, I blurted out a great big "Are you kidding me?" and instantly tried to smooth it out with an "Oooh, I'm so sorry."

Then I said, "Doc, I'm going to go out on a limb here. I have to ask you something."

"Sure, go ahead," he said.

"Has this been coming on for a while? I mean, have you been unhappy for some time?" I tenderly asked.

"What makes you ask me that?"

"The night at the Four Seasons. I sensed you were very unhappy," I said confidently.

"Well, I sure was happy to see you, even if I had to see you with another man," he quickly came back with.

"Thanks, but I mean you personally. Something was very wrong back then, wasn't it?" I asked.

"See, you get me. You knew it. You sensed it. I want to see you, I have to see you and talk to you face to face. I've wanted to open up about all this for some time, but I don't have anyone I can really let it all out to. When can we get together? I think we can both use a little entertainment and a lot of old friendship," he knowingly declared.

"Just say when and where," I quickly responded.

We made plans to meet in Chicago in a few days, and they couldn't have passed quickly enough. By now it was summer, and I was pretty tan. Just after my divorce, I decided I needed a change, and I dyed my hair several shades of blonde. It was a pretty good look for me, and up against a tan and a gorgeous white summer backless outfit that showed off my extra slender, toned body, it looked extra good. Doc picked the restaurant we were to meet at, a great steak and seafood place in an upscale western suburb. I was very familiar with it. As I pulled up, I noticed the VALET sign, so instead of hunting for a space, I pulled up. The valet approached me, and as I expected to hear a simple "Good evening, ma'am," my mouth dropped as he added, "You're here to meet with Doc, right?" *What?*

"Yes, I am," I cautiously replied, "but how did you know that?"

"Doc said that the most stunning lady in the world will be arriving around seven, so when I saw you pull up, I knew it had to be you." He laughed. "I was told to put your car right next to his," he said, indicating there was no need for a ticket. Now I ask you, is that a major move or what?

As I entered the restaurant, he was there waiting to greet me, arms extended, ready to hold me, and we embraced in a long, tight hug. No kisses, just held each other cheek to cheek while he whispered how good it was to see me, how fantastic I looked, and how much he loved the blonde hair.

"You take my breath away, Contessa," he whispered lovingly as he kissed my hand and held it tightly. He motioned to the hostess, who led us to "his" booth. Not tucked in any corner, but very front and center, which was very *Doc*. He had to be noticed wherever he went. It was not arrogance on his part, just so effortlessly his style.

Over champagne, appetizers, and a fabulous dinner, we caught up on our children, what changes I'd made in my life, and what my plans for the future were. He talked about his practice, which was expanding, his travels, various new medical situations he was involved in around the world. I'd always had great admiration for his passion toward his work. He made me want to be a doctor too! I always knew that his first love was his practice. I think it was obvious to everyone but him that he would never be satisfied that he'd done enough. He was quite gifted, knew it, and always strived to go further. He just loved talking about his work, so I let him go on. I wasn't about to make any inquiry into his marital status. I thought it best to let him bring it up in his own way.

Finally, he did. He told me of the growing gap between him and his wife that had become undeniable and increasingly unbearable to live with. They were in two different places, and she gave up trying to participate in his world. He did not hesitate elaborating on his marital situation. Although I was surprised in all the details he disclosed, I didn't like what I was hearing. I was sure that the specifics of my recent divorce opened my eyes and enlightened me to the mind of high profile men who are surrounded by "yes" people and ass kissers. They become so full of themselves they sometimes forget who was there with them to help push them up as they were climbing their proverbial ladders. In short, Doc was a medical superstar, and he had the personality to match (and maybe even exceed) his renown genius. He was written up, honored, awarded, and paid homage to by many all around the world. Then he went home to his wife, living a typical suburban-wife-and-mother lifestyle, who had the nerve to put on a few pounds while raising three kids. Yes, there appeared to be a few other issues, but nothing I would say was insurmountable. I think I shocked the shit out of Doc when I interrupted him.

"Okay, I get the picture, Mr. High Profile Doctor. You got it all. Granted, you worked for everything and now you want to enjoy the fruits of your labor, which is fine. But your wife has a different role in caring for you, your children, and your home. While you want her to be all up in your ass, let me hear how compassionate you are to what *her world* is like on a day to day basis, or is that too boring for you?"

His mouth dropped. "Whoa, I wasn't expecting that!" he said sheepishly.

"Doc, I get that you're married to your work, but you're also married to flesh and blood. Her job as wife, mother, and caretaker for the family is 24/7. I can relate firsthand to how tiring it is, willingly giving all the pieces of yourself away every day. But how long can anyone go without getting something back in return? How do you think she feels seeing you come home in your tuxedo when she's probably in pajamas, whipped from housework, kids, their schedules, homework? What do you do to make her know she's appreciated?" I took a big chance with all that, but I didn't care. I wouldn't be able to look myself in the mirror if I didn't say what I believed needed to be said, what he needed to hear.

Doc sat there silently for a moment. He smiled while outlining my face with his soft, well manicured hand. "Nobody else I know would have the guts to say those things to me but you. You're right. I guess maybe I have been a bit of a schmuck."

"You think?" I threw back at him. "Did you ever stop to think that it's kind of hard living with a superstar when you are nothing but a mere mortal? I think you should try building her up a little for a change and then see if that positively affects some of the other things you're whining about," I finished.

"Jeez, I knew tonight would be memorable, but I never thought it would be because I got my ass kicked!" he joked.

"And I never imagined that I would be saying anything like this to you, but trust me, my friend, you need to hear it. Doc, you know I adore you. What I'm saying to you is somewhat because of how much you mean to me. I'd like to think that we are the best of close friends more than anything else, ever, and if you accept that, you have to accept that I will always tell you what I think and not just what you want to hear. Secondly, after what I just went through with my own marriage, I'd like to think I've learned a thing or two. A marriage is about two people. I mean, there are likely to be other issues involved, but please be fair and don't be afraid to come down to earth and live on her level once in a while."

"I think you just saved me a bundle on a marriage counselor," he joked.

"Good, then you can afford more champagne," I joked right back.

We talked more about some of the other issues, possible solutions, as well as music, dancing, travel, kids, and so many other things, till we eventually got the signal that the restaurant was closing. Do I have to mention how impressed I was when Doc asked the hostess to signal the valet to bring both our cars around? As we exited the restaurant, there was his Mercedes parked next to my BMW. "Look, even our cars look like they belong together," he said as he walked me to my car. He held me tight as he said goodbye, and I could have easily let him kiss me. I wanted him to so badly, but no, that wouldn't be right. Not now and not this way. I really did learn something (hang on, it's on the way), and I had to prove it to myself. Only if and when his issues were worked out. But for now, it would have to be fine with me for Doc to be my dear and very special friend.

"You're an extraordinary lady," he told me as he stroked my long blonde hair, "and you have your own place in my heart." He kissed my forehead. Nobody I had ever known had made me feel as special as he did. Ever.

We said good night and drove away. At the onset of the evening, I guess I really didn't know what to expect. I was just so excited to see Doc for the very first time in a personal atmosphere, and alone, where we could experience each other as friends. Okay, I admit I wanted to look as hot as I could, and maybe that was wrong of me, but I should get points for not allowing it to go in a direction that it very well could have, right? I replayed the night all the way home, and as I drifted off to sleep, I was fine with everything. Our relationship was now defined. Special friends who, I admit, were playfully sensual with each other. But that was all it was…just play.

We enjoyed telephone conversations now and again. We were never at a loss for words or general interest in each other and always had so much to say. Doc seemed to work things out with his wife, and they were back together, but there were still a few problems, which we discussed frequently. I honestly wanted him to work it all out and never cut him any slack or coddled him about his ways. He told me I kept him in check. He was great for my ego too, which needed a little boosting.

I began noticing certain feelings and cramping that were the warning signs of a cyst and/or tumor, and I knew it was time for a checkup. Of course, now that I was on my own again, I went to see Doc. I know a lot of people couldn't have that personal relationship with the doctor that examine, operate, and treat them, but I was completely okay with it. My feelings were confirmed, and I had several cysts that had to be removed. Even though I still maintained a home in Michigan, I would have the surgery in Chicago, at one of his hospitals. Most of my family and friends resided there, so if there were any complications, they would be around to help me. I arrived at the hospital with my long blonde hair picture perfect, flowing softly around my shoulders. Although no makeup was allowed, I gave myself a facial the night before, to make sure my sun kissed skin was glowing. Okay, I put on a little lip gloss, so what! Known for my taste and fetish for glamorous lingerie, I wore a beautiful silk lounge set. Several nurses commented favorably. The same nurses also communicated that they were under strict orders by Doc to make sure I was kept extra comfortable. I was surprised of the open attention he actually drew to me through his staff. Doc came in to see me before they started prepping me, first of all not to ask, but to tell me what music he selected for my surgery. He chose to get the Led out. *Sweet!*

Doc predicted a simple surgery; he advised me that it shouldn't take more than two hours. My brother and cousin were in the waiting room. One hour passed. Two hours passed. Three hours passed. As my relatives sat in the waiting room, suddenly Doc appeared and first apologized for them being led to the wrong waiting room on the opposite side of the hospital. He then explained there were several complications they discovered as surgery was underway but he had them under control. Surgery would go on for another few hours. It wound up taking over five hours in total, but the outcome was positive. I was taken to my private room, arranged by Doc, one that the nurses called the VIP room. We Italians are full of traditions that even extend to hospital stays. You must take good care of the caretakers, so they in turn will take good care of you. I became conscious a day and a half later, to find my relatives had overtaken my room with homemade Italian goodies, beverages, and lots of conversation. They showered the nurses with these Italian delights, which the nurses loved, and my room seemed to be the happening place. The minute my eyes were open, the relatives gave me an account of what the complications were and what all had transpired.

After surgery, Doc addressed my family, filling them in on what the surprise complications were and what he did to address them. Doc assured my family I would be fine, but that I would be hospitalized for a few days. As with all surgeries, you never really know exactly what you're dealing with until you are on the table, and this time they found a few surprises and had to remove a lot more than anticipated. Doc ordered me this private room and instructed the nurses to be extra attentive as I was his "special" patient. Because he had operated on me so many times, he knew I would be asleep for quite a while but came in to check on me several times before he left for the night. He popped up the first few times while still in his scrubs. My cousins expressed they went weak at the knees while he talked to them, conveying the situation. To this day, I still laugh out loud when another cousin of mine remembers blurting out to Doc, "I think I need my uterus checked." Doc's attention to me and charm to them left the relatives with their tongues wagging. Doc came in one more time to check on me with his suit on, telling the cousins he would be leaving for dinner but would stop back later. My older brother was also there; by now, he was in a state of shock over Doc's attention. The year before, my brother was deathly ill due to an allergic reaction to medication. He was hospitalized for almost a month and nearly died. It was difficult to pin the doctors down for discussion, and it was my personal threat to them that made his doctors finally sit down and answer my brother's questions regarding his situation. Needless to say, my brother was a little agitated seeing me get all this attention.

"For Christ's sake! I was fucking dying and we had to threaten the fucking doctors to get them to sit down just talk to me, and this doctor is falling all over her!" my brother exclaimed.

My cousin joked back, "She's a lot cuter than you are," which made my beloved brother laugh along with them.

While I lay there sleeping off the anesthesia, the family remained in my room. Around ten o'clock that evening, Doc appeared again, and they all practically passed out when he announced, "I just wanted to check on her one more time before going home." He also offered that he had to leave town in the morning (jeez, this was becoming a pattern!), but rest assured, the nurses would take very good care of me and he would be calling. *No, shit!* my family thought. Realizing I was out for the night, they all finally left. The nurses, I was told, were a little sad that the party was over, as they got a big kick out of having my family there, listening to the banter and wisecracking. I woke up the next afternoon to a party going on in my room with all the cousins and several nurses. They enlightened me as to the complications and what all had transpired medically, and as soon as the nurses were out of the room, the cousins were fighting one another to tell me how crazy they were about Doc and what he had done, that he had to leave town but he would be calling me. Within one day of my family meeting Doc and witnessing his attention, the family phone lines were burning up and news of the entire episode spread throughout the entire family. It was such a juicy gossip story that when I returned home to recuperate, they asked me about him before even asking me how I was feeling. Cheap thrills, I guess!

Before long, I was feeling fine and it was time for my follow-up visit to Doc's office. Even though it was routine, he always had his assistant present in the room during his examination of me. Having him do what he needed to do could have been construed as a little awkward, given our circumstances, but his assistant was there and our private, corny joke was that we never needed to become intimate because he'd already been in and out of me a million times! After this exam, while still in the presence of his assistant, he told me he needed to discuss a few things and I should meet him in his office for consultation after I dressed. I couldn't get dressed fast enough.

With one hand closing the door, he reached out to me with the other, pulling me to him and hugging me. "I can't tell you how I've missed you. I've thought about you so often, and it was hard not to call you. I have to see you. I made sure that you were my last patient so I'm free to leave now. Meet me for dinner, will you please?" he asked, almost begging.

Of course, I would, so off to "his restaurant" we went, in separate cars. The valet at the restaurant remembered me, as did the staff, and I was quite flattered. We talked about my condition, and I was confident it was all fine, especially under his care. We laughed over my hilarious family and their antics. He commented that the nurses loved our traditions and had a blast with the cousins. He apologized for having to leave the next day, but another joke between us was his leaving town was somewhat protocol by now. I expressed my appreciation for all he had done and told him I'd have to work very hard at repaying him.

In a voice that could melt butter in the snow, Doc pierced me with his chocolate eyes that were no longer sad. He commanded, "Be with me, just be with me, Babes." Doc reached for my hands and held them tightly in his.

Whoa! I certainly did not expect this at all and was so overwhelmed I couldn't speak. Tears immediately welled up in my eyes.

"I can't talk about this here. Can we go?" I asked.

We left the restaurant, got into his car, and drove a short distance away. I just had to get out of there for fear everyone would hear my heart pounding. I could have easily said, "Sure, let's go someplace right now," but what stopped me were the lessons that now I knew I finally learned from my last marriage. I certainly wanted him, but if I were to have him at all, I wanted it to be the right way. How torn, how hard it was to be alone with him and refuse him. But not now and not like this. I was glad there was no time to plan out my response; it just came pouring out.

"Doc, I adore you, and yes, yes, yes, I want to be with you. I would be lying if I didn't admit imagining us being together in all sorts of ways. But I can't be the other woman. I can't, and I won't."

He gave me the short rendition of what was going on in his marriage, which didn't seem good, but nonetheless, he was still in it.

"Doc, you have to make a decision," I managed to get out with tears pouring out of my eyes. "Let me go tonight and you take time to think things through. You will always be in my heart no matter what, but I can't let it go further while you officially belong elsewhere. If I hear from you, I'll know that you cleaned your house. If I don't hear from you, no harm, no foul. After all, we agreed that our relationship was first based on friendship. No explanations will be necessary if that's the case. Agreed?"

Thankfully, the gearshift of his Mercedes was in between us, for if his purposeful embrace weren't enough to have me surrender completely, the kiss that followed surely was. *Oh, shit!* His lips were beyond what I had imagined over all these years. They say that a man's sexual prowess is in his kiss. His was more than perfection; it was the epitome of lovemaking all by itself. So intense was his kiss that I feared the orgasm I experienced from it would never happen again. Powerful. What a tug-of-war was going on in my head! Here I was, on the receiving end of the most passionate, delicious, and seductive kiss I'd ever had. What could I do but respond in kind? It seemed to go on forever. The pleasure I was feeling at that moment did not stop me from realizing the reason not to let it go further was more about protecting myself than giving in to what would please us both. No, not this way. And so with all the self-control I could muster, I pulled away and, referencing the gearshift, said, "Well, that's one instrument you haven't used on me yet." We both burst into laughter. When in doubt, I can always rely on my famed and unparalleled sarcasm to get me out of an I-don't-know-what-to-do situation.

"Babes, we have to be together," he whispered to me ever so softly.

"That ball is in your court," I managed. "But I'm going to leave you now." I gently kissed him on the lips again, then on his cheek, got out of his car, and walked back to mine without looking back to watch him drive away.

Summer ended without word from Doc, and I was okay with it, assuming he was trying harder at his marriage. But as we approached winter, there came his usual out-of-the-blue phone call, always making me stop dead in my tracks. He called to first tell me that he and his wife were officially over, second to tell me that he had confided the entire story of "us" to one of his closest friends, who urged him to go where his heart was, and thirdly, to ask if I would accompany him to his annual "guy" skiing trip to Aspen. That was one hell of a phone call!

Rewind a minute, Doc. I needed details, which he readily provided. In response, I was sorry—but yet not really—about his marriage and asked how his kids were handling it. I was dying to hear what was said to his friend and what the reaction was. He told his best friend that he was taken with me the minute we met so many years ago and we had developed an extraordinary bond over all these years. He went on to disclose it had undeniably grown into more and he could no longer suppress his feelings. Music to my ears. Lastly, while I was so flattered that he would want to take me to Aspen, I would not go. Now, here's a real lesson that I learned the hard way from #3: In a situation like this, of course you'd want to bolt right into his arms and go anywhere he wanted, as we imagine the man of our dreams whisking us away to live happily ever after. Stop it! Wash those stars out of your eyes! When you've just ended a relationship, the best thing you can do, in my opinion, is to take some time for yourself alone. Take it slow, get your thoughts straight, get settled into your new single life, and clean your house before you invite someone else to join you in it!

I thanked Doc for his invitation but said that I wouldn't go with him. This would be a great opportunity for him to relax and hang out with the guys by himself. I'd look forward to hearing from him upon his return. Doc responded that while he was disappointed I wasn't going with him, he agreed with and applauded my philosophy, reiterating how he admired my good sense and strength. He called me from Aspen, and our conversation was just as playful as ever, but a new dimension of sensuality surfaced in our conversations. I was seeing a side of him I had only imagined was there, but aaahhhhh, did I dare to dream I'd ever experience it? After Aspen, he had several business trips in a row to attend. By now Doc was world renowned and spoke on his medical procedures and theories around the world. His calls were frequent, and each one became more loving, as well as provocative, and I believed him to be sincere. He wondered why, though, I never called him. He provided me with every single possible way to reach him at any time. No, I didn't need to do that. He could call me me when he had time, I reminded him. He praised me for urging him to spend some time alone, emphasizing that on this series of meetings and speeches, he certainly was, but was realizing the merit to it. He repeatedly confessed missing me, and we were definitely on track to rendezvous upon his return.

That moment couldn't come quickly enough. We would meet at the Four Seasons, as Doc expressed he wanted to return to the night he saw me floating down the escalator. Doc made all the arrangements in his usual exemplary manner. He reserved a lavish suite with a private dinner waiting for us. What followed is extremely difficult to put into written words, but I will try. Sit back, close your eyes, and imagine the most tantalizing, spellbinding lovemaking session you've ever encountered either personally, on paper, or on film. It begins ever so gently, so very softly, with electrifying kisses so beguiling, some soft, some long and lingering. Kisses that start on your lips and caress every inch of your body, going south, until they land on the most perfect spot. Suddenly you are on an island, in the hot sun. You are lying in a soft, grassy nook, under the sun. The soft breeze is caressing you, just enough to leave little goose bumps all over your silky body. Those goose bumps slowly become throbs, and your heart begins to beat faster. And the faster your heart beats, the more your body pulsates, faster, harder, and back down to that spot. And you begin to feel as though the ground you are lying on is trembling—and maybe it actually is—louder, louder. Then you realize there is a volcano near and bits of lava begin shooting out, slowly at first, but soon bubbling up faster, louder, and your heart is beating in time with it until you cannot stand it anymore. You feel yourself screaming, screaming just as the volcano is erupting and spilling all over the meadow you are lying in. And then you lay there resting as the ocean tide splatters a wave over you. You feel a slight chill, but you lie there panting, trying to catch your breath, and the ocean's wave consumes you like a blanket of serenity. Your body is floating, and you are in a lingering state of calm. You cannot speak. It's a tranquility that you've never experienced before. It's heaven.

Two hearts, two souls, and two bodies that hungered and longed for each other all these years feasted on each other with more rhythm than an orchestra. Adventure, exploration, and explosion, one after another, filled every inch of that Four Seasons suite with complete harmony, rapture, and perfect bliss. Never had either of us experienced such a night of passionate lovemaking. It was worth the wait too, even better than surgery we joked. However, as much as I basked in the glory of the bond we had now sealed, I was well aware that we could never become a conventional couple, or at least not for a very, very long time. I knew his children and his practice would always be first, and I was fine with that. Truly, I was. My confidence in his feelings for me was enough, and to be very honest, I never even thought about anything more between us than just knowing those feelings existed and being together whenever we could, taking all the pleasure we could of just being together. I knew in my heart it would never be on a regularly structured basis; that just wasn't Doc. Although he couldn't or wouldn't readily see it, I knew that the last thing he needed at this point was another commitment. He needed to be free. I have learned in my lifetime that allowing someone their freedom will actually keep them closer to you. Okay, I was willing to go on that theory. It worked for us. Although Doc's schedule kept us from seeing each other for periods, we were always in touch via phone, and we each went about our lives. There was a special place in our hearts for each other, and we were both happy being able to run with our careers, knowing we were there for the other.

Fast forward a few more years. My beloved Little Contessa was stricken with a life threatening disease. As we learned of her diagnosis, our worlds were crushed in one day. Of course, the first thing I did was call Doc and explain the situation. This was not the first time he came to my rescue, and his serene manner took over my hysteria and he immediately mapped out a strategy for what needed to be done in addition to what he would do to expedite the process. Doc called several of his associates to confer on what the best possible solutions would be. Never in my life did I need support and comfort as I did now, and Doc was there to give it to me. His tender and compassionate approach to calm me down as well as assure me that things would be rough but would eventually work out positively was exactly what I needed to hear. No other person could make me believe it more than Doc. My faith in him personally as well as professionally, plus the tone of his voice and the words he chose to soothe me, gave me strength in order to deal with the depth of this situation. All I could do now was pray. Doc called back within a few hours, telling me that Sloan Kettering would be calling me soon for discussion on immediate treatment and I was to relay everything to him afterward.

The worst of Little Contessa's medical crisis went on for several years; however, today we have every reason to believe that her health is and will remain good, with continued observation by professionals. That's a whole other story that is far more significant than any of this, but it became part of my relationship with Doc, and therefore relative at this point in his story. The next few years were consumed and devoted to my daughter and doing whatever I could to aid her situation. I couldn't mentally focus on anything else; however, Doc checked in with me regularly, always offering his medical counsel as well as personal comfort and support, which I wanted, needed, and greatly appreciated.

Years later, a young couple I knew was having trouble conceiving a baby. When I became aware of this information, I immediately recommended them to see Doc and offered to call him for an introduction of them and their situation. The first thing he inquired about was Little Contessa, who by then was well on her way to full recovery. And of course, he then wanted a full update on me. We took care of the young couple and then got down to business. By this time, I was confident enough of Little Contessa's good health, and I had purchased a new condo in a hot downtown Chicago area. Music to his ears. We met, resumed our passion, and this time, Doc vowed he would not let me go. My birthday was approaching, and that same weekend, he had to speak at a conference in Las Vegas—what better way for us to celebrate my birthday than a weekend in Las Vegas, he concluded. *Vegas, here we come.*

Doc was already there, attending to his business affairs when I arrived. He arranged for a limo to pick me up and called me just as we were on our way to the hotel to make sure I was on track. He was about to begin his speech, which would be followed by several meetings that would take a few hours. We would meet afterward, and the rest of the weekend would be mostly ours. He pulled some strings to get us dinner reservations at the most sought after restaurant in Las Vegas. All I had to do was get settled in, enjoy the spa amenities that he arranged for me, and primp myself for a night on the town with the most dashing, dynamic, and romantic fella in Vegas! I was definitely up for the task!

Upon checking in to the suite, I quickly unpacked the carefully planned attire I brought along for this soiree, our first trip together. How thrilled I was knowing that Doc made every detailed, first class arrangement and that I would delight in every second of it. I would enjoy the massage waiting for me then powder, press, and curl myself enough to dazzle the shit out of my man upon his very sight of me. Following a masterful massage, I returned to our room and began preparing for the evening. Formfitting black satin cigarette slacks with a soft velvet pattern, topped with a sculptured black velvet top laid across the bed to be lightly misted with the cologne Doc went nuts over. Red suede platform pumps, red jewelry to accent the outfit, giving it a very high class, sophisticated look. Now, just a few curlers in my hair to fluff it up and jump into the steam shower, followed by the special body scrub, mist, and lotion that guaranteed extra silky skin. I wrapped myself in the giant hotel robe that covered me like a cashmere blanket. *Aaahhhh, this is heaven,* I thought as I sank into a lounge chair with a huge smile on my face, basking in the glory of all this.

Snuggled in the massive chair, I still felt the smile on my face as I turned, opened my eyes, and glanced at the clock. "AAAAAAAGGGG- GGGHHHHHHHH! OH MY GOD!" I screamed. What I thought would be a moment turned out to be two hours, only minutes before I was supposed to meet Doc. How the fuck could I fall asleep when I'd been dreaming about being away with Doc for years? *I don't fucking believe it!* You never saw anyone move so fast; lightning didn't flash this quickly! With my hands trembling, I managed to get some makeup on, pulled out the curlers, throwing everything everywhere when the phone rang. I didn't even have to hear his voice to know it would be Doc.

"Are you ready, Babes?" he asked.

"Uhhh, yes, I was just walking out of the room," I managed to get out as I was trying to pull my clothes on.

As I ran to the elevator and all the way down in it, my head was flooded with excuses for why I was so late. I was notoriously punctual, especially for Doc. Like a linebacker running for a touchdown, I dashed through the crowd of the hotel. Admittedly, I am a lady who likes to make an entrance, but sprinting through the lobby of one of the most exquisite hotels in Las Vegas while dressed to the nines, plus being in four inch heels, was not what I was shooting for.

It didn't even occur to me to stop running even as I approached the spot where we were to meet. I just kept running. People were jumping out of the way before I even got close to them, and before I knew it, there was an open view of me that led right up to Doc waiting patiently, with his hands crossed behind his back, whistling. What broke his nonchalant look was his outburst of laughter at the sight of me running in his direction.

"What the hell are you doing, you little nut?" he said, laughing.

I can't imagine what an idiot I must have looked like, especially to him, who was never, ever out of place. I was trying to collect myself, panting, almost in tears. A million excuses ran through my mind instantaneously, but suddenly the real story began to spill out, and the more I talked, the more he laughed, and in no time, I was laughing along with him.

"Hey, Babes, why are you so upset?" he asked.

Quivering voice, fighting back tears, I explained that I just wanted everything to be as perfect as I knew his plans for our time together would be.

And right there in the lobby of the Bellagio, in the middle of so much activity, he held me in his arms, caressed my hair, and gently whispered in my ear, "Babes, it's just me, it's just Doc. I've waited years for you, what's a few more minutes?" as he kissed me ever so passionately. Although the hustle and bustle of Las Vegas was all around us, the world consisted of just the two of us as long as his lips were upon mine.

We were soon to realize the best laid plans were meant to go south, as we discovered our reservation was gone because we were so late. It was incredibly difficult to get reservations at Prime, and I felt horrible about losing ours. Doc's attitude was "Hey, we're in Las Vegas, where the possibilities are bound only by lack of imagination! So let's get this party started," Doc enthusiastically commanded. And start we did—champagne here, champagne there, champagne everywhere! An appetizer here, an appetizer there, and so much champagne, I hadn't a care.

We were making the rounds and sampling the best of what Vegas had to offer. Remembering it was my birthday, Doc insisted on a stop in a lavish jewelry store. If I weren't floating already, I sure was by the time we walked out. Upon leaving the jewelry store, we sparkled all the way to a restaurant that Doc was familiar with. I never flinched at him selecting the cuisine, but this time he ordered Kobe beef burgers. I was surprised at this, because he knew I didn't eat red meat.

"First of all, have I ever steered you wrong? And second of all, we're gonna eat these burgers and scram—we're gonna need this protein. We've got things to do," he whispered to me with a slight slur, which I heard for the first time and found so very charming. Doc loved teaching me things, and I was an eager pupil. His description of the Kobe burgers as well as his feeding them to me was ever so sensual. Enough so that our server practically asked us to leave and get a room. *Okay, fine, we're outta here! C'mon, Doc, let's scram!*

I don't even remember going to our room, but trust me, I remember in finite detail what went on when we got there. The pinnacle of lovemaking, the culmination of all that was wild, tender, and titillating all wrapped up in one experience. We left our imprint all over the suite, as if to mark our place in time, leave behind a tone, an example for all the lovers that would follow in our footsteps here. There was a melodic flow to every welcomed and receptive move we made. There were no hesitations, no awkwardness, every intense gesture executed in utter perfection, and this golden night taught me exactly what perfection truly was. The spender of this night proved the theory that you lose all sense of time in Vegas, for this night seemed to go on and on and on…

The intensity in which our feelings were acted out was almost too much for either of us to bear. I didn't need to hear Doc tell me how much he loved me and wanted me, but it sure did send me flying higher than I ever imagined. I can still feel his breath and hear his soft voice tell me of all the places we would travel to as I accompanied him to various lectures and conferences around the world. I can still feel him caress me, pet me, while painting his idealistic picture of our future together with me "on his arm." Listening to Doc's rendition of what was to come hurled me into a chilling flashback. What he was describing would have been, should have been music to my ears. But instead, warning lights and sirens went off in my head that literally scared the shit out of me, snatching me away from this harlequin romance novel moment. What I was hearing was a replay of my last marriage (be patient, it's coming!). While I believed his words to be heartfelt and surely meant to please me, they sent me back to a place I had previously been, a place I vowed never ever to allow myself to go back to. I thought, *Thank you, God, that finally I learned to look at a romantic situation without those rose colored glasses on.* Finally, my vision was crystal clear. In this very moment, I realized that had it not been for all my past mistakes, all the tears I shed from love gone wrong, I would never have finally allowed this lightning bolt of reality to strike me.

A type A personality, Doc was a wild mustang who could never be corralled, although he didn't see himself that way. While Doc was an emotionally committed person, any partner of his would have to understand his need to be free. To love this man and keep him, you'd have to be comfortable and content knowing your relationship would be void of responsibility on his part. What made Doc most happy beyond his work was a "c'est la vie" lifestyle, which included only the best looking, best dressed, best connected, party pleasing crowd with a high level of savoir faire. Doc craved the spotlight, needed the drama and crescendo of a weekend such as this one. That was the allure for him. The regular and the mundane simply were not in his repertoire and would bore him to death. I realized that long ago and was fine with it. One of the reasons our time together was so special was that it was limited; it was uncertain and always impromptu, thus more appealing. To have his committed heart was enough for me; we would each then be able to go on with our lives yet be together whenever our schedules allowed. If that momentum was consistent, so would more weekends such as this. I believed Doc's tender whispers of our future were genuine and what he truly wanted, but they were also naive. Succumbing to his dreamy visions would require me to relinquish the person I was, the life I'd worked so hard to build for myself. Giving in to Doc's tender whispers would gradually have me become the wallpaper in his office, giving way to the very same monotonous life that he just left, which would inevitably lead to him looking for new stimulation. No, thank you!

Those were the thoughts that prevented me from falling into a blissful sleep, to dream of riding off into the sunset with my knight in shining armor. I drifted off, all right, but right into reality, which would ultimately have a better ending.

While rolling over, Doc happened to glance at the clock. He was to speak at a breakfast meeting shortly and was mortified to see the time. Never having seem him frazzled, I found it hilarious to watch him running around, trying to put himself together, with an obvious hangover, in order to get there quickly. I would have paid money to hear him pull this speech off, but deep down I knew he would. Harried as he was, he still came to kiss me goodbye, promised to call me later, and ran out the door. I lay there thinking, thinking, thinking, reveling in the magic of last night, yet trying to ignore the cloud of reality that was looming over me. Try as I might to discard it, I had to acknowledge its presence. As much as I loved him, as much as I wanted to be with him, I could not, would not allow myself to surrender who I was, what all I'd achieved, and all the things I still yearned to do, only to merely be Doc's arm candy. Not that he ever made me feel that way; it was just my version based on past experience. I knew I would have to be the strong one in order to maintain my integrity and hopefully sustain a beautiful love affair that had no real or positive hope of going past this weekend without dragging my heart through the mud. It was completely up to me to save myself. That said, my next move would be critical. I decided it would be best for me to walk away now, right now, before he got back and persuaded me to stay, which would be ever so easy for him to do. Leaving now would allow me to keep the memory of this weekend in the dearest pocket of my heart as well as maintain the virtue I'd most definitely lose if I stayed. Surely, this would be better than to play it out the way Doc told himself was an actual possibility and (a) give up myself, which I had just fought so hard to regain, and (b) plunge into an unrealistic relationship that would die a slow and eventual death, possibly never equaling the sublime of this weekend, and (c) preserve my edge.

After a long chat with myself in the shower, I was convinced that leaving now, before Doc returned, would be the right thing to do, because face-to-face, he would easily melt me and I would be lost. As I was packing, Doc called. I listened halfheartedly as he described how he mastered his speech despite his pounding hangover, what other medical notoriety was in attendance to hear him, the meetings that would follow after this breakfast that would tie him up for the rest of the day. Careful to keep my voice strong and hide the tears that were now streaming down my face, I managed to tell Doc I was leaving. Long pause.

"What do you mean? Why?" he asked.

I surprised myself as I spontaneously concocted and blurted out a story about receiving a business call that required me to get back home right away to address this business issue of significance. I added that if I hurried, I would be able to catch the next flight. Doc tried to persuade me not to go, and the more I emphasized this was such an important business issue that had to be addressed, which he was not hearing, the more I realized leaving was the right thing to do. Although Doc inquired about and took an interest in my business affairs, they would always be far less important than his. Doc expressed his disappointment, that last night ranked among the best in his life, and that he couldn't wait to be together again. He went on to describe his thoughts on our next adventure, that he would call me soon because right now he needed to get back to his associates. We would chat about it later, and he reminded me that his upcoming travel schedule was pretty hectic but hopefully we'd be able to work something out soon. *No problem, Doc!* Typical Doc. He closed by saying all the right things. Safe travels, stay gorgeous, and a few other things I couldn't even hear because the tears were pouring out of me like a faucet and all I could concentrate on was muffling them.

Yes, difficult as it was, leaving was the right thing to do, and while I never looked back, I basked in the glory of this weekend for a very long time. The more time that passed, the more confident I was in my decision to leave. In my heart and my mind, leaving allowed me to freeze a moment in time to keep perfect forever, as opposed to torturing myself over something I could really never have the way it should be. It was the only way this fairy tale would end happily.

A true love will definitely last a lifetime. Doc was the love of my life even though our relationship didn't play out the way most people would want. Funny thing, though, after leaving, I never once cried over him until I wrote this chapter. The warmth and comfort he provided me kept me fulfilled through many a cold, lonely night. For a very long time, I accepted Doc as he was. What's that old saying? "See him as he is, love him as he is." And I did. He was someone who loved the idea of being in love and being committed to a high caliber lady (as he put it) without actually having the responsibility of being a committed partner. I finally learned, after all these years and so many mistakes, to put my head before my heart and realized that while Doc could fulfill many a fantasy, I still had wants, needs, and desires that were part of the real world, my world, that he could never satisfy. Most importantly, this relationship taught me that you should never have to forfeit your whole self or your dreams in order to find true happiness in a relationship. An honest, healthy, and true relationship would and should merge your desires with those of your partner, or at least allow for both to be appreciated.

I loved him over many years and love him still, but I've learned that I love me more, and that's okay. We have playfully and affectionately kept in touch, but never as we were in Las Vegas. I've made a conscious decision to put myself first, never ever to give up who all I am to satisfy somebody else's needs. That would be the best way to conserve one of the most memorable relationships I've ever had. However, as I write this chapter, I'm aware that I am finally letting Doc go completely and saying goodbye, for good.

The Rock Manager

Honesty really is the best policy!

I saw a plaque in a store once that I just had to buy. The plaque read, "Truth is like surgery. It hurts but it cures. A lie is like a painkiller. It gives instant relief, but side effects can last forever." I love this analogy, as it reminds me of what my dad always said regarding the truth. He always told us, "You might not like the truth, but it'll keep you on the right path and enable you to make the right decisions." The point of this chapter is, Would you rather be hurt by truth or happily deceived by lies? I've always been a put-your-cards-on-the-table kind of person. Just say what's necessary, deal with the situation, and move on. Done. In doing so, you eliminate drama or the need for it. The truth keeps life neat, clean, and simple. Move on positively with your life. Unfortunately, much of the drama and dishonesty in the world revolves around relationships. I think that because people have a hard time with their real feelings, they try to avoid confrontation, or they just find it easier to lie, make up stories, say anything to get what they want out of a relationship until they don't want it anymore. *Ugh,* it could all be much easier if people would just be honest about their feelings, their partners, and their lives. I didn't think I'd ever meet a man with that simple character trait, the straightforward, easy, and uncomplicated human ingredient that is missing in so many: pure honesty. Nope, didn't think a man of such caliber existed. A man of sheer integrity, virtue, and just plain goodness. Not until I met the *Rock Manager*.

I was well into a few years in my position at Citibank. By this time, I was a middle level manager, accountable for the banking instrument sales of the northeastern section of our country. I managed sixteen states, having individual sales reps within that region, each with their own territory. We worked on the design, implementation, and execution of marketing programs to boost sales of our products as well as create special programs and contests for additional customer (and sales) perks. Adding to my existing customer base and addressing needs current customers had were among my priorities. I interacted with principals and decision makers of banks and bank holding companies within that region of our country. I loved my job, as once again I worked in an extremely aggressive environment, in which I thrived. Our offices were new, plush, and very contemporary. I had wonderful coworkers, whom I so enjoyed working with, team oriented professionals, both within our own territories and interterritory. We shared our experiences regularly. "Your issues today could be mine tomorrow" was our philosophy, and regular brainstorming and sharing was part of our culture. I attended the American Institute of Banking and received the required certifications. I also engaged in many other management courses and training programs that would allow for growth and development within the organization. Although our offices were in Chicago, the sales managers were required to report to New York City now and again for various trainings and meetings or to work with our counterparts there. The Big Apple was within my sales territory, so I had other reasons for going there a bit more often as well.

I traveled now and again throughout my territory, making presentations to either prospects for new business or existing clients for various promotions or special marketing programs. In addition, there were semiannual regional sales meetings for our individual sales teams plus our company wide annual sales meeting, which was always held at top notch resorts, usually on the West Coast. Consequently, I got to see and experience the best parts of our country, traveling first class, staying at the finest resorts and clubs. My regional team and I were consistently in the running for sales of the month, quarter, and annual awards, usually placing among the top three categories. The awards were usually an extravagant gift of some sort accompanied by a monetary bonus. Once again, I loved this fast-moving, aggressive company and was absolutely crazy about the position I held there.

I was in an extremely happy place. By this time, I was divorced from Will and joyfully living alone with my Little Contessa, who had blossomed into a beautiful, poised young lady in high school. I was so proud of her. She was a model teenager, well liked and respected. A good student, she always received glowing remarks from her teachers and counselors. Little Contessa was very active in student government. Her organizational, planning, and execution skills were pretty sharp, as demonstrated in her student council role. She was key in arranging a variety of student functions and platforms. Quite popular, Little Contessa had tons of friends, both male and female, who all had wonderful things to say about my little girl. Friday evenings, I usually took Little Contessa and friends out for some sort of recreation. Roller skating, movies, or maybe just out to eat, and the evening often ended up at our house with a loud, festive pajama party. High-spirited, exuberant, and loud as they were, I never minded having the girls spend the night, and I tried to spoil them all with treats and, of course, a super duper breakfast in the morning. There were a few girls Little Contessa was especially close to whose parents welcomed her to stay at their house overnight when I had to travel occasionally. I really appreciated that, which was another reason I didn't mind having the weekly PJ parties. I enjoyed having a way to reciprocate the help that I received, plus I really welcomed having the girls in the house.

This was a pleasant time for both of us. I was rid of Will and all the drama that came with him. I was blissfully happy and in good standing with my company and position, earning a salary I only could have dreamed about, plus wonderful benefits and fantastic perks. I wasn't dating, nor did I ever even think about it. My main focus and attention was to Little Contessa and work. I kept a part-time waitress job for extra money, which went right into the college fund I had set aside for my daughter. It wasn't a question of if she would or wouldn't go to college. It was only a matter of where. Not attending college was not an option for her. Life was good for us.

Little Contessa developed a flair for fashion at a very young age, and her love of flipping through *Vogue* or any other fashion magazine grew with age. I was an expert seamstress and, through the years, made many a party dress. She would tear out a page and, with those large puppy dog eyes and irresistible smile, playfully ask, or tell me, I'm not sure, "Mommy dearest, wouldn't you love to see me wear this to the next dance? You're so good I know you can copy it exactly! I need it in two weeks!" And off to the fabric store I would go and buy everything I needed to copy her choices to the tee. By her junior year, there were many more events planned as fundraisers, most of which were planned by Little Contessa and the other student council members. I wanted her to be the best dressed there, and if I had anything to say about it, she certainly would be.

On a Saturday night one early spring, I was home sewing, putting the finishing touches on a gorgeous black taffeta dress for Little Contessa's upcoming dance. Accompanying the simple dress style was a bolero jacket, for which I designed a pattern of beading and would spend this night applying. Little Contessa and I shared a sense of style. Keep the main piece uncomplicated and classic, and put the wow factor on the accessories. The beadwork was all done by hand, something I was really good at. It was very relaxing, and I enjoyed it. I cruised the cable TV channels, hoping to find a good movie so I could plop on the sofa and begin my hand-beading. To my surprise, an HBO music special was starting in a few minutes. It was the fortieth anniversary of Atlantic Records, and all their recording artists were being featured live at Madison Square Garden. Just what the doctor ordered! I've always been a lover of all kinds of music, but I must admit it's classic rock that gets my heart pumping. This HBO special would feature a wide variety, especially some of the oldies I loved. I watched and I sewed, stopping for moments at a time when either a favorite band or song was featured. Finally, the highlight of the evening would be coming on next. One of the most renowned rock 'n' roll bands of the seventies (and one of my personal favorites!) was about to take the stage. This band, who do not need to be named, defined rock in the seventies and thereafter. Front man and lead singer's voice has been called one of the greatest in the history of rock 'n' roll. This legendary band had not performed together in a decade, since their celebrated drummer passed away. I had to put the sewing down. I couldn't miss one single beat!

When their set was completed, I, along with the entire audience, both live and those riveted to their TV screens as I was, jumped up and screamed, "Encore!" They still had the magic, mystifying sound and the hypnotic, haunting vocals of the lead singer (ahhh, let's call him Richard). Richard was present and accounted for. By this time, Richard had moved on, formed a new band, and treated the audience to a few of his new sounds, new songs, and new group. They were about to begin a tour in the United States. They rocked it. This segment of their performance alone would have ensured a successful night of entertainment. With that, the special ended, and I continued on with my sewing. I went to bed that night feeling as though I had just been to a fabulous concert. Having been so thoroughly entertained that night, I slept like a baby.

The next morning, I had to pack for a few days in New York City. It was time to present my quarterly sales reports and projections to headquarters. Normally, I looked forward to this quarterly meeting, as I usually traveled with one of my teammates, but I would be making this trip alone and wasn't happy about that. When you travel with a counterpart or team member, you can better enjoy the after hour time, especially in such a grand city like the Big Apple. It's somewhat lacking to dine in even the most fabulous restaurants by yourself. While I dreaded going alone, I was excited and prepared to present a very positive account of my sales figures for the quarter ending and a favorable forecast for the quarter ahead. I packed for myself and got Little Contessa ready to spend the time at her friend's house until I returned. My flight wasn't so early that Monday morning, so I enjoyed making my little teenager a nice big breakfast before she headed off to school. Just as I finished cleaning up the kitchen, my corporate limo pulled up and whisked me off to O'Hare Airport. Yes, it was first class all the way with this company. The rationale was not about opulence; it had more to do with efficiency and saving money. The corporate mindset and dual purpose of a limo was that if a limo picked us up at their massive corporate discounted rate, the company would save on the exorbitant airport parking fees plus ensure getting us there on time. No argument from me, that's for sure! I just reveled in a limo ride—pick me up, carry my bags, and transport me to the front door of the airport. Hence, my travel style had clearly developed!

Many flights were delayed this day, and I soon realized mine was not taking off on time. *Ugh,* I just wanted to get on with it and get this trip behind me. We had a choice of flying into three airports, JFK, LaGuardia, or Newark (New Jersey). After some experience, my personal choice became Newark. It was a smaller airport, baggage claim was a breeze, and the drive into New York City was usually pretty smooth, as long as you timed it right. Once my flight finally took off, I got settled in and had a nice little siesta that lasted most of the ride to New Jersey. As usual, we landed and I collected my bags without incident, and there was my limo driver, waiting with my name clearly written on his hand sign. I usually took the same outbound flight, and I guessed that the delay in takeoff put us closer to late afternoon rush hour traffic; therefore, the ride into New York City was going to take forever. My assumption was correct. No matter where in the country you may be, no matter what you view as "heavy traffic," I can promise that you've never experienced a real traffic jam until you've been in New York City rush hour traffic! We moved at less than a snail's pace, and I sat there gazing out the window, definitely void of a smile on my face. I was starving and realized the highlight of my evening would be to eat dinner alone in my hotel room.

As we approached Manhattan, the traffic literally came to a dead stop. We were at a complete standstill, not moving at all. A sea of limousines and taxis surrounded my limo. My head went back and forth, gazing out at the river to the right and back to the black limo's and bright yellow taxi's ahead and to the left, hoping something in the scenery would change. In the lane directly to the left of me was a long black stretch limo that was just about side by side to mine. Its sunroof opened, and out popped the glorious and distinctive golden mane of Richard, who had just entertained me two nights ago on the HBO music special. He rose from the sunroof, with camera around his neck, taking pictures of the river. He faced me in order to do so. Flashback to my days at Four Seasons, where we were trained never to call attention to celebrities, and my tenure there allowed me to be quite comfortable speaking to an assortment of notoriety. They're just people like you and me, right? I immediately instructed my limo driver to open my sunroof, stood on the seat, popped my own nicely coiffed head out, and gave an extremely nonchalant "Hello!" to Richard, who was still taking pictures.

"Well, hello, yourself, gorgeous!" he replied.

Ahhh! Did I mention that I could listen to that British accent all day long? It didn't dawn on me that across the lane was Richard, the voice of the rock gods. All I knew was that I was bored to death and I saw a face I could talk to! What the hell! Seize the moment, right?

"I saw your reunion the other night. You were amazing, and your new band is awesome. I loved hearing your new songs," I told him.

"Thank you, Miss," Richard said politely. "Were you here at the show?" he asked.

Did I mention that I could listen to that captivating British accent all day long?

"Oh, no. I was home, watching on HBO," I answered.

"And where is home?" he probed.

"Chicago," I proudly responded.

"Ah, Chicago, my kind of town, Chicago is!" he sang playfully.

"Mine too, but I must say New York City is pretty special as well," I offered.

"Yes, it is. What big plans do you have while you're here?" Richard asked.

"I'm here on business, so basically just meetings," I sadly responded.

"What is your business?" Richard continued probing.

"I'm a manager for Citibank," I proudly told him.

"Wow! You're a banker! And such a pretty one at that," he teased.

"Well, I work with banks, I'm not actually a banker," I corrected him.

Seeming to let that comment go right over his head, Richard continued an easy and frisky conversation with me. As traffic was a gridlock, he asked me where I was staying, how long I would be here, what my dining preferences were, how I liked my job, if I traveled often, and several get-to-know-you questions. We even talked of banking business a bit. I felt as though I was having lunch and chatting with a new friend. When he asked what my plans for dinner were, I explained that since I was here alone and spending all this time stuck in traffic, I'd just have dinner alone in my hotel room. That led to a most unexpected question.

"Well, then, you're such a likable lady. How would you like to go for a ride and have dinner with me?" Richard asked.

"I'd love to, if we ever get out of this traffic nightmare. Where are you having dinner?" I asked.

"In London," said Richard with a poker straight face.

"You're joking," I gasped.

"No, actually I'm not. I'm on the way to my plane, and I'd like nothing more than to scoop you up and show you the sights of London. You're very interesting, and I think we'd get on quite well, don't you?" he both stated and asked.

Richard had an extremely relaxed manner about him; he seemed to be a playful and gentle soul, and a genuine one at that. I wonder how many, if any, ladies would have forsaken their responsibilities and just went with him. Tempting as it was, though, I had to refuse. "Your offer is very enticing, Richard, but I'll have to decline. I'm meeting with my superiors early tomorrow, so I'm afraid dinner in London is out of the question," I laughingly replied.

Richard continued asking me questions about my work.

"Such dedication is commendable, Contessa! I love meeting passionate people—I mean in regard to your work, of course! You make the world of finance sound stimulating," Richard went on in his own very mischievous way, and my laughter at his impish grin seemed to encourage him on. "Passion and stimulation—are you sure you won't reconsider?"

I felt as though the ear-to-ear smile on my face would never go away.

"There are no words to thank you for your very tempting offer, as well as for this very entertaining conversation, but it looks like we are beginning to move along," I said sadly.

"A pity for sure, Lady Contessa, but I shall hold our delightful chat in memorable esteem," Richard said as he blew me a kiss and traffic moved along.

I came back down inside and settled into the supple leather seat, replaying what had just happened. I found myself laughing out loud, thinking of what my friends would say about this encounter.

I finished out the week in New York, dazzled my managers with my presentation, who responded favorably, and returned home confident that big commissions and a bonus were heading my way.

It's always hard to get caught up after you've been out of the office for a few days, so the following Monday, I arrived quite early. Soon my teammate Erica popped her head over the cubicle wall.

"Hey, Contessa, how was New York?" she cheerfully asked.

"Go get your coffee and have a seat. I've got a story for you!" I announced.

Erica was a sweetheart of a gal, and we got along very well. While I managed the northeast section of the country, she managed the southeast portion. We worked together on various projects and took over for the other when either of us was out of the office. We enjoyed the company of each other and often had lunch together. I told Erica of my weekend sewing, watching the HBO special, leading right into my limousine encounter with Richard.

"Oh my God! This would only happen to you! Richard has a concert here in a few weeks. My husband and I are going. You've got to come with us!" Erica demanded.

"Richard's new band is playing in Chicago? Where? When?" I asked.

"Memorial Day weekend at Poplar Creek," Erica declared.

"Okay, so how come you know about this and I don't? You don't even watch MTV! Where and when did you get your tickets?' I asked.

Erica went on to explain that her husband, Mike, was a public relations manager for Atlantic Records!

"You never told me that! No wonder you're always going to concerts!" I screamed.

Erica elaborated that she purposely didn't tell people that because they'd had their fill of folks hounding them for tickets for various concerts, knowing that Mike could get them. Mike was responsible for all advertising, promo radio spots, group entertainment, etc. for groups performing in Chicago. Erica insisted that I accompany her and Mike to Richard's upcoming concert, that my encounter with him in New York was an omen, that something wonderful would come of it. We would have great seats, and afterward, Mike would take us backstage for me to see Richard again.

"Sounds great, Erica, but two issues. First of all, there's no way in hell Richard would remember me. I mean, the guy must meet a zillion people every day. I don't think I left that big a stain on his brain. Second, I'm sure there's a crowd of groupies and girls hanging around his band, and you know that's not my style. I'd love to see the concert, but please don't feel obligated to bring me backstage," I said.

Erica gave me a "don't worry about it" gesture, and we carried on our chat with work related things. We ultimately did solidify our plans to go to the concert and dropped the whole backstage part of it. In my mind, we were going to what was promised to be a great concert, having awesome seats (compliments of Mike's job!) on the start of the summer season. I was looking forward to hanging out with Erica on a personal basis and meeting her husband, whom I'd heard so much about.

I told the whole story to family and friends, who all agreed with Erica. More would come of this; it was a prelude to an adventure. I made myself a perfect outfit for an outdoor summer concert. Short summer skirt with a matching off-the-shoulder top. Black, of course, with just a little sparkle. On the surface, I was very cool about it all, but secretly I was hoping something exciting actually would happen, just as the others predicted. Mother Nature gave us the perfect weather for concert day, and as promised by Mike, we found ourselves in ideal seats. The opening act was Cheap Trick, an awesome band from Rockford, Illinois, with several great hits to their credit. Their latest single, "The Flame," was currently at #1. So it was a bonus to get to see them as well, and they did not disappoint. Richard and his new band took the stage and took us all hostage. They were amazing.

After the first encore, Mike instructed Erica and me to follow him. I really just thought we were leaving to beat the crowd. No, we were heading backstage. Mike was intent on making sure Richard saw me. I was a bit uneasy about it and expressed my feelings. Mike insisted, and besides, he was required to check in with Richard to ensure all went well with the PR Mike put together for him. I didn't want to seem like a groupie. Mike dismissed my concern as we plowed through the crowd. We got backstage, and Mike knocked on the dressing room door. To all our surprise, Richard himself answered it. He took one look at me and screamed, "It's *you*, the banker! I told all my mates of our encounter. I told them all about Lady Contessa, the lovely banker I met!" Richard exclaimed all this as he grabbed my arm and dragged me into the crowded dressing room. Mike had an all access pass, so he and Erica were right behind me.

"Guys, remember the pretty banker I told you about? Here she is! Isn't she a love?" Richard introduced me to his band. They were all kind of shy and soft spoken, but truly very nice. This was their first trip to the United States, and they confessed to be a bit overwhelmed. Richard knew Mike from previous PR situations, and Erica jumped right in to the how-do-you-do's. He couldn't get over the coincidence of Mike being his Chicago PR manager and Mike's wife being a coworker of mine. In an instant, we were all engaged in a lively conversation. Richard and I veered off to a corner, away from the roadies, record label people, and variety of other folks related to the tour. He wanted to know all about my personal and professional life, developing winning strategies, while he related it all to managing his own business affairs. Richard was quite impressed with me and wasn't shy about letting me and everyone in the room know it. Before long, it was time to leave. Richard informed me that there was a private party being held for him and the band at the Park Hyatt Hotel, downtown Chicago.

"Contessa, you are such an intriguing woman. You must come along. You'll ride along with me in my great big stretch limo," he said, laughing.

"I'd love to, Richard, but I drove here and can't leave my car," I reported.

"Then you'll meet us at the hotel. Wait here and I'll get you a pass," Richard instructed as he called his road manager over and delivered the instructions. In just a few minutes, Richard handed a pass over to me, along with his secret code name to deliver to the doorman at the hotel upon my arrival. It was like a covert operation, all so very exciting. How could I refuse?

I don't know if I drove or floated down the Kennedy Expressway, heading toward the Park Hyatt, but given this late hour, there was no traffic at all, and before I knew it, I had arrived. I gave the private pass Richard provided me to the doorman, who confirmed its authenticity, informing me the valet would take my car and another doorman would show me to the private party area. Richard was keeping an eye on the door, and once I entered, he immediately scooped me up, introduced me around, and offered me all the fineries the Park Hyatt had to offer. We found ourselves tucked in a corner, having the most enjoyable conversation about everything under the sun. Richard was a huge fan of my beloved city, which was a huge part of our conversation. Did I happen to mention that I could listen to an English accent all day long? He loved the detail I gave him about the various areas I was so familiar with. He then surprised me by suddenly asking if I'd like to go for a walk. On this magical summer night, I couldn't say no, and soon we were walking in the breeze along Lake Michigan, discussing everything from the trials and tribulations of working parents to the tortures of relationships.

So here I was, walking along the lake with the voice of rock, and I was having a flashback of my Four Seasons days. Celebrities are people just like you and me, and I was discovering that this legend was one of the most heartfelt, kind, and engaging men I'd ever known. Get past, if you can, his mesmerizing good looks, infamous golden mane of perfect locks, hypnotic blue eyes, dimpled, twinkling smile radiating mischief, tenderness, a "whole lotta love," and you'll find a tender, authentic, spirited, and fascinating teddy bear. He surely was a tall cool one! No wonder his celebrated lyrics were so relevant; they came from real life. Richard didn't just talk—he listened. He was so invested in our conversation you'd think I was the celebrity! He could have stayed at the private party being held for him, surrounded by prominence and many ready to blow smoke up his ass, but instead, he didn't hesitate to show his interest in me, admitting his intrigue was in never having met a "regular" and self sufficient lady who was successful in business, particularly a single mother. Consequently, he wanted to know every single thing about me, my work, my life. We found common ground in coming from scant beginnings, finding a passion, and rising above. He loved people. He was deep. He didn't appear to say things he didn't mean in order to appease his audience. He was something I was doubtful that existed. He was a good man, an honest man, and a man I hoped would become a good friend.

As all good things must come to an end, as we sat on a beach front park bench, watching the sun come up, I announced I must be going home. Richard asked me to stay on at the hotel, that he would get me a room. I declined and explained that as we discussed, I was the mother of a teenager who had a sleepover at a friend's house and I was to pick up in just a few hours. I thanked him for his gracious offer as well as for the entire night.

"Well, this surely won't be the end for us. I'll be in touch, love! There are surprises in your future," Richard promised. He took my phone number, and we hugged long and tight, ending with a soft kiss on the cheek.

I don't remember ever actually seeing the sun rise, but I clearly recall such a beautiful sight that morning as I drove home. I couldn't believe I wasn't even tired. I made some tea as I got home, sitting alone on my sofa. I had a few hours before I would pick up Little Contessa from the sleepover. I needed time to replay the events of the last twenty four hours. I wouldn't necessarily say it was a surreal experience, but more of an out-of-body adventure. Did I really just spend the night as a guest of the greatest voice in rock, or did I just meet a great guy and make a new friend? The reality was both!

As the story of my encounter spread, the response was the same from all. "This would only happen to you, Contessa!" I got a big laugh out of it. I tucked it away in my mental memory bank, with a special note of what a fun, fabulous experience it was, and that was the end of it. But it didn't take long for me to find out that no, it wasn't. The fun continued as phone conversations with Richard became a regular part of my week, with lots of information exchanged, particularly in reference to Brett, Richard's manager and very, very close friend. Richard spoke of Brett with the highest regard, no matter what the context. Brett had an extensive business background, was involved in the production of a multitude of entertainment projects, and managed several other high profile bands. Who? you might wonder. Well, let's just leave it at several high profile bands! Richard told me all about Brett, their relationship, what admiration he had for Brett's managerial ability, his business acumen, his quiet authority, and most of all, his honesty. Richard admired, respected, and loved Brett, considering him as family. Richard explained that Brett had been separated from his wife, who was described as a stark raving mad woman, for several years. The relationship between Brett and his wife had been strained for a very long time, that the wife had her eyes on someone else, a real tangled up drama pit that Brett preferred to stay away from rather than to deal with at all. Brett was a workaholic and poured himself into this tour, consequently avoiding the situation. Richard was confident that if Brett met the right woman, he would clean his house and unfinished business, get a divorce, and be done with the whole shit show.

"Brett sounds fabulous, and I'd love to meet him. But I think you know by now I'm a private and drama free person. I don't want to get in the middle of anything, particularly if it would cause problems for him, or even you, for that matter," I told Richard.

"Just be your charming self, Lady Banker, and leave the rest to me," Richard said with that mischievous voice of his. I envisioned his impish grin as he uttered this directive to me.

Our conversations covered a wide range of subjects, including schedules, and before I knew it, I was on a plane headed for Louisville, Kentucky, to meet Richard, the band, and Brett! Upon arrival at the magnificent Adams Mark Hotel (gorgeous hotel, screamed of Old South grandeur), I was handed a note from the front desk clerk. It was from Richard: "You must be famished, meet us in the café." How thoughtful was my friend! I didn't know who the *us* was; I reveled in just being there, so I kind of didn't really care. I threw my bags into my room, did a quick check in the mirror, fluffed up my hair a bit, and off I went to the café. There was Richard sitting at a large round table for eight with some of the band. It was obvious that he was quite in charge of this band of merry men, as his laughter (does anyone remember laughter?) and happy-go-lucky demeanor filled the room. I was greeted by all in a friendly, welcoming way, and I immediately got caught up in the current events of the tour and how well it had been going. We all loved the South and marveled at the hospitality of its people and the splendor of this magnificent hotel. Suddenly, Richard announced, "And here comes the boss!" Without even turning around, I knew he must be referring to Brett. A bit of a chill ran through me, as if a premonition of excitement just became reality. And then I heard him speak.

I've always had a "thing" about voices. They can allure me, deter me, or even leave me cold altogether, depending on their sound. I am always drawn to a voice of distinction. Dean Martin had a smooth, velvety voice that was all his own. Frank Sinatra's voice was undeniably his trademark. Get the picture? Then I heard Brett, and he went right up into that same distinguished category. A calm and gentle yet solid, disciplined, and strong voice of authority. A voice that melted me the second I heard it.

"This must be the banker I heard so much about," Brett said. "Hello, I'm Brett," his creamy voice announced. Before I uttered one syllable, he held my hand in his and kissed it ever so gently. Would it be plagiarism to say he had me at hello?

I began, "I'm delighted to meet you, Brett! I'm—"

"Oh, I know who you are, Contessa," he interrupted. Turning to Richard, Brett continued, "But as complimentary as you've been, Richard, you didn't place enough emphasis on her beauty." Brett turned back to me. "I must apologize for having you meet me after my morning run. I'm sure I look frightful! I didn't realize you'd be arriving this early."

Frightful? No way! Standing before me was a tall, extremely fit, very handsome man, toned and tan, with silvery hair and piercing green eyes that immediately had me under his spell. A man who, after jogging several miles in the intense Kentucky heat, was too cool to even sweat! It was instantly apparent that Brett walked and spoke softly but carried a great big stick, his authority unquestioned and irrefutable. Frightful? Hell no! Anyone who didn't "get" Brett the moment they met him was either blind, stupid, or both.

Brett did not sit down and join us. "Is your room satisfactory?" he asked.

"Oh, yes, thank you, Brett. It's lovely," I responded.

"Good. We want to make sure that our lovely banker has everything she requires at her disposal. Enjoy your lunch, Contessa, and relax a bit. We have a special and long evening planned that I'm sure you will enjoy," Brett advised.

And relax I did. While I basked in the comfort of this elegant Southern hotel, there was a knock on my door. It was a messenger delivering a lovely card from Brett, indicating how pleased he was to finally meet me, asking me to be in the lobby at six o'clock sharp. I took extra time to polish, press, and curl myself, making sure I was absolutely breathtaking and irresistible for my host as well as the evening festivities. A final check in the full length mirror assured me I achieved my goal. The outfit I chose for this evening was a buttery soft strapless leather dress with a matching jacket. The light melon color accentuated the golden brown tan I worked hard on these last few weeks, which blended nicely with the platinum highlights I put in my long, thick hair. Small simple earrings and my trademark ring on the right hand were the only accents I added. Completely confident and in check, I left for the lobby. I mistakenly pressed the M (for mezzanine) button in the elevator instead of the L (for lobby), which took me to a level one floor above the lobby. It was quite a serendipitous mistake, for I suddenly found myself at the top of a long winding staircase, looking down at Richard, Brett, the band, and security. I was Scarlett O'Hara at the top of the Twelve Oaks staircase, staring down at Rhett. I mimicked that scene to embrace the incredible wonder of this moment. Richard caught sight of me and blew me a kiss and a wink, a sign I was certain indicated confidence that his matchmaking efforts would prove fruitful. Engaged in conversation with the security team, Brett noticed me descending the stairs and just walked away from them in order to be at the foot of the last step just before I got there. I was the belle of the ball, being greeted by a prince. It just didn't get any better than this!

Brett was an incredible and exceptional man. Strikingly handsome and fit, he was a man of tranquil authority. His manner was so easygoing and engaging no matter what the circumstance or company he was in. A kid from the streets of London, he combined the artful, razor sharp savvy abilities one can only acquire while hustling in a hood with the acquired intellect of a worldly scholar. While he didn't hold academic degrees, Brett was an avid reader with a wide range of literary preferences. He could quote Gandhi or Shakespeare at any moment and render the quote relevant to the issue at hand, thus making his point in an artful way. I was mesmerized by him. The blend of his company with Richard's playful and fun loving nature was a party all by itself. The boys in the band were delightful as well but a bit shy and on the quiet side, as this was not only their first tour but, for some, also first time ever away from home. Our hosts brought us to an absolutely sublime restaurant that opened our eyes to the best of Kentucky, with delicious tastings, delightful dinner music, and Old South warmth that could charm the devil himself.

Ever the commander in chief, Brett designated the seating and placed me in between he and Richard. The conversation throughout dinner was an ideal mixture of Richard's whimsical exchanges with all of us as well as the local servers and restaurant staff, the band's curiosity and wonder of America, as well as a few more intimate moments between Brett and me. We enjoyed both frisky and serious chatter, and I took pleasure in having my point of view being embraced. While the fun and laughter continued throughout the night, Brett and I managed one-on-one discussions. We shared our humble beginnings, with each of us delving into the other's story in great detail. Brett and I probed each other on our goals, ambitions, successes, what drove us, and found several common denominators. We discovered that we had a great deal in common. We were both business driven. We shared the philosophy that success is wonderful but you must remember to give back to show gratitude for whatever you're blessed with achieving. Brett elaborated on his philanthropic endeavors, declaring his actions-speak-louder-than-words philosophy. You need to get involved and show you care about these needy entities. He could not stand anyone being bullied and was always the champion of the underdog, as was I. And what really touched me the most was his feelings about honesty, in absolutely everything about life. We each confessed to be workaholics, had a great love of movies and, of course, music.

After dinner, security took us to a local jazz club, where a few old jazz notables awaited us, literally bringing tears to Richard's eyes. There was lots of musical interaction between Richard, the band, and the locals. A good time surely was had by all.

Arriving back at our hotel, I thanked Richard and Brett for a fabulous evening and said good night to the boys. Brett extended his hand out to me. "I'll see you to your room, Contessa. I want to make sure you get in safely," he said. I was so high from this night, but what do I do now? I don't even remember the conversation as we headed toward my room—too many thoughts racing through my mind. Brett was an absolute dream! Could I fall into his arms and melt like butter? Absolutely! But the voice inside my head reminded me of the many times Brett told me how unique I was. Both he and Richard consistently told me I was exceptional in many ways, that I was unlike any lady they had ever met. Okay, then, as we walked to my room, could I assume that the "expectation" would be for me to invite Brett in? Most likely, so that's exactly what I decided I absolutely would not do. We arrived at my door, and before I could say anything, Brett covered me with his arms, kissing me in a way that was true to his nature, soft and gentle yet powerful. And I responded in kind. *Whew!* The man knew what he was doing!

"I'm delighted to have had the pleasure of your company this evening, Contessa, but I'd like it to be a bit more private next time, please," Brett said softly as his green eyes pierced me.

While melting fast, I thought it best to conjure up some of my trademark sarcasm as the best way to break his spell. "Right! I think next time we could leave security at home."

We both broke out in laughter, followed by another juicy, lengthy kiss.

"I want you to get a good night's sleep and dream of possibilities," he whispered.

"Possibilities?" I asked.

"Yes. Possibilities of you and me enjoying each other," Bret answered.

I stared deep into those seductive green eyes of his for a moment, kissed him softly on those luscious lips, and without saying a word, turned to enter my room. *Wow!* As if he were watching me, I did exactly as I was told, snuggling into bed and thinking only of him and this magical night. I didn't have to fall asleep to dream; I lived one tonight.

I woke up to find an envelope on the floor, slipped under my door. It was a card from Brett. The front of the card showed two cartoon little piggy characters passing each other by, with the caption "Not too long ago, we were perfect strangers," and the inside showed the two characters playing together, with the caption "Now we are perfect friends!" Brett also included all his personal contact information, including the name of his secretary and agenda for the next month, asking me to coordinate my schedule with his for a dinner date, only this time it would be just the two of us. Unbelievably, I wasn't surprised—deliriously happy, of course, but not surprised. I immediately got the feeling this was how he would handle things, direct and to the point. Right up my alley.

I met Richard in the dining room for breakfast. He was waiting for me with that impish grin on his face, ready to hear my thoughts on Brett. He was such a sweetheart, and the more I got to know him, the more I realized he was an old fashioned romantic. But first things first.

"What a fabulous time I had last night, Richard! You planned an amazing evening. Thank you so much," I said as I embraced him with a big hug and kiss.

"Cut the bullshit, Contessa! You know what I'm dying to hear!" he demanded.

"Ah, yes. What do I think of Brett?" I giggled. I also teased him a bit by slowly pouring and preparing my coffee.

"Come on, then, let's have it!" Richard playfully demanded.

"Richard, the man literally oozes everything any woman could ever want. I don't even need to get to know him better to know how genuine he is," I finished.

Richard did a little happy dance in his seat. "Fantastic! I just knew the two of you would get on well. Then you'll be staying on with us? You'll come along to Alabama tonight?"

"I can't, Richard. I'm keeping my flight that leaves this afternoon. Remember, I've got a teenager at home. One night away on a non business trip is all I can do," I finished as I nibbled at the breakfast goodies Richard ordered for our table.

"See, that's what's so intriguing about you. Most women would toss everything aside and jump all over Brett, me, the private jet, and everything else that comes with us. But not you. You're grounded and responsible. Does Brett know you're leaving?" he asked.

"Yes, I told him." I went on to explain the card I received. "I was hoping to see him at breakfast to say goodbye."

"Hmmm, for someone who just met the man of her dreams, you don't seem that excited. Come on, now, talk to your old Uncle Richard."

"Excited? How could I not be? *Excited* is an understatement! But I'm also practical. Richard, I barely slept because I kept pinching myself over all this. You, our friendship, this trip, and now Brett. He's absolutely amazing! But, Richard, I am not a jet setter. I can't keep up with the lifestyle you both lead. I'm a single mom with a career, and they take priority over everything. I'm being realistic, and I just don't see how this can work out," I confessed.

"Contessa, listen to me. Nobody is closer to Brett than I am. He never would have given all his personal information to you if he weren't truly interested in you. He's a man who makes things happen. Give him a chance. You're in New York often, and so is he. Do what he asked, keep in touch with him, and just go with it. You won't be sorry, you'll see," Richard advised.

"Thank you, my friend," I responded as we hugged and kissed. I was just about to get up when Brett entered the dining room.

"I thought I'd find you both here. What have you two been plotting now?" Brett asked.

"Good morning to you, brother Brett! I've been bestowing some pearls of wisdom on our dear Contessa. And now my work is done, so I will leave you two alone for a proper farewell," Richard joked as he reached over to me for a hug and kiss. "Bye, darling girl. We'll see you again soon." Richard left.

"I was hoping to see you before you left today, but I didn't want to ring your room and wake you," Brett said.

"Great minds think alike, I guess. Those were my exact thoughts," I told him.

"I couldn't let you leave without knowing I'm serious about seeing you again. I'm a decisive man and know what I want when I see it. I don't have time for games. I'm sure it's difficult juggling work, travel, and a teenager at home. I can see and fully respect what a hands-on mother you are. But I hope you'll keep an open mind for opportunities and some adventures for us, Contessa. Let me know that you want it, and I'll make it happen."

Brett's words mesmerized me.

"Yes, Brett. I want it," I responded, stroking his hand, hoping those few words would seal the deal, followed by a soft kiss. "But now I have to be going in order to catch my plane," I reminded him.

"Ah, yes. I've arranged for security to take you to the airport," Bill advised. Of course, he did, and once again, I wasn't surprised. He walked me back to my room and called security to come pick up my bags. Once they arrived and he directed them, we shared a very passionate kiss. It was almost as if he purposely waited to, true to his nature, express his quiet authority, indicating to security that they would be seeing a lot more of me. I would learn this was his unique style.

I was so glad that Little Contessa was old enough to share this experience with me. The trip, the excitement, and the new man. She seemed very approving, which was important to me. I, lovingly, got the feeling she welcomed the idea of me in a relationship, for personal reasons, of course, but also so that some of my helicopter mom time would be eaten up! As I gave her a blow-by-blow account of it all, I found myself realizing that I had given Brett a green light to a relationship. I decided I would review my work schedule and see if I could rearrange my next scheduled trip to New York sooner, in order to coordinate with Brett's being there. The itinerary he gave me included a few stops in Chicago, as well as cities near it. I began to think that yes, maybe this could work. The gods were aligning, as I found it relatively easy to modify my schedule. I was in fact able to reschedule my next trip to New York City, citing the reason was one of my largest clients (whom I had already rescheduled with—shhh!) having to change our meeting date. At this time, we sales managers were presenting the summer promotions to clients. I won the sales contest last year and was on track to win again this year, so anything to accommodate my clients was perfectly fine with my manager.

When Brett called, I was able to review my newly adjusted schedule with him. I was anxious not only to talk with him (ohhh, that voice!) in general but also to hear his immediate, thrilled response to my rearranging my business affairs in order to accommodate his agenda and allow us more time together. I was very relieved to hear his genuine excitement in my doing so. Brett was quite complimentary in my cleverness to achieve the desired results and thus allowing us these couple of days to enjoy. He promised that I wouldn't be sorry for the extra work. Brett was ready with dinner plans for us and also invited me to his condo, which overlooked the west side of Central Park. In two weeks I would meet him in New York City, but I made it very clear I had reservations at the Parker Meridian, my favorite hotel. In his business, I was sure Brett encountered plenty who were ready to jump on his (and Richard's) bandwagon. I wanted him to know I was in no way one of those, was very emphatic about my independence, and liked it that way. I was convinced, and he demonstrated he was impressed by that. In addition, I thought it was a good idea to not be so available, so "in his face" all the time, to shine a light on my life as well as his. Once our schedule plans were coordinated, we enjoyed a lovely conversation of a completely personal nature. We exchanged our work worlds and a wide variety of other things that allowed for us to know each other better. Conversation was fluent, diverse, and fun. It also became a regular part of my evenings, regardless of where in the world Brett was.

News of this budding relationship spread like wildfire throughout my family and social circle; however, I kept it quiet at work. The only person I confided in was my coworker Erica, who knew about Richard right from the start. I knew I could trust Erica to keep it quiet. She was a loyal friend, a levelheaded and professional gal who fully understood it would not be a cool thing to advertise in the extremely conservative environment we worked in. We did whisper about it over lunch and did our best to maintain our composure over the whole thing.

Two weeks couldn't have passed any slower, but finally I was on a plane headed for New York City. Accompanied by my kick ass summer promotion presentation, I reviewed it in detail while on the plane, and by the time we landed, I was ready to dazzle my top client. Rather than roll out one blanket promotion for all clients, I developed a knack for creating personalized strategies tailored for each client based on their sales trends, region, and staffing structure, which included mini awards for managers as well. I incorporated promotional emphasis, mini competitions for products of ours that were in somewhat of a slump, with incentives for the bank tellers. Increased sales for these products grew my commissions. The results were bonuses for managers and tellers in my customer branches and increased financial reward for yours truly, not to mention my star rising among my counterparts. Win, win, and win. The presentation went extremely well, and the client signed off on it, which meant a big commission for me as well as a huge jump start to winning this quarter's sales competition. Between this triumph and knowing I'd be seeing Brett in just a while, it was difficult keeping my feet on the ground!

Adhering to Brett's instructions, I called him as soon as my workday was complete and I returned to my hotel.

"Is the excitement in your voice due to a successful business meeting or for having dinner with me?" Brett playfully asked.

"I guess you'll have to wait and see," I teased.

"I'll give you an hour to rest and one more to get out of your suit and into something elegant, and I'm certain it will be worth the wait," Brett commanded.

I just love a man who can take charge in such a smooth and chivalrous manner.

"See you in two hours!" Brett finished as I laughed out loud.

While I wasn't sure exactly what Brett had in mind for our evening together, I knew that he admired polished sophistication. In his world of rock, he saw too much of women in jeans, T-shirts, and the likes of "rock clothes." A lady dressed in a stylish, classy, feminine way was a turn-on to him. That said, I packed a few choices that would accommodate whatever or wherever we went Brett's plans took us. The final decision was a backless black silk slip dress hugging me in all the right places, which was worn with an elegant tuxedo jacket. One small crystal pin—a scorpion, in honor of my zodiac sign—on the lapel was the only jewelry worn this night. After all, you have to have a little sparkle!

I made it down to the lobby just as Brett's limo pulled up. Quite the gentleman, Brett got out of the car to properly greet me in the lobby. I melted as I heard that velvety voice of his utter "You are a vision" as he gently kissed my cheek. A sidebar note: yes, the mere sound of his voice turned me into butter, but I never let Brett know it. Yes, I graciously accepted his compliments, but without gushing and "gooing," letting him know how he made my knees knock! Nope, an endearing thank you, a sincere smile, or a light brush to the cheek and a soft kiss was just the right response.

Brett escorted me to the car and conveyed the evening's plans. "We are off to the 21 Club for dinner, and afterward, we'll head to the Palace Theatre to see *La Cage aux Folles*. I was pleased to learn how you love the theater. Nothing beats the London theater, but New York is a close second," Brett joked. "I've been wanting to see this for some time and glad to see it with you."

I was delighted.

An extravagant, fabulous dinner followed by a phenomenal Broadway play would have been quite enough for one night, but Brett had more in store for us. We exited the theater, and there waiting for us was a carriage driver right out of the *Cinderella* fairy tale book, holding the door open for us to walk right in and be seated in this very plush carriage.

"You must see the beauty of the city under the twinkling stars over Central Park West," Brett advised me. "I need to make the best possible impression so that none of those wealthy bankers you interact with steal you away from me," he finished.

I turned to him ever so closely, stroked his cheek, and said, softly assuring Brett, "Don't worry your pretty little head over that happening."

His response was a long and passionate kiss. I felt as though he put everything into that kiss, as if it were do-or-die, a kiss with power that overwhelmed me. Brett then directed the driver to take us to his condo.

There was champagne on ice waiting for us, Brett indicating that he left certain instructions for his housekeeper before she left for the evening. As the tour of his condo continued, I could see the housekeeper addressed all of Brett's directives. The fireplace was crackling, the curtains drawn to show off the sparkling stars in the sky, and an ever-so-soft hint of roses was in the air. I made myself comfortable on the oversize, sumptuous leather sofa while Brett poured our champagne. We toasted to a beautiful evening, perfect in every way.

"Not quite perfect yet," Brett whispered. "No, still a bit to do."

Brett took me in his toned, muscular arms and kissed me with a flawless blend of passion, expertise, and command. He picked me up and carried me into his vast bedroom, carefully laying me on his massive four poster bed, which was covered in rose petals, kissing me all the way. *Oh, so that's where it's coming from!* I thought.

"Contessa, you are a very beguiling woman," Brett announced, "and I'm falling in love with you."

It takes quite a lot to leave me speechless, and this admission was almost too much for me. I felt my eyes fill up with tears. "Oh, Brett, really? Is that true?" I cried.

"Why are you crying, love? Does the thought of my being in love with you bring you to tears?" Brett joked.

We both laughed.

"Tears of joy, silly. I just can't believe I'd be that lucky. And well, it's a little scary to me," I confessed.

"Believe it, Contessa, and I promise you'll never have reason to be scared," that lyrical, powerful voice of his assured me. I did believe his promise. I trusted Brett was not a man who would say these things so frivolously. His words left me completely surrendered and enthusiastically responsive to his very mastered, tender, and virtuoso seduction abilities. Brett made love to me in a way that, at least up until this point, I had never experienced. As in everything else I saw him put his hand to, Brett was a maestro in the bedroom as well. No surprise.

After a marathon lovemaking rollick, we lay there blissfully wrapped in each other's arms. If I were a smoker, I would have been puffing away!

"Like I said, a perfect evening," I blurted out.

"No, love. Still a tiny bit lacking," he responded.

"Darling Brett, there is nothing lacking in the magic you showed me this night," I assured him.

"Yes, Contessa, there is," Brett repeated as he poured us more champagne. I gave him a puzzled look. "I meant it when I said I was in love with you, and although you haven't actually said the words, I'm assuming you have deep feelings for me—"

I interrupted, "Brett, I—"

"Shhh, let me finish," he said. "I love your spirit, your heart, your humor. I admire your strength, your independence, and your tenacity. The way you embrace people, all people. You relate to everyone—food servers where we dine…you hang out with our roadies, you can be the badass in the boardroom yet be the classiest, most sophisticated lady in any venue. I love that I can share my trials and tribulations with you, while you understand and offer resolve. You ask for nothing and give everything of yourself effortlessly. So now I'm asking, "Will you join my circus of a life and bring a bit of sanity to it? I love you so and can only hope you feel the same toward me."

"Yes, Brett, I think I fell in love with you the moment I met you! But I was reluctant to say anything, afraid to believe for a moment that you could ever love me back. I'm fine with just enjoying—no, reveling—in every moment we share. Your life is so enormous compared to mine. I feel like the most boring person compared to you. Single, working mom. That's it," I confessed.

"Hey, now, no discriminating against working mums!" Brett humorously interjected.

"Ha, ha. You know what I mean. My life is so simple it's hard to imagine someone as worldly as you would be attracted to that," I added.

"No, not simple, Contessa. Accomplished, focused, and sound. That's how I see you and how you live your life. You need to know how attractive that really is, especially to me. Truth be told, I could use a bit more of that. So come on, now, say the words I want to hear or tell me what I need to do to get you to feel as I do," Brett asked.

"I'm so flattered by everything you've said, Brett. And yes, I love you, I do! The only thing I will ever ask of you is to be open and honest with me. Give me that and you'll have all of me in return," I promised.

"All of you? Really? I'll take you up on that, starting right now!" Brett commanded.

He embraced me once again and began a very long, tender, yet sensual, erotic, almost pornographic stretch, one that left us both almost needing oxygen.

We've all read books and certainly have seen the fairy tales, the Cinderella stories. Handsome, wealthy Prince Charming swoops up the lesser, helpless (well, maybe not exactly *helpless*) girl and puts her in the castle, where she will never want for anything ever again. Not that I ever expected or imagined it could happen, but this was my fairy tale. For the next year, things between Brett and me went along blissfully. Brett saw to it that we were able to spend a good deal of time together. He came to Chicago whenever possible, even if just for a day. I was so excited to have Little Contessa meet him. I was deeply touched to see him a bit nervous to meet her, wanting so much for her to like him. Brett easily won her over, though, as I had no doubt he would. The three of us had some good times over dinner during his occasional visits. Little Contessa did like him. It was her first experience with celebrity, and she was impressed that he was so very down-to-earth, easy to talk to, and not only interesting but interested in her as well. Brett enjoyed seeing my day-to-day life and was respectful and proud of how I managed things both at home and work.

Brett also arranged for me to fly to him when he couldn't get away. We were constantly reviewing our schedules, making sure there was no lengthy stretch of time that we wouldn't be together. I loved spending time on the road with Brett, Richard, and the band whenever I could get away for a day or two. Richard was the most fun to hang out with. I will always remember him fondly. A lover of life, such a deep thinker, and an extremely kind, playful, soft hearted guy who was always ready with a joke, a tale, and that one-of-a-kind, signature smile. I enjoyed being part of the working crew, mostly looking after the band's wardrobe and making sure all their dressing room needs were taken care of. "Everyone works!" Brett always said. I loved all of them and tending to any chores that Brett assigned me. I also loved being aboard Richard's private jet! Jeez, after that, even first class on a regular plane was a drag!

Brett was a man of distinction and presence. Anything he had his hand on was left with his aura, his feel, and his tone. With me too. So much so that I didn't even mind it too much when our schedules didn't allow us to be together for an extended period. He gave me so much of himself it was like a part of him was always with me. Brett was quite appreciative of the fact that I fully understood his responsibilities and time commitments. In turn, he was just as compassionate if I was unable to hop on a plane to meet him someplace on the road. After all, I was always busy being a mom, and my work was a constant challenge. Those were my two priorities, and both required most of my attention. During these times, Brett made it a point to keep in constant touch, ensuring that I really felt he was with me in spirit. Our long, intense phone conversations were a mix of sharing our business of the day, and afterward, things got pretty heated when moving on to late night, more intimate chatter. That made our reunions all the sweeter, or hotter, depending on how you looked at it. All in all, our relationship was great and we developed a wonderful rhythm to scheduling time together as well as remaining close while physically apart. I was confident, completely content, and perfectly comfortable in our relationship. Life was good.

But as they say, all good things eventually come to an end, and later that year, our relationship did. We had a fabulous weekend in Chicago. Brett was able to break away from the tour, as Richard's tour was hovering around two cities nearby. Brett always stayed at one of the finer hotels downtown, and as usual, he planned a weekend full of fun, entertainment, close conversation, and of course, intimacy. If you were to ask me if anything seemed a little funny that weekend, my answer would be absolutely not. In fact, it was more than perfect. No hint or clue whatsoever that soon we would be history. Just prior to my leaving the hotel, Brett ran down his schedule for the next few weeks, indicating it was jam-packed. In addition, he had to return to London for about two weeks, to his head office. Explaining what all was going on, Brett asked me to be patient with getting in touch with me, what with his busy schedule plus the time difference. No problem, I assured him.

The ax dropped on a Wednesday evening. I was reviewing quarterly sales reports. Little Contessa was down the hall at a friend's house. Every time the phone rang, my heart began to pound, hoping it would be Brett. No such luck, up until now. My heart soared when I heard his voice. He first apologized for not being able to call me for so long, but then in typical Brett style, he cut right to the chase.

"Contessa, I've decided to get back together with my wife," Brett began.

I thought a building fell on me, but I managed to remain calm and let Brett continue.

"I've told you what a hot mess she is and was truthful with you when I said I've wanted a divorce but just never seemed to make the time for it. Plus, I'd be lying if I said I wouldn't miss the millions she'd take me for. But since I returned to London, I've heard from many of our friends who all report that she's been obsessed with getting back together, particularly after learning I was involved with you. We did a lot of talking, and she's admitted to all her mistakes. I've decided to give it a go one more time, give her one last chance.

I'm so sorry, darling girl. There's no other way to tell you but straight out," he finished.

My heart was about to burst right out of my chest, but I managed to speak in a level, calm tone. "Brett, you may be the smartest man I've ever known, yet you're falling for one of the oldest tricks in the book," I told him.

"What trick is that?" Brett asked.

"The 'I don't want you, but I don't want anyone else to have you either' trick. Isn't it funny that she became obsessed with you as soon as she found out you were in a serious relationship? Up until then, it was fine for her to have affairs galore, even with one of your friends. She was fine knowing you were buried in your work, but the minute she discovered you were happy with someone else, she was suddenly desperate to get you back. Brett, you can't fall for this." I was desperate to control my tone.

"Contessa, I've always admired your intuitive nature, and I fear you're spot on. It's crazy, I know, but I absolutely must see it through in order to have a clean conscience about it, once and for all, no matter which way it goes. I can't ask you to understand, I can only tell you what's going on in my head. I would never disrespect a woman like you by being dishonest or deceitful about things. Contessa, I meant every word I've ever said to you. I've enjoyed being with you more than you'll ever know. But this is something I absolutely must do. Please don't hate me. I'll never forget you or all the joy you brought into my life," Brett finished.

It was hard to believe the words that I was about to utter, and even more unbelievable was how relaxed I was while saying them. "Hate you? No, Brett, I could never hate you. Matter of fact, I respect you now more than ever," I said.

"Why is that, Contessa?" Brett softly asked.

"I told you all I would ever ask of you was honesty, and you gave me that. A man in your position could have easily pulled the wool over my eyes, went back to your wife, and kept me on the side, or tried to, anyway. But not you. You're too honorable for that. I admire you, Brett, and want to thank you for not putting me through what could have been torturous. But you're gonna miss me! Just wait and see!" I even managed a chuckle.

"I don't doubt that. You're an extraordinary lady, Contessa," he said.

"Please tell Richard I said thank you for making one of the happiest years of my life possible," I asked.

"If he ever speaks to me again after I tell him of my plans, I will. He can't stand her, and he just adores you," Brett confided.

"I always suspected he may be just a bit smarter than you," I teased. But I had to end this conversation; I had to be the one to let go. "And with that, I will thank you for an absolutely fantastic chapter in my life. I wish you nothing but happiness. If anyone deserves it, it's you. Goodbye, Brett."

I immediately hung up.

I sat there for a few minutes, feeling nothing. Blank. Empty. Staring at the wall. I finally got up to make myself a cup of Nighty Night tea. If there ever was a night I'd need it, this was it. As I sipped, I reminisced the course of my relationship with Brett. It was fun, it was fabulous, and it was an enchanting dream, a memorable chapter that would always warm my heart and I would cherish. I was sad, of course, but there were no tears, no hysterics, no drama. Instead, I was consumed with feelings of gratitude for even meeting Brett and sharing his life this past year. After all, how many young women do you know who have had an opportunity, an adventure like this one? I can only smile thinking about it all. Words of a song I loved suddenly came to me.

A fool will lose tomorrow
Reaching back for yesterday
I won't turn my head in sorrow
If you should go away
I'll stand here and remember
Just how good it's been
And I know I'll never love this way again

No sadness, no regrets, just happy memories. And do you know why? Because it was so very honest! Brett never promised anything he wouldn't deliver, and he delivered everything he promised. That simple. I fully realized that old saying: honesty really is the best policy! The truth is the most basic, raw element in the world. You can't argue with it, and you can't debate it; it's just there for you to have and accept. Accept and move on, which was exactly what I did.

Many years had passed, and by this time, I was happily married to husband #3 (be patient, we're almost there). Now living in a small city of Michigan, my husband and I were at the grand opening of our town's new performance arena. A state-of-the-art venue that would attract a wide range of talent, which this town was in desperate need of. I found myself thinking of Richard and told myself he would play here one day. Richard often spoke of buying an old brown truck and touring America, playing very small venues, where he could really connect with his audience. Sure enough, one day I heard lunchroom chatter that Richard teamed up with his old guitar partner, was touring the United States and appearing at our little arena for the next two nights. Of course, I was certain Brett would be with him. This was such a small town, with only one grand hotel that was worthy of their celebrity, and I was confident they'd be staying there. I began reminiscing about Richard, the band, and Brett. How could I not? I closed my office door and allowed myself some deep thought. I would really love to see them, but to be completely honest, I would really love to know the outcome of Brett's decision to go back to his wife. I knew all the aliases they used while on the road as well as the way to get either Richard or Brett directly. My hesitation was that I was a dedicated wife now and would never do anything inappropriate or detrimental to our marriage. Would it be wrong to ring up an old friend who was in town? Just to catch up? What harm could a phone call do? My husband was out of town, and I really wrestled with it. What would he do if he were in this situation? Hmmm, I think he, as well as most men, would definitely go for it. Decision made, I called the hotel and used the name and correct dialogue to get Brett directly. After two rings, I heard the voice that still sent shivers through me.

"Hello, Brett," I said with a big, fat smile on my face.

"No way! Contessa? Is that you?" he asked in a disbelieving tone.

With a burst of laughter, I answered, "I'm amazed that you remembered my voice!"

"Silly girl! I could never forget you or your beautiful voice," he admitted. "My God, I can't believe this! How in the world did you find me?"

I explained and continued on with the short version of where I was in life. I told him of my marriage, my career, Little Contessa, and how I arrived and got settled in Michigan. I got to a point where it was his turn to enlighten me.

As if he were reading my mind, he stepped up. "Well, I think I know what you're dying to hear about, Contessa. Thanks for allowing me a minute to eat the crow I'm choking on. You were right. About it all. It was a bloody disaster. She just wanted to know that she could get me back. That she still had power over me. It was all about her ego," Brett confessed.

"I'm really sorry, Brett. Truly, I am," I said.

"You're being gracious. Don't be sorry. I'm not. I had to do it, had to see it through to get her out of my life once and for all, move on with a clean slate. What did you used to say? *Clean house.* Yes, I needed to clean my house. The only thing I truly am sorry about was that I lost you in the process. And I've thought about you. I even tried calling you, but your number was disconnected. I wanted to give you the opportunity to scold me with a very appropriate 'I told you so.' But not to worry, Richard gave me plenty of that!" he added.

"I wouldn't have said that then, nor will I now, Brett. I just want to know if you're happy," I asked.

Brett went on to tell me that yes, at this late time of his life, he was deliriously happy. A few years ago, he met and fell in love with a lady in South America. They had a daughter and were expecting a son in a few months. I was honestly and genuinely thrilled for him. That was something I thought of when we were together as well. Children of his own were the one thing in life he wanted, that all his success and money couldn't buy, nor could I give him either. When we were together, I wondered how, knowing I couldn't give him what he wanted most, a child of his own, that would ultimately affect our relationship. Brett went on to tell me all about his five year old daughter, who had him wrapped around her little finger. I could hear the pride and joy in his voice. He would name his son after his deceased brother, whom he was so very close to. Yes, Brett was more than happy; he finally had everything he ever wanted personally. His business had grown and diversified into several areas he used to talk about engaging into. He was managing several more groups, he bought the rights to a World War II book I remembered him speaking of, and had plans to make it into a film. He had it all, and nobody deserved it more than he did. Of course, he also brought me up to speed with news of Richard. All was well with him too. I was so glad that I called. Yet just as with our last conversation years ago, I knew I'd have to be the one to let it go.

"Brett, I am so very glad we had this opportunity to talk. Please know how happy I am for you," I told him.

"Why don't you come to the show tonight? Richard will pass out when I tell him you're here," Brett asked.

"I'd love to and appreciate you asking, Brett, but no, I can't. My husband is out of town and it just wouldn't be right. But know that this conversation has meant a great deal to me. In so many ways, just as you did. I think it best to leave it here. Please understand," I asked.

"Of course, I understand, Contessa. And I want you to know that I share your feelings. I'm grateful to you for calling. Most women wouldn't have. But then you're certainly not most women. You are truly one of a kind. I've never forgotten you, nor will I ever. You taught me what a real woman is all about, and I think of you with great admiration and affection. Be well, love," he finished.

I'll stand here and remember just how good it's been, and I know I'll never love this way again, echoed in my head.

"Bye, Brett."

While no relationship is perfect, this one was pretty close. It was amicable, harmonious, humorous, compassionate, passionate, and enlightening. It was fun, it was adult, and it was confident. Most of all, it was honest! The only thing this relationship lacked was an element no relationship needs but unfortunately too many have: drama.

And yet it ended. Of course I was heartbroken, but the honesty, the no bullshit, no drama way in which it was handled caused no ripple effect to me at all. I was able to accept and move on effortlessly, without wanting to throw myself off a bridge. Period.

So, ladies and gentlemen, please pay attention to the moral of this story: relationships can certainly be difficult, but you can make them much less difficult if you remember to keep them honest and drama free. When love is good, make honesty your best ally to keep it that way. When problems arise in your relationship, be open and honest about your feelings, deal with them directly, and things should work out. When love goes wrong and you need to break free, whether you're the breaker or the *breakee*, just be honest and direct about the issues and you'll see how much easier, neater, and less theatrical it is to make the break and move forward positively, for both of you.

After all, honest really is the best policy!

Husband #3

The winner takes it all!

I was out to dinner with a few of my girlfriends. We were in agony, listening to the ongoing drama of one of our friends who just had a bad breakup with her boyfriend. Seemed we were always listening to her many crisis situations with this guy, but that's what girlfriends do, right? She began a relationship with a guy who, unbeknownst to her, was married. When my friend found out her new beau was married, she was upset, of course, but the guy convinced her he would soon be leaving his wife. Well, now years later, that didn't happen. He strung her along all this time, and she recently found out he was seeing yet another woman and was "cheating" on both my friend and his wife! The story we were yawning to was how she finally ended it. One of the other girls closed the conversation with "Honey, if you got him that way, you'll lose him that way!" Words to live by.

Some time passed before we gals were able to schedule another ladies' night out. It was winter in the Windy City, and wouldn't you know it, the night we had planned on getting together, a snowstorm was building all day. By mid afternoon, we were all calling one another to decide if we should keep our date. It was decided that yes, we would brave the weather. At this time, I was managing a sizable commercial real estate office in an upscale northern suburb. Having brought this firm up to speed with the latest technology in computers, communications, and employment practices, I had full charge of the company's accounting, payroll, benefits, employees, fleet, and properties. I loved my firm, my job, and my coworkers. Little

Contessa was now in college, and I had multiple side jobs (waitressing, banquet serving, store demonstrations) to pay her college tuition. My side jobs kept me pretty busy most weekends. I rarely had a chance to see my girlfriends, and even though my first choice was to go straight home, get comfy, and curl up in my jammies, I really needed a girls' night. That said, I left the office a bit early and headed out in what became a blizzard to meet my friends. There was a new French hotel in the area that had a fabulous restaurant inside. The restaurant was getting rave reviews; we were all dying to experience it, so that was our intended destination, if this blizzard didn't bury us alive en route!

I was the first to arrive. It really was as beautiful and ornate as reported. I made myself comfortable in the luxurious lobby, to make sure we gals saw one another upon arriving. There was a bar just off to the side of the lobby. A very proper and handsome gentleman in a tuxedo approached me, asking if I wanted anything to drink. Jokingly, I asked for hot chocolate, and before I knew it, I was sipping on some. It was heavenly on this cold, blistery night. I sat there sipping, and suddenly, another man sat next to me. This man was tall, thin, and not very handsome. He was not wearing a dashing tuxedo as my server, but instead a rumpled suit that I was certain to be a wash-and-wear. He appeared to be in desperate need of a barber, with patchy stubble all over his face. Did he shave in the dark? I wondered. His silvery brown hair was long, unruly, and all over the place, clearly no style at all. His glasses were so outdated and ill fitting all this dork needed was a Band-Aid on the nose piece. As he sat down in the chair next to me, I noticed his pant pocket was torn. Poor bastard, he was a mess. What wasn't a mess, though, was his confidence, his style, and his demeanor.

This disheveled stranger just plopped down next to me and introduced himself. "Hi, I'm Jeff. I assume you're waiting for someone, and I hope it's not a date."

Always rooting for the underdog, I was amused. "I'm having dinner with friends." I smiled.

"Thank God! I see you're not wearing a ring. Single, I hope?" he asked.

"Wow, you get right to it, don't you, Jeff?" I laughed.

"You can't get what you want without going straight for it. I noticed you immediately as you blew in. You were a vision, even covered in snow. I just had to meet you." He sure sounded like a very self-assured man, but his body language and tone were in direct contradiction to his appearance. I was intrigued. "So I know you're single and you like hot chocolate, but I sense there's so much more about you I'm going to love getting to know," he continued.

"What is it you'd like to know, Jeff?" I laughingly asked. This guy was hilarious. I couldn't yet figure out if he was just another macho Casanova or he was serious. I had to keep it going.

"Your name, to begin with. The rest I'll take my time in learning," he went on.

"Contessa. My name is Contessa," I replied as I took another sip.

"Very fitting, Contessa. Your name has beautiful movement, just as you do," Jeff continued.

We sat there engaged in fluent get-to-know-you conversation, exchanging a bit about our lives. Jeff was from Michigan, was president of a distribution firm, in Chicago for a meeting that wrapped up today. He was waiting in the lobby for his group to meet for dinner. Jeff liked to talk, but he listened just as well. He was not shy at all and seemed to be working hard at making a remarkable impression. Turned out, he was quite magnetic. He asked lots of questions about me, my life, where I worked, and in what capacity. He said he had been divorced for several years and the father of two daughters, and he told me all about them and their interests. They were both in college on the East Coast. It turned out to be a very pleasant conversation that ended only as I spotted two of my girlfriends come through the lobby entrance.

"Here they are!" I announced as I waved over to the girls. "Jeff, I thank you for the company and conversation. Enjoy your dinner and the rest of your time in Chicago," I told him as I began to walk away.

"Remember this night, Contessa. I know I will," Jeff said as he took my hand and kissed it. *Wow,* for the hot mess that he was, he really had game.

The girls and I greeted one another, and our loud chatter began immediately.

"Who was that guy you were talking to?" one of the gals asked.

"Now who did you meet?" asked another.

"You guys are gonna love this story!" I laughed.

I looked through the glass wall of the restaurant and was able to see the group of men gathering in the lobby, who I assumed were Jeff's associates. I couldn't help but smile. Jeff was a character, all right. It was a fun encounter. I proceeded to tell the girls, and we howled with laughter and continued on to have a very festive, badly needed girls' night out.

The snowstorm diminished through the night, allowing for a smooth ride into the office the next morning. This day, I was to give our office receptionist her annual review. Linda was a lovely, eager young woman. She was a bit rough around the edges, not the best at her job, but I saw hunger and willingness to learn in her, plus I was trying hard to coach her up a few notches. Seated in our conference room, I acknowledged and complimented Linda on the progress she had made since last her last review. I also outlined key points that she really needed to work on. A particular annoyance to me and the other managers was the manner in which she transferred phone calls. She frequently forgot to screen them, putting calls through to the various managers without announcing who was on the line. We managers were constantly complaining about that. My specific directive to Linda was to follow simple steps in accepting and transferring incoming calls. Politely ask who it is and from what company. Put the caller on hold. Intercom the specific manager to whom the call is intended, checking to see if that manager could or would take the call. We reviewed this easy instruction in detail, and that concluded the review.

Not ten minutes after I got settled back into my office and involved in the day's work, my intercom rang. It was Linda.

"Contessa, you have a call on line 1," Linda announced.

I took a deep breath, trying not to explode from having just directed Linda on this very issue! "Linda, who is it on line 1?" I calmly asked.

"Ooops! Sorry, I'll find out," Linda responded.

A minute later, she came through the intercom again. "It's Jeff," she said triumphantly.

"I know several Jeffs! Jeff who?" I demanded.

Linda didn't bother to explain this time. Another second later, she buzzed me again. "It's Jeff who you met in the bar last night," she said with a laugh.

"*What?* Oh my God!" I gasped. "Hold him for a minute, then put him through." *What the fuck!* I thought to myself as I did a quick review of last night's conversation with him. I was absolutely certain I did not give him my work number! How the hell did he find me?

My line rang again from Linda putting the call through. I guess I was about to find out.

"Good morning, Contessa," that deep, strong voice said, greeting me.

"Jeff? How ever did you find me?" I shockingly asked.

"You told me about your job. I looked up your company. I apologize for not giving a more dignified response to your secretary, but when she pressed me for information, I realized I didn't tell you my last name. Anyway, I just couldn't leave without trying to find you. I hope you enjoyed our talk as much as I did. I'm in Chicago often for business, and I'd love to keep in touch," he said.

"You made quite an impression, Jeff, and yes, I did enjoy our time," I assured him. "Tell you what. You can call me next time you're in town, and depending on both our schedules, we'll see what we can do. Sound good?"

"I get you're not going to give me your home number. That's okay. You're cautious. That's a good thing. I knew you were a smart lady. I'll keep in touch with you at work. Sound good, Contessa?" he responded, mimicking me.

"Sounds fine, Jeff." I laughed.

"Uh, I love saying your name!" Jeff confessed.

"Then I'll look forward to hearing from you, but right now I am in the middle of something important, and I'm going to have to let you go," I told him.

"I'm just glad we connected, Contessa. I'll be in touch. Bye now," he finished.

I sat there thinking for a moment. *Now that's what I call making an impression!* Our casual conversation last night included things anyone would discuss upon first meeting. Where you work, in what capacity, marital status, kids, hobbies, etc. I am not one to give out my phone number. If I meet an interesting guy and find a mutual attraction, should he ask for my phone number, I would turn it around and ask for that gentleman's business card and reach out to him, if I so desired. I would communicate that way until I felt comfortable to provide him personal contact info on myself. Jeff went out of his way to find me. He got my attention.

One day the following week, I was busy in my office when my intercom rang. It was Linda. "Contessa, something just arrived for you and you've got to come out and see it!"

I wasn't expecting anything, so I was wondering what this could be. Upon entering the reception area, I saw a gorgeous, gigantic, and fragrant floral arrangement.

"Wow!" I exclaimed with shock. "For me?" I asked Linda.

"Hurry and open the card. I can't wait to see who this is from!" she said.

The card read, "Every dream begins with a dreamer. I've been dreaming of you every night. Can't wait to see you again." It was from Jeff. The card included his office number, home phone number, and email address, asking me to contact him.

Once again, he got my attention. I returned to my office and called him.

"Boy, you really do know how to surprise a lady, don't you?" I told him.

"You're a lady who deserves attention. I'm trying to ensure you'll keep thinking about me, so I thought one rose per day should do it. They should last until I return to Chicago. I'm hoping to have the pleasure of your company over dinner so we can really get to know each other," Jeff said.

"I'd be delighted, Jeff," I said as we continued on with a short and whimsical chat.

The more we talked, the more interesting and intriguing he became. Consequently, a man I wanted to get to know better. Yes, I'd be very receptive to a dinner date soon.

Jeff continued to call regularly, and our conversations were getting more and more fun, personal, and substantive. I found myself anxious for his next call. Soon I gave him my direct line and, before long, my home number.

Time flew by and before I knew it Jeff was back in town. We would meet for dinner this evening. I felt like our evening chats were like dates, sometimes going on for most of the night. I already felt as though I knew him well. I was thrilled to finally see him in person for our first physical date.

Jeff did not disappoint. Not on this date or any of the many that followed. He was crafty in manipulating his schedule to allow him to be in Chicago more often. Jeff applied thought and detail into all the plans he made for us, always giving me notice and allowing for my approval. The best and varied restaurants, theater, and sporting events, and sometimes merely allowing the many sights of Chicago to entertain us. We thoroughly enjoyed each other, sharing our lives, our hearts, and our deepest thoughts and emotions. We became very close and compatible in every way. Emphasis on *every way*! He had deep personal thoughts and emotions, and I sensed he was dying to share them with someone. I also had a feeling that his efforts were not appreciated, that he was severely taken advantage of in the past. He certainly was no onion with many layers to peel, but a man who was so open about everything he was quite easy to read. Jeff demonstrated impeccable manners in some areas. Never failing to open doors, seating me before himself, allowing me to order first, and always putting me on the inside of any walk we took (a very old fashioned but charming custom, to shield the lady from harm) were just a few examples. In direct contrast, though, were a few things about him that had me scratching my head, things that both embarrassed me as well as amused me. Jeff talked with food in his mouth, often allowing pieces of food to go flying out. He chewed like a cow—so loud that I often looked around, wondering if anyone else noticed. He left an outline of crumbs and food debris all over his clothes, the table, and around his seat. But crazy as it sounds, I didn't mind. Jeff wasn't perfect, and that was fine. He was a regular guy, with apparent flaws that were sort of endearing.

Slowly I began sprucing Jeff up a bit whenever we were together. We both enjoyed shopping and dressing him up a bit. I also applied my hair styling abilities to put a finishing touch on his new look, which Jeff was quite pleased with.

"Nobody ever spent this much time on me," Jeff explained. "I gave all my attention to my ex-wife and my girls. I guess I never paid any attention to myself because they didn't give any to me. I never knew what it was like to have someone fuss over me the way you do. And I love it. And you know what? I love you too!" he confessed.

Music to my ears, and I responded in kind. That was that; we were in love, and it was wonderful. Jeff made it to Chicago every other weekend. I scaled back my weekend job, alternating every other weekend to spend time with him. He was very complimentary and supportive of me working an extra job to pay my daughter's college tuition. Jeff applauded my independent nature and tenacity in achieving what all I wanted for both my daughter and myself. As they say, absence makes the heart grow fonder, and that was true in our case. We enjoyed lengthy phone calls, sharing everything, and were never at a loss for words. When Jeff called me from home in the evenings, I talked him through cooking. He often called me from his office as well, with me on speaker phone while he worked. It was easy to tell when he was in his office. He had a squeaky old chair that made the loudest noises whenever he moved in it. I teased him, saying he must be working for a very cheap company because they couldn't afford some WD40 oil for that old thing! We shared everything and were never at a loss for words.

It was Jeff's habit to call me upon returning home after spending a weekend with me. It was very late this Sunday night when he called, saying he was at home and speaking of things directly related to his home and him being there. He expressed endearing words on the weekend we just spent together. Suddenly, I heard that big loud squeak from his chair.

"What was that?" I quickly asked.

"What was what?" he sheepishly responded. *Squeak, squeak!* There it was again!

Remember we talked about those rocks falling on your head a few chapters ago? Forget the rocks; a ton of bricks just fell on my head.

"Oh my God, Jeff! You're not at home! You're in your office!" I shouted.

"No, no, I told you, I'm at home," he nervously tried to assure me. The more he talked, the more nervous he got, the more he wiggled, and the more his chair squeaked. I could literally hear him shaking in his seat. And I knew why.

"LIAR! You're a fucking liar! You're married, aren't you? You couldn't go home to call me, so you went to the office! That's the only reason why you'd lie about where you were at midnight!" I screamed.

"No...I, uh...oh, shit!" Jeff nervously mumbled.

"Oh my God! I'm right, you're married! You fucking asshole! You've been lying to me all this time!" I screamed. My heart was pounding, and I started heaving.

"Okay, yes, but please, Contessa, please let me explain," Jeff begged.

"I don't want to hear anything. I don't want to know anything. You lied to me, and all I wanted from you was truth! Jeff, lose my number, leave me alone, do *not* contact me at all! I AM DONE!" I finished and slammed the phone down.

I sat there in shock, going over and over so many of our conversations where Jeff distinctly referenced things relative to his divorce process, being divorced, managing his kids, etc. What did I miss? What didn't I see? I repeatedly asked myself. I was furious. My anger was partially directed at myself because even though these days my antenna was raised, I obviously missed something, and by now I thought I was smarter than that. However, Jeff was the main reason my blood was boiling. I could not believe the detail, the stories he told me, the entire scenarios he concocted as to where he was when he called me. He was clearly very good, I'll give him that, but a lie is a lie is a lie (especially one of this magnitude!), and I wanted no part of the story or the drama that went with it. The most confusing aspect was that I really did believe him when he said he was in love with me. The emotion, the tenderness, the gestures, and the feelings that accompanied those words made it so real. I didn't expect anything beyond that; I had no expectations or aspirations of marriage to follow. I was completely content and happy to be in a committed relationship, and the way we shared time together was just fine with me. *Jeez, is there a Pathological Liar University someplace that I don't know about that enables people to become so good at this stuff?*

My usual method for deleting something from my mind was to bury myself in work. I stayed a little later at the office each night, and I returned to my secondary weekend job every single weekend. However, forgetting was not that easy, as I came home each night to telephone messages from Jeff on my recorder, letters of explanation in the mail several times a week, and even flowers delivered to both my home and office. I never returned the phone calls and tore up the letters without even reading them. I returned the flowers that were delivered to both my home and office. Well, except for one time, when Linda's mom was in the hospital; I let her have the flowers to take to her mother. They really cheered Linda's mom up, so they were put to good use. I wanted no part of him, and I wanted him to know that.

This went on for about nine months.

Then one day I received a large thick manila envelope from Jeff. My curiosity got the better of me, and I opened it. To my surprise, the envelope contained copies of Jeff's recent divorce papers, with a very long letter attached. I left the package sitting on the dining room table for about a week, without even reading it. The following Sunday, I was off, due to a scheduling snafu. I sat there staring at the envelope as I sipped my tea.

I called my long time best friend, Kathy, and gave her the update. "Oh, just open it already!" Kathy demanded. "He must really love you. If he didn't, he wouldn't bother with you after all this time. Guys don't hang in there when they get kicked in the ass. He's going crazy. If nothing else, you should hear what he has to say, at least to know what's going on in his head."

Kathy was the best common sense thinker I knew. We had known each other since we were kids, and she was well aware of my feelings toward Jeff and what I believed to be a cardinal sin, lying. Kathy was also my partner in crime as a single working mother whom I shared everything with, so she was well versed in the entire Jeff situation. Her insistence to read through all the information made sense. I kept her on the line while I read. Apparently, after I found out Jeff was married, he actually did file for divorce, and here were copies of the filed papers, detailing all aspects of it, including the settlement. He hid nothing. The handwritten letter Jeff included told the story of his unhealthy marriage and that his sole reason for staying in it was "for the kids." Kathy and I both groaned, each sharing thoughts we both agreed on. Men can be so dumb! Between the two of us, we knew many guys who leaned on this same feeble excuse not to put their big boy panties on and go through with what they say they want: their freedom from the bitch they married. Either they are too lazy, too stupid, or too full of shit, Kathy and I agreed.

The letter went on to describe that Jeff felt "love at first sight" upon meeting me. He wrote his intentions were always to tell me, but fear of losing me paralyzed him. He went on writing that our time was always so wonderful he couldn't find the right words or moment and thus just kept putting it off. Blah, blah, blah. "Please, please, please call me. You're all I can think about. I love you and miss you so much." I thought it was all bullshit, good bullshit, but nonetheless, bullshit!

Kathy melted. "Awww, Contessa, I really think he's legit. He's pouring his heart out to you. He's begging you to call him. He doesn't sound like a player. Everything you've told me about him says he's a good, down-to-earth guy, kind of dorky, but a good guy." We laughed. "Seriously, I've never heard you talk about any guy the way you speak of him, how you make each other feel, what all you have in common, how interested you are in each other. I know you. You're mad because he lied to you. Okay, I get that, but hear him out. I mean, he obviously got a divorce, so he must really love you. If he didn't, he wouldn't be bothered. See what he has to say and then tell him your thoughts before you close the door completely," she finished. Once again, Kathy made perfect sense.

I sat on it for about a week. Kathy's words kept ringing in my ear, and I finally agreed that she was right. I decided I'd call Jeff to either see his point of view or officially end it once and for all. I waited for the weekend. If he was so distraught over me, let's see if he was home alone on a Saturday night. He was.

"Hello, Jeff" was my unemotional greeting.

"Contessa, I've missed you so much! I have so much to tell you, and I've just been dying to hear from you!" he cried out.

"I'm listening," I said, to allow him to begin.

Jeff reiterated everything he had written in all his letters. He married someone he didn't really love, that his domineering mother pushed the marriage on him, as Mommie Dearest felt she was "suitable" for their social circle. Jeff said he went along with it for two reasons. First, to get his mother off his back. Second, for fear of not having another opportunity for marriage, as he was pretty insecure. When kids came along, he doted on them, making life with the wife more tolerable. Work was another escape for him, and his frequent travels made the time he spent at home more tolerable. This went on for almost two decades, and he resolved himself to live a loveless life, a fantasy family life for the sake of the kids. Jeff went on to say he often felt like a walking dead, merely going through the motions in his roles of husband and father, completely empty inside and emotionless until he met me. Fear of losing me got the better of him; what little confidence he had diminished over the years, and being with me brought his self-esteem back. He kept planning to tell me but chickened out every time. When I found out and cut him off, he went directly to his attorney and began the divorce proceedings, which got pretty ugly, his wife trying to turn the kids against him. Finally, they worked it all out and the divorce was finalized.

I said nothing as Jeff finished. There was a brief pause for both of us.

"Contessa, I love you! I fucked up, royally, I know, but you have to give me a chance to make it up to you. I realized what a naive fool I was for staying with my witch of a wife for the sake of my kids. They knew the marriage was a charade, and they couldn't care less so long as all their desires were met. I stupidly thought that sacrificing my happiness for their sake would be appreciated. Truth is, I wasted too much of my life trying to please people who never appreciated me. If I hadn't met you, I would have rotted in that sentence of a marriage. But I'm free now, free to love you and finally experience someone loving me. I guess I really never knew what true happiness was until you. I was dying a slow death, and you brought me back to life. There's nothing I won't do to make sure you never regret forgiving me. Please, please tell me you will!" Jeff cried.

"It's not that easy, Jeff. You broke my one cardinal rule: honesty. If I can't trust you, in all you do, I just can't have a relationship. I think you learned pretty quickly that I'm not a desperate woman. You know I hate lying and, even more than that, I despise drama. My life is clean and neat, and I intend to keep it that way. I need trust, Jeff. I can't go forward without it. If you lied about being married, what else might you lie about?" I explained.

"Not a damn thing. You know it all now. Contessa, I'm begging for another chance. I love you, your fire, your spirit, your zest for life. I want to marry you and experience it all together," he said.

"Whoa, slow down, Jeff! You're moving way too fast! Those are all the right words, but they won't allow me to forget what happened. I need time. Let's just take it slow and see how it goes. That's about all I can say right now," I told him.

"I can wait if I have to. Contessa, if you tell me you still love me, I can wait forever. You're worth it. And I'll prove those are not just words, you'll see," Jeff said.

"Yes, I do love you. But you lied to me and you hurt me, Jeff, and I'll never forget that! I need time, okay?" I asked.

We left it there. I had to let this marinate for a while. Jeff called me every night, but I only took his call about twice a week. He came across as genuine in his ongoing attempts to get back into my heart. I still loved him and wanted to run back to him, but I had to be sure he'd be completely honest going forward. The ice was melting slowly, but a chunk of it remained inside me. I guess I was waiting for a sign of some sort, something that would trigger me to go in one way or another. To either realize that nope, this wouldn't work, because I'd never be able to trust him again, or be hit by the proverbial lightning bolt to confirm I just couldn't live without him.

In the meantime, I got a call from a fella I used to date inviting me to a party at his very upscale, prestigious country club. Chuck was a very successful, high profile businessman who was handsome, debonair, and fun to be with. He had all the attributes that a single man needed to attract the finest lady. However, he had an arrogant side, which was a huge turnoff to me. We always had a good time; I just couldn't stand to be around the pompous attitude he often displayed, and I ultimately stopped responding to his calls. A fundraising gala was in the works at Chuck's club. True to his nature, he noted Chicago's most prominent would be in attendance. Chuck said he wouldn't dream of attending such an important event with anyone else but me, adding, "Only one who can awe should accompany me to this awesome event, and, my dazzling Contessa, nobody can impress more than you!" Translation: "This is an important social event, and I need good arm candy!"

At any other time, I probably would have declined the invitation; however, due to my current bewildered state, I decided this might be just what I needed. In addition to all the Jeff drama, I'd been working every weekend for quite a while. A weekend off to attend a high society event with a prominent member, being wined and dined, sounded lovely to me. I planned my dress, hair, and makeup with extra special detail. Chuck's goal was to impress, and I wanted to make certain that he, first and foremost, was completely mesmerized by my finished product. With somewhat a short notice, I went through my closet to see what I could throw together to wear. I chose a gorgeous, just-above-the-knee, form fitting smoky gray satin dress with a low cut back (Chuck's favorite). Together with beautifully jeweled shoes, purse, and wrap, it was a perfect choice for the occasion. As I was doing my makeup, the phone rang.

"Hey, doll, it's Chuck. Just wanted to let you know my limo will be there to pick you up at six," he proudly announced.

"Wonderful, but if you aren't in it, you'll be dining next to an empty chair," I promised.

"Aw, c'mon, doll! I have a tee time at two o'clock, and I'm bringing my tux to the club so I can change there. Not sure if I'll have time to come get you," he said.

"As your invited guest, I'll walk into your club on your arm or not at all. The choice is yours, doll!" I volleyed back.

"You're a tough cookie, Contessa, and I love it! Never fear, your knight in shining armor will arrive in his chariot at six sharp," he said, laughing.

Chuck looked so dashing in his tailor made tuxedo and was extremely complimentary of me as well. During the drive to the club, he expressed delight in being with me, that he had lots of plans for us moving forward.

The club was everything you would envision a ritzy country club to be, and this night it was decorated to the hilt. As Chuck introduced me to many of Chicago's movers and shakers (and some wannabe movers and shakers), I glossed over a sea of little black dresses (and some big black dresses, LOL!). Sunglasses would have been appropriate to shield your eyes from the sparkle of the diamonds in the room. I was seated among several high profile couples, and the conversation was unpredictably boring. A macho pissing contest over who had the bigger boat, who spent more money on their last vacation, and who had the better wine broker. The ladies were pleasant, but their mindless chatter was limited to playing "guess the designer" around the room and exchanging technicians and services at various several notable spas. I actually thought dinner conversation would be more informative and enlightening in the world of business, given this crowd. Very disappointing. As the men got up and headed toward the bar to continue bragging and have a cognac, I stayed on with the ladies, where things got a bit more festive and the claws came out. After I had successfully answered the barrage of questions (who I was wearing, where I got my hair and makeup done, how serious it was between Chuck and me, what charity work I did, etc.), their conversation shifted to who was sleeping with whom, who had what work done, and the like. Not appealing to me at all. I excused myself and headed in Chuck's direction. I overhead several of the guys crowing about the sexual adventures they had with the club staff, that as long as you kept the tips coming, they'd keep you coming! And roaring laughter followed. I wanted to throw up. I had to get out of there. I got my wrap, went outside to find Chuck's driver, climbed into his limo, and left. I didn't even say goodbye to Chuck.

My heart was pounding. I felt tears falling over my cheeks. I could only think of one thing: Jeff! I loved him, and now I knew I wanted him and only him. I called him as soon as I got home, even though it was quite late. I was delighted to realize that I woke him up.

"Can you promise me with your soul that you'll never lie to me again, that you'll be completely transparent in everything about us?" I asked.

"Till death do us part, Contessa! I swear to you on my life, if you believe anything, believe that! I love you. I want you back. I want to marry you," he pleaded.

"Then let's start over, with some lessons learned. I love you too, Jeff!" I cried.

We talked well into the wee hours, opening our hearts once again, sincerely and genuinely committing to each other as well as making significant plans to move forward. We would mix up our weekend schedules in order to be fair, balanced, and respectful to our commitments. He would visit me, I would visit him, a weekend open for each of us to work, and another for us to each visit our college kids. It was an ambitious but well rounded mutual strategy, and we found it worked out well.

When Jeff visited me, I made it a point to socialize with my friends. We were perfectly fine alone with each other, but I felt it important for him to be part of my whole life and those close to me who were in it. He easily integrated with my friends, and we always had a great time with them. The singular most important person I wanted him to meet and get to know was, of course, my Little Contessa. That was a bit difficult, though, as the college she attended was five hours away. I shared our relationship with her, frequently telling her all about him and our time together. Little Contessa was delighted that I was happily involved in a solid relationship.

Jeff always planned a variety of things to do when I went to visit him, sometimes with another couple, but mostly just the two of us. It seemed to me that Jeff didn't have many friends outside of work. I attributed that to his work and travel schedule, as well as the fallout of friends that sometimes comes with divorce. Jeff was dedicated in showing me the best of his town while trying to entice me to leave Chicago and join him in his. Not that I didn't daydream about it, but the reality was, my daughter and my work were in Chicago. Although Little Contessa consistently told me that her plans were to move out on her own after college, I didn't want to think beyond that time. The world seemed so right at this moment, and I just wanted to bask in it. My career was where I worked all these years to get it to be, and I had a wonderful job that I loved. My daughter was doing well both academically and socially in college, and I was deliriously happy to see her have opportunities that would lead to a very bright future for her. Things had worked out perfectly with Jeff and me. We were madly in love, and I was confident that our relationship was on solid ground. I told myself that if this was as good as it got, I was fine with it. I didn't dare to ask or expect more.

A year passed, and the bond between Jeff and me grew even stronger. We maintained and enjoyed a regular schedule of being together, with few hiccups. We shared a love of our work, and surprisingly, that became a key topic of discussion more and more frequently. Jeff was a senior official for a sizable industrial distribution organization, reporting to its CEO. It was a privately held company, as most in that industry were. At this time, many of those types of companies were focused on acquiring similar, smaller companies. Jeff became the key figure in designing acquisition strategies that would not only grow his company in size but also diversify its portfolio of products and services as well. This innovative twist he added to the company's acquisition binge was well beyond the calculations of his competitors and would prove to catapult his firm high above the rest. As I had always been a fan of inventive, forward thinking concepts, I loved talking to Jeff about his plans. Knowing my career background and accomplishments, Jeff became increasingly curious of my experience in human resources development, knowing that the company I worked for hadn't had this module prior to my employment there, and it was my principal assignment to establish it. Jeff's industry was primarily made up of small mom-and-pop shops that were not subject to the various employment mandates that larger organizations were. Consequently, Jeff began formulating plans for one more element to his organizational growth plan, to develop and implement a human resources component, something entirely new to this industry. It was so exciting to learn about I felt that my little bit of input made me a small part of it, and I was thrilled.

It was an exceptionally warm spring, and Jeff planned a getaway to Mackinac Island. This would be our last weekend for a few weeks, as we both had to collect our girls from their college dorms and get them home for the summer. I had never been to the island before, and as usual, he had it planned in great detail. We took the ferry over and were greeted by a grand horse and carriage. We took a slow trot around the island before arriving at the Grand Hotel. I was captivated by the charm and scenery as well as the fragrance of the lilacs that were almost in full bloom. We spent the next day biking, stopping at a particularly gorgeous cliff with the most fabulous view. There was an old fashioned bench there, and we sat for a while, taking in the beauty of this island and its picturesque appeal. It was all so magical. Suddenly, Jeff bent down on his knee, pulled a little box from his pocket, and asked me to marry him.

"Contessa, you pulled me out of a coma and showed me how wonderful life could really be. You've already shared more of me and with me than anyone else who's ever been in it. I feel like I can accomplish anything so long as you're with me, and together, there's no telling what we can do. I love you more than I can say, in every way imaginable. I am not asking, I am begging you to marry me," Jeff asked.

I was completely overwhelmed and began to cry. Jeff handed me the box.

"Go ahead, open it," he instructed. Inside was a gorgeous diamond ring that Jeff took out and placed on my finger as I sat there crying, laughing, kissing him, and trying to get words out of my mouth.

"Jeff, I…I…I'm speechless! I don't know what to say!" I screamed.

"Just say *yes*, silly!" he said as he kissed me more passionately than ever.

"I love you, Jeff, you know I do. But what about my daughter, my job? Can we just stay committed to each other?" I pleaded.

"I promise you, we'll work it all out, just like we worked everything else out. Together we can work anything out," he said.

I sat silently for a moment. "Yes, yes, yes, I'll marry you!" I screamed as we kissed, as though we were the only two people on that enchanting island. One thing we never had to work on was our adventurous lovemaking, and this night, in honor of our engagement, set a new precedent!

For the rest of the weekend, I basked in the glory of marrying Jeff. However, on my way home, reality and my priorities set in. My daughter came first, and I wanted her blessing as well as assurance that she wanted to go forward and be comfortable with her plan to live on her own after graduation. I wanted to hear directly from her that she would be all right with me living in another city. Then there was the financial side. I had a wonderful job with a great salary. While we weren't wealthy, I supported us nicely, and my supplemental jobs allowed me to pay her college tuition and expenses. No way would I give up the financial security that I worked so hard to establish for so many years. It had nothing to do with love or trust; it was rationality, common sense, and reality. Having Jeff's genuine commitment, his love, and his promise of trust was enough for me. I thought about just staying engaged and going on as we had been.

Over the summer months, Jeff was back and forth to visit, meeting Little Contessa. He didn't immediately bowl her over, but she warmed up to him over these summer months. My little girl was on the protective (and cautious) side of her mother, and it was endearing to me to see that part of her. Jeff pressed on to set a date, but I held off. I was glad that my daughter ultimately approved of him, also pleased to have a better feeling for the relationship between Jeff and me. However, the financial issues remained a big concern to me, and I would not go forward without discussing them further. I would address this conversation with Jeff in more detail after I packed up Little Contessa and brought her back to school for senior year.

"Jeff, you know how hard I've worked over all these years. Being a single parent, working multiple jobs, going to night school, fighting for every step to be where I am now. I've always provided a safety net for Little Contessa and me, and I can't abandon that. My salary, my 401(k), my benefits—I can't merely let them go. You cannot expect me to just walk away, go to another city, and start all over again with no guarantees," I declared.

"Your independent nature is one of the things I love about you, Contessa. I never expected that to change. Don't worry, I have a plan," Jeff said.

He went on to describe the last phase of the corporate growth plan he developed. Jeff purposely waited to disclose this piece until after I agreed to marry him. He proposed implementing a human resources department, which I would spearhead, reporting directly and only to the CEO of the company, just as Jeff did. It would be yet another layer of distinction that would elevate the company far above all competition plus realize the value-added benefits that an HR department contributed. The salary and benefits were very appealing. Jeff emphasized this would be a huge challenge, but he had full confidence that nobody was more suited to undertake this challenge than I was. He had already proposed this plan with all senior management members within the company, and they all agreed to it. Nobody loves a challenge more than I do, and I have to admit, this was a very enticing offer. I was thrilled at the prospect of undertaking this intriguing operation, but I needed to hear what Little Contessa's thoughts were. I couldn't make this move without her blessing. Ultimately, I did get that, and plans were soon under-way to set Little Contessa up in her own apartment when she came home for Christmas break.

I worked on a five year operating plan for the human resources department implementation and submitted it to the company's CEO. He approved it, as well as all other salary and benefit options that I negotiated. Done and done! However, one more detail lingered, and I couldn't shake it out of my head. I don't mind taking a chance, especially when I'm rolling the dice on myself. But it was a huge risk. What if, for whatever reason, things didn't work out between Jeff and me? I mean, shit happens! Then what? I'd relocate back to Chicago and start all over again? Nope, I'd have to have a security blanket in order for me to make this move. After much thought, I came up with one. I would present it to Jeff when we spoke tonight.

Jeff was on a high this night, reveling in how well our plans were falling into place. He continued to press me for an actual wedding date, opening the conversation by trying to get me to pick a date.

"Jeff, there's one more thing I really need before I can do that," I began.

"Jeez, sweetie, I thought we covered everything. What's up?" he asked.

I had never, ever asked a man for anything, nor would I ever, but this wasn't asking a favor. This was all about me being the one who was making all the changes, me taking all the risk. It wasn't about trust; it was all about rationally thinking through the situation and providing a safety net for myself.

First explaining my rationale for the request I was about to make to Jeff, I finished with, "Jeff, we are taking bold steps in merging our personal and professional lives. The risk is all mine, the changes are mine, and if, for any reason, it doesn't work out, the problems to put my life back together again are all mine. That said, I'm going to need you to provide me with the security of two times my annual salary. This is business Jeff, not personal." I wasn't being a bitch; I was being smart, and I knew he could handle it.

Silence.

"I get it. I told you I'd do anything to marry you, and I meant it. I'll send the check tomorrow. So when will you set a date?" Jeff asked.

"As soon as the check clears!" I laughed.

"Contessa, you missed your calling. You should've been a lawyer." He laughed back. This would not be the first time he made that reference.

The next eight months were fast and furious. I secured a lovely apartment for Little Contessa to live in after graduation. We moved all my home furnishings over before she left for her senior year of college. We were both pleased with her new setup. I packed up my personal things and headed off to my new home in Michigan, where

Jeff happily waited to greet me. We rented a house in a lovely area for one year until we decided where to plant ourselves permanently. I was adamant about not living in the house Jeff shared with his ex wife. *No way!* I wanted a clean, fresh start; *clean and fresh* would never be applied to the house they occupied. Jeff agreed. I had two whole days to get settled in before starting work.

The headquarters consisted of two buildings; Jeff's office was in one, mine in the other. The first few weeks, I held a series of meetings with the employees, introducing myself, the new direction of the company, the addition of the HR department, and what the benefits of this new sector would bring the company. The five year operating plan was well received by employees, realizing there would be a greater emphasis on them and their work environment. When Jeff said their company was a bit behind in the HR area, I didn't think he realized what an understatement that was. I couldn't believe what I walked into. The company was void of even the most basic tools every organization should have to instill their mission, structure, and guidelines for employees. No employee files, no employee handbook, work rules, or corporate framework. Absent of any formal processes for hiring, terminations, reviews, salaries, etc. I knew this would be a startup enterprise, but I never would've guessed it would be as bad as it actually was. My strategy for climbing this mountain was to start by implementing the most essential items and building from there. To create documentation on 150 employees, review medical benefit and 401(k) programs to strengthen them, update the word processing platforms and train staff to utilize them, spend time in each department, citing areas of deficiency and implementing improvements— these were among the very first of my new challenges. Traveling to over a dozen branches, training a manager in each on all new policies and systems, was next. Soon I was off to Texas A&M University to study quality management, a program that would become paramount to the industrial distribution arena. In a crash course, I successfully completed a full semester. I would use the tools from this course to create a blueprint and guideline for all employees, practices, policies, and procedures. Next on the list was to establish a working relationship with the corporate attorneys who specialized in employment law and were noted as the best in the city. My work would have to pass these employment experts before being presented to Jeff first, as President, then our CEO, for his personal approval and ultimate implementation. I would work very closely with our legal team to achieve the ultimate goal of the human resources adaptation saving money, keeping the company out of court, and creating a more structured, progressive work environment. A daunting task, to say the least, but I had full confidence in my abilities to achieve the goals that lay before me. Jeff was my biggest fan and supporter as well as a huge help to get the few reluctant good ole boys on board, those who were not accepting of change. My plate runneth over; days were very long, but it was still very invigorating!

On the home front, Jeff and I were flourishing. There was no period of adjustment; cohabitation was splendid from the start, despite our differences. We were the reincarnation of Felix and Oscar. Jeff was worse than the original Oscar to my neater-than-neat Felix. He was completely oblivious to what a slob he was, and I became accustomed to picking up after him, like a mom cleaning up after her son. Leaving dirty clothes and wet towels on the floor, used dishes on the table, magazines and mail thrown all over the counters…*Ugh!* But I took a deep breath and followed him around, cleaning up the constant mess he made. It was even a little comical to me that he had no clue as to how things got cleaned up. I said to myself, *No situation is perfect, and if this is the worst of our relationship, I can deal with it, as we are so happy overall.* Integrating work with our personal life seemed to have strengthened our bond. Discussion on what was being planned, rolled out, accomplished, plus next on the list was ongoing between Jeff and me. Rather than get bored, we thrived on it. We worked hard and played just as hard. We were both very athletic and played tennis and golf; we biked, hiked, bowled, and played just about anything that kept us moving. We found both humor and solace in the same things. Jeff was extremely romantic and made sure we had time for new experiences. It was all very close to perfection.

However, into everyone's life a little rain must fall.

Jeff's mother was the consummate Wicked Witch of the West, Cinderella's stepmother, and Phoebe Tyler rolled into one. Forever pointing out her aristocratic (and fabricated) ancestry, Madge was an arrogant and condescending narcissist who took great pride in communicating her importance and self imposed stature on everyone she encountered. While she was stiffly courteous to me in Jeff's presence, she let me know in no uncertain terms that I was the white trash her son dragged here from Chicago whenever she and I were alone. I must admit her act was good; she even fooled me for a while. I never revealed that I had her number. *Let her think she scares me,* I thought. Jeff expressed to me that she had always been an overbearing, meddlesome bitch of a mother who had made his life, as well as his beloved father's, miserable. Jeff also told me his mother just wasn't happy unless she was directing everyone to do exactly what she wanted. He put up with it for years, just to shut her up. Having this knowledge made it a whole lot easier to deal with her. I countered her stupid, haughty digs with a smile and accounts of how happy Jeff and I were, particularly in the bedroom, which I knew drove her out of her mind! Touché, bitch!

Jeff had two daughters, who were younger versions of Madge. With the same high-and-mighty tone and tactics as their grandmother, Gabby and Abby sharpened their tongues and lifted their noses up a bit higher whenever they were around me, which, thankfully, wasn't very often. I found great humor in listening to them constantly toot their own horn, pat themselves on the back, and look down on everyone around them, particularly me. Apparently, nobody else ever complimented them, so they felt they had to do it themselves. They were very direct in conveying that I could never mean more to their father than they did, and why he "settled" for me was a mystery to them. In response, I expressed sorrow for them, thinking that a loving relationship is a contest, followed by the sharpest, most sarcastic tongue of all: mine. It only took a few retaliations by me for them to realize they were no match for my biting payback, and I'd always be ready for them. All this behind Jeff's back, of course, and soon they got the message not to provoke me. Always chasing their love, Jeff was merely a lapdog for them, and a sad one at that. The girls hung the divorce of their parents over Jeff's head, using it against him as a tool to secure their whims of the moment. A new car, a trip, shopping sprees, extra spending money—he was their cash cow, and they played him like a violin. Thankfully, their visits were few and far between, lasting only long enough for them to sing the blues and get whatever it was that they came for. As soon as he fell for their act and provided whatever their whims were, they were gone. Sensing the ongoing pain they caused Jeff, I made it a point to be extra affectionate and loving to him following the departure of his evil offspring.

While I loved my job and all its challenges, the office was not void of such menaces either. The employees immediately saw improvements in their workplace and consequently were vocal in their satisfaction. However, there were three vice presidents, whom I take pleasure in referring to as Moe, Larry, and Curly. These three were direct subordinates of Jeff. Moe, Vice President of Sales, was a handsome man in his fifties, married, but always on the prowl and let everyone know it. He traveled a great deal and frequently came back with stories of conquests while on the road. He believed himself to be Jeff's best friend. Larry, Vice President of Operations, was also a married man in his fifties. Larry was a devout Christian, and while he bragged of his ethics and devotion to Jeff, he was, in actuality, as shady as they come and would throw the Good Lord Himself under the bus to save his own skin. As Vice President and Treasurer, Curly also pledged his loyalty to Jeff, but I came to learn he had many under the table kickback deals in the works with various entities the company had dealings with. Among them was an arrangement with their local insurance provider, who paid Curly to keep the corporate insurance in place without question on the rising premiums. Jeff and I occasionally socialized with the three VPs and their wives, and in that circumstance, they made sure Jeff saw them fawn all over me. Anything to please their boss and assure him all was wonderful. I know that it's kind of normal to blow a little smoke up your boss's ass now and again, but these three could have alerted Smokey Bear with their bullshit! And as Smokey says, where there's smoke, there's fire! They were all aware of Jeff's bad marriage, bratty kids, over-bearing mother, and low self-esteem. I watched and observed. Their smoke signals targeting Jeff's ass were to bolster his confidence in their loyalty to him. In turn, he would never question what they were doing or why they were doing it. If something went wrong, the three stooges pointed a finger at someone else and Jeff accepted it. As a result, they got bigger paychecks, bonuses, vacation time, and many other extra perks.

The three vice presidents reported directly to Jeff, and it was known throughout the company they pretty much ran the day-to-day operations. They were aware that the programs I was working on would be integrated into their areas, and I immediately encountered resistance from each of them. I was determined to remain calm and focused and believed I could break them down by virtue and results of these positive new programs. I was relentless in my pursuit to have them see the overall benefits for the company. I kept their opposition to myself. Jeff was a bit naive when it came to them, and it would serve me no purpose to go running to him, complaining that his three top VPs were not playing ball with me. I had to figure this out on my own.

One day, Moe called me, asking me to meet him in Curly's office. I got there to find Moe, Larry, and Curly seated alongside one another, with one empty chair in the middle of the room reserved for me.

"Good afternoon, gentlemen. We didn't have a meeting scheduled, but for you I'll be flexible," I began with a grin.

"Contessa, we thought it was time you learned how things work around here," Moe, the head stooge and ringleader, began.

"Oh. So we're here for you all to enlighten me, is that correct?" I sarcastically asked.

"Look, honey," Moe continued, "we've been here from the beginning. We have an established relationship with Jeff. We run things the way we see fit. We tell him what we think he needs to know while he's running around buying up smaller companies and cutting deals with other big owners."

"Yeah, it's a well oiled machine, and we're gonna keep it that way," Larry chimed in.

"And your point is?" I asked.

"If you think you're gonna bust in and take over, we're not gonna roll over for anyone, let alone some broad. If you think you can waltz in and take charge over our operations just because you're sleeping with the boss, think again, lady!" Larry finished.

I sneered at Curly and asked, "Don't be shy. Surely, you must have something to contribute."

"Look at it this way. We're trying to save you a whole lot of time and energy. Forget about this company. Jeff's a member to the best country club in this area. Go to the club, go shopping, spend his money like his ex-wife did. Sit back and be the trophy wife he's been looking for," Curly added.

"The bottom line here, Contessa, is that our operation's been in place for a long time. We have things just the way we want them. We're not gonna allow you to get into our business and stir things up," Moe declared.

To say I was livid would be a massive understatement. I was a volcano about to erupt. Knowing an explosive response from me would be welcome to them helped me to remain calm. "Gentlemen, I'm a put-your-cards-on-the-table kind of person, so I'd really like to thank you for making the picture crystal clear," I responded.

"Does that mean you'll quit?" Larry asked.

I got up from my chair and walked over to them, sticking my face directly in theirs. "No. That means I'm going to be up your ass higher than a Preparation H suppository, and there's not a fucking thing you can do about it. You forget I was brought here by your boss to oversee an operation sanctioned by both the president and the CEO. Either you're hiding things, you're threatened by a girl, or both. So I'm going to do what I was hired to do regardless of you three. Feel free to threaten me anytime, guys, that's like vitamins to me. And if you go running to Jeff complaining like little bitches, you'll only piss me off more than you did today, and I promise that won't end well for you. You wanna play? I'll play. Bring it, fellas. I'm ready."

I stormed out and went back to my office. I was suspicious of them from the start, and this discussion proved they were all up to no good. Why else would they be so vehemently opposed to a new entity that would only bring about positive changes and enhancements to all? I vowed then and there to get to the bottom of whatever they were up to. But I wouldn't go to Jeff with this. No, I couldn't complain to him about the people he was closest to, revealing they were taking advantage of him. That would only turn Jeff against me. I could never figure out why Jeff was so insecure around these three. Despite his undisputed intelligence, he seemed to have little confidence in administering authority, even when it was warranted. I thought perhaps because the stooges knew Jeff for so long, watched his mother, wife, and kids keep him under their thumb, they figured they could do the same. I have to admit that they were extremely good at blowing smoke up Jeff's ass, which was why, I suppose, he felt they were so loyal to him. That was the only conclusion I thought made sense, which made it all the easier for Moe, Larry, and Curly to continue with their conniving, greedy, and dishonest ways.

So here I sat, assessing the new world I was in. The mother-in-law from hell, the evil stepchildren, and the coworkers who were trying to oust me from the very position their boss put me in to help him achieve his business goals. All this while Jeff and I were planning our wedding! I was determined to make it all work. We ultimately decided on a very small simple wedding with our children and parents. The wedding would take place on Mackinac Island, very near to where Jeff proposed to me. I was so excited to have Little Contessa with me for a long weekend. We went for a long walk together, enabling us to catch up. She was happy in her job as well as her apartment. The relationship with her boyfriend had grown and flourished so much that they decided to move in together. Little Contessa expressed she was in a very happy place. I was delighted things were going so well for her. It was now my turn. Ever my rock of judgment and voice of reason, my little girl did not fail me.

"Mom, it sounds like everything is okay between you and Jeff but it's a mess all around you. Are you truly happy? Is this what you really want?" she asked.

"Yes, I am. I feel like it's just so right this time. We're really happy together, particularly when it's just us. Yes, I want this, I want him. My only challenge is managing the shit storm around us," I said.

"Looks like a pretty big storm, Mom!" Little Contessa laughed. "I mean, your work situation is bad enough, but the personal side isn't much better. Jeez, Gabby and Abby are so plastic and phony. The act they're putting on to be nice to me is actually pretty funny. Not that I care, but what did you threaten them with?" We laughed. "And Madge! I sat there for an hour listening to her brag about herself. I can see where those girls get it from. They must not have any friends who compliment them, so they do it themselves, right?" More laughs. "I know you can handle them all right, but I really worry about the guys from work. Sounds like they've really got it in for you. That's going to cause more serious problems for you and Jeff," Little Contessa went on.

"That's the tough one. I'm convinced these three have things going on they wouldn't want Jeff to know about. The scope of my work should uncover anything that isn't right. When I find something, I'll deal with them directly. You know Jeff can't handle confrontation—they know it too—so I'll keep things to myself and just do my own thing," I finished.

"Okay, well, right now your thing is to get married, so let's go and get ready," she ordered.

"I love you, baby girl!" I responded as I kissed her forehead.

The next few years passed so quickly. Jeff and I maintained an exhaustive schedule, traveling so much we never spent an entire month at home. He was achieving his ultimate goal of making our company one of the biggest, best, and most innovative. His acquisitions were now branching out to other states. A financial wiz, he put the financial deals together, and I trained new staff on corporate structure. The human resources department was now a staff of seven. The programs I developed were rolled out and widely accepted. As the company grew, so did the scope of my work. The national association for our industry ultimately recognized the need for a Human Resources Board and asked me to be its director. I was joined by four other HR directors from the largest companies in our industry, which was about to go international. Together we developed criteria that would become the industry protocol for hiring, terminations, job descriptions, personalized review processes, benefits, employee manuals, and processes on procedures for just about all possible situations. It was hard work, but extremely gratifying, particularly when the favorable results became apparent.

Jeff and I were proud of how well we worked together. We became a great team, Jeff initiating financial structures for acquisitions and me folding the newly acquired smaller firms into our company. We were acknowledged as the dynamic duo by many directors from the national association. Although our travels were quite taxing, our accomplishments were, in some ways, groundbreaking to the industry and made our efforts worthwhile. We were personally and professionally very happy, thriving on the success we were realizing. An added benefit, being on the road separated us from the negativity that surfaced from his mother, daughters, and the stooges, who, now and again, did cause us to argue. I bent over backward being kind, personable, and embracing to all of them, but my efforts were met with resistance from all ends. Why couldn't they see that all I wanted to do was make Jeff happy and to blend us all together? It was understandable why the stooges didn't want me around; they knew I had them figured out. But the mother and daughters? I certainly posed no threat to them. Nonetheless, I continued trying to win them over. Our travels were mostly together; however, our roles required separate trips as well. I didn't mind when Jeff was away, as it gave me extra time at the office as well as an opportunity to do things around the house. Jeff would entertain his mother, get a little more tennis and office time in, and (*ugh!*) have dinner with one or all the stooges when I was gone. It seemed to be a good balance.

I worked closely with two corporate attorneys to secure legal approval before any of my written material became policy. Our legal team concluded that most corporate lawsuits were the result of not having written policies or guidelines to be followed, and that was the primary focus of my work. I developed a wonderful working relationship with the lawyers within the firm. Attorney Scott covered worker's compensation issues. All situations related to either wrongful discharge, harassment, or discrimination were handled by

Attorney Matt, the employment law specialist. The training I conducted with managers included a strong emphasis on these areas. Conceivably, if all policies and procedures were followed, lawsuits against the company would diminish, saving thousands of dollars in both legal fees and settlements. The distribution industry was riddled with lawsuits, primarily worker's compensation claims, due to very lax procedures, training, and management. The bulk of the newly implemented quality control procedures becoming part of the culture was specifically aimed at preventing such cases. In just these few short years, I was successful in overturning every single case that was brought against the company, proving positive that incorporating policy, procedure, and structure in place was beneficial for all.

I came across many worker's comp claims that seemed odd to me. The payouts didn't match insurance records, and they lacked supporting paperwork. After reviewing a multitude of legal, insurance and payroll records, I discovered that Curly approved all payments without inquiry, probing their validity or reporting to the attorneys, costing the company tens of thousands of dollars. In addition, a few of the payouts were to employees who had already left the company and were apparently left on the payroll by Curly! He must have forgotten that my department kept impeccable employee records. Curly obviously collected their checks and pocketed the money. Larry approved all payroll sheets, so he had to have been on it as well. I immediately notified Scott of the situation, and further research unveiled Curly would work payment of insurance claims out with Larry, splitting the money with him. The mystery was how they explained these large payout chunks to Jeff, but it was inevitable that Larry cooked the books and made up some cockamamy story to satisfy him. Jeff was by no means a dummy, but he was notoriously weak around the stooges and always backed off from them if it meant any type of confrontation. If either of them even slightly suspected Jeff was becoming suspicious, they simply started talking about "other career opportunities," which initiated Jeff to quickly back off. They had his number and played him.

Moe caused significant legal issues as well. A conceited womanizer, he was very condescending to women and had no filter as to what he said or to whom he said it. Moe thought nothing of openly throwing out disgusting remarks regarding body parts of several female employees and what he'd like to do with them. Despite my training, constant reminders, and arguments about sexual harassment in the workplace, Moe merely laughed my efforts away, as did Larry and Curly. They considered themselves above anyone's authority; they had their own rules to live by and would not be challenged by anyone, least of all me. I brought the seriousness of this issue to Jeff, but he disregarded it as "Oh, that's just his way, he doesn't mean anything by it." From the beginning, I warned Jeff that I would not, under any circumstances, defend the company on a sexual harassment case.

A potential discrimination case had been building. One of our specialty divisions had more than doubled in size. Elaine, the existing department manager, was a highly intelligent lady who ran her department with the utmost precision. Having been the manager from its start, Elaine had the knowledge, expertise, and management skills the department required. The staff respected and adored her. It was decided that we would split the department in half and hire another manager. We promoted John, an existing salesman from that department. This division fell under Moe's supervision. Moe set John's salary almost three times above that of Elaine's plus gave him a company car and several other perks Elaine was not receiving. I spent countless hours arguing against it, pointing out Elaine was way more experienced and had already ran this department successfully for many years. Starting a new manager, particularly one of the opposite sex, at such a higher pay grade was inviting a lawsuit. Like employees ultimately do, Elaine eventually found out John's salary. She was outraged and blew up in my office, demanding that I talk to her boss, Moe, about the unfairness of the situation and her demand for equality in both pay and perks. I did just that, to no avail. Elaine became increasingly agitated over it, repeatedly arguing to do something about it. After several attempts with Moe proving futile, I took the issue to Jeff, something I had never done before. Jeff shrugged the situation off, indicating that it fell under Moe's jurisdiction and I should work it out with him.

"How would it look if I tried to intervene in supervising Moe's subordinates, especially with pressure from you?" was Jeff's answer.

"It would look like you recognize a very discriminatory situation that's putting the company in jeopardy and, as Moe's boss, you're directing him to make it right!" I snapped back.

I warned Jeff that Elaine was becoming more and more unglued over it, and I had a very bad feeling something damaging would come of this, that she was like a time bomb waiting to explode. I reiterated that if Elaine initiated a lawsuit, I would not defend the company, as this was both harassment and discrimination. The issue caused several fights between Jeff and me. After a while, I just gave it up, hoping and praying it would never amount to anything. Jeff began traveling a bit more on his own, and at this point, I was so consumed with work I really didn't care.

Naturally, I disclosed the entire Elaine situation to Scott and Matt. We strategized on how best to bring all the violations to Jeff's attention, adding Elaine's story as a potential disaster but something we could turn around if we did the right thing quickly. They proposed disclosing everything in an open forum at our next senior managers' meeting.

"Contessa, better let Matt and me take the reins on this. You exposing Moe, Larry, and Curly will cause a war, and you'll be the only casualty. Let us do the dirty work," Matt suggested.

"If we approach Jeff alone, he'll turn his head to it like he always has. We've been very aware of the hold those three have had on him for years. I guess it's easier for him to believe they are his soldiers rather than his enemies. Since some of this involves theft of company funds and falsifying payroll records, we're going to recommend resignation without benefits in exchange for prosecution. We need to expose them openly, in front of their peers, for all to acknowledge the significance of what they did. At that point, no way could Jeff back down from them once the other managers realize how far they took things," Scott finished.

"Great strategy, guys. I appreciate you trying to keep me out of it, but you do realize once the proof is offered, they'll know it came from me," I added.

"Contessa, we've known Jeff for many years now. We're aware of what kind of family life he's had. He caves with confrontation. We've seen him run from it for years. It's easier for him to look the other way and pretend everything is great. We know what a positive effect you've had on him, that you truly love him. He's never been happier. You've done so much for him and the company, as well as the industry, but you shook things up in the boys' club and nailed them. We're not married to their boss, so we have no fear of retaliation!" Scott laughed.

"Ha, ha! You're right. Whatever you say. Our meeting is in two weeks, and Jeff will be away for most of that time, so I won't feel so guilty about keeping all this to myself," I finished.

I was having a busy Friday afternoon after an unusually busy week. Jeff was scheduled to get home from a week long trip, and I was really looking forward to a quiet, relaxing weekend alone with him, hoping we could smooth out some of the rough edges plaguing us as a result of all the work bullshit. I called Jeff's office to see if he had returned. His secretary told me he did but was in a closed door meeting with Moe. Okay, at least I knew he was back. As I was beginning to wrap up my day, Elaine came charging into my office. She was disoriented, mumbling one minute and yelling the next. Something was very wrong. She had a crazed look on her face; her eyes were bulging from her face. Elaine began ranting about her co-manager, John, and Moe trying to force her out.

"You promised you'd take care of it! You promised you'd save me! I counted on you. You were my only hope, the only one who could help me!" Elaine screamed.

I jumped up and ran to her, hugging her. I rubbed her back while she cried hysterically. I told her I would get her some water and we could talk, to please just sit and relax for a moment. I ran out, quickly, instructing my assistant, Suzanne, not to leave her desk, that something was wrong with Elaine. The entire staff heard Elaine's rant, and the office was frozen. When I returned to my office, Elaine was getting hysterical, crying and mumbling things I couldn't understand. It was all about the salary situation, but I was able to make out a repeating "You promised, you promised" from her. Suddenly, she began throwing herself against my wall, banging her head on the door repeatedly, screaming, "He's gonna throw me out!"

I ran out to Suzanne and told her to call an ambulance, then call Jeff and tell him to get over here immediately. Everyone heard Elaine screaming out; I didn't blame anyone for not coming in to help me console her. It was a pretty scary situation. I couldn't get Elaine to calm down, and finally, she ran down the hall to Moe's office and began tearing it up.

"I'm not garbage! He wants to throw me away!" she screamed while throwing things around and hurling herself against the wall.

Suzanne eventually came in to try to help out, but not even the two of us could restrain Elaine. While everyone was aware of what was happening, it was only Suzanne and I who saw that psycho, crazed look on Elaine's face. Finally, she stood there, frozen, and urinated on the floor, afterward letting out a hysterical scream, followed by more crying. I got her to sit down and ran out to get some water as the paramedics arrived. When Elaine saw them, she really flipped out and actually went into a seizure. They restrained her but alerted us that because Elaine caused destruction on private property, they had to call the police. I begged them not to, but they insisted, saying it was protocol. I whispered to Suzanne to call Jeff, find the stooges, and get their asses over here.

She called Jeff's office. His secretary said Jeff was in his office, now with Moe, Larry, and Curly. The door was closed and he wouldn't answer his private line. In what was actually minutes but seemed like an eternity, the police arrived. I begged, I pleaded with them not to take her away, to please let the paramedics take her to the hospital. "She needs medical attention, not a wrap sheet!" I pleaded. They insisted it was their duty. They actually handcuffed Elaine, and she really went berserk, kicking, screaming, and fighting the officers. Looking me right in the eyes, with that crazed look, she screamed, "Save me! Save me! Save me!" The officers put her in the car, took a report from me, and took her away to jail. I immediately ran to pull her file for her husband's work phone number, to explain what all had transpired. He went ballistic. I offered any and all assistance to him, but he told me what I could do with that offer and hung up.

I thought my heart was going to pound out of my chest. I was outraged. I stormed over to Jeff's office. Everyone was huddled together, buzzing about Elaine. The door was closed, and without even knocking, I burst in. There were Jeff and the three stooges, all giggly and laughing. I knew they were making jokes about Elaine. They could see I was furious and not in a laughing mood.

"You think this is all so funny? Big bad asses you think you are, but you hid in here like pussies!" I screamed at the stooges.

"Contessa, calm down. The employees will hear you," Jeff said.

"They should hear me! You want to run the show, but when the shit hits the fan, you all run for cover. Fuck you all!" I continued yelling.

"Contessa, watch your language and lower your voice!" Jeff demanded.

"Fuck you too! That poor girl just had a nervous breakdown in my office, in my arms! And this is on all of you!" I pointed to Moe. "I warned you a million times, I offered suggestions that would fix everything, but no, you snubbed your nose at me. Big shot, right? Well, guess what, big shot? Her husband is out of control over this, as he should be. He's going to sue us for everything—discrimination, harassment, and anything else that'll stick. And the good news is that he'll win."

"Contessa, this is your strong suit, you work so well with our attorneys. You'll find a way out of it just like you always do," Jeff demanded.

"Jeff, I'm talking to you as my boss, not my husband. This situation has been brewing for the last three years. In all that time, I've done everything I could to rectify it, and you all shrugged it off. So let me say for the very last time, I will not—repeat *not*—be part of defending this company for destroying Elaine's life when all she wanted was fair treatment. Go fuck yourselves, all of you!"

I dashed out, slamming the door behind me. I knew the employees heard me, and a few applauded as I departed. So much for a quiet, relaxing weekend. How Jeff could allow this—after all the warnings from me, Scott, and Matt—was beyond me. I believed he was just as responsible as Moe was, as he had the authority to intervene, as Moe's boss, to diffuse this situation, and he did nothing. A woman's life was now turned upside down.

I drove around for some time, not wanting to go home. The thought of looking at him made me sick, but I ultimately had to. Upon arriving home, I didn't even get the door closed when Jeff came crashing down on me.

"How dare you talk to me that way! Especially in front of my vice presidents. Who do you think you are?" Jeff demanded in an icy tone I hadn't heard before.

"I'm also one of your vice presidents. But I'm an honest one, a dedicated one, and one that stands up for people, for what's right," I softly responded.

"You're supposed to stand by *me*! That's what's right. And you will stand by me and the company by defending it against any action we get hit with. *That* is what's right! And you will apologize to my vice presidents for talking to them the way you did. That's also what's right! Are we understood?" he finished.

I couldn't believe my ears. Who was this man? I didn't recognize the person hurling these directives at me.

The biggest argument of all followed and went on until neither of us had much of a voice left. I spilled the entire story of how Moe, Larry, and Curly had been ripping off the company. I included that all the evidence was in the hands of Scott and Matt, who were soon to present it to the senior managers. He now knew everything. Instead of thanking me, showing appreciation for exposing people pretending to be loyal to him, he exploded. Jeff refused to believe his "devoted" friends would deceive him and the company, that no matter what, he would never press charges against them. Worse than that, his biggest concern was over the bad publicity he would get, having this happen right under his nose. Who was this cold hearted, egotistical bastard?

We slammed doors in separate bedrooms.

Exhausted as I was, I couldn't sleep. I got up and tiptoed to our room, where Jeff was sleeping like a baby. Go figure! It was about three in the morning, and I wandered the house. While in the kitchen, I noticed Jeff's briefcase lying open on the counter. I am not a snooper. I had never, ever gone through Jeff's things. But as if a force was guiding my hand, I reached into the zippered pouch inside the case and pulled out a bunch of folded up, scrunched up papers. I began opening them up as my heart pounded harder and louder. On notepaper from various hotels Jeff had stayed were names and contact information, some with dates and times, of women he apparently made contact with while traveling.

If the events of this last day weren't enough, I knew in that very instant my marriage was over. Jeff had been traveling more than usual lately. Arguments over work related issues were increasing. My God, he was doing the exact same thing as he was when I met him. Running from confrontation at home and finding comfort elsewhere. I was devastated. I was crushed. I was gasping for breath. Thoughts flooded my head. I'd always had a strong ability to function well in crisis mode. Lord knows, I'd had plenty of practice. I prayed that attribute didn't fail me now! I knew exactly what I had to do. I quietly sneaked into my room to grab clothes. I dressed and headed for the office. I knew the security codes, so getting in at this hour was no problem. Once in my office, I began loading files into my trunk. Since I did all of Jeff's expense reports, I loaded the last three years' worth. The expense records would include dates of travel, where he stayed, phone bills, and with them I could check things he was reimbursed for against nonbusiness entertainment he received. I worked with the phone company on the design and implementation of a new interbranch phone system, which included cell phone records for every manager in the company. I loaded phone bills for the last two years. I took Jeff's credit card receipts as well. I worked fast and furiously. I finished just as the sun was coming up. I succeeded in getting back home before Jeff even woke up.

I made some tea and sat on the deck.

Jeff awoke and ignored me as he ate breakfast. How this asshole could even eat was beyond me! Jeff got dressed and left. Good! I needed to be alone to think. I actually laughed as I noticed his briefcase still open on the counter. What an idiot!

I knew this would all blow up the instant Jeff discovered those notepapers were missing. The clock was ticking on that. The records were safely locked in my trunk, so I had no worry of him finding them or realizing I even had them, as they were kept in my locked office file cabinets. My mind raced with thought until I finally dozed off. I woke up to a quiet, dark house. It was late, and Jeff hadn't returned. I didn't care, but I did wonder where he was. Sunday came and went without Jeff coming home. Fine with me, as it allowed me to rethink and fine tune my plans. I woke up Monday morning to Jeff entering the house. Without saying a word, he showered, put on a suit, collected his briefcase, and left. I was certain he would soon discover his missing little black book notes and would act.

I immediately called the attorneys to inform them on the Elaine story as well as Jeff's reaction. They were shocked but convinced that once he saw the proof, he would see it differently and come to his senses. Both attorneys said they would schedule a meeting with him immediately and would follow up with me later. I advised them of the horrific arguing that followed, reiterating that there was no way I would defend the company should this become a lawsuit. Knowing how hard I worked to rectify things on Elaine's behalf, Matt and Scott certainly understood. They were sympathetic to my situation, citing what an awkward position I was in. No kidding! I had the weight of what happened to Elaine, the shock of my husband/boss demanding that I disregard the unethical nature of it and go to bat for the company, apologize to the assholes who caused the problem, and all this while just finding out my husband was obviously cheating up a storm! What a weekend!

Soon after that conversation, Jeff called. I hardly recognized his voice. His tone was an icy cold that I had never heard before. He was direct and to the point.

"I'm filing for divorce. At some point, I'll come by to collect my things. You are no longer allowed on company grounds," he said, as if reading from a script.

In the calmest tone I could muster, I responded, "If you're firing me, you're going to have to send me a letter of termination, stating reasons."

Click. He hung up.

Even though I expected this in some manner, it was an excruciating blow. So just like that, it was all over. I stood there silently, praying for strength to do what I needed to do, in order for justice to be served. For Elaine and now for me. Okay, it was on!

First call was to the locksmiths to change all the locks on the house. Next, change the security codes on alarm system. I unloaded the records from my trunk into my home office, which became command central. With cell phone records and expense reports, I put a pattern together. My hotel expertise allowed me the skill to obtain copies of itemized bills from each stay, which included the hotel phone records. These hotel folios were faxed directly to me. The records proved links to the numbers I found in Jeff's briefcase, along with restaurant receipts from those cities. Believe it or not, some restaurants keep records on credit card payments, attaching the food order to the payment receipt. These would be helpful in proving Jeff was not entertaining business associates, or at least not the industry associates he claimed on his records. The only business he had going on was monkey business, which was not reimbursable and illegal if submitted for company reimbursement. I had those forwarded to me as well. I worked nonstop for four days straight, putting this puzzle together. I could not and did not sleep.

On day five, Jeff arrived home and became all bent out of shape when his key didn't fit into the door. He furiously banged on the front door while I quickly hid all the files I was working on. I looked a wreck. No sleep for days left me with bloodshot eyes and hardly any voice. Jeff immediately went into a rant over me changing the locks.

"You said you were leaving. I have no idea what craziness is going on with you. I have to protect myself," I responded in a whisper.

"Sit down. I have something for you to sign," Jeff demanded very coldly.

I sat as he threw papers at me, demanding I sign them right then and there. I sat there pretending to be defeated and broken. I knew I looked the part. I wanted Jeff to believe he already got the better of me, that he had nothing to fear.

"Jeff, I haven't slept in days. I'm too dizzy to even see, let alone read and sign these. Please give me a few days to look them over," I pathetically asked.

Jeff told me he would check with me in a few days. With that, he gathered some of his things and left.

I carefully read through the papers. His grounds for divorce were irreconcilable differences. He wanted me out of our home and out of his business. If I needed a kick to get me through this, here it was! My blood raged. "You mother fucker! You cold hearted bastard!" I screamed. "You think you're gonna throw me out after all I did for you, your fucking family, and your company? You ungrateful fucking prick! I'll show you who you're dealing with, if it takes my last breath to do it!" I vowed.

He obviously had somewhere to go. *He isn't one to be alone. He must have a girl stashed someplace,* I thought. I hired a private detective to have him followed. Now more invigorated than ever, I worked at lightning speed to piece together the puzzle of Jeff's philandering, which stretched across a multitude of cities, over a two year period. By the end of the next day, I had all the pieces in place. I took the longest shower in the world and passed out. Next day, I heard from the private detective I hired. Yep, Jeff had a girlfriend and he moved right in with her.

I compiled my investigative masterpiece and hired James Arnold, a divorce attorney dubbed the F. Lee Bailey of divorce in our area. After hearing the details of our marriage, my work for the company, and what all I had been subjected to, he assured me it would be an open-and-shut case, particularly with the evidence I brought with me. Within a week, a date was set for our divorce depositions to be taken. Since Jeff was the one who filed, his would come first. Mr. Arnold and I rehearsed how his line of questioning Jeff would go. I advised him exactly how and when to get right up in Jeff's face and yell, knowing that was extremely unnerving to Jeff. By the end of the week, we had it down.

Surprisingly, Jeff didn't use one of the corporate attorneys. Perhaps he finally learned about discretion and didn't want his personal dirty laundry aired to them. Jeff's attorney began the process asking the normal questions and factual information. The final question was, "Why do you wish to dissolve your marriage?" Jeff's response was a cold "She puts her work before me and no longer takes interest in me or my needs."

Give me a break!

Now it was my attorney's turn.

Mr. Arnold carved out a rose petaled path for Jeff and led him down it like the pro he was known to be. He had Jeff in the hot seat for over three hours, shoving the information I compiled down his throat. The cheating, lying, falsifying of expense reports and receiving reimbursement, firing me without cause, discrimination in the workplace, all of it. Mr. Arnold included that we were prepared to have an open trial in which all our findings would be publicized in maximum efforts. Such an event would be the cherry on my cake of settling all accounts. Both Jeff and his mother would be mortified at the thought of scandal, that their precious, concocted lineage would be damaged. I reveled in watching Jeff squirm, hearing his voice break, seeing his jaw quiver! If you really want to piss off your legal representation, lie to them or don't disclose the entire story. Jeff did both. His lawyer's face turned a glowing red, his veins hanging out of his neck, looking like his head would explode, until finally he called for a recess. Mr. Arnold and I sat there whispering and giggling about it all. About twenty minutes later, Jeff's attorney reappeared. He announced that Jeff would tear up the papers he initiated and would agree to my terms, whatever they were. Mr. Arnold handed my list of demands over, which included keeping my house and everything in it. The attorney assured us he would draw up new papers that included my requirements and have them processed immediately. All I had to do now was wait about ten days for that to happen.

Just like that, it was done. Over.

Isn't it funny—we went through so much over a long period to be together, and it was all over in a four hour meeting. So sad. But I still had some things to do.

I had an empty feeling as I walked to my car. I sat in it for a moment, collecting my thoughts. I drove to the home of Jeff's ex-wife. I needed to apologize to Lea. I rang her doorbell, and Lea's boyfriend answered. I explained I would like to speak to Lea but would certainly understand if she wouldn't see me.

"Hang on, I'll get her," the boyfriend said.

In a minute, Lea appeared and very graciously invited me in. Between the nature of this small town, plus Gabby and Abby working on Jeff, I was certain she was fully aware of the situation between Jeff and me. She was.

"Lea, I owe you a huge apology," I began.

Lea gave me a confused look and asked for what. I explained how Jeff and I met, that he flat out lied to me about being married, and went through the whole story.

"I want to apologize for any pain the situation may have caused you or that I may have inadvertently caused you. I didn't understand the emotions, the feelings you must have had while going through it, but believe me, I sure do now! Lea, I want you to know how very sorry I am, and I hope you can forgive me."

Lea could not have been more gracious. She assured me it was all good, that she moved on with her life and she was quite happy, especially not having to deal with Jeff's mother any longer. We both got a big laugh out of that. Lea and I exchanged a few very funny Jeff stories, and in the end, we embraced with a friendly goodbye. I actually felt uplifted upon leaving. Asking Lea for forgiveness was a necessary step for me, a first step in moving on.

Within the next two weeks, Mr. Arnold informed me that he received the new divorce papers, that my requirements were all met, and that all I had to do was come in to sign them. I did so that very day. "Congratulations, Contessa. You're now free of that piece of shit. I'll have these processed immediately. I must tell you, though, in all my years of practice, I've never had such a drama free, open-and-shut case that closed so easily. That was due to the information you put together. It had to be heartbreaking for you going through it all, and I commend you. You made my job enormously easier. Actually, it was pretty entertaining. So what will you do now?" he asked.

"I'm going to get my head and my life back together," I told him. I then went home and quietly fell apart, succumbing to the mental exhaustion that I had been riddled with over these last few months.

Sometime later, as I had been enjoying peace and quiet while mulling over considerations as to what to do next, my former assistant, Suzanne, called to advise me that she forwarded mail addressed to me marked "Personal and Confidential" that she thought was something legal. When it arrived, I found it was the notice of charges filed against the company on behalf of Elaine. The charges included discrimination, harassment, emotional distress, and creating a hostile work environment. Spot on! Just as I predicted. I read the papers thoroughly. The suit named the company plus Jeff, as President, along with Moe, as Elaine's direct manager, personally as the defendants. I knew exactly what I had to do.

I called Elaine's attorney. He was aware of who I was and my role in trying to help Elaine these last few years. I first inquired how Elaine was doing. The lawyer advised me that she did have a nervous breakdown, had been hospitalized since the event at the office, that it was quite rough for a few months and would be some time before the possibility of reaching a full recovery. My heart broke for her, but hearing that made what I was about to do much easier. I advised the lawyer that I was now divorced from Jeff and since had absolutely no association with the company. I enlightened the attorney on all the facts regarding Elaine, that I worked with the corporate attorneys on her case, that they were also disgusted by the situation and would still have the supporting evidence on it.

"I'm familiar with the protocol. My advice to you is to first revise these papers and increase the monetary settlement you're seeking times five. Then notify the defendants that you will subpoena me, that I will be your star witness. I absolutely guarantee that you'll never even go to court and you'll get whatever you go after," I advised.

There was a moment of silence.

"You've got guts, lady! Are you sure about this?" he asked.

"I'd bet anything on it. Elaine deserves this and more for what they put her through," I said. I asked him to give my heartfelt regards to Elaine, that I wished nothing but happiness for her future.

That felt awesome!

It wasn't about revenge (okay, maybe just a little); it was more about justice! It was the right thing to do for Elaine. Hopefully, Jeff and his stooges would learn that you couldn't mistreat people without ramification.

A few weeks later, I received a call from Elaine's attorney. He took me up on my recommendation, and just as I had predicted, the case was settled out of court, in Elaine's favor. The attorney was holding the check for Elaine in his hand. I was delighted to hear that and expressed my delight, asking him to once again convey my very best wishes to Elaine and her family.

Sometime later, I received a call from Jeff. I almost didn't pick it up, but then my curiosity got the best of me. I barely spoke, just asked what he wanted. Pleasantries followed. "How have you been?" "I'm so sorry for the way I treated you," "I hope we can be friends," blah, blah, blah.

"Cut to the chase, Jeff. What do you want?" I coldly asked.

"I need you to come back, Contessa. *We* need you to come back. The team you put in place is doing all they can, but the leadership and interaction with the branches is missing. I'll pay you anything you want. You can write your own ticket," Jeff pleaded.

I roared with laughter! Now *this* was karma!

"Jeff, you thought way too much of your arrogant self and far too little of me. I fell for it once, and only a fool would fall for it twice. You said you loved my strength and spirit, but then you wanted to turn me into one of your 'yes' men, and you couldn't deal with it when I didn't play along. You chase the people who use you and shit on the few who are genuine to you. I never could figure that out, but I no longer care. There isn't enough money in the world to entice me back. And now, please go fuck yourself and don't ever call me again!" I triumphantly told him and hung up.

Once again, I laughed out loud, but my laughter turned to tears. I sobbed harder than I had up to this point. I finally let it all out. I sat there feeling victorious in both my divorce and helping Elaine. Neither was a card that I asked for, but they were the hand I was dealt, and I played them well. I won, albeit a bittersweet victory, for sure. The man I loved turned out to be a serial, sociopathic liar and cheat. A man who found it easier to throw me under the bus because I wanted him to face the music and deal with things. I wasn't one of many who told him whatever he wanted to hear in order to gain his trust. A man who could only feel important by surrounding himself with people who blew smoke up his ass in order to take advantage of him. A man who betrayed my honest heart. It was all a tough pill to swallow, but I knew I'd get over it in time. He would stay stuck in a constant shit storm of his own making. I could see now that this was his way. When the going got rough, he got going.

While we had no contact whatsoever, I did come to learn that he went on to several other relationships, bringing the same type of drama to every single one of them. Some people never learn.

The takeaway? Issues present themselves in any relationship. It's weathering those issues together that tests the strength of the relationship. However, when a relationship starts out with drama, be wary! It's hard to build lasting trust on something that begins with a lie. You can't change the spots on some leopards, so pay attention to those spots as soon as you spot them!

The Director

Happy days in LA!

I am vehemently against any type or form of abuse: sexual miscon-
duct, biased, discriminating, or demeaning treatment to or of
anyone in any manner, inequity in jobs and pay scales, etc. There
is no way I could look at myself in the mirror or sleep at night if,
should any of these situations appear before me, I looked away from
them. Hopefully, I made that point in the previous chapter. Wouldn't
the world be a better place if all such conduct could magically be
erased? But alas, until then, I believe anyone exposed to it must act,
do whatever they can to prevent, stop, and/or reveal it. Wearing a
certain color and pinning something to your lapel to show support
is fine, but the key word here is *act*! If you really want to support
the cause, take action, do something. Every situation varies, each
circumstance is its own, but I believe with all my heart that a uni-
versal approach to end this behavior is to address it at the onset. We
may not be able to control the actions of others, but I do believe we
can deter their attitude, change the way a culprit thinks if a different
approach is demonstrated right from the start. Let the guilty party
immediately know they could try, but they won't get away with it.

Following divorce from Jeff, I took a bit of a badly needed break
to relax, rethink, regroup, and reconnect with life. I didn't immediately realize how much of an impact the whole Jeff ordeal had on
me until it was all over. At that point, I fell apart—and I mean really
fell apart! Few people realized what a bad state I was actually in, but
I was very aware. Three divorces. Granted, unusual circumstances
with each. But I refused to be a victim or a woman playing the blame

game. Was it me? What could I have done differently? I must be doing something wrong! I didn't have answers to these questions, and I knew I needed help to get them; that was the only way I could heal myself and move forward positively.

I sought the help of a therapist, which turned out to be the best money and nine months I'd ever spent. The therapist was a strict elderly lady who put me and all my emotions through the ringer. She shoved my face in the mirror, and I didn't like some of the things that I saw. We worked on fixes together, and it turned out to be just the medicine I needed. I eventually got the answers I sought, made a few decisions, and finally felt ready to embark on a new path, a new chapter in my life. I evaluated the skills I had amassed over the years, thought about my passions, and decided on what I believed would be the most advantageous way for me to pursue both.

I had always had a love of reading and writing. In the corporate world, I had written a wide variety of publications and corporate documentation. I began a business writing résumés. My services included additional assistance in job searches, interview, and cover letter guidance. I was enjoying this work but wanted to broaden my scope. I began creative writing classes, engaged in writing groups, and commenced writing short stories. I attended writers' conferences of a variety of sorts, which provided fabulous networking opportunities. Contacts I had made led me to writing magazine articles on human resources, networking, marketing, branding, and self-assessment/improvement. I found it extremely rewarding, particularly when my clients confirmed achieving their desired results.

While attending a creative writing conference, I met a literary professor from UCLA. We worked on a project together for a class that was well received by the others students. The professor and I exchanged many ideas and began working on a script for a play. We shared our work via emails, and before long, the script was complete. We would soon meet at another writers' conference in Las Vegas.

The professor and I met in the lobby of our hotel, where we discussed our project and strategizing toward production. In the midst, the professor noticed Harry Shepherd, the famed writer and director of countless successful televisions shows and blockbuster movies, checking in at the front desk. Mr. Shepherd was the keynote speaker at this conference.

"Look, there's Harry Shepherd! Man, would I love to corner him and talk him into investing in our play!" the professor declared, explaining he met Harry once before and would feel comfortable approaching him.

"Oh, yeah, he's the keynote speaker tonight," I said.

This celebrated man would easily be identified, if not by the sight of him, then surely by his highly recognized voice laced with New York twang. Harry was an older guy, much larger in person than I had seen on both small and large screens. I probed the professor as to how he would go about pitching our play. Asking for money was never one of my strengths; I was always more of a figure-it-out-yourself person. That said, I left the professor with those decisions. He assured me that was the way it was done. We continued our discussion as Mr. Shepherd walked toward us. When Harry got close enough, the professor jumped up to address the famous director.

"Harry Shepherd, great to see you! We met last year at your theater. I was a guest of…blah, blah, blah."

The professor's voice became muffled to me as I felt Mr. Shepherd's intense leer burning a hole right through me. It made me very uncomfortable. I motioned to the professor we'd finish later, that I was leaving. He paid no attention at all, as he was in schmooze overdrive. The professor's blah, blah, blah to Mr. Shepherd went on as I gathered my things to leave. I proceeded to walk away when suddenly I heard Mr. Shepherd blurt out, "Wow, look at that heart shaped ass! Honey, come back and let me get a better look at that work of art!"

I stopped dead in my tracks. This conference was a casual event. We were all dressed mainly in jeans and casual tops. Nothing sultry or provocative, just everyday casual attire. Without a second of hesitation, I turned toward the men with fire spewing from my eyes and addressed the director.

"What did you say?" I venomously asked while slowly walking closer to them.

"I said I'd love to get better acquainted with that fine ass. Lots of things I'd love to do with it," he proudly repeated.

The professor cringed as I got closer to them. We didn't know each other all that well, but the professor knew me well enough to know I didn't take shit from anyone. Nothing would provoke my temper faster than disgusting behavior like this.

"How about if I acquaint you with my fist right between your eyes first?" I shouted as I raised my fist to his face.

The professor just about passed out. The director's mouth dropped.

"Who the fuck do you think you are, you ignorant piece of shit?"

"Do you know who I am? Do you know who you're talking to?" the director arrogantly asked.

"I know exactly who you are, Mr. Shepherd! Too bad you don't know who *you're* talking to, you asshole!" I snapped back and got right up in his face. "Maybe you get away with that shit in LaLa Land, but where I come from, that kind of talk doesn't fly! Got that, Mr. Director?" I finished.

Mr. Shepherd turned to the professor. "Who is this girl?" he asked.

I didn't even give the professor a chance to answer. "I'm someone who could teach you how to treat a lady!" I snapped. "So keep that in mind as you address the impressionable young writers hanging on your every word tonight!" I finished and walked away.

The professor followed up with me later and gave me a hard time about what happened and that, because of it, he couldn't even consider pitching the play to Mr. Shepherd. My response was, if funding this project was contingent upon being a great big ass kisser and turning a blind eye to such behavior, I wanted nothing to do with the project. He agreed we would work out other funding options. The professor went on to say that Mr. Shepherd asked a million questions about me and, although was taken back by my actions, he actually applauded them. Interesting.

The keynote address began by Mr. Shepherd telling the story of meeting a very gusty lady in the lobby this afternoon who prompted him to mind his manners, to watch his words and actions, particularly when addressing a lady. I was amazed at how he took our encounter and turned it into a lesson to writers, to always be ready to learn something about words and communicating them.

"So if I crack a joke or say anything offensive to anyone here, I'll apologize in advance and blame it on my bad sense of humor and lack of etiquette, as pointed out to me today," he said while looking directly at me.

The audience laughed, thinking it was just his comedic nature talking. I was the first one out the door the minute the speech ended.

While back in my room later, I answered a knock on my door. It was one of Mr. Shepherd's assistants, asking me to meet him in the lounge for a drink. My response was a quick "Please thank your boss and advise him that I don't accept invitations through a third party." She left.

I was meeting three ladies I'd met at this conference for dinner in one of the hotel restaurants. We were having a lovely time discussing the events of the conference. One of the ladies had a background in human resources, so we had a great time exchanging stories. We had already ordered dinner, but suddenly our server appeared with another drink for me. I was surprised and explained that I hadn't ordered another.

"This was sent over by a gentleman," the server responded.

"Please send it back and tell the gentleman to take a closer look at our table, that there are four of us here and he should have offered all of us a drink instead of only me," I responded.

The ladies roared with laughter.

We continued on with our dinner and good time. Suddenly, Harry Shepherd appeared at our table.

"That's three times in one day you told me how rude I was. What do I have to do to impress you?" he asked.

"Go to charm school!" I snapped.

A second of silence was followed by a roar of laughter from the director. "I think you've got a future in show business! Lord knows you've got the guts for it. I'd like to talk to you about your writing goals. I'd also like to see some of your work. Would it be possible for us to meet at some point?" he nicely asked.

I began, "Mr. Shepherd, I—"

But he interrupted. "Please call me Harry."

"Harry, I'm truly flattered and would be happy to meet you in the open lobby area, where we met earlier today. Do you remember where that was?" I asked.

"How could I forget!" he answered.

"Wonderful! How about tomorrow after the sessions are over?" I asked.

We agreed on the time. Harry bade us all a good night and left.

As I explained the entire story, the ladies roared with laughter. "I bet Harry just about died when you shoved your fist in his face! I would've bought a ticket to that show. Good for you, Contessa. Some of these Hollywood big shots think they can treat women any way they want," Heather commented.

"Maybe because the casting couch has been successful for so long they think nothing of that mentality. If they dangle the carrot of stardom in front of a pretty girl, they get whatever they want," Lori added.

"It's not only Hollywood, it's everywhere. The unfortunate thing is that too many women either want a job badly enough to submit to anything for it or they just don't have enough confidence in themselves to achieve it any other way, so they grab the carrot. Or maybe both. Who knows? Either way, it's sad," I said.

"Well, men wouldn't get away with it if more women stood up to them like you did, Contessa! Jeez, I wish I could've seen that!" Barbara laughed.

"I've had a carrot or two dangled in my face over the years. It would have been very easy to grab it and take the offer presented to me. It wasn't always easy, but thankfully, I had the sense to tell the guy to fuck off. There's no way I'd allow anyone to think they could buy me or treat me like a piece of meat. I have a definite line in the sand about that, and if it's crossed, I'll act on it. I don't give a rat's ass who the culprit is!" I told them and changed the topic to the conference.

When we asked for our check, our server informed us that Harry already picked it up.

The next day, I was to meet Harry in the lobby after my last conference session. It ran a bit late, and that didn't stop me from leisurely walking over to our meeting spot. Yes, I could be a bitch and got a kick out of having the great director sitting there, waiting for me. As I approached him, Harry stood up to greet me, extending his hand out to shake.

"Hello, I'm Harry Shepherd. I think we got off to a bad start, and I'd like to begin again," he announced.

"Thank you, Harry. That's very nice of you," I said.

"First off, may I apologize for what I said. I have to admit, I sometimes get a little full of myself. Usually a crack like I made to you will get me a different kind of response. You know, the young girls recognize me and they think it's an invitation to a part in a movie, so they just go along with it," Harry admitted.

"I appreciate your apology. As for your explanation, I can't believe you'd even admit to that. It's disgusting," I told him.

"You're an impressive lady, Contessa. Can we hit the reset button, get to know each other? The professor told me you were from Chicago. Didn't surprise me. You're a tough cookie. Strong women from the Midwest. My wife is from the Midwest. Good people with good heads on their shoulders from there. Tell me a little about yourself. I want to know more about you."

I could see he was trying to be a good boy with his Sunday suit and manners on, so I took the edge off my tone. "There's not much about me to tell, Harry. I'm a business woman who decided to leave the corporate world and change my direction to the literary world. I met the professor a few months ago, and we're working on a play."

"Yes, he told me, and I was sure he was about to pitch me to get involved when you stole the scene." Harry laughed. "I hope you put that in the play somewhere. It was amazing."

"The professor is the writer. I'm taking the reins on the production and business end of it. That's more my forte," I said.

"You know, I have a bit of writing experience under my belt. I could really help you out," he offered.

"Uh, no, I don't think so," I answered.

"Most anyone would jump at that offer," he said.

"I'm not most people. I mean no disrespect, Harry, but I'm pretty independent. I watch, learn, and go on my own. And besides, I'm thinking that your help would come with a price tag that I'm not willing to pay," I told him.

We continued the conversation by exchanging stories of Chicago, our backgrounds, our families, and my collaboration with the professor. It was not only pleasant but really quite funny as well. In the end, I was glad I came to meet him. Harry wished me well and handed me his card with all his personal contact information, insisting that I keep in touch.

"I'll let you know of any progress on the play," I responded.

"You know, when a man gives you fifteen ways to contact him, the lady usually responds by giving him her number in return," Harry declared.

"If we move forward on the play and I find myself relocating to LA, I will surely let you know. I promise," I assured him, without providing my phone number. I thanked him for the chat and left.

The professor and I continued to work toward our goal of having the play produced. We were finally successful. I would have to relocate to Los Angeles to oversee production. Always excited for a new adventure, I looked forward to this open ended move, knowing it would be temporary, but unsure of how long "temporary" would turn out to be. I looked into corporate housing, rentals, etc., finding good information, but still had lots of questions. I decided to call Harry, who was delighted to hear my good news. I appreciated all the various suggestions and insight on housing suggestions he offered. Harry asked me lots of questions about the production itself, the business plan, timing, etc. He was complimentary of how we put things together.

"You seem to have it all under control. I applaud your strategy and business instincts, particularly this being your first production," Harry said.

"I'll be in LA soon for about a week to start putting things in place," I advised.

Harry immediately suggested a few different hotels in close proximity to my activities. He offered to show me around to get better acclimated to the area.

"I'll accept your graciousness on the condition you fully understand we are just friends and that you'll remember to be on your best behavior. None of that dirty mouth talk," I told him.

"Are you kidding? You think I forgot your fist in my face?" Harry laughed. "I shared that with some of my friends, and they were on the floor, laughing. They're dying to meet you."

"I just want to be crystal clear," I reminded him.

I had so much to do I was moving at lightning speed, but finally I arrived in Los Angeles. I got settled into my hotel and agreed to have dinner with Harry that night. He arrived in the lobby right on time and welcomed me with open arms. He took me to a lovely Italian restaurant. Although it was jam packed, the hostess appeared out of nowhere, and as if Moses were parting the Red Sea, the crowd divided in half, allowing us a clear path as she led us to our table. Now, I'd seen women gush over celebrities before, but I had never, ever seen anything like how this gal threw herself all over Harry. After slobbering all over him, she finally left.

"She must be a fan of your work!" I sarcastically said.

"Well, there's a little story that goes with her," Harry said.

"I'm sure! Do I want to hear it?" I asked.

Harry mentioned the filming of one of his most prominent movies, one that I had seen many times and loved.

"We just wrapped up the movie when this restaurant opened. There really aren't many upscale Italian restaurants out here, so a friend and I came to check it out. She was all over both of us. She made it very clear that she would do anything—I mean *anything*—to get a part in one of my movies. I explained that we were in the editing process of an upcoming film and needed to add a scene or two, asking if she would be interested. She jumped on it, or jumped on us would be more like it. We still had several of the sets in place, so we had her come in and shoot a few scenes." Harry explained the fake scenes he shot with the hostess.

"I've seen that movie a million times. Neither of those scenes were in it." I paused, and before Harry could comment, I figured it out. "Let me guess, those scenes wound up on the cutting room floor."

"Yeah, but not before we all did a little partying!" He laughed. "In the end, I told her we had to make some cuts to make the timing right but that I'd use those scenes as a screen test for future reference."

"So she'll keep thinking she has a chance at another part, right?" I asked.

"You're a very smart girl," he proudly admitted.

"And you're a pig. No, you're an offensive pig!" I said.

"Hey, she wasn't forced, we didn't pressure her. All we did was lay out an invitation. She came, and I mean she really came, and went all on her own. It was her choice." He laughed again. "That's the way it is in this town. You'll see."

The hostess returned with a bucket of champagne. I noticed her creativity in shoving her very evident breasts in Harry's face. She took forever to open the champagne and set the glasses up, but finally she left. Harry laughed as I shook my head in both disbelief and disgust.

"Aw, come on now. Let's drink to the success of your career in show business. May you triumph in your first production. And don't forget, I'm here to help you in any way I can," Harry toasted.

"I appreciate that, Harry, but I think I'll roll the dice on this alone," I said.

I was consumed with work, organizing production details and strategies, hiring, and setting up temporary housing. One week just flew by, and before I knew it, I was home finishing up details there so that I could bounce right back to Los Angeles for good. Another whirlwind, but one I loved, as I approached a new endeavor. Harry called me regularly, checking on progress. He gave me many helpful hints on where to go for various things I'd need, suggestions on production staffing, public relations, and pitfalls to watch out for, which I really appreciated. Overall, Harry complimented me on my production efforts. He applauded the business plan I put forth and assured me that in a town where few were true friends, I could count on him to be one. Finally, I was on a plane headed back to the City of Angels, ready to embark on a new path. I was over the moon with excitement to experience this new adventure.

I hit the ground running, getting settled into my apartment and diving right into production. They were long, intense days averaging around fourteen to sixteen hours. I had to decline the many dinner invitations Harry extended, but he certainly understood. Dinner? Who had time for dinner? We were living on a few hours of sleep and fast food that was within blocks of the theater. A show runner got takeout for the crew each night as we slaved away on set design, production details, and rehearsals. In time, things got more buttoned up, and I was finally able to relax a bit. I got a chance to check out my new surroundings. Harry had a group of pals that met regularly at an old fashioned pancake place not too far from my apartment. He was dying to have me meet his friends, and I promised I would as soon as I had time. Harry described this group of five prominent show business retirees in such a hilarious way I was really looking forward to meeting them as well.

Things were going well enough for me to take a day off, and I told Harry I'd meet the gang for breakfast. They squeezed an extra chair into their usual round table for six to accommodate me. Harry didn't have a chance to introduce me, as one by one they stood up to greet me, announcing their names. Greg, Alan, Rick, Rod, and York couldn't have been nicer, funnier, or more gracious. They shared their backgrounds and impressive careers in both movies and television. I hung on their every word as they told me very animated stories of old Hollywood. They were absolutely delightful, and I was having a blast with them.

"Harry told us we had to be on our best behavior with you, and now I can see why. You're a lovely lady, Contessa," Greg said.

"Yeah, he also reminded us to keep our hands under the table or you'd lay us out!" Alan added. "We died laughing when he told us how you lambasted him when you first met!"

"Lambaste? That was more like castrate!" Rick joked.

"I told her she needs to write that scene into her work someday. It was priceless!" Harry chimed in.

"Contessa, it's understood how you'd be insulted by a crack like what Harry made to you. This town is crawling with girls, women who make it crystal clear they would do absolutely anything for a role, and they jump on the smallest bit of attention or opportunity they get, especially from a known director. Normally, Harry's crack would have gotten him a very entertaining evening," Rod explained. "Not only did you shock the shit out of him, you really got his attention as well!"

"Yeah, they all want to be movie stars! Admittedly, we're wretched creatures, us guys, and we're guilty of using tricks of our trade for female favors. But truth be told, we get away with it because women act so desperate for it. Fame is sought, chased, and lusted after so badly around here that offering this for that is an easy bargaining chip. Been that way since movies began," York declared.

"I'm sure it's very different in the corporate world, where you come from. I'll bet you never had any experiences there," Greg suggested.

"No, not really. Unfortunately exploiting women is alive and well in the corporate world too. I think the difference is that the corporate world provides more structured avenues to take action against it. And yes, I had a very specific encounter with a boss trying to take advantage of me," I told the group.

"Really? Did you punch him in the face?" Harry asked as they all laughed.

"No, but let's just say I handled it," I said.

"It's the culture around here. You're gonna see more of it, and I know it bothers you, but don't pay any attention, just look away," Harry said.

I couldn't believe my ears! Don't pay attention? Look away? This is the culture around here? Good Lord! Where was I?

"Well, right now, I'm looking at my watch and I really have to run. Gentlemen, I had so much fun. It was truly a pleasure meeting you all," I said.

The group invited me to join their breakfast club, and I graciously accepted.

Opening night was a full house. It was a high profile audience, many celebrity friends of the professor's, cast, and crew. Standing to participate in the roaring applause at the finale were Harry and the breakfast club. We hosted a party in the theater lobby, and I was delighted that Harry and the gang stayed to enjoy it. They delivered praise and felt we had a hit, that it would complete its scheduled four week run. If I was a nervous wreck prior to opening, I was now on cloud nine, celebrating this rewarding night. Harry proudly introduced me to many of the notables in attendance, all of whom he knew well, all congratulating me as producer on a winning play. He whispered how proud he was of me, how he valued our friendship, and that he had big plans for me, which we would discuss soon.

The play completed its run to mediocre success. Not bad for a first time producer, and I learned a great deal. I was truly exhausted and thought this was a perfect time to return home for a bit. With fall approaching, it would soon be cold, and I needed to decide what to do next. Harry was upset when I told him I'd be going home for a bit, expressing fear that I wouldn't return. I assured him I would, as I still had time left on my apartment lease and thought it would be fun to take time off from any business, to just hang out and enjoy Southern California. I missed my little girl, who was now a happily married lady with a thriving career in sales. Little Contessa supported my going to the West Coast and new experience. She was happy for the positive result there, but we both missed each other and needed a good catching up.

It felt wonderful to reconnect with my daughter, my home, and my friends. We exchanged stories of my LA experiences, Little Contessa's own business dealings, her job, her company, how she was loving married life, etc. We were all good. I did invite her opinion on whether I should extend my stay in LA for a bit or just pack it up and return home for good. I filled her in on Harry and the breakfast club, which she got a big kick out of.

"Really cute old men, but dirty old men for sure!"

I fully explained them all to her and Little Contessa encouraged me to return and just relax for a while.

"Mom, you've always said that when in doubt, do nothing until you're sure of your next move. You worked your ass off all these years. Take a break, stay there for the winter, and enjoy the sunshine. Go have some fun," she advised.

I agreed, and after a few weeks, I returned to the West Coast. Harry made sure to secure dinner plans with me on my first night back in town. I have to admit, I looked forward to just going out without looking at the clock, worrying about how much (or little) time I had to sleep. Harry took me to another spectacular LA restaurant, and we were greeted by another gorgeous, voluptuous hostess and another act of "boobs in your face."

"Don't tell me, you offered her a part, she gave you a peep show!" I shook my head in disgust.

"And then some!" Harry laughed.

"Harry, it's not funny. It's revolting and rude of you to keep flaunting your stories of sexual encounters in exchange for fake movie roles, knowing how offensive I find it. When are you going to learn that behavior is going to bite you in the ass someday?" I said.

"I love to see you get all riled up! I love your fire. It's enchanting."

I couldn't tell if he was serious or making fun of me.

"Okay, so you said you had something very important to talk to me about. Spill," I said.

"I was really impressed with the production you put together. You demonstrated exceptional business skills, did a fabulous job of directing the crew, and even came in under budget. That's something even my producers seldom do! I think you'd be a great addition to my theater team," Harry offered.

"Work for you? In what capacity?" I asked.

"As production manager for my theater. I think you'd be fabulous. I think the staff could learn a lot from you, and in turn, you'd learn the theater. A win-win situation for us both," he suggested.

I hesitated. "Wow! I wasn't expecting anything like this," I confessed.

"Well, you'll take the job?" Harry asked.

"Harry, I'll have to think about it," I said.

"Just name your salary. You pick the scripts, whatever you want," he said. Harry reached out and put his hand on mine.

I pulled away. "Harry, I sincerely hope this isn't what you and the boys call a bargaining chip! You know I'm immune to that stuff," I said.

"Of course, I do. But think of what an opportunity this could be for you. You'd be my protégé. Think of the perks," Harry offered.

"From what I've learned, your perks come with strings attached. I'm skeptical," I hesitated.

"I can introduce you around. You'd meet lots of influential people. People in the business who could advance your career. Parties, a little fun, and playing around might do you some good, in several areas. You just might enjoy yourself. I can make it all happen for you," Harry offered with an impish grin.

"*Boom!* And there it is!" I yelled. "How many ways, how many times do I have to lay it out for you? I don't need this! There's nothing I need or want from you that I can't get for myself. There's nothing I'm so desperate to have that I'd sacrifice my dignity for! I want no part of this! I love ya, Harry, and thanks for the offer, but you're a piece of shit! This town is full of shit!" I got up from my chair to leave.

"Please don't go. Sit." Harry grabbed my arm and begged me to stay. "Listen to me," he asked. "You know, nobody talks to me the way you do," he told me.

"I know, and that's why you like me," I responded.

"I don't like you, Contessa, I love you!" Harry confessed.

Whoa! I certainly wasn't expecting this! I froze as Harry went on.

"You're right. That is one of the reasons I'm so attracted to you. I've had lots of successes, but I've also had lots of failures, especially in my theater. And I think one of the reasons for that is I'm surrounded by ass kissers. Some of them even rip me off. I don't say anything, but I know it. Nobody has the gumption to disagree, make a suggestion, or show me a different point of view. I guess sometimes it takes an outsider with a fresh set of eyes and mindset to see things more clearly. I see that in you. I watched you put the blueprint together for your play. At first, I said to myself, there's no way she'll pull this off. But I watched you work. You organize, you direct, and you listen. Your approach, your style is so refreshing, inspiring. I talked this over with the boys, and they all thought it was a genius idea. We could be a great team. Please say you'll take the job," Harry asked.

"Harry, I'm flattered. Really, I am. This is a huge commitment. I'm still not sure if I want to stay here. I just want to kick back for a while. How about if I think it over for a month?" I said.

"All right, then. I have one month to persuade you," he declared.

"Can we order now? I'm starving!" I said.

"Of course. I wouldn't want that fine ass of yours to shrink," he joked.

"You are such an asshole!" I laughed.

The next month, Harry made me his constant companion. He invited me to his theater, named the Eagle, after his teenage Brooklyn gang. I became a regular there, as well as his office, which was across a courtyard from the Eagle. Harry had me sit in on several production meetings. I have to admit, it was exciting to get a feel for how their team worked and gave me incentive to think about his offer more seriously. I was asked to read scripts and give my input for possible production selections. Harry took me to parties, movie premiers, and casual gatherings. Through him I met many industry professionals as well as celebrities, some of whom referred to me as Harry's protégé, *wink wink*, which drove me nuts. He seemed to take pride in that assumption, which drove me even more crazy! I insisted that he set the record straight, but he laughed and joked about it.

"I have a reputation to maintain," he would joke. "Nobody would believe me, anyway. Remember where you are." He laughed, to which I consistently told him what an asshole he was.

That was the negative side of his offer. Would I be taken seriously on my own merit, or would I just be Harry's girl? The glitz, the glamour, the parties were fun, all right, but nothing that I felt I needed regularly.

We both loved tennis, and we played with several of Harry's neighbors (all industry well-knowns) regularly. Mostly all comedians. There were times I could barely hit the ball being doubled over from laughter. They were all incredible folks, and I was quite appreciative to meet them, playing a sport we all enjoyed together. We hung out with the breakfast club regularly, which was always fun and entertaining. In the middle of it all, Harry and I had long discussions about the various business elements he exposed me to. I asked a lot of questions and learned a great deal from our discussions. I really appreciated being asked my opinion on various things, and while we sometimes had dueling attitudes, we respectfully listened to each other. While I learned much from Harry, he admitted learning a thing or two from me as well. We had, in fact, become truly close friends who loved and respected each other. I was thoroughly enjoying myself both personally and professionally, but mentally I was struggling with the decision I had yet to make. The good was very good; in fact, the good was incredible. However, the sexist element that shadowed the environment was too much for me to bear. I flipped back and forth with the pros, which were many, and the one and only con, wondering if I could exist in a culture dominated by sexual "favors" and abuse. This was so different from what I had experienced in the corporate world, most recently at Jeff's company, where I was able to correct the discriminating and abusive behavior. I was reminded of my favorite prayer, one that got me through many a dilemma: "God, grant me the courage to change the things I can, the serenity to accept what I cannot, and the wisdom to know the difference."

My ultimate decision was made shortly after mentally reciting this prayer, and the thing that weighted my decision came from a very unlikely source. Unbelievably, or maybe even miraculously, while lost in thought over all this, I was startled by the sudden loud ring of my phone. It was Little Contessa.

"Mom, are you sitting down?" she gleefully asked.

"Actually, I'm lying down." I laughed. "Good news?"

"The best news! I'm pregnant!" Little Contessa screamed, and I immediately joined her.

"Oh my God! I'm so excited!" I cried with joy, followed by all the normal questions. "How are you feeling?" "How far along are you?" "Natural birth?" etc. Little Contessa had lots of questions for me as well, referring to my pregnancy with her. I was over the moon with joy over this news, and I couldn't stop telling my little girl how happy I was. This news solidified my decision. Without a doubt, I would wrap it up here in LA and head back home to prepare for my first grandchild.

I met Harry for lunch the next day to tell him of my decision. We were seated outside a gorgeous outdoor restaurant by yet another beautiful young hostess. I sat there watching yet another display of the antics that seemed to follow us being seated at every restaurant he took me to. Although I have to say, this hostess took it to a whole other level. She took extra care in tucking Harry's napkin on his lap, right in front of me! *Ewww!*

"If I didn't see it for myself, I wouldn't believe it!" I said in disgust.

"What can I say? They all want to be a movie star!" He laughed.

"I actually feel sorry for any woman who feels she has to fill her résumé with overt behavior instead of credible work experience," I said.

We were in the middle of discussing the last script Harry asked me to read when the hostess returned with our drinks. I was completely appalled as she did an encore performance of her napkin-in-Harry's-lap trick before leaving, as he smiled and whispered, "I'll try to arrange that screen test next week," to her and patted her ass as she walked away with a triumphant grin. That was it for me!

"Harry, I made my decision. I'm going home as soon as I can wrap things up here," I announced.

"No! You can't mean that!" Harry cried out. "You can't go. Why? Why would you leave when everything is going so well?"

"First and foremost, I just found out my daughter is pregnant! I'm going to be a grandmother, and I'm thrilled about it," I told him.

"Okay, so you stay here, you go back for the birth, and then you come back. I've got plans for you. We work so well together. You're my shining star! Even the guys say it. The kid's not even gonna know who you are for a few years!" he pleaded.

I was not happy with this response. "The correct response would have been you congratulating my family and expressing your happiness for us. And guess what? My own shining star is on its way, and nothing could mean more to me. I had hoped you'd understand," I said.

"I know, I know, you women go crazy over the whole baby thing. But you just can't walk away from the opportunity I'm offering you. You deserve it. You have the talent. I respect you! You can write your own ticket, be the boss, pick your perks, anything you want. You see how these young girls throw themselves at old farts like me. You see how ready and willing they are to do anything for a part or a job. Well, I'm handing it to you. I'm putting a golden opportunity to make a name for yourself right in your lap," Harry went on.

"Harry, I've earned several names and titles in my lifetime that I'm pretty proud of. And the best one of all has just been given to me, grandmother. A grandchild is going to be put in my lap, and that's all I care about," I said.

Harry's tone turned a bit more tender. "Haven't you enjoyed the time we've spent together? I thought we always had fun. I've tried to show you a really good time so you you'd stay. I really wanted you to love being here as much as I love having you here," he told me.

"Harry, you've been great. I really appreciate everything you've taught me. Our time together has been wonderful, in many ways. Nobody can make me laugh the way you do. I like it here, but honestly, I don't love it," I confessed. "My decision has nothing to do with LA or you or anything else here. It's all about my family. I had to work my daughter's whole life. I've always felt guilty about things she wasn't able to do or things I couldn't do with her when she was young because I either didn't have money, time, or both. But things are different now. My daughter is a successful professional, and I'm going to be there for her. I'm dying to be a full-time grandmother so she doesn't have to worry about some of the things I had to when I was a working young mom. And I want my grandbaby, or babies, to know that nothing in the world will ever be more important to me than them. It's just that simple," I finished.

"So there's nothing I can sweeten the pot with to make you change your mind?" Harry asked.

"You should know by now dangling a carrot in my face will only piss me off," I reminded him. "Be happy for me, Harry. That's what friends do. You are still my friend, right?" I asked.

Harry reached across the table and took my hands in his. "I will always be your friend, Contessa. A friend who loves you and respects you. There will always be a special place in my heart for you. You became a bright light in my life, and you made me very happy, even though you always swear at me and call me every name in the book."

We both burst out in laughter. Only Harry could throw a joke into such a heartfelt speech.

"Tell me, it's not just all business for you, is it? I mean, you feel something special for me too, don't you? I mean, you're one of the few genuine people I've been able to have any kind of an honest relationship with. You tell me what I need to know, not what I want to hear like so many others around me. You're not a bullshitter. You never asked for anything, didn't want or need me for anything. You just put up with me. It warmed my heart to know I had a true friend in you. Tell me my instincts were right," he went on.

I was so touched by Harry opening up like this, reaching this deep into our relationship. I got a little verklempt. "Of course, Harry. You'll always be my dear, dear friend. And yes, Harry, I love you too!"

"The breakfast club is gonna be devastated. They like you more than me, and they're probably gonna say I did something wrong to make you leave. Promise you'll stay in touch and come back to visit us?" he asked.

"Yes to both, my friend," I promised.

"I mean, you gotta come back. I'll go crazy if I can't see that heart shaped ass of yours! Finest ass I've never had!" he joked.

"You are such an asshole!" I said.

"I love you too, kid!" He laughed.

"Harry, I want you to promise me something too," I asked.

"Name it, kid. Anything you want," he said.

"Change your ways. Stop all the disgusting behavior. Stop the lying about parts in movies for sex. You say that's the way it's done around here. Change can start with you. Make a difference. Just stop it! You have daughters, you have granddaughters—how would you feel if someone tried to pull that crap with them?" I pleaded.

Harry was silent for a moment. His eyes actually teared up. "You made your point, as always. I get it, kiddo," he said.

Soon thereafter, I wrapped up the shreds of remaining business and joyously headed back home, never once looking back. I'll always have fond memories of my phenomenal adventure in the City of Angels, but a little angel of our own was on its way, and there was much to do in preparation.

My time in Los Angeles was exciting, fun, and filled with one-of-kind experiences, many of which were largely due to knowing Harry. In many ways, it truly is a magical place. The sparkle of the town is everywhere. But all that glitters is not gold—at least not for me. I saw beyond the celebrity. I saw a side of the environment that wasn't so glamourous. I saw very bad behavior by powerful men taking advantage of women who perhaps felt there was no other way for them to achieve their goals or escalate their career. I saw women yield to what Harry said was "in the air we breathe around here," and that was extremely sad and disturbing. I liken it to "what came first, the chicken or the egg?" syndrome, and I do not have a solution. I only have hope that someday this dark cloud gets washed away with some of the beautiful rays of sunshine this beautiful city is known for.

Harry and I always kept in touch. I did visit him several times over the years and proudly announced that there was a new man in my life, one that he could never compete with. Like any proud grandmother, I carried a picture book of my beautiful grandson, showing my little angel off to Harry and the breakfast club. It was always great to see them. We always had a good time, but I looked forward to getting back home to my own little star. The last time I was in LA, Harry and I had a lovely dinner together, sharing family stories, catching up on business, and reminiscing. We said our good-byes, and Harry asked me for a favor.

"Name it," I said.

"Just walk away and let me get a good look at that heart shaped ass of yours!" he asked.

"Harry, you are such an asshole!" I reminded him.

"I love you too, kid! Be well."

The Friend

Be careful what you wish for; you just might get it!

During my high school breakup with Mousie, I began to spend more time with girlfriends I had made from different neighborhoods. I wanted a change of scenery and had options available, so *what the hell*, I thought. This breakup period was the perfect time for adventure. My cousin introduced me to several girls who were classmates of hers at an upscale, all girls Catholic high school. They were a nice group of girls—a little classier, definitely better dressed, but not too street smart and pretty much spoon fed. Nonetheless, we all got along great. Like me, they hadn't been out of their own environment much and therefore were somewhat limited as well. For instance, when the gals in my neighborhood needed to go somewhere, we hopped on a bus. When these girls wanted to go somewhere, they were driven by their mothers. I think there was only one mother in our entire neighborhood who actually had a driver's license, let alone a car!

This new neighborhood was called Ross Park and located about forty-five minutes, or two bus rides away from my home. The Ross Park neighborhood was a bit more posh than ours. Homes in this area were more expensive and stylish, newer cars parked along the sidewalks, schools were of a higher caliber, and dads were clearly professionals. Unfortunately, some of the people in the area thought the "posh" applied to them as well.

This was a moment in time when weekend dances were pretty popular. On any given Friday, Saturday, or Sunday night, kids had a choice to various dances held at church centers, VFW halls, or school

300

gyms. Some dances featured live local bands, while others used speakers and played records (remember them?), with early versions of DJs. A weekend dance venue became popular based on the music, the crowd, and the venue itself. This was how kids from various neighborhoods met and mixed. Or not. My new stomping ground had a church center that was ultimately named The Zoo, and you get only one guess as to why. Needless to say, it was quite favored, the "in" place to spend your weekends!

I was really enjoying my new circle of friends as well as hanging out at Ross Park. The girls were enjoyable and entertaining, plus they had their own clique of guys. Hanging out with a new group of teenage guys wasn't a hard thing to do, and there was plenty of them to get to know. Boys will be boys, I guess, and in any given group, one could always count on the stereotypes. The clown, the muscle man, the movie star, the quiet one, the hothead, the brain, etc. I got to know them all. They were a high spirited bunch who loved to dance and strut their stuff at each of the weekend dances. My father personally knew a few parents of my new girlfriends, so he didn't mind me going to Ross Park dances. Dad allowed me to attend sleepovers at some of the girls' homes as well, which usually followed a dance. That was half the battle. The other half was something to wear, learning to fix my hair and do my makeup, which never came naturally to me and something I needed to work on diligently. I was discovering that glamour is really hard work, a painstaking task in which I was not skilled in, but I was learning that practice makes perfect.

My girlfriend Mary Ann was dating the "it" guy, the hottest guy in their neighborhood. Johnny was the leader of the Ross Park area. He had it all—strikingly good looks with gorgeous, dark, chiseled Italian features, money, style, with great clothes that showed off his incredible physique, and if all that weren't enough, he was the owner of an awesome white Cadillac, lined in red leather, which he chauffeured us around in. Yep, he had it all, in addition to being one of the best dancers around. Being noted as a great dancer puffed up a male reputation just as much as all the aforementioned attributes. Johnny was also known for one little thing that was not a very attractive quality: he had a volcanic temper that didn't take much at all to set off. He was really a nice guy to all his friends, but those who knew him knew what little things would trigger his temper, and they avoided those things like the plague. In social settings, mainly dances that brought guys from other neighborhoods around, the tiniest situation could ignite Johnny's legendary temper. When that summer wind came blowing in and summer's events were underway (dances, carnivals, festivals), guys did tend to get a little territorial about two things: their turf and their girls. Messing with either resulted in a fistfight. Outsiders who were visiting a new sphere of influence for a dance or other activity came to know the guys to whom that "turf" belonged and what they stood for by way of what they would fight over. Somewhat of a boundary line as to what you could or couldn't do in that neighborhood. Crazy, right? You bet, but this mindset was pretty much in the air long before the Jets and the Sharks brought it to the forefront, as well as long after.

Mark was Johnny's best friend, wing man, and constant companion. Mark was Italian as well, only with lighter features. He had a soft, fair skin tone and a demeanor to match. Mark was tall and slender, with straight light brown hair. His warm round eyes were full of expression and lined with the thickest lashes, matching his always perfectly styled hair, well, perfectly. So emotional were Mark's eyes they sometimes seemed to do the talking for him, which I really didn't think he minded. He was a pretty quiet guy. His lips were not large or emphasized, just ideally shaped, covering his flawless pearly whites. Mark stood out from the crowd in more ways than just his lighter features. He was soft spoken and quite reserved. Mark always demonstrated a bit of sophistication which, at that time, I couldn't have even identified in him; I just knew he was different from the others in a mysterious yet positive way. It was his manner that definitely intrigued me. Mark was very stylish, always seemed to know what the next trend was, and it was clear that his keen sense of style led many of the guys (even Johnny) to follow his lead when it came to their attire. His quiet, unpretentious nature was so different from the attitude of the other guys I knew, which told me Mark was self assured and oh-so-very cool that he didn't need to compete with the other guys. He was a guy who didn't say much, but when he spoke, people listened. Mark was the calm to Johnny's storm, the Dean to Johnny's Frank. He was the peacemaker when Johnny's temper erupted. Mark was the sheriff who broke up the fights as well as the ambulance that rescued Johnny from many a scrape that could have ended in catastrophe. He was a solid guy. Mark could make the knees of any girl go weak just by flashing his radiant smile at them. He had a natural polish and finesse to him that separated him from all the others.

Mark was a confident person who could stand silently among stallions, all of whom were racing to the finish line in order to be the leader, the star. A group in which each strived for their next possible achievement that would allow bragging rights, which would put that guy at the top of the leader board. Particularly teenagers, and most particularly teenage boys. Everyone was looking for that one thing that would project them and allow them the mark of distinction they all attempted. Consequently, each made their mark in their own category. This one was the best looking, that one was the best dressed, another was the best prankster, athlete, brainiac, etc. Mark often demonstrated tremendous poise as he stood back to let Johnny shine. He was not the one who needed to know how many girls were admiring him—although so many were! There were the things I noticed about Mark, the things that made him stand out as the "cool one." I'd be lying if I said it wasn't Mark's undeniable, dreamy good looks that first attracted me to him. As a matter of fact, upon my laying eyes on him for the first time, the sound of my girlfriends' chatter was immediately drowned out by Roberta Flack's "The first time ever I saw his face…" taking over my sense of hearing. But as I got to know Mark a bit more, I found his quiet strength, soft, suave manner, and the worldliness he often demonstrated were what drew me to him. I was determined to get to know him much, much better.

Even though it was Johnny's awesome white Cadillac, it was usually Mark who was behind the wheel. Johnny wanted Mary Ann in the middle while he sat in the passenger seat. Since we gals always traveled in packs, it was this elegant car that we were shuttled about in. From dance to dance we cruised around in style with Mark at the helm. I didn't have to announce my feelings for Mark to any of my girlfriends; perhaps it was the dazed and confused look I had upon my face whenever he was around that gave me away. I designed a plan. The front seat of the Cadillac was always reserved for Mark, Mary Ann, and Johnny. I let the other girls know that I would be the first to enter the back seat. Nobody ever argued with me, as I had my own way of declaring myself. As Mark drove, he would often have to look in the rearview mirror, and I would be right there for him to see. I actually told myself that if he looked long enough, I would catch his eye.

Mark demonstrated perfect manners and was always pleasant and gracious to me. We even danced a bit now and then. There was the occasional conversation, just between the two of us, that sometimes went on and on, which allowed me to hope I stood a chance with him. I managed to steal him away at a dance once in a while; sometimes I even got him to take a walk with me, listening more than I spoke. I considered it quite a feat to even get him talking, as he was really a man of few words. I frequently rehearsed questions I would ask him if I had the chance, in order to keep the focus on him and keep him talking. His voice was so smooth! He had been to Italy and several places in Europe, which naturally fed my own sense of adventure and desire to see the world. Conversation was never something that I struggled with, especially when it was interesting and appealing to me. Thus, our walks and chats were never dull, but rather vibrant and fluent, with an easy flow between us. We talked most about our families, different neighborhoods, customs, etc. He was very respectful to his Italian heritage and expressed how much he enjoyed talking to a girl who felt the same way. Family was extremely important to him, and he shared emotions about his parents' recent announcement that they were divorcing. I wasn't surprised to see such a soft side to him, highlighting what an internally strong guy he was. I felt particularly proud that he shared this with me, as I came to learn later that he hadn't even told Johnny about the divorce. It takes a lot for a guy to open up like this, and he chose me to do it! Most other guys would never reveal such things, thinking it would diminish their masculinity. But it came naturally to Mark, as did my probing, which gave way for more revelation from him. I was always more comfortable talking about somebody else's life than my own and quickly saw the benefit of throwing the conversation into his lap. Mark commented on how good it was to be able to talk to a girl about real things that had actual meaning and his honest thoughts about life. He referred to the unimportant babble that he usually heard spewing from many girls' mouths, normally all about themselves. I felt accomplished in making this kind of connection with him and was certain no other girl had. I was confident that a solid relationship was developing between us and was patient to allow it to grow. I knew Mark had plenty to choose from, but I never saw him go after any one particular girl. All he would have to do was point his finger at any girl and they'd run, not walk, right to him. Being a positive person, I believed I could make him like me; I mean, even though we were always in a group, we were still together quite a bit, so why wouldn't he?

One night following a dance, Janet, another girlfriend in our group, had a pajama party. By this time Mary Ann had gotten hot and heavy with Johnny and the plan was to sneak Johnny and Mark into Janet's completely remodeled and furnished basement, where we would all be sleeping. That was an effortless task, as Janet's mother was upstairs, sleeping soundly in their lavish, multilevel home by the time we arrived home from the dance. Just in case, though, we were careful not to make any noise that would wake her. We just wanted to hang out and watch TV with the guys. Mary Ann and Johnny had other plans, and they took those plans to a secluded part of the basement. Harmless, really, just a lot of making out and panting. Mark and I got deep into a conversation, and he asked if I wanted to walk outside for a bit. "Sure," I responded as I quickly scrambled for shoes. We walked outside on this gorgeous summer night, eventually settling on Janet's porch, conversation flowing like sumptuous bath water that I drifted away in. I didn't need Calgon to take me away; all I needed was Mark.

Then suddenly and without warning, Mark kissed me!

Oh my God! This wasn't just a kiss; it was *the* kiss! I was dizzy and not even sure if I was dreaming. Yes, this was really worth waiting for and all I thought it would be. Mark expressed how much he enjoyed talking to me and, being several years older than I was, how mature I was for my age. He said I sounded like I knew exactly what I wanted in life and told me how attractive that was to him. He continued that he was so easily bored with the silliness of most girls my age and called me "focused," which, to be honest at that time, I didn't even know what the word meant. I looked it up later, though, just to be certain of his compliment. Our make out session lasted for some time, until Johnny surfaced and announced that they had to leave. Mark gave me a very soft goodbye kiss without saying another word.

I literally floated back into the basement and fed the girls exactly what they were starving for, including every single detail of every single second between Mark and me. This was it! I screamed. I got him! I was on cloud nine, until one of the girls asked me if he took my phone number. "Well, no," I confidently responded. "He had no time to ask, since Johnny scooped him away so fast, but I know I'll see him again at the dance next weekend, and of course, he will ask for it then."

I would have bet my life that it would all work out the way I wanted it to.

The next week was one long dream of the new romance I was a certain Mark and I were beginning. I was so confident that next weekend we would talk more, kiss a whole lot more, and that I would be crowned Mark's girl. I couldn't have worked harder to prepare myself for this upcoming coronation. I wanted to be utterly irresistible for my new beau. *Irresistible* was never a word I would use to describe myself, but this latest event, Mark's attention to me seemed to encourage me to think I could actually be. I looked through my rose colored glasses and literally had our whole lives planned, right down to the picket fence and 2.5 kids! I was still floating the following weekend I arrived at Mary Ann's house. As I unloaded my things to spend the weekend there, I noticed she was a little nervous and fidgety. I asked what was wrong, and she easily dismissed me with an "Um, nothing, I just have a headache." As I babbled on about my attire, hair, and makeup for the weekend, what Mark and I would talk about, how I still felt his lips on mine all week long, I saw her eyes drop to the floor, and I knew then something was up.

"Okay, spill," I demanded. "Something's going on, and it's not a headache."

With her eyes still downcast and speaking in a very faint voice, Mary Ann softly mumbled, "He's gone."

"Gone? Who's gone? What are you talking about?" I demanded.

"Contessa, I'm so sorry to have to tell you this, but Mark is gone. His parents' divorce became final. His father went to Italy for the summer and took Mark with him. I found out earlier in the week, and I struggled with how or when to tell you. You were so happy all week long I just couldn't say the words over the phone. I'm so sorry, but I just didn't know what to do," Mary Ann explained.

Snap! Just like that. Over. As I stood there trying to pick my mouth off the floor, I was surprised to hear my own thoughts over the loud pounding of my heart. *So this is what shock feels like,* I thought. A numbing feeling consumed me, and whatever else was coming out of Mary Ann's mouth was muffled and incomprehensible to me. My heart was pounding so hard and loud I felt my chest heaving. I had to get air. I had to walk.

"I gotta get out of here," I told Mary Ann. I knew I was going to lose it and wouldn't allow that to happen in the presence of anyone. I always remembered my father's words: "Never let anyone see you at a weak point, never let anyone see you cry." I ran out and just kept running. I found myself nearing the beautifully landscaped Ross Park, found a bench, and sat on it alone while the tears over this devastating news poured out.

Many of my father's words were ringing in my ears right now, particularly what he preached about knowing the truth of a situation. So Mark would be gone all summer. Who knows? Maybe even longer. Nothing I could do about that. But I asked myself, *Am I going to sit here and sulk over him all summer, or am I going to file it away, move on, and enjoy my summer break?* It was not like I just said that to myself once and I bounced right back. I had to have this internal conversation over and over and over in order to convince myself to shake it off. What really nagged at me was the fact that he didn't say anything to me. He must have known this was about to happen; we got so deep into all sorts of conversations, especially family stuff. Why wouldn't he mention that he might be leaving for a while? Our night together on the porch was so special. The intensity of our conversations was just as significant as our kisses. He must have known he'd be leaving in a matter of days. Why leave without any indication he would soon be gone? How could he tell me how special I had become to him and then just vanish? Why not just explain the circumstances surrounding his departure? They were certainly understandable. How long would he be gone? What would happen when he returned? If he returned? He could have told me he was leaving; maybe even write to me, knowing that he aroused my sense of adventure and travel, which we frequently talked about. The more I thought about it, the more pissed off I was starting to get. He could have handled a simple situation differently, but instead he blew a whole bunch of smoke up my ass and then just let me deflate! Yep, I was getting madder by the minute. Soon my anguish turned into a "fuck him!" attitude. And in that instant, I quickly learned two things. Lesson 1: Don't fret over things you have no control over. I also chastised myself because I let myself jump the gun a bit. Lesson 2: Never assume! Don't tell yourself you're in a relationship until the words and actions occur first, leaving no doubt in your mind.

Needless to say, summer vacation went on, and so did I. My girlfriends eventually discovered that Mark returned, but by that time school had resumed, so did my relationship with Mousie. I won't say that I completely forgot about Mark; I simply channeled him away in my memory bank as someone who spent a minute in my life, teaching me a thing or two along the way. I must admit, though, now and again, I would think of him, wondering what it would be like to meet up with him as an adult.

Fast forward twenty years. Now in my mid thirties, I entered a new chapter in my life. I was single, and Little Contessa would be returning to college at the end of this summer. I was enjoying a great career in management and felt as though everything I had worked for was beginning to materialize. This was the period in my life I referred to as my time. Little Contessa was in college and doing well there, thriving in her environment and enjoying college life. I had worked very hard to get her there, juggling several jobs at a time. I rarely had a night out with girlfriends or any kind of social life. I'm not complaining at all, just saying. My entire focus, everything I had done up to this point, was for us, mostly for her, that she would have a better life, with more opportunities and choices than I had. I always put her and whatever she needed first, knowing "my time" would come later. Well, here it was.

At this point, I was in a good place, happy with life in general. I was grateful for the challenges that came my way as well as having overcome them, for they led me to the success I had experienced up to this point. Physically, I think I was at my peak. Always on the slender side, always maintained a healthy lifestyle and diet. No smoking, alcohol on special occasions and always a workout routine in place. My hair was long and highlighted with blonde streaks. I know, quite different from my regular dark auburn color, but I was definitely one to mix it up now and then. Besides, this was a new period for me, so what the hell? For the first time in a very long time, I was feeling satisfied about my life and thought it couldn't get any better. I was calmer, knowing that I had already achieved many of my goals, mostly being able to put Little Contessa through college; she was the very first in our family to attend college and live away from home. No mother could have been more proud of their child. With Little Contessa living away at school, this was the very first time in my life I had lived alone. We had a very nice apartment in a great suburban area, my finances were manageable, and I was ready to experience a little of what I had thought of years ago, my time. This was mutually scary and exciting for me. A time that would allow me to explore, have adventures, have some fun, and discover who the real me actually was.

My dearest girlfriend Kathy, a friend since high school, was also now a single mother. We were both in the same place in our lives; we got each other. We were a great team. Kathy was a very attractive tall, slender blonde, hilarious in nature, always finding the humor in any situation. She was a hard working waitress at one of Chicago's most reputable restaurants. Although Kathy worked hard, she was always ready to have some fun. Good to balance life out, we'd say. We coordinated our schedules so that we would have at least one

Saturday night out every few weeks. Kathy was privy to what was happening on the Chicago nightlife scene through her clientele, and the info allowed us to plan where we went on our girls' night out. There was always a new summer hot spot in the city, and this summer, it was a very posh new club called Cairo. Of all the places Kathy and I experienced, Cairo was the most elegant and appealing. With three levels, Cairo offered something for everyone or everything for someone all in one night. Cairo's decor was fresh and red hot. A very sensual Moroccan themed environment—colorful, deep jewel tones accented in lots of gold and sparkle. The opulence of the entry level was particularly alluring, with just the right amount of grandeur to make you feel special just by being there. Its long, winding bar glowed from all angles. There were small seating areas for groups or little tables for two along the side of the main bar. Soft music played, and it fit the theme of the club, both relaxing and exciting the patrons. Cairo had the sensuality and allure of the city it was named for, put you in the mood no matter what mood you were in when you arrived. You could drink at the bar, or if you met someone and wanted to take it to a more private level, you could move over to the table area, where an audible conversation could take place. The second level depicted dark caverns, where couples had their own table to drink, canoodle, or whatever. The third level was for private parties, which I never experienced but heard plenty of stories about. Cairo was Chicago's answer to Studio 54.

Kathy and I were both quick studies. The place to be was at the main bar on the entry level. Managing a seat there on any night was a monumental feat, but if you were lucky enough to bag a seat regularly, then you made it; you were in. As single moms without much extra money, we knew we had other assets that would pave the way for us to obtain main bar status. For the first time in my life, I was feeling confident about my looks, my manner of dress, and certainly my ability for stimulating conversation. I made sure I was well versed in many areas in order to be aptly conversant in any crowd. Listen attentively, speak in a self assured manner, and most importantly, keep conversation going. I had already learned that conversation was a very powerful allure, so best to make it linger, make it last, and make it unforgettable.

Kathy and I were pretty well rounded in that we were a good balance of brains, beauty, wit, and humor, which proved to be quite a winning arsenal. I became known as the queen of sarcasm, a handy tool that always accompanied me and proved to be a great quality for drawing power. We always made a notable entrance, and to ensure a spot at the main bar, we called ahead to let the bartenders know we were on the way. Both of us being food servers for so long, we knew that getting to know the bartenders personally, plus slipping them a little extra dinero, would get each side what they were after. For me and my partner, Kathy, it was a seat at the main bar. Profitable for the bartenders, because the wealthy male clientele was quick to shower attractive ladies with lots of champagne, followed by huge tips. Yes, the bartenders took great care of us; after all, we might have only slipped them a few bucks, but they came to realize we were fun gals who could get a guy to have the best champagne flowing all night long. It was a great tag team. The main bar was status; it was where the fluffiest plumes engaged, where all the stars sparkled. It was the focal point of the club. This was a great time and place to meet guys of diverse backgrounds and professions, some merely to chat with for the evening, some with dating potential, and others to network with for possible career opportunities.

Now that I was experiencing Chicago's club scene for the first time in my life, I was extremely grateful for the sewing prowess I had developed over the years. I certainly didn't have the money to buy expensive clothes, but I absolutely had the skill to create my own knockout numbers that cost a pittance to make and gave me the confidence to strut my stuff amid the best dressed in town.

One Saturday night in particular, I was wearing a new dress I had just completed earlier that day. A black and gold lamé slip-on mini dress with an off-the-shoulder sleeve that was quite the style at that time. Steep platform shoes to show off my slender legs, a black bracelet, and large black hoop earrings were the only accessories I needed. It was one of those nights when my hair was cooperating, due to the lack of humidity in the air. I added very little makeup to my sun kissed skin—just enough to emphasize my eyes and lips, which I considered to be my best features. I was to meet Kathy at Cairo around ten that night. I was feeling exceptionally happy and carefree this night. I remember thinking how perfect my life was and how grateful I was for it.

I pulled up to the valet area, and there was Nico, the little old valet attendant, whom I developed quite a relationship with. I tipped Niko well enough with cash, as well as with a sultry facial caress and kiss on the cheek to ensure he would place my car in a certain area whereby I would have ready access to it whenever I wanted to leave. He often told me that he didn't want my cash tip, that it was just enough for him to breathe my fragrance and feel my soft touch for him to be my slave. "Ah, bella, bella, I always wait for you, mia bella, every other Saturday at ten o'clock," he would sing. Nico was a cutie pie.

The air on that perfect, warm summer night seemed to whisk me to Cairo's entrance. I could hear the music. I could feel the vibe even before I entered. Cairo was that special. I felt special this night too; it was going to be an exceptional evening, I kept thinking for some reason. Standing tall, shoulders back, confidence level at a peak, I sashayed in and approached the bartender I knew (and liked the most) with a smooch on the cheek, asking for my usual sparkling water and lemon, which he readily provided, along with a seat smack dab in the middle of his VIP main bar area. I immediately reciprocated with my usual twenty dollar tip. There were several other hellos from a few regulars there, and it took no time at all to settle in and be the center of attention. It became quite natural to me. I felt at home there.

While in the midst of conversing with a few friends, I suddenly heard my name called out. Surprised, I searched the crowd to find the voice. I heard it again. I scanned the sea of faces, and then, I froze. In an instant, I was fifteen again, consumed with my first feeling of shock upon hearing that Mark had departed to Italy. That same shocking feeling now overwhelmed me as he stood there, calling out to me. It's hard to leave me speechless, but seeing Mark again did the trick. He was heading my way, so I thought it best to pick my mouth off the floor, as I would need it to speak to him. Here he was, more handsome than ever. His perfect hair crowned a golden, tanned face, exposing that flawless bit of age in men that makes them even more distinguished, easier on the eyes. Dressed casually cool in an open collar white shirt with the signature eighties sleeves rolled up, and well tailored black slacks, he approached me with open arms and a huge hug. I remembered his embrace. The feel of his body was just as it was that night—tight, toned, and muscular. No middle age midsection tire on this guy. I remembered the way my hands could glide through his still silky, stylish, still there hair. Hugging him back, I inhaled as you would homemade pastries in the oven. Ahhhhh, he was just as mouthwatering! Yes, I remembered every inch of him. After all, it was only a mere twenty years ago since I kissed him on that porch while basking in all the pleasure he gave me just by being next to me, by being interested in me.

"Hey, gorgeous, this is an awesome surprise!" Mark shouted as he hugged me again, even tighter than the first hug. The music was playing, the crowd was buzzing, but it all fell into the background as he began conversation. "I almost didn't recognize you and had to look twice, but when I saw those eyes and those lips, I knew it was you. I love the blonde hair," he added as he gently stroked my long locks. "You're stunning, Contessa," he whispered softly. "What a beautiful woman you've become."

Was it actually Mark speaking to me, or was it Dean Martin singing to me personally? I sat there listening to him, taking it all in. I responded in kind and mentally wiped the fifteen-year-old look off my face, replacing it with a poised and confident "I'm a big girl now" demeanor. Mark suggested champagne, since our meeting was certainly cause to celebrate. Who was I to argue? As we clinked our glasses, we began a melodic serenade of where our lives took us up to now. It was effortless, it was fluent, and it flowed, just as the champagne did. There was only one difference. Years ago, we were kids aspiring to be this and that, laying out our hopes, dreams, and goals. Now we were adults, experiencing the plans of our youth. We'd been out in the world for some time. We were much more worldly, or at least I know I was. And certainly much wiser, an additive that was the frosting on the cake of my night.

Mark realized significant success, having developed a new advertising placement concept, creating his own agency. He seemed to be at a content place in his life. I didn't ask about his personal life or status. I certainly wouldn't go there and thought it best for him to offer that information. I assumed that would come out at some point. I wasn't about to get too personal either. For all I knew, this might have been a chance, one-time meeting that was fun but over at the end of the night. I was prepared to treat it as such. Either way, I was basking in it. Normally, I'm a one-flute-of-champagne girl, but this night I lost count of the bottles and corks that my bartender friend popped for us. Just as Mark was ordering yet another bottle, I reminded him that I had to drive home. With that, Mark cited what a gorgeous summer night it was and asked if I would like to go for a walk. Absolutely, I would! As we made our exit, I thought about karma; good thoughts and actions out into the world, the same back at ya! I never spoke poorly of him all those years ago; I never put blame on him or wished him ill, even though I was terribly hurt. More to the point, I looked inside myself to see what I learned from the experience and found it was my own fault, my own assumptions that led to my heartache. Now I bumped into this old friend, whom I had the wildest crush on, in the utmost best of circumstances, and have the benefit of a fun, frisky, easy reacquaintance without one single moment of awkwardness. It was fate, for sure. The music played on as we left.

We walked around Cairo's neighborhood and continued this utterly delightful conversation with questions to each other about others we used to hang out with. Whatever happened to this one and that one from our old crowd? I really hated to end the night, but I did have to drive home all the way to the suburbs. I announced that I should get going.

"Hey, you're not just going to leave me here on the street, are ya?" he jokingly asked in the smoothest voice. "I mean, if you're sure you really have to go, you have to at least give me a ride home. I want to spend every minute I can with you," he said as he caressed my face.

"Of course, I won't leave you here on the street, silly. I can't risk another twenty years flying by before bumping into you again," I joked.

We walked to the car lot, where Nico was just about to close up for the night. "Good night, mia bella signora," Nico said as he blew me a kiss and winked. Mark quickly and tenderly responded to Nico, "No, signore, lei e'la mia bella signora," which translates to "No sir, she is my beautiful lady." Could this night get any better?

We drove the short distance to Mark's house, a beautiful white townhouse in a very prestigious area. As he pointed to his house, I pulled up and double parked, prepared to say goodbye but hoping he would at least ask for my phone number before getting out. I surely didn't want him slipping away without it, like last time. "Aren't you going to come in?" he asked.

"Mark, this night has been beyond spectacular, but I have such a long drive and you poured all that champagne down my throat." We both laughed. "So I think it best that I just get going," I decidedly responded. No way was I going to step one foot inside his house. I knew what would happen if I did, and I was not going to make it that easy for him.

"Oh, come on, please, just for a little while. I'm having such a good time. I can't tell you how good I feel seeing you again, how happy I am to talk to you again. Please, please, just for a little while," he seductively begged.

Okay, I caved and parked the car, but I insisted that we just sit outside on the porch and enjoy what was left of the fantastic evening air. As we made ourselves comfortable on the top step, I was stunned as Mark reminded me that this was where we left off.

"What do you mean?" I coyly asked.

"The last time I saw you was on Janet's porch. We sat out there on a beautiful, hot summer night, just like this one. Amazing, isn't it? Here we are again. Alone on a porch on a beautiful, hot summer night." He was not really whispering, but his words were a melody to me, as though they were uttered by breath alone, without the use of vocal cords.

"Yes, I remember that night quite well" was all I could say. I wouldn't dare ask about his sudden departure to Italy; best to leave that alone. But ahhh, would this night end with the same overwhelming kisses as it did all those years ago?

We were instantly engaged in more fluent conversation without one moment of silence, this time getting a little more personal. Mark offered that he was divorced and had two daughters, to whom he was completely devoted. He didn't go into what went wrong with his marriage, but he spoke kindly and respectfully of his ex-wife. To me, his courteous attitude toward his ex-wife spoke volumes about him. I had never heard a man speak of their ex so admirably. He went on and on about his girls and how much they meant to him, what his aspirations for them were. I could easily see what a dedicated father he was. It was so refreshing. With that, I told him all about Little Contessa and the short version of the demise of my marriage as well as my single-mother saga. Tales of single parenting kept us gong for quite a while.

I really had to pee and had been holding it for way too long but couldn't any longer, so I asked him to direct me to his bathroom. He escorted me in, and I did my thing. Before exiting the bathroom, I did a check of myself. Hair, good. Makeup, still in tact. Just a bit more lipstick before I, hopefully, kissed him good night, and in anticipation of that, I popped a breath mint in my mouth just in case. When I came out, there Mark sat on his succulent leather sofa but quickly jumped up and offered to show me around. "You know, it's really late, and I need to get going," I timidly responded.

"Aw, come on, just a little longer. Let me show you the whole house," he pleaded.

I was putty.

Mark began a tour of his contemporary and tastefully decorated, impeccable home and office space. It was easy to see his classic style everywhere, and I was particularly drawn to the many photos of his children, which he took delight in showing me, explaining each photo in detail. Even their pictures were specifically arranged in a certain way, adding to the decor of the room. His love and devotion to them was obvious and heartwarming. Like I needed anything else to make him more attractive!

I was mentally demanding myself to be smart and leave just as soon as the tour was over. It would be way too easy to jump into bed with him, and I certainly did not want that to happen—not yet, anyway. The voice inside my head was screaming, "Okay, enough! Now, get the hell outta here!" Finally, I worked up the strength and announced, very emphatically, that I really had to leave and unwittingly included "Before you have an overnight guest." *Oh, shit!* I really didn't mean to say that! I was just so tired and trying to make a graceful exit.

"Well, that wouldn't be such a bad thing, Contessa."

We stood there just staring into each other's eyes for a minute before Mark grabbed me, held me tight in his arms, and kissed me ever so passionately. That kiss was endless, and we fell onto his creamy leather sofa, allowing it to go on forever. When we finally came up for air, I looked deep, deep into his beautiful round light brown eyes and caressed his perfect lips. Mark could have kissed me into anything, but I fought to keep it together, to hold my ground. I just kept thinking, *God, please give me strength, give me strength, give me strength!*

"Mark, you have no idea how much I would love to stay, but I'm not going to," I softly told him. "I really need to leave now." I tried to find my legs and get up. My heart was pounding so hard I thought he would actually hear it.

The power of his kisses and my hope that he wanted to see me again intoxicated me more than all the champagne we drank this night. My heart grew heavy as I headed for the door without him indicating anything about us seeing each other again. That realization actually gave me the strength to keep on going. I would've rather died than be a one night stand of his, so as long as I knew I had to leave, I was going to do so with dignity. As I walked, I reiterated how wonderful it was to see him and reminisce. With one hand on the doorknob, I turned to look at him one more time, when he embraced me yet again and hugged me ever so tightly.

"Please tell me this isn't it," he finally asked. "Please tell me I can see you again."

I didn't even realize I was holding my breath, waiting for that, and when I heard it, I think I exhaled endlessly. I couldn't speak; I left the words up to him.

"You didn't think I was going to let you leave without getting your number, did you?" he asked as I was still exhaling.

Thank you, God!

My car seemed to have turned into a magic carpet, because I felt I was floating all the way home. It was actually sunrise by the time I got home, but ask me if I cared. I didn't even want to take my clothes off; I just wanted to keep everything the way it was. I sat on my sofa and replayed the entire night in my head. If I really was dreaming, I didn't want to ever wake up. Mesmerizing as it was, I finally drifted off into a very deep sleep. When I woke up, I actually had to think for a minute if last night was real or not. I loved the mental replay and put it on rewind several times in order to convince myself that it was. Now the big question was, would he actually call me? Of course he would, right? I mean, why wouldn't he? Not to be arrogant, but it was all perfect. We were both single, professionals, have history, similar backgrounds—we have so much in common, including daughters, even mutual friends. It was just an ideal situation. Who would dispute that? Oh God, please let him think so!

Sunday was a blur, just one big flashback of the night before, plus the anticipation of my phone ringing with him on the other end. Alas, the phone did eventually ring, but it was Kathy calling to explain and apologize for not showing up at Cairo to meet me. She got her period, got very nauseous, and just couldn't leave the house. This was before the days of cell phones, so there was no way for her to call me. Not to worry, I assured her as I delighted in repeating the whole story to her. Kathy screamed with excitement for me and assured me that yes, he surely would call. But as the night dragged on, the phone never rang again. Exhausted and knowing how busy Monday mornings at the office were, I took the longest hot shower, jumped into bed, and called it a night.

As the office manager of my firm, I had a private office and a direct line. I gave that private number to Mark, along with my home number. While I was in the midst of one of the most miserable Mondays, suddenly my private line lit up. I had a feeling it would be Mark. I put my best professional voice on but sugared it with a little sultry tone. Yes, it was him all right! He got right to the point and asked me out to dinner that evening. As much as I wanted to run right over, this would not be a good night for me. I wanted to be my best, and I was still dragging a little from the weekend, plus this day was taking a toll on me and I would probably have to work a little late. In addition, the next day would be worse due to some of the mishaps of today. I told Mark that the next two nights would not be good, and I suggested Wednesday. That worked for him. We set the time, and I gave him directions to my house.

I made sure I was able to leave work a little early on Wednesday, just to get home in time to primp myself for my very first actual date with Mark. Not knowing where he was taking me, I chose a casual but stylish pant suit that was safe, chic for anyplace. I had just enough time to fluff up my hair and put a fresh touch on what little makeup I wore. As I was triple checking everything, the doorbell rang, and I buzzed him through the intercom, letting him know I would be right down. I didn't think there was reason to invite him up; perhaps I would save that for later when he brought me home. As I approached the lobby of my building, there appeared what I pretty much expected. A big black shiny new Cadillac with Mark standing on the passenger side, holding the door open for me. Ahhh, be still, my heart! Again dressed in his signature casual, cool style, all I could think about was how gorgeous he was, and that gentlemanly manner of his didn't hurt the situation either! He complimented me on the way I looked, indicating once again how much he loved my long blond hair and my simple yet sophisticated style of dress. Coming from such a dapper guy, this compliment meant a lot to me.

We arrived at a lovely Italian restaurant not too far from my house. I'd seen it, heard of its great reputation, but had never been there before. I informed Mark that this could not be a late night, as I had an early meeting in the morning and had to be focused.

Nestled in a cozy little booth, sitting next to each other, we fell right into place, and our easy conversation mostly targeted our professional lives and eventually migrated to our children. Mark went into detail on the various things he was involved in and what led him to building his current business. He was just as interested in my career, whom I worked for, what my job entailed, and what my aspirations were. I was blown away by his interest, which appeared to be genuine. I included that while I had a solid position with a major firm, I was contracted with several marketing companies to manage corporate booths at various Chicago trade show venues. This part-time job allowed me to meet a broad range of people and provided vast insight into a wide variety of people and industries. Mark complimented me on my focus and ambition. He was impeccable through dinner. Mark ate European style, which went well with his persona. Class act. Thoughts of how perfect we were together consumed me. We had such a natural rapport, we had the same love and devotion to our children, and with that, Mark would certainly be compassionate to me for what all comes with single parenting, something I needed to have in any relationship. In the single world these days, you often meet someone you have an interest in and they run as soon as they find out you have kids. Or they can't deal with the fact that your children are your first priority. Good riddance to that shallow mind. With Mark, it was embraced. We were both in exactly the same stations in our lives. Never a lapse, never a single awkward moment. Instead an ongoing delightful serenade that played on. After dinner, Mark declined coffee, and I was flabbergasted to hear him ask me if I would make him coffee at my house. Oh, shit! I can cook you a twenty course meal with my eyes closed, but I make the worst coffee in the world! I always kept coffee in the house but asked my guests to make it, as coffee was not my forte. I took a big gulp and dived in. *Okay, here goes nothing.* I instantly thought this would be a good opportunity for Mark to meet my daughter, who I knew would be home by now. I advised him that Little Contessa would be home from work, *just* in case he had ideas besides a cup of coffee. Mark expressed delight in meeting her, as she was home for summer break from college. Little Contessa would be returning to her downstate college soon, and having told her the whole story of our history, I thought it would be great that she would get to meet him.

My daughter and I lived in a very nice apartment complex in Arlington Heights, an affluent suburb. Ours was a spacious two bed-room, two bath apartment that was decorated very simply. Tasteful, though certainly not anything grandiose. One thing for sure: anyone who knew me could vouch for the fact that my home was always warm, welcoming, and extremely neat! I was proud of our little home, but it was nothing compared to Mark's rich and luxurious Chicago townhouse. Oh, well, I was grateful to have worked my way up to affording this. *So here it is, Mark, take it or leave it.* As we walked in, I heard Little Contessa on the phone in her room. I asked Mark to have a seat while I let her know I was home, and with com-pany. I popped my head in her room to let her know I brought Mark home with me and would she please come out and meet him when she got off the phone.

An Italian tradition is coffee and sweets after dinner. Although I was more health oriented and didn't personally follow tradition, I usually had something in the freezer I could pop in the micro-wave, just in case any company stopped by. While I was preparing the sweets, Mark graciously complimented me on our very mod-est home. We sat in the living room with the TV on and chatted when my daughter came in to join us. I introduced the two, and Mark immediately made note of the resemblance to her dad. Little Contessa was surprised to learn that they had known each other. Mark explained that he was born in the same neighborhood as her father and they went to the same grammar school but then he and his family moved away to the Ross Park area as he entered high school and they lost touch. Little Contessa discussed her college curriculum and campus life but then excused herself and retreated back to her room. I apologized for what was most likely the worst cup of coffee he probably ever had, but again his chivalrous nature told me it was fine. *Don't worry,* I thought, *my cooking will surely impress you and make up for the bad coffee.* By this time, it was getting late, and Mark announced he should get going. I walked him out to the lobby. I just had to get another chance at those lips.

Mark asked me to walk out to the car with him so he could give me a proper goodbye. Of course, I would. It was so easy to slide over on his plush leather seats once he reached out and grabbed me around my waist, pulling me close to him. If his kisses were sugar, let me die of diabetes!

"I had to have more of your lips to hold me over until I could see you again," he whispered. "Do you have plans this weekend?"

"No, I don't," I managed.

"Well, you do now!" he commanded. "I'll plan everything and call you with the details."

Don'tcha just love a guy who takes control! One more kiss, finished by a peck on the cheek, and we said goodbye. I melt like butter for an action man! Nothing wishy washy about Mark. Direct and to the point was just my style, leaving nothing to be questioned. I was in heaven.

I knew exactly what this weekend meant, and it couldn't come fast enough. I've always been known to primp a lot regularly, but a special occasion required exceptional dolling up, and this Saturday night was just the night to go balls out. I became a master at highlighting my eyes, which were one of my more noted features, so this night I applied individual false eyelashes, which really make your eyes pop, yet with a very natural look. My freshly washed and blown dry hair was thick, long, and silky, parted to the side and tucked around one ear, allowing the large silver hoop earrings to show. A very natural but sultry look, which was my style, and one that I learned Mark loved. A solid navy blue summer knit dress, backless to the waist, with a navy and white bow at the base of the back. No need for a bra; the girls were in solid position. And the panties I chose were quite unique, most importantly void of showing panty lines; cannot tolerate them, not sexy at all, which ruins any look. Simple yet elegant and complimentary to my figure. Certainly just right to whet Mark's taste buds as well. Since he made dinner reservations at one of his favorite downtown restaurants, I of course would drive to his place to meet him.

Oddly enough, as I was getting ready, the excitement faded and was replaced with a more calming confidence. We both knew where the night would take us. I would have been kidding myself to think otherwise. And why not? We were both single adults, and there was no disputing the electricity between us. We had a history together and so much in common. *Tonight's the night*, I kept singing to myself, so I really didn't care where we went, because I knew where we'd wind up. It was all so right, I thought as I drove, and the closer I came to his house, the more relaxed and positive I became.

I don't think I need to go into the details of Mark's elegant manner in public, his finesse over dinner, and how our interaction with each other was effortless, natural, and just flowed. Let's cut right to the chase. Mark asked me if I'd like to go to his place, maybe sit outside, sip champagne, and enjoy this warm summer night.

"Sounds fabulous," I happily replied.

With that, we flew home in Mark's big shiny black Cadillac. On the way, he showered me with compliments of a wide variety. He added that he felt like the luckiest man in the restaurant to be there with me, that he knew he was envied by every other man there. *Great foreplay, Mark! Oh, yeah, tonight is gonna be quite the marathon!*

All things come to those who wait, a wise person once said. Someone else, who might have been even a little smarter, said that all things happen for a reason and we have to be patient to find out what that reason is. Both of these wise old sayings are relative here, and time is the only teacher to have their wisdom sink in. Here we were, sitting comfortably on Mark's porch, having pre-prepared dessert and champagne, talking about everything under the sun. I could never have handled this all those years ago. I was in no way equipped for this, and it was only now that realization hit me. Those were the years for dreaming. Time had taught me, and now was the time to make dreams come true. Each of us needed to channel through our lives to get to this point—just the right time for us both.

While Mark went inside to replenish our drinks, I sat there so completely relaxed, allowing the evening summer breeze to blow my hair comfortably back as I gazed up at the thousands of sparkling stars above me. The only thought rolling around my head at this glorious moment was how Mark would make his move, and it most definitely would have to be his move. I didn't have to ponder that thought very long though. I opened my eyes to find that he had returned to the porch with two fresh drinks. He sat there beside me, just watching me bask in my moment. He put the drinks down over to the side, reached over, and embraced me, stroking my hair and caressing me. It was an indescribable moment that sent shock waves through me. I responded favorably with a blazing glare that told Mark that I agreed with his obvious intentions. We had talked enough; words were no longer necessary. His tender yet sizzling, lingering kiss told me how much he wanted me, and I believed not just for tonight. That was more a maneuver than a smoking hot kiss and was part of Mark's choreography programmed to take us from the porch into his luxurious bedroom, which had been prepared for our arrival. As if our vivacious conversation, playful banter, and sexual undertones weren't enough foreplay, the candles, rose petals, sensual aroma throughout the air cinched it. Soft music followed us to this room that was soon to become a steam bath, but I had no idea what it was; all I could hear was the sensuous voice of Roberta Flack once again singing in my head, telling me that the first time ever I saw his face, I felt the earth move. And move it did!

Having already acknowledged I would never have known how to handle such a learned man as Mark years ago but now, in the sophomore stage of my adult single life, I was confidently more than equipped. I will add, though, that while I was now quite a bit more worldly, I was always prepared and receptive to learning more. I was certain I would inevitably grow from being with Mark. What ensued was a wondrous revelation for each of us. A powerful encounter of optimum magnitude that resonates with me even to this day. In time, I became convinced that it was our matched prowess in several areas that was part of Mark's attraction to me. We were hungry for each other in multiple ways, beyond our combined sensual, sexual nature, but for our equaled passions for life, adventure, and the world. Yes, a perfect combination and a very harmonious relationship steadily grew over the next few months. At that moment in my life, I was blissfully happy, felt completely appreciated, wanted, and most of all, respected. I believed I was getting very close to realizing my lifelong and strongest desire, to be bound to a genuine, honest, and loving man, maintaining a solid relationship. The world was completely in tact.

I was in the midst of an extremely busy week at work, having to stay late several evenings. By the time I got home each night, I was exhausted. In the middle of the week, I realized I hadn't heard from Mark, which was unusual. Normally we spent each weekend Mark was not with his children together. I had the utmost respect for the way he cared for his girls, and his dedication made me care for him even more. That said, the weekends we were not together led to more endearing feelings for him as opposed to to an irritant, as most other women would view it. Mark often commented on my acceptance of his situation and cited that as a reason for his not being able to sustain a relationship up until this time. Not a problem with me! He would call me, and our chats would always include a definite plan for when we would be together next. Never did an entire week go by that I did not hear from him. Until now. By Friday, I got concerned. I wrestled over whether or not to call him. Would I be interfering if he was just spending more time with his kids? Would I seem like I didn't care if I didn't call? What to do, what to do! I certainly would never want him to think I didn't care if there was a problem situation going on, so after still not hearing from him by Saturday afternoon, I decided to call him. He didn't answer, and I left a lighthearted message, just saying hello, hoping everything was all right, and asking him to call me when he could.

I sat there curled up on my mediocre sofa, nestled in my jammies, trying to watch TV, but the movie I was really watching was going on in my head. It was a replay of the entire time Mark and I spent together, starting back from twenty years ago. I kept going back to that summer when I found out Mark had left for Italy. The memory of how shocked I was to hear the news sent a chill down my spine, and suddenly it hit me, leaving me with the same chilling shock wave. *Mark doesn't say goodbye!* I jumped up with this realization. For whatever reason he had, it was over. I just knew it. Given all of Mark's graciousness, all his gentlemanly manners, his unparalleled sophistication, and what I believed to be genuineness, that flashback from years ago threw me into the reality of today. A future with Mark was not to be. The rerun played over and over as I reviewed it, trying to see what sign I could have missed. Was I wearing the rose colored glasses I thought I threw away long ago, or was I just a fool, wishing for and wanting something so badly I allowed myself to believe it was actually happening? I drove myself crazy on that sofa the entire weekend thinking it through. Still not having heard from Mark by Sunday evening, I was convinced I was right. I was now questioning whether there ever really was a relationship in the first place. Was I just walking through a daydream? Jeez, if I could only talk to him, I knew I could get him to open up and talk to me, tell me what the issue was.

After a few nights of tears, replays, wishing Mark would call, and beating myself up, I gave myself one final slap in the face to snap out of it and just shake it off. What bothered me most was that I was just left there hanging, again! If only I could talk to him one more time, I would at least find out what his reasons or issues were. I wouldn't even think of trying to change his mind; I mean, if he already made a decision to discontinue seeing me, so be it, but I would sure like to know why, as well as give him a piece of my mind. And no way would I sink to calling him again. Nope.

But after several more days passed, I knew I wouldn't be hearing from him. Okay, it happened, and now it was over. *So move along, little doggy. You've got things to do, and there's no time for sulking.* I fell into a fairy tale, and while I believe it to have been genuine, I realize now that I told myself it was more than what it actually was. What can I say other that I went with my feelings and played the situation out? In the end, it was Mark who made a decision, and while it ended abruptly and ungraciously, the fact was, it was over. You can't predict somebody else's feelings or actions, and you cannot force a situation if both parties aren't completely engaged. I needed to accept it and just file it in my "stupid things men do" binder. I had no answers or control over it and deduced right then and there I would not waste any more time on it. I did, however, know that I was worth more than this and confident that while my heart was broken, it would be put back together someday and by the right person. I decided that in the future I needed to be more guarded with my feelings and thus added another layer to the growing wall around my heart. I tucked this experience away, and when asked what happened, I would crisply reply that we just broke up, and my tone told the person asking to ask no further.

Fast forward to another twenty years. No kidding! I was having a lengthy phone chat with Dana, one of my childhood friends. Our busy lives didn't allow us to see each other often, so our phone calls were always pretty long. Catching up on our work, families, kids, other friends, etc. always allowed for welcome and lively conversation. Dana mentioned the delight in the new girl her son was dating, that this was the happiest she had seen her son in a long time. Dana also mentioned that the girl was Italian and the two young people had actually known each other since they were children, because both sets of parents were friends.

"How nice," I replied. "Who are her parents?"

Dana was quick to tell me their names. The immediate high pitched shriek I let out almost sent Dana to the ear doctor!

"What? What's the matter? What's wrong?" she cried out.

It took me a minute to grab ahold of myself. The new girl in Dana's son's life was Mark's daughter! I roared with laughter as I quickly began the short version of the history shared between Mark and me, mainly from the early years, leaving out most of round 2, particularly the ending. I called it a casual reacquaintance of two old friends that evolved to a short lived, pretty casual affair that just fizzled out. No big deal. I would rather jump off a bridge than let on what a hurtful situation it turned out to be for me. Besides, it was so long ago I hadn't even thought of him in so many years, and I had let go of all those feelings, anyway.

I wouldn't dare ask anything about him, but Dana offered that Mark was still single after many on again, off again years with his ex-wife. Although they divorced many years ago, they reconciled and broke up a million times for several years. They finally called it quits for good some time ago, and Mark had not been involved with anyone since. He was living alone in a nearby suburb, pretty much just focusing on work and hanging out with old friends, many of whom were longtime friends of mine as well. Dana and I had been trying to get a group together for dinner, but with everyone's hectic schedules, it hadn't materialized yet. She announced a great idea. Why not plan something and include Mark? What a surprise it would be for him to see me, she thought, and she asked if I'd be okay with that. She added, "You guys would make a great couple. You have so much in common and know so many of the same people. It would be great if you two could get together."

Although I hesitated for a minute, all I could think of to say was, "Well, you know me, Dana. I love being with friends." I mentally froze. Did I really want to see him again, or ever, for that matter?

"You're hesitating. You don't want to see him, do you?" Dana asked. She knew me so well.

Sure, why not? I thought. I wasn't a love sick puppy anymore, and truth be told, I became receptive to show him what he missed out on. Yes, we were twenty years older, but I still looked pretty good, often taken for many years younger than what I actually was. In addition, I had many successful accomplishments under my belt that I was quite proud of and wouldn't mind sharing with him. So yes, I admitted that I'd love to see him and let a claw or two out. Mark would see a sassy side of me, a side that had been well seasoned over the years.

"No, really, Dana, it would be great to see him," I assured her but suggested that she run it by her husband to see what he and the other guys thought and let them decide. I certainly didn't want to come off like a desperate woman throwing myself at him, and I could easily see how he could think that with the way things left off between us.

Dana got back to me within a few days. Her husband, Tony, and the other fellas agreed that getting Mark and me together was a great idea. *Hmmm, this is getting interesting,* I wickedly thought to myself. Dana would call me in another day or so once the men finalized the where, when, etc. I have to admit, the thought of seeing him again became tantalizing, for various reasons. First of all, I admit I was curious, and who could blame me? Where was he in life? Was he still drop dead gorgeous? Second, I had accomplished quite a bit since we last saw each other, and everyone who would be at this dinner knew it. I wouldn't mind sugaring the conversation with a little bit of where I'd been and what I'd done. Maybe the tables had turned; maybe he would be in awe of me this round. Lastly, just how would he react over seeing me? That was the million dollar question. Was I being conceited and even a little arrogant in my thoughts? *For sure, but hey, I'm human, and I'm a bit of a scorned woman, so get over it.*

Game night. My heart was not at all a-flutter this time as I got ready for dinner. It was an unusually hot summer night, and I was well tanned and very toned. My hair was long, still pretty thick, and a beautiful auburn. I chose body hugging clothes—light, casual, and simple, but "classy" sexy. It was going to be a sassy night, and I had to dress the part. Besides, if ever there was a reason and opportunity to flaunt whatever I had, this was it. *I'm no saint and can even be a little bitchy, but at least I'm an honest bitch!*

Dana, Tony, and I were the first to arrive at a casual little Italian restaurant in a nearby suburb. Tony knew the restaurant owner and asked him to set up tables in a certain way to accommodate our entire group. The three of us were seated. Tony mentioned that the guys agreed not to tell Mark I would be here tonight. I found that to be hilarious and burst out in laughter. Dana and Tony didn't understand why it was so funny to me, and before I could even start to explain, we heard a loud "Hey, guys" come from behind. It was the rest of our friends, and Mark was smack dab in the middle of them. They were behind us, so Mark didn't immediately notice me. It was important for me to see the look on his face when he first caught sight of me. As I turned around, our eyes met instantly. He stopped dead in his tracks.

"Oh my God!" he yelled out with a huge grin on his face, running to me with open arms. While he squeezed me hard, I embraced him more casually. "I can't believe it! Contessa, it's wonderful to see you!" he kept repeating. Mark was more animated than I'd ever seen him. I guess we all change a little with age. It was clear to all that Mark was very excited to see me.

With several seating choices, Mark plopped down right next to me. He looked fantastic. While most guys add a few years of extra gut or love handles, Mark appeared to have gained twenty years of debonair! *Ugh, this isn't going to be easy.* It was a fabulous night of old friends mixing, mingling, laughing, and reminiscing over great food and drinks. Before dinner was brought out to us, Mark stood up to make a toast to friendship and then put the spotlight on me, adding in Italian, how blessed he was to have maintained the old friends and even more blessed to have an old friend return to his life, especially one who, as he turned to me, seemed to have found the fountain of youth! The gang roared with laughter and drank to that toast. Damn, he was good!

While the conversation remained lively and ongoing, Mark and I had a few individual sidebars on our kids, travel, careers, and what our current lives were like. Once again, it was so easy to be with him, but I kept my guard up. While our conversation was fluent as ever, I pounced on every single opportunity to infuse the witty sarcasm I was known for to be part of it. Not that I was in any hurry to end this happy night; my wonder was of how he would leave it.

The night flew by way too fast, and before we knew it, the staff was flickering the lights, indicating it was time for us to end this extremely pleasurable evening. We kissed and hugged each other, promising to do this again soon. Just as I began thinking what an asshole Mark was for not giving at least some indication that he was sorry for treating me like gum on the bottom of his shoe he just had to get rid of, he grabbed me tight around the waist and shuffled me off to the side.

"I really want to see you again, and soon. There are things that need to be said," he whispered in his golden tone. I just stared at him without saying a word. "Contessa, please. I have to see you again. How about this weekend? Please give me a chance to explain some things," he pleaded. There was no longing in my eyes; perhaps they were even a little icy, which, if he didn't pick up on before, my response made clear.

"Tonight was great, but honestly, I don't think that's a good idea," I said with a sly smile.

"You don't understand. I don't just want to see you, I *need* to see you," he begged.

I have to admit, I was basking in this. I hesitated for just another moment and offered, "I'll tell you what. No need for us to get together, but if you really feel the need to say some things to me, call me." I turned and began walking away.

"Wait!" Mark grabbed my arm. "Give me your number."

"Did you say wait?" I laughingly asked. "I have waited, Mark, twenty years! Get my number from Dana!" I said as I turned and walked away, feeling quite pleased with myself. I felt my actions were justified, and I kinda liked seeing him squirm. If for no other reason than curiosity, I did want to have this conversation but just didn't want to make it easy for him. I was pleased to share some of the angst he caused me all those years ago.

My phone rang bright and early the next morning. It was a very excited Dana. She had so much to say and also to ask. She conveyed that the whole group was happy to see Mark and me together, that they thought we made a great couple, and how nice it would be if something serious developed between us. They all commented on our individual little chats throughout the night, as well as this being the first time they saw Mark with someone who commanded the crowd more than he did. Dana noticed that Mark and I went off to the side for a private chat. She wanted to know what that was about. Dana added Mark already called her, asking for my phone number. Dana held off providing it, though, saying she would have to ask my permission before she gave it to him, another reason for her call to me now. She wanted to know, why didn't I give it to him last night? I expressed my appreciation for having the "blessing" of the group, joking it was nice to know they sanctioned a relationship between Mark and me. The only lame excuse I could conjure up as to why I didn't give him my number was that I didn't have anything to write it on, so I suggested that he just call her for it. That explanation seemed to work. I gave my permission for Dana to give Mark my number. Now, to see if he actually called.

The whole thing was really out of my head, and I spent the entire day conducting my business as usual. After dinner that night, I had plopped on the couch to watch one of my favorite shows when the phone rang. Caller ID showed it was Mark calling. I let it go into voice mail, waited a few minutes, and then listened to his message. In his usual silky voice, Mark was practically begging me to call him back, reciting his phone number three times, asking that I call him right away no matter how late it was when I got his message. I finished watching my show. I gave myself a facial. I took a long, hot shower. I prepared my calendar for the rest of the week. Finally, I called him. Mark expressed gratitude for my call, even admitting he doubted that I would.

"Why?" I coyly asked. He confessed realizing the shitty way he left things all those years ago was horrible and cowardly, that he wanted an opportunity to explain and hopefully make things right between us. "I'm listening" was my dry, monotone response. He had to clear his throat before beginning. In all the years I had known him, I'd only seen him collected and assured. I had never seen him rattled, which, I must admit, I was thoroughly enjoying.

"When we got together, I was divorced from my wife, as you know. You also know how much I love my daughters and how I agonized over having them only part-time. Their mother started dating someone the girls didn't like at all, and it got to be a very serious relationship. My kids were begging me to come back home, to try to patch things up so their mother would get rid of the other guy. They begged me to put our family back together again. Well, call me crazy, but I actually thought I could, that I could make it work. I moved back in with my ex-wife. We didn't remarry, but we tried to put all the bad stuff behind us and began to live like a family again. The kids were so happy, and I admit that for a while I was too. I really wanted it work for the sake of the kids. You know how much family means to me. I've shared my feelings with you about how devastated I was when my own parents broke up. When I saw how happy my kids were because their mom and I were back together, I became more enthusiastic about trying to keep it going. But in time I realized that I was forcing it. I wanted it to work so badly for the girls that I told myself it was something that it really wasn't. After a few years, I just couldn't take it anymore. And by that time, the kids were teenagers, doing their own thing anyway. You know how that goes."

"Anything else?" I wryly asked. I wasn't going to let him off the hook so easily. He came this far, and now he'd have to go all the way.

"I know. Why didn't I call you and explain?" he half asked, half stated.

"Bingo!" I answered.

"I didn't want to hurt you. I guess deep in my heart I knew I was making a huge mistake. I wrestled with the decision for a very long time, and unfortunately, it was during the time you and I got together. You were my deterrent, and you made things harder for me because I really did have strong feelings for you. My ex-wife and I had so many issues deep down I knew we couldn't resolve them. But I kept telling myself it was what the kids wanted, and I didn't think you would believe me. I had such deep feelings for you, such respect for you. You always demonstrated high standards, and I just didn't think you'd understand or respect the reason for the choice I made," he finished.

"And because you didn't want to hurt me, you thought that just leaving me hanging would be less of a blow? You had so much respect for me that you couldn't or wouldn't give me any explanation as to why you were abruptly ending a relationship that you yourself said was almost too perfect to believe? You had so much respect for me that you couldn't give me the benefit of the doubt that I just might understand? Okay, since this is a confession call, I'll confess that I was just as dumb as you were. I wanted it so much I told myself there was something there that really wasn't. Well, no worries, Mark. I got over it," I coldly responded.

"Contessa, you weren't dumb. There was something there. So now what?" Mark assured me and asked.

"You mean you're finally giving me an opportunity to make a decision?" I snapped.

"Contessa, we were meant for each other, you know that. I believe in fate. Why is it you came back into my life now, when all the bullshit with my ex-wife is behind me, my kids are grown, and we're both at good places in our lives? C'mon, you have to admit it's our fate to be together. Why else would you have come to dinner last night?" he pleaded.

"Because I was hungry and love to dine with friends," I sarcastically answered.

"That's just one of the things I love about you, you sarcastic little wench! Please, please let me see you again. We can pick up right where we left off. Can't I at least have a chance to make it all up to you?" he begged.

"It's not that easy, Mark. I can't speak for you, but I'm not the same girl you left behind. I don't forget easily, and I'm even more independent now than I was in our last round. I'll be honest with you, I'm very guarded these days," I finished.

"I can see that, and I certainly understand. I promise, if you just give me a chance, I'll make you forget the past and I'll break down any barriers you have. I'll make you trust me and have faith that it's real this time," Mark responded.

"I need to think about this, Mark. Give me time. If I change my mind, I'll call you" was all I could say.

I spent the next few days thinking hard about this whole thing. Dana was calling me constantly, wanting to know more details, but I was pretty casual about everything. I never wanted to disclose what all had happened years ago. Knowing Mark and how hard he strived to satisfy his children, I somewhat believed the story as to why he went back to his ex-wife. However, no matter what his reasons were, there would never be an acceptable reason or excuse for leaving me hanging like he did. Simple honesty was all I would have needed. Then I started thinking about where I was at in my life at this point. It was all good. I had realized much success and enjoyed a very comfortable and pleasant lifestyle. I was personally and financially independent. I had many wonderful friends in my life. While I had the pleasure of enjoyable male company regularly, there wasn't a steady significant other. Hmmm, it was comfortable with Mark. The same rapport we experienced years ago was still evident. We still had so many friends in common. We were getting older. I started to soften. *Okay, why not give it a go? Worst case scenario: it doesn't work out and I chalk it up to chapter 3, the final episode.* I decided to give it a try.

I called Mark the next evening. He seemed overjoyed when I told him I'd like to see him. He immediately made several suggestions as to where to go and what to do. I countered those suggestions with offering dinner at my place. I wanted to test the waters on my own turf, without us having our "Sunday suits" on and a whole lot of ambiance to enhance things. He loved the idea. I was prepared to start over and just see where it went. I had no expectations, but these days, it wouldn't take much for me to determine if there was a chance in hell for this encounter to go anywhere. I'd seen it, done it, and dated it all by this time and felt pretty secure in the fact that I would know in one night if there was any merit to continuing.

I was no longer intimidated by a meager home. I lived in a downtown Chicago high rise with a very prestigious address. My condo was impeccably furnished, everything first class. I was very proud of it. Once Mark arrived, he commented on how stylish my place was. I prepared a fabulous Italian meal with several courses. As usual, Mark looked dapper as ever, and of course, one of his accessories was his signature bottle of champagne. He made his way into the kitchen and found champagne glasses, commenting on their beauty. I took pride in mentioning that they were Italian antiques. Dinner was delightful, and we were both very relaxed and enjoying the evening. Truth be told, it couldn't have been nicer. I even managed to forget that I had him on trial. I remembered his love of coffee and dessert after dinner and suggested he relax in the living room while I prepared it. As much as I had progressed in life, I still hadn't mastered the art of making coffee, and we both got a kick out of that. As I was preparing coffee and dessert, I suddenly heard Luciano Pavarotti softly playing. Mark wanted to surprise me, having remembered that I loved Italian opera. As we listened, he took me in his arms and kissed me ever so passionately. Nothing changed. His lips were just as intoxicating as ever; the electricity of his kisses had not diminished with time. The guy still had it! I sat back for a moment, just to take it in. I didn't want to talk; I just wanted to enjoy it.

"You are even more beautiful now, Contessa. You are even more desirable than ever," he whispered. I leaned in for more. "I have another surprise for you," he announced as he got up from the sofa. He put his shoes and jacket on and went for his car keys.

"Where are you going?" I asked.

"I'll be right back. You're gonna love this one," he answered.

"Oh, yeah, well, it better not take you another twenty years!" I joked.

Mark roared with laughter and came back to kiss me. "I'll be right back," he whispered.

About fifteen minutes later, there was a knock on my door. Of course, it was him. I opened the door expecting a surprise, and boy, did I get one! He reentered with a suitcase, a very large suitcase!

"What's this?" I asked.

"I thought I'd stay for a while," he casually answered.

I tried hard to keep my cool, but *What the fuck!* was raging through my head. "*What* do you mean stay for a while? That looks like you're planning on moving in!" I snapped.

"Well, I thought I'd leave a few things here. We can talk about me moving in later on," he all too casually announced as he proceeded to open the suitcase and begin unpacking it.

Oh my God, this is not happening! "Slow down, buddy. Take your foot off the gas!" I ordered.

"What? What's wrong?" he asked.

I can be pushed and remain polite up to a point, but, ruffle my feathers, push me over my line, provoke me, try to control me, and you're gonna get it!

"You drop me like a bad habit twenty years ago, I see you once, and you're all ready to move in to my house? Are you kidding me? Either you think I'm that stupid or you're that special or both—I don't know. What I do know is that nobody is moving in to my house unless I invite them, and I didn't invite you! No, this is not happening." If my words didn't sink in, my tone should have, but as I was yelling at him, he kept right on unpacking! He pulled out an eight-by-ten framed picture of himself dressed in full Mafia garb, including a fedora.

"Oh, come on, babe. We worked all that out. We got past that. You said you loved me, and now I'm back. You got a hammer?" he asked.

"I loved you twenty years ago, buddy. That's the only thing that's past! A hammer? What the fuck do you want a hammer for?" I yelled.

"I had this picture made for you to hang up. Isn't it great?" he said, admiring himself.

"Oh my God, you've been watching too many *Soprano* reruns!" I grabbed the picture and threw it back into the open suitcase. I then grabbed his arm and led him to the living room. "What the fuck do you think you're doing? You are *not* moving in with me! Something else is going on, and don't tell me I'm crazy! For once, why not just tell the truth? Spill!" I demanded.

As he looked downcast for a minute, he took a breath and started. "Okay, here's the deal. Everything I told you was true. Only I left out that I've been out of work for some time now, and the day before we all went to dinner, I found out I was losing my house. Things haven't gone too well for me lately, and I have to be out of my house by the end of the month. But I really do believe it was fate that brought us together again for us to have another chance, especially now that we are older and have nothing to distract us from each other."

I couldn't believe what I was hearing. There was that truth stuff again! "And to my ears that translates to you thinking fate brought us back together so you could jump right into my comfy life, my home, and have me take care of you and all your baggage! Well, forget it, honey!" As I spoke, I was grabbing his things and throwing them all back into his suitcase. "How fucking stupid do you think I am?" I yelled.

"Hey, you're pretty sexy when you're all fired up!" he joked.

"You know, you might have gotten away with this twenty years ago, but these days it takes a lot more than a silky voice to make my knees weak, so here's your suitcase. You're all packed now, so beat it, and don't let the door hit you in the ass! Go, and do not ever call me again!" I spewed.

"But I'm the love of your life, babe!" was Mark's last desperate statement. He said it with definite seriousness! All I could do was gasp when I heard that one.

"No, you're not, but you could've been, you arrogant asshole. Now go!" I demanded.

I opened the door and threw his suitcase in the hallway, adding that he had one minute to get to the elevator before I called security to remove him. He honestly looked shocked and befuddled. He actually couldn't understand that I didn't want him, or his troubles, especially after the way he left me twice before. He left. Good riddance. Jeez, it was better to have left the story alone the way it was at the end of our dinner; at least it had somewhat of a fairy tale feel about it. But this was just fucking unbelievable!

I'm not sorry I saw it through. I was curious to see how it would go with him, and I think I was right to satisfy my curiosity. If I didn't, I might have wasted more time with him only to lead up to what happened this night. I admit that for one fleeting moment, I thought, wouldn't it be great at this stage in my life to have a partner I was so comfortable with, had history with, shared mutual friends with? Yes, that would have been great. However, I'd be damned if any man was gonna storm into the home I'd made for myself and take over, especially a man who had hurt me before. No way. And most importantly, I think I finally saw Mark for what he really was, the smoothest Casanova, the best dressed conniver, who didn't do anything without his putting his own agenda first. One who left his conscience at home when he went out to play.

The moral of this story is that no matter how badly you want someone or something, no matter how much you love that person, or think they love you, want them, desire them, or believe how perfect you'd both be together, you absolutely cannot force it to happen. Like my dear old dad used to say, it's like trying to shove a ten pound bag of shit into a five pound bag! It has to come naturally and mutually. If love is real, it will evolve all on its own and you'll know it's truly from the heart. If you have to work so hard and hold your breath for every single bit of what you kid yourself into calling growth in a relationship, it just isn't the real thing. It's not a bad thing to have a line in the sand. Make sure yours is drawn, and don't let anyone ever erase it from you. If that line gets crossed, stick to your guns and allow the person who crossed it to know there are consequences. Live your life by the standards you are comfortable with. Believe whatever it is you are looking for will come to you naturally and eventually. Don't hesitate to take whatever steps you need in order to bring closure to a situation that isn't working for you, no matter how silky the voice trying to tell you otherwise is!

The Upshot

I've always believed that I'm the luckiest girl in the world. I have a wonderful life, and I'm in an extremely peaceful and happy place. It sure has been a bumpy road to get here, but I wouldn't have had it any other way. Nope, I wouldn't ever trade one of the many stumbling blocks that tripped me up, whether from life itself or my own stupidity, for anything. These things sure do turn life into a roller coaster, but wouldn't life be completely dull without a few thrills and spills, twists and turns?

Henry Ford said that "failure is the opportunity to begin again, only more intelligently." That pretty much captures the essence of each chapter of my life, as well as this book. Assess previous events, focus on the positive, store the negative as lesson learned, and move on positively. I've developed an annual year end ritual between Christmas and New Year's Eve. I reflect on the year about to end and review what worked and what didn't. Did I achieve the goals I laid out for myself (because establishing at least one annual goal is important)? Why or why not? I ponder that question, look for the answers, and write down new goals for the upcoming year. This tradition is part of my ongoing self-assessment, and one that I've found to be immensely helpful in many ways.

My greatest source of happiness comes from my family. Little Contessa is healthy, happily married to a wonderful man, and together they enjoy a great family and home life that any parent would want for their children. In addition to watching my daughter's happiness blossom, nothing on this earth has given me more pleasure than watching my beloved grandson grow and develop into the finest of young men. He is a kind, respectful, and intelligent teenager, a phenomenal athlete with a big heart, a great sense of humor, and a young man who is well liked by all. I've cherished every second I was able to spend with him. I want him to know he has brought more joy to my life than one could ever hope for and that I am immensely proud of him.

I am blessed to have a few genuine, longtime friends, those who have shown me time and again that they love me, warts and all, who have been a constant source of love, appreciation, and support. These few are authentic; they are the real deal, the truest meaning of the word *friend*. They know who they are, and more importantly, I know who they are. I've heard that if you can count true friends on one hand, you're lucky. I can, and I am. I try very hard to reciprocate the love, support, and appreciation they have so selflessly extended to me. I count them among my many blessings.

I continue to look for ways to give back, as I was taught so many years ago. Whether by monetary donation, volunteering time and attention, or mere compassionate guidance and counsel (when asked), it's important to share yourself wherever and whenever you can. A good deed is hopefully appreciated by the recipient, but I have found giving, sharing, and lending a helping hand have been both rewarding and fulfilling for me in many ways as well.

My dating life is alive and well, albeit somewhat casual. I have found that just living your day-to-day life will allow attractions to come your way. I've had the pleasure of meeting lovely gentlemen in grocery stores, restaurants, the gym, the golf course, and department stores. I've never been one to actively seek out or chase a dating life. I believe in letting it come to you; just live your life and let it happen. At least that's what has worked best for me. I would love to find that one special guy whom I'll enjoy being committed to, but I won't be sad if that doesn't happen. I've experienced and enjoyed many loves in my life, and while none have resulted in a happily ever after, I have to say, the ride love's roller coaster took me on is one that I'm grateful to have taken. Wouldn't have traded it for anything. Didn't some wise person say that it's better to have loved and lost than never to have loved at all?

In conclusion, may I share a few of what my gal pals have deemed "Contessa-isms," or words to live by in order to keep your life neat, clean, drama free and happy:

- Honestly will always be the best policy.
- Keep your life drama free. When a negative situation presents itself, put your cards on the table and deal with it directly and completely. One of my all time favorite quotes is by Mae West (now that was a badass lady who had her shit together): "A lady who knows the ropes won't get all caught up in things." Think about it.
- Clean your house before you invite someone to join you in it. Tie up the loose ends of a relationship before you begin another one. A bit of single time never hurts either.
- Relationships are definitely hard. We all have to be the willow once in a while. Give it a try; you'll find you won't break.
- The best laid plans can be thwarted by curveballs life throws us. Learn to adapt and move on. "Though nothing can bring back the hour of splendor in the grass, glory in the flower. We will grieve not, but rather find strength in what remains behind" (William Wordsworth).
- Be receptive to voices outside your own. A different point of view can be extremely valuable.
- You can't change yesterday, but you can surely learn from it to better direct your tomorrow.
- People will treat you the way you allow them to. Be true to your standards.
- There are givers and takers in this world. Beware of fair weather friends; those who suck up to you merely to enjoy your generosity, but seem to forget your number when you are in need.
- Wear pretty pajamas to bed. You never know who you'll meet in your dreams.

And last but not least:

- The best revenge is your own success! Don't harbor anger and bitterness. Keep your focus on tomorrow not yesterday. Dedicate yourself to achieving your goals and ambitions compassionately and honestly. Believe. The rest will fall into place.

About the Author

Contessa is a retired business woman who enjoys family, friends and travel. Her career experience has contributed to writing and publishing various marketing, networking, self improvement and inspirational articles. Contessa's love of biographies and vintage romantic melodramas fueled her passion for writing, focusing on stories that entertain, encourage and uplift. Contessa attributes her success to strong faith, determination and a tenacious commitment to setting and achieving goals. She believes that hardships should be embraced as opportunities to develop and grow as people, that we should welcome challenges as possibilities to thrive.

Contessa's philosophy on life is that it can change in a minute and it's up to us as individuals to analyze and channel new circumstances into favorable, constructive conditions that will ultimately help us reach our objectives. Always maintain a positive mindset. Learn to make lemonade from lemons. Don't bitch, moan (nobody likes a whiner), complain (never protest or criticize unless you have an alternate solution) or place blame. Never depend on anyone else to make your life what you want it to be. It's all up to you. We all make mistakes on our life's journey. Contessa encourages us to embrace them as lessons and factor them into a strategy towards realizing our dreams. A plaque hangs in Contessa's office that reads "Believe in yourself and the magic will happen." She does, and it has!

CPSIA information can be obtained
at www.ICGtesting.com
Printed in the USA
LVHW031429200519
618456LV00004B/502

9 781643 509174